Saline District Library
3 4604 91094 6069

P9-CRD-225

A Good Death

A Good Death

Christopher R. Cox

MINOTAUR BOOKS
A THOMAS DUNNE BOOK
NEW YORK

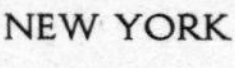

This is a work of fiction. All of the characters, organizations, and events portrayed in this novel are either products of the author's imagination or are used fictitiously.

A THOMAS DUNNE BOOK FOR MINOTAUR BOOKS.
An imprint of St. Martin's Publishing Group.

www.thomasdunnebooks.com
www.minotaurbooks.com

ISBN 978-1-250-01231-9 (hardcover)
ISBN 978-1-250-01232-6 (e-book)

First Edition: February 2013

10 9 8 7 6 5 4 3 2 1

For Maria and Timothy

Love is eternal. It has been the strongest motivation for human actions throughout history. Love is stronger than life. It reaches beyond the dark shadow of death.

—Vera Caspary, *Laura*, 1944

One

Somewhere between the airport and downtown, in the steamy, sinking warren of Bangkok's broken streets and stinking canals, my taxi driver began complaining. Loudly. Four hundred baht had seemed a fine fare when I slumped into his dented Toyota sedan after midnight, but now he found the thirteen-dollar amount wanting. He thought seven hundred baht a better price for a foreigner to pay. *Farang* always paid more. Why wouldn't I pay more? So he had left the airport expressway, haggling while he sped along a secondary road, scattering stray dogs that had come to forage on heaps of trash beneath the faint street lighting. The Grand Babylon Hotel was nowhere in sight. Around me the night stretched away, black and molten. The moonlit reflection of rice paddies, perhaps. I had no idea where I was or where we were headed. Cambodia or Burma didn't seem out of the question.

"First we go to Patpong," he insisted. "Buy beer. Buy Thai lady massage." He pumped his fist, cackling. "Good lady make you forget bad airplane. Then we go to hotel."

He pounded the steering wheel and, without slowing the car, turned to judge my reaction. His grin was an uneven stream of silver fillings, his eyes just dark, speed-dilated pools.

"For you," he said, "six hundred baht. Special price."

Now we were getting somewhere.

"Four hundred," I said evenly.

He moaned; the cab accelerated. We vaulted a short, arched bridge over a dank creek. Then we abandoned paved roads for a muddy lane through a slum of lean-to shanties.

"Patpong," he insisted. "We go Patpong. For you, six hundred baht."

I quietly unlocked the back doors, checked my pockets. Wallet. Passport. Tickets. Thai phrase book. Swiss Army knife? Inside my suitcase, which was rattling around inside the trunk of the taxi. Not good. I scanned the brooding night for clues of my whereabouts. Less than an hour after landing in Thailand, it looked like I might get rolled in the middle of nowhere.

"Forget Patpong," I said. "Take me to the Grand Babylon. Sukhumvit Road. I'll pay you five hundred baht. No more."

Exhaustion gnawed at the edges of my patience. I hadn't slept the entire flight. I felt dulled, devoid of ideas, with a screaming headache—the consequence of a recent on-the-job injury—scouring my skull. Hardly the condition required to nail this case. I had less than a week to find my subject—if she was still in Thailand. If she was still alive. I needed to get to the hotel and then check in with my client. It was after midnight local time, so it had to be around lunchtime back in Boston. A lot can happen in the thirty hours it takes to fly from Boston to Chicago to Tokyo to Bangkok. Given its current meltdown, the Thai baht had probably plummeted another 10 percent against the dollar. I owed another day's compounded interest on my mounting bills. And my subject had more precious time to deepen the mystery of her whereabouts.

The driver clucked and unleashed a stream of Thai invective, no doubt agitated by the kingdom's economic predicament and the cheap-bastard American customer sprawled across his backseat. He pulled a few g-force turns on rutted tracks, accelerating to scatter mud, trash, and chickens until we finally emerged onto a divided six-lane thoroughfare still crowded with traffic at . . . who knew what hour it was? I had forgotten to set my watch to local time. But it now had to be after one o'clock in the morning. My disoriented system craved a turkey club sandwich.

"Sukhumvit," he pronounced.

I rolled down a back window and drank in the stew of internal combustion and infernal temperatures. In the distance, thunder groaned like a hospice patient. Thailand didn't waste time. As soon as you arrived, it plunged you into its labyrinth of heat and intrigue, scents and secrets, traffic and lies. Hard to believe that just a day ago I had held all the trump cards. I knew the streets. I spoke the language. Best of all, I understood the people. I sensed their motivations, mined their frailties, capitalized on their vanities. I'd had the knack as a reporter; the talent now also served me as a private investigator. I had always enjoyed the chase: the paper trails, the clandestine stakeouts, even the cold-call inquisitions. I had pulled surveillance in darkened cars and smoky bars, nursed cold coffee and warm beer for hours, watched and waited while crooked businessmen and cheating husbands discarded their careers and discounted their marriages. Once, I had done it for the story. And now, since the news business had betrayed me, I did it for the money.

The promise of the first decent check in months had brought me to Bangkok to chase Linda Watts. With any luck the case might also put my new career on the fast track, above the usual PI drudgery of matrimonial investigations and workmen's-comp claims. Had I known my subject when I was writing for the *Ridgefield Beacon,* I might have given Watts's life the long, heartwarming feature treatment. She had been born in an uncharted village in Laos, a country few Americans could even find on a map. What notoriety Laos had achieved came from the dubious distinction of being the most heavily bombed country in the history of warfare—this despite the fact that it was officially neutral during the conflict in neighboring Vietnam. Linda had fled this carnage not long after the Communist victory in 1975 and spent half a decade in a grim Thai refugee camp. She had come to America with her uncle, her sole surviving relative, in 1980. In the States, hers was the quintessential immigrant success story: a welfare childhood in California, Minnesota, and finally Rhode Island, accented by academic excellence. That performance had earned Linda Watts a full scholarship to Boston College, where she had graduated cum laude in finance. She had then taken a job with BankBoston and begun a steady rise through the ranks—loan officer, assistant vice president—ascending a year ago to the position of vice president in the firm's small-business-lending area.

But her life had recently gone off-track in perplexing ways, which explained why I was riding through Bangkok's darkest, outermost limits in a taxi driven by a methamphetamine-addled maniac. In April, just three months earlier, Linda Watts had broken off her engagement. A month later she had gone to Thailand on vacation. Then, in mid-June, her body had been found in a cheap guest house in a gritty part of Bangkok favored by backpackers and budget travelers. The official cause of death: a massive heroin overdose. She was just twenty-eight years old, according to her records, which seemed part of the mystery as well. Her age was just an estimate. No one kept vital statistics in the distant reaches of the Annamite Mountains, where Linda Watts had been delivered into a violent, primeval world.

A Bangkok OD had not been the news anyone expected; it certainly wasn't what my client wanted to hear. The Cotton Mather Mutual Life Insurance Company stood to lose several hundred thousand dollars settling Watts's life-insurance policy and the claims-department manager was having none of it. She had told me as much:

the timing and circumstances of Linda Watts's death were highly suspicious. The two-year contestable period on Watts's original policy—$250,000 face, $500,000 with the double indemnity—had barely passed. Then there was the conflicting association of traits: bankers, especially achievement-oriented immigrant bankers, were sober, cautious people, she argued, not mainlining junkies.

Linda Watts was not dead, my client said flatly.

But where was she, then? Mather Mutual had paid me to find out, and quickly. I had the company's thin case file as guidance: a few Thai documents, her original life-insurance application form, an old photograph. I could make little sense of the Thai-language papers; I had yet to tire of looking at her picture. Linda Watts was striking, even within the confines of a college-graduation portrait: copper skin and high cheekbones, wide mouth and pillowed lips, startling blue-gray eyes and auburn hair tumbling over her shoulders in thick waves. She looked more Native American—Apache perhaps—than Asian, which only added to her mystery. More than her appearance, however, something about her solemn attitude haunted me. That college photograph should have reflected one of the greatest achievements of her remarkable life, yet she looked as if she had just been diagnosed with a terminal illness. Was she out there, a wan face in a land of smiles, daring me to find her? Knowing I didn't have much time?

We drove in silence for a few miles, then the taxi driver resumed complaining.

"Please, sir. Five hundred baht, no profit. Why not more? Why not six hundred?"

He shifted to a curbside lane, as if to exit and make another off-road sales pitch.

"Six hundred," I said wearily. "Now shut up and drive. But to my hotel. No Patpong."

What was another few dollars to a client like Mather Mutual? I didn't know it then, but I had lost the first of many rounds with Thailand.

I lay back on the overpadded rear seat and fought the urge to sleep, to surrender to an emptiness beyond dreams. The driver hummed happily as we moved along Sukhumvit Road, a major thoroughfare lined by a bulwark of small office buildings, retail shops, and hotels that stretched into the night for miles. I struggled to formulate a plan of action for the coming day—U.S. embassy, Bangkok medical examiner, Thai immigration—but kept dozing off. The driver finally turned onto a narrow lane between two office blocks, swung around a dry, shattered fountain that had claimed less-alert hacks, and skidded to a stop in front of the Grand Babylon Hotel. I counted out his precious six hundred baht and lurched into the spacious, silent lobby. My artless entrance roused the slumbering night manager at the reception desk, but not the hotel's overnight security—a uniformed Royal Thai Police patrolman—dozing blissfully on a teakwood bench next to the elevator.

After the manager slowly copied out the details of my passport, a drowsy bellboy appeared from a back room. We rode a cramped elevator that smelled of ammonia to my third-floor room, where he demonstrated the disappointing amenities: harsh lighting, basic-cable television, plastic telephone, tiny minibar. So much for the veracity of the guidebook I'd relied on to select this "business friendly" hotel. With a tip-hungry flourish, he opened a sliding glass door to a narrow balcony. I stood at the threshold, felt the greasy night seep into the cool room. The boy pointed across the traffic circle to a building identical to the Grand Babylon but for a flocking of black mold on its walls and Crayola-colored lingerie fluttering like erotic semaphore signals from scores of balconies.

"Maybe you like lady massage?" the bellhop asked. He grinned, the expectant pimp.

I felt like a long-distance runner who had begun his finishing kick far too soon and now staggered painfully down the last, interminable stretch to the finish line. Waves of fatigue pummeled my body, eroded my thoughts. Mather Mutual, Linda Watts, Thai ladies—they all would have to wait. I gave the boy a crisp, new fifty-baht note and called it a night.

Two

I didn't awake until midmorning, when the thick fug enveloping the room and the dull hurt across my face goaded me from a bed that reeked of recent, purchased lust. Still stiff from more than a day in economy-class seating, I slowly stepped onto the terrace and regarded the city. Its scent was at once ancient and industrial: charcoal smoke and spoiled fruit, diesel fumes and wet concrete. Although a putty-gray scrim of smog filtered the morning sky, my bruised left eye still caused me to squint to try to make sense of this chaotic, corrupt capital. Good news had rarely been contained in any story I'd ever read with a Bangkok dateline—a litany of fires in sweatshop factories, floodwaters in the streets, illegal wildlife on restaurant menus.

This had all started with an irate husband. I made my living chronicling the disintegration of marriages, and Porter Moyle should have been an easy fee, even on short notice: a corporate lawyer having a midlife crisis on an out-of-town business trip. It didn't get more obvious. My client, Dolores Moyle, had rung me about nine o'clock on a Sunday night, a little more than a week earlier, while her husband was in the shower. I was still at the office. Hell, I'd been living at the office, the middle floor of a three-decker in Somerville's Union

Square, since Christmas. Ever since Dianne had finally left me. At that hour it was too late to arrange for any operatives to back me up in Washington, D.C., where Porter Moyle was heading the following morning. I took the case anyway. I needed the work.

It had been barely a year since I had quit the *Beacon,* after the managing editor killed a project I'd labored over for weeks. There was absolutely nothing wrong with the story except that the main subject—an ethics-challenged real-estate developer—happened to golf in my publisher's regular Friday-morning foursome. My investigation wouldn't do, especially in a clubby Connecticut town like Ridgefield. So I sent the story to the nearest competition, a daily in Danbury, and cleared out my desk even though I didn't have the fuck-you money to cushion the abrupt shock of unemployment. When my subsequent job search went nowhere, my father had grudgingly taken me aboard his one-man firm. And a strange thing happened: I found that I liked detective work, could even endure close quarters with the old man. I enjoyed seeing my name on the letterhead of Damon & Son Investigations nearly as much as I had seeing my byline attached to a page-one story. But my wife had worshipped Connecticut. Dianne hated my new line of work, my unpredictable hours, and especially our shabby, urban address, which was nowhere near Harvard Square, let alone Central Square, in Cambridge. Too unseemly, she sniped, rummaging through other people's secrets. It was bad enough working as a poorly paid reporter and chasing small-town news. As a private investigator, she complained, I'd become a full-blown cynic. She left me with a five-figure Visa bill and went back to grooming the dogs of Fairfield County's rich and dysfunctional. I knew nothing about love, she said. She was right, as always. And, working matrimonial cases, I never would.

I had made the subject at Logan the next morning among the herd of suits awaiting the eight o'clock shuttle to Washington. At fifty-two, Porter Moyle pushed six feet two inches and 240 pounds and wore his thinning, graying hair long, well over the collar of his khaki summer suit. He had the look of an old tight end gone soft, relegated to golf with clients and the odd game of squash. I placed his stylishly dressed companion—about five feet six, Mediterranean complexion, with the carriage of a club-level tennis player—in her early thirties. She had come to the gate ten minutes after Moyle. I went back to reading the *Herald*. There was plenty of handwringing about the impending Hong Kong handover and the sunset of the British empire. Mike Tyson was getting eviscerated in the press for biting Evander Holyfield's ear during Saturday's fight. And the Red Sox were swooning again, already fifteen games back of the Orioles.

Moyle and his mistress had played it coy in Boston, with no interaction in the crowded lounge, and boarded the plane separately. Once we were airborne, however, their party began. It was easy enough to get video with the matchbox-size pinhole camera concealed inside the Red Sox windbreaker I wore. The camera was a beauty: a ninety-degree viewing angle, low-lux rating, and excellent picture quality. The couple sat three rows behind me and I just stood in the aisle, pretended to secure my bag in the overhead luggage bin, then walked past them to the bathroom. Guys like Moyle always got sloppy out of town. Deluded by lust, arrogance, and a few Bloody Marys, he made my job easier. He had forgotten a cardinal rule of infidelity: never allow yourself to be seen in public with your tongue in the ear of a woman who is not your wife.

When we landed at National Airport, I tagged the couple into town in another cab. Porter Moyle avoided the quaint romance of a Georgetown bed-and-breakfast for the Willard InterContinental, a beaux arts pile two blocks east of the White House favored by politicians, potentates, and law-firm partners out to impress their girlfriends. The rascals and the cheaters always stayed in the best places. After the subject had registered, I asked the receptionist for the next-door room on the eighth floor. Twenty dollars convinced him I wasn't a jumper. Moyle and his mistress were already in the sack by the time I hooked up my microcassette recorder and stuck it to the shared wall with a suction microphone. They carried on in impressive fashion, much longer than the normal, adulterous three-minute rutting. Then I heard another set of aroused voices. It took a few moments of theatrical sex talk before it dawned on me: Porter Moyle had rented some soft-core porn flick on Spectravision. The interlude seemed a good time to check in with Dolores Moyle. Her secretary answered and put me on hold until my client had wrapped up a conference call.

"How bad is it?"

It was Dolores Moyle's style to cut right to the chase. She already knew the truth. Most spouses do by the time they come to me.

"Your husband met another woman at Logan, and then flew here with her. They just checked into the Willard."

"Where we honeymooned," she said, as if surprised by this insult.

"I photographed them together on the flight. I also have pictures of them in the lobby here. And I recorded some compromising dialogue."

I didn't have the heart to tell her how compromising.

"Take a room if you have to. Try 815. Nice views."

"That room's already occupied. I'm sorry."

"Get everything you can," she said, her voice filling with cold fury. "Everything."

Porter Moyle had made a very costly mistake. I hoped he had deep pockets. A decent attack-dog divorce attorney could use this evidence—photographs, recordings, tickets, receipts—to establish, in devastating detail, the continuity of an affair. It always ended badly for cheating husbands, if the PI was any good.

After my client hung up, I went downstairs and hired a taxi outside the Willard for a flat half-day rate. The old man had taught me that hailing cabs piecemeal while on surveillance was too risky and conspicuous, while renting a car for an urban situation invariably meant parking problems. I got into the cab, and waited. When Moyle appeared fifteen minutes later he wore a fresh blue dress shirt with his suit and the smug aura of a man who has just indulged in vigorous, illicit sex. I tailed him over to K Street, the business after his pleasure, and watched him disappear into one of the interchangeable buildings along the steel-and-glass gulch that was prime habitat for lobbyists and corporate lawyers. The buttoned-down kind of place where I might have worked had I taken my mother's advice and gone to law school instead of running away to Europe after college.

An hour later, Moyle reappeared and took a cab north into Adams Morgan, a funky neighborhood of ethnic markets and restaurants. The woman waited at the sidewalk table of an Ethiopian restaurant—probably her idea, gleaned from a glossy travel magazine. Moyle seemed like a steak-tips-and-fries kind of guy. The couple ate with their hands, scooping food with clumps of flat bread. Soon they were nibbling the slop off each other's fingers. I knew where this was leading: back to the Willard. I quickly wearied of taping their afternoon-delight orgasms. It was deflating, the prevalence and predictability of infidelity. I couldn't remember a matrimonial case where I hadn't gotten the goods on a subject; there had never been any relief or reassurance that a spouse was absolutely clean. They had all cheated. They invariably treated their lovers with more passion and consideration than their partners. And consequently, they all got crushed in divorce settlements. Small wonder Dianne considered me such a cynic on the subject of long-term love, or that I had since shied away from any sort of relationship, even casual, personal-ads dating, after she filed for divorce. Narcissism and infatuation steeped the sordid world I worked in; my profession held no proof, no affirmation of trust or commitment.

I went downstairs to the hotel lobby, found a wing chair by a sunny window, and settled in for the duration. I don't know how long I'd been dozing before someone was shaking my shoulders, commanding me to wake up. Standing over me was a woman in her late forties, wearing a dark-gray power-suit ensemble. The sandpaper-and-honey voice ordering me to snap out of it could belong to only one person. My client.

"The concierge kindly pointed you out. Is your nap rate the same as your day rate?"

"The subject—your husband—went upstairs a few minutes ago," I bluffed.

"Then we have time to talk. I suppose there's a lot to catch up on since we spoke this morning."

"This isn't a good idea."

"Nonsense. It's my marriage."

"I'll have to break off surveillance. A confrontation could jeopardize your case."

She glared at me.

"I'll make the decisions."

"You're paying for my expertise as well as my time, Mrs. Moyle. Your presence here won't help."

She didn't budge. An elevator settled and opened its doors. Porter Moyle stepped into the lobby and into his wife's view. Too late.

"Dolores," he said, clearly shocked. "What a nice surprise."

He walked over, arms extended as if ready to embrace his wife.

"The Willard, Porter? You little shit."

Break it off. Don't let it heat up. Avoid a confrontation.

"Who's it this time?" she persisted. "Another paralegal? A waitress?"

"I've been in meetings all day. What are you talking about?" He turned those broad shoulders my way. I probably gave away three inches and at least sixty pounds. "Who's this lungfish?"

He studied us, trying to place me. It took a few seconds before his glib, defensive smile disappeared and the color drained from his face. He remembered. Logan Airport. The shuttle. The lobby. Lunch.

"What're you trying to prove, Dolores?"

"What do you think you're hiding, Porter?"

Porter Moyle gave me an accusing look.

"You've been following me around all day."

"I just met the lady in the lobby."

"Bullshit. You've been bird-dogging me since Boston."

"I'm just down here on business, sir."

He moved closer, as if sizing me up for a clothesline tackle.

"What kind of man follows other men around? You get off on stalking me?"

"For a man in a khaki suit, you've got a very vivid imagination."

"You screwing my wife, too? The two of you up to something?"

"Shut up, Porter," Mrs. Moyle hissed. "You're the only dog here."

She took a step toward her husband, swung, and missed with an open-palm slap. I turned toward her, trying to figure a way to play this scene. I never gave up a client. I never compromised an investigation. And I never saw Porter Moyle's roundhouse punch whistling toward my face.

At least the blowout fracture had been a boon for my business. On Wednesday afternoon, two days after the confrontation at the Willard, Dolores Moyle had walked into my office and offered me another, better case. I wouldn't have to tail her husband anymore; she had filed for divorce. She felt indebted to me for my work and for my facial injuries. She wanted to alleviate my pain, she said, to supplement the Percocet with a well-paying assignment. The job she proposed wasn't a domestic case, not even workmen's comp. It was better, far better: overseas life-insurance fraud. As head of the claims department for the Cotton Mather Mutual Insurance Company, Dolores Moyle had the authority to retain any investigator she deemed fit. She was going to make me forget all about Washington, D.C., and the Willard punch-out. She wanted to send me off to look into a very suspect claim. Big-game hunting, she called it. The quarry was a young woman with questionable intentions.

Over the years, Dolores Moyle recounted, she had used my father's firm for a few disability jobs; he had always delivered thorough, professional work-ups. But, aside from following her husband to D.C. and getting my lights punched out, I was an unknown quantity. And to her way of thinking, the Watts case already presented enough unknowns. She paused to light a menthol cigarette with a flourish that indicated: Tell me about yourself. I waited for the infernal wail that signaled a run from the nearby firehouse to subside. Then I sketched my background: college in North Carolina on an athletic scholarship, an English degree. Journalism school had been out of the question—I couldn't pass the minimum forty-five words per minute on the typing test—so I'd majored in Conrad, Hardy, and Kipling. Then I told her how I had come to join my father's firm, passing up law school for several summers on the European running circuit, followed by a succession of dead-end jobs—proofreader, technical editor—that culminated in my job at the *Beacon*. While I didn't have a journalism-school diploma, I had several compelling qualifications: I could string together a few coherent sentences; I would work for virtually nothing; and although I typed slowly, my copy was clean. And the *Beacon* editor was a friend of an old college teammate of mine. That had landed me a job as an entry-level general-assignment reporter. Then, all I'd had to do was not screw up too badly while covering the endless meetings that were the staple of small-town news, and keep my own name out of the local police blotter.

"Any experience beyond matrimonial investigations?"

"Plenty: security checks, disability and workmen's comp, missing persons."

These were a detective's staples. The work was fairly routine and the clients always paid the bill. Furthermore, they didn't materialize in luxury-hotel lobbies and compromise an investigation.

"I've also done workups, pretext calls, canvassed neighbors and relatives, checked financial records, checked criminal records, checked court records, run stakeouts. Anything else, I'm a quick study."

"Any military service?"

"I didn't go into that family business."

It only seemed like I had served. As a kid, practically every year had meant moving to a new army base and enrolling in a new school, but always the same cheerless dependent housing and lousy, understocked PXs.

"And where is the illustrious Sergeant Damon these days? It surprised me when you answered the phone instead."

"Retired to Florida a few months ago. He's the dockmaster at a marina down on the Intracoastal Canal. He's living the Parrot Head dream: got a thirty-eight-foot Chris-Craft and a forty-year-old girlfriend."

"An army lifer with a boat?"

"Dry land didn't treat him very well."

"He also had police experience. You?"

"I was a mall cop one Christmas."

"I'll take that as a no."

I spoke about my contacts within the Boston Police Department, the Massachusetts State Police, even the Federal Bureau of Investigation and the Drug Enforcement Administration. I had retained my father's sources. Many of these lawmen had served in the military, too, and that bond had carried over into cop life. After three tours in Southeast Asia and my mother's ultimatum, Master Sergeant Thomas Jackson "Stonewall" Damon had finally packed it in and used his service connections to get onto the force in Boston. He loved the action, loved being a cop. The only drawback to civilian life, he once told me, was not being able to call in air strikes. But his police career had foundered after he collared a politically wired gangster holding a gym bag full of cash and a one-way ticket to Honduras. Despite pressure from police headquarters and, by extension, city hall, he had refused to make the arrest go away. So when he began getting passed over for promotion, he turned in the badge, got a PI license, and began playing his web of contacts.

"Are you familiar with life-insurance policies?"

"I don't have one yet."

"You really ought to consider it. At your age, it's still very affordable."

"Maybe when there are people who depend on me."

"I'm asking you all this, Sebastian, because I have a serious overseas case."

"I've spent some time abroad. And I've worked enough insurance investigations."

"This won't be a European vacation, or workmen's comp fraud. What do you know about Thailand?"

"Pretty mountains, prettier beaches. The military coups are usually bloodless. Their currency, the baht, is about to go in the toilet. Monsoon season should be starting soon. So I will have to move fast if you want me on this case. Before the deluge begins."

And that's when she told me about Linda Watts, the particulars of her American odyssey and the peculiarities of her Asian death. An uncle, Bounliep Yanglong, who lived in Providence, Rhode Island, and was listed as the policy beneficiary, had just put in a half-million-dollar claim. Moyle handed me a manila folder containing several official-looking documents. There was a copy of Watts's original life-insurance policy as well as paperwork submitted by her uncle. Beneficiary claim form. Coroner's report. Death certificate. Cremation certificate. I reviewed them quickly. Most of the proofs were incomprehensible, written in the graceful, looping characters of the Thai language. The American embassy in Bangkok had yet to send its completed form, the "Report of the Death of an American Citizen Abroad," but Mrs. Moyle doubted this last document would shed any new light. The State Department paperwork was invariably an English-language regurgitation of the official foreign story, she said.

I pressed her for further details about the death of Linda Watts.

"*Alleged* death," she immediately corrected me. "Work on your skepticism, please. Two weeks ago the Bangkok police were called to a guest house in a part of town favored by the backpacker crowd. You know: the trekkers, the dopers, the burnouts."

I knew the type. During my time running in Europe, I had seen them in cafés and vegetarian restaurants, clad in ethnic textiles and flaunting indigenous tattoos, nattering on about Goa and Morocco, giving righteous attitude to package tourists. Dolores Moyle, who had the taut physique of a serious jogger, wanted to know a bit more about my track career as a "rabbit." I'd been a pacesetter in Europe, I explained, hired by meet promoters to push more elite middle-distance runners to faster performances, especially in the mile or the fifteen hundred meters. Spectators didn't pay to watch tactical races; they wanted to see record-setting times. Rabbits ran too hard too early to have any hope of winning, however. We dropped out of the race, our work done, long before the bell lap. Malmö, Zurich, Brussels. It was decent money, with less training and pressure than in college, and left plenty of time for a languid Grand Tour. There were far worse ways to spend postgraduate life than running a few laps on a long, warm midsummer evening in a beautiful, historic city once or twice a week.

She considered these details.

"I need someone who won't quit. Someone who won't be satisfied just to have a payday."

"That won't be a problem," I assured her.

"The Thai authorities say Linda Watts' body was found after another lodger complained of the smell. They had to break down the door to her room. Dead nearly a day. Syringe still in her left arm. The body had already started bloating and rodents had made a mess of the soft facial tissue. The police confirmed the identity of the body from her passport. So did the American consul. The U.S. embassy notified the uncle in Providence. He had her cremated at a Buddhist temple in Bangkok."

I glanced at the file. The official evidence had failed to sway Dolores Moyle.

"The woman was a banker, not a waitress in a bike-messenger bar," she continued. "Linda Watts didn't dye her hair purple, pierce her nipples, or brand her arms. She earned more than sixty thousand dollars a year, plus an annual bonus. She had a quarter-million-dollar term life-insurance policy. And three months ago she added ADB, an accidental-death benefit.

"The double indemnity boosted her payout to five hundred thousand dollars. She also changed the beneficiary from her fiancé to her uncle, her closest next of kin. I love my uncle, too, but I'm not setting him up for life when I die. And then she goes to Bangkok and ODs? She didn't think this through. A drug overdose makes the ADB contestable. And if this isn't an OD, maybe we have a suicide on our hands. Was she despondent? You need to make absolutely sure Linda Watts really died, and died from an OD, before we cut the check. See if she's done a buildup, too. Maybe she's taken out small policies with other firms as well, hoping to run the same insurance scam. I don't want Mather to cough up a goddamn dime that we don't have to. This is not a good death. My gut says the whole case stinks."

Mrs. Moyle had a bullshit detector for shady claims and it had gone off hundreds of times during her career. It's why she now occupied a corner office in Mather Mutual's Back Bay headquarters. Thailand made her suspicious, she said, although it couldn't compare to ethical cesspools such as Nigeria, Haiti, or the Philippines. Life-insurance fraud had become a Third World growth industry. Government officials were pliable. Official documents were for sale. Accidents were frequent. And insurance companies were too lax. Mrs. Moyle launched into a spiel she had probably delivered at more than a few industry conventions:

"We're part of the problem. Companies leave themselves wide open. Underwriting standards are far too liberal. Premiums are at least ten percent higher because of these scams. We rely on brokers and forget that the applicants—not the insurance companies—are their clients. The brokers write policies they shouldn't write and we pay out on claims we shouldn't pay. Our accountants figure that paying up is cheaper than hiring investigators to look into borderline cases. And most companies evaluate these claims the wrong way. They put their least-experienced adjusters on the smallest claims. But a lot of the fraud is on the one-hundred- or two-hundred-thousand-dollar policies. That may be short money over here but it's a small fortune in a dump like Lagos or Port-au-Prince or Manila. I make sure my adjusters look at the cases, not the amounts."

"If she's alive, I'll find her."

"She's alive. The facts say otherwise, but paperwork has a nasty habit of hiding the truth. You find this woman. Quickly. Personal-injury attorneys love to get involved in these cases, toss around threats of punitive damages. All the pain and suffering to their clients caused by our heartless delays. Any day now her grieving uncle will retain a lawyer."

"I'll need a letter of authorization from the uncle before I can start pulling documents."

"In the file."

"Then everything would seem to be in order. About my fee . . ."

"I hope it's in the same neighborhood as the Washington job."

"It's a more distant neighborhood—and it could get even rougher. I'd like to do a workup here on the subject: interview the insurance agent, the uncle, co-workers, significant friends. Let's say two days here, a maximum of five days overseas. My Stateside rate is five hundred dollars for an eight-hour day. Overseas, it's eight hundred."

What did I know? I had never caught an international case and simply threw out a number.

"That's five thousand dollars, plus airfare and expenses. I'll fly coach if it'll make it more affordable for your firm. I don't require a four-star hotel, either. But I won't be hamstrung if I need to move around or have to pay cash for information. I'll ballpark the fee at nine thousand. Total."

She scanned the room as if mulling the amount. She already sensed I was living out of the office and, worse, had no other work pending. She'd been here nearly twenty minutes and my phone still hadn't rung.

"I can get Insight Security to do this one for six thousand," she countered. "They're our usual firm for Asian cases. Based in Bangkok, too."

"I can go eight."

"Seven thousand. Consider this case an investment in your future."

"Seventy-five hundred. I've heard the future won't be cheap."

"I do feel bad about your eye. Agreed."

After expenses, the fee would cover my monthly nut for at least three months and let me make a dent in the Visa bill. The interest payments alone on the plastic debt were killing me. We stood to shake hands and I gave her my standard advisory, the same one

I had recited Sunday night before agreeing to tail her husband: I never guaranteed results. I only guaranteed effort.

"I'm counting on both. You don't seem the type of man who disappoints people."

She smiled and patted my bruised face.

"Get to work, and finish strong, Sebastian. Unlike that rabbit."

And then she was gone, although her Chanel perfume lingered in the room, a piece of pressing, unfinished business. The lilt of bossa nova from the ground-floor Brazilian *mercado* finally broke the silence. I sat down at my desk, took a deep breath, and opened the scented file filled with alien scribbling that was about to send me to another world.

MEMORANDUM FOR THE FILE

Re: Watts, Linda (Case 97-013)
Subject: Interview with Vincent Cammarata
Date: Thursday, July 3, 1997

My first interview was with Vincent Cammarata, the insurance agent who wrote the original life-insurance policy for Linda Watts. His office is located at 5½ Prince Street, Boston, a storefront in the North End.

Cammarata told me there wasn't anything unusual about the subject's policy, aside from the fact that his client was Asian. In this Italian enclave, insurance agents don't write much business with Asian immigrants. Linda Watts was a walk-in; she had come to Cammarata in early 1995 to take out coverage. In most cases the underwriter prospected for clients, Cammarata said, although customers sometimes initiated contact. Cammarata occasionally advertised in Boston's ethnic weekly papers; he thinks Watts must have seen one of his ads. His business was only a short walk from her Financial District office.

Cammarata gave Watts a standard screening procedure. She completed an insurance application, answered questions about family medical history and preexisting conditions, and took a blood test. The original policy, in the amount of $250,000.00, listed her uncle, Bounliep Yanglong of 1109 Westminster Street, Providence, Rhode Island, as beneficiary.

The subject did not hold additional life-insurance coverage. Cammarata had checked with the Medical Information Bureau; Linda Watts wasn't doing a buildup. He had no further reservations about writing the policy. Cammarata insisted in the strongest terms that he would not have written the policy had he known Linda Watts used drugs.

When the subject became engaged to Bryan Ward, of 3 Joy Street, Boston, nine months ago, she made her fiancé the policy beneficiary. In late March, however, she reinstated her uncle as sole beneficiary.

Cammarata didn't question the added-death benefit that Watts took out on her policy in late March—the same time she changed her beneficiary back to her uncle. Even under current underwriting standards, Cammarata explained, the increased coverage put Watts's insured-versus-earnings ratio at a little more than 8 to 1, which was well within the 12 to 1 industry guidelines.

Cammarata considered Linda Watts to be a "prudent" woman, wary of international travel and especially concerned about the welfare of her uncle, whom she considered unemployable.

Three

It was after eleven o'clock in the morning by the time I had showered and scrubbed the flight and fatigue from my system. I dressed and walked out to Sukhumvit Road, where I bought two skewers of grilled chicken from a sidewalk vendor and then hailed a cab to take me to the American embassy. It seemed the logical place to start. I wanted to get a copy of their report on Linda Watts and a briefing on Bangkok's bureaucracy of death. The taxi driver swung a U-turn across a half-dozen lanes of traffic and pointed his battered sedan toward downtown. As he coaxed the old car through traffic, I double-checked the contents of my documents case: Watts files, notebooks, Bangkok map, Thai phrase book, 35 mm camera, microcassette recorder. I used the tape player to record interviews, surreptitiously when necessary. The camera was for the photographic survey that would accompany my investigation. It was also my de facto photocopy machine; I didn't know how many Thai agencies would have electricity, let alone office equipment.

On short notice, my sources had assembled a thorough workup of Linda Watts: bank statements, credit-union reports, telephone records. Every young adult should have had her sterling character and solid-gold credit rating. Her savings and checking accounts held nearly three thousand dollars; her 401(k) account had already amassed thirty thousand. She dabbled in a few mutual funds that invested in blue-chip American corporations: total worth, four thousand dollars. Beyond converting five hundred dollars into American Express travelers cheques and withdrawing another twenty-five hundred in cash, she had no large bank transactions in the weeks leading up to her departure for Thailand. She had paid off her car loan—on a used 1993 Mercury Sable, a sober white four-door, no less—a year early, according to her credit report. She had no criminal record. She gave nearly 5 percent of her net income to various charities: United Way, Catholic Charities, the Emma Lazarus Center. Linda Watts looked clean, virginal enough to run for public office. She had left her life in perfect order. Too perfect, perhaps.

My unease was fueled by more than just my client's cynicism and suspicions. The autopsy report indicated that the decedent weighed four kilos less—a difference of nine pounds—than Linda Watts had indicated in her insurance application. It also measured the corpse at the metric equivalent of five feet four inches—an inch less than Watts had claimed on her application. Then again, people always lied about their physical details. I had also played a hunch and called an acquaintance working in the circulation department of the Boston Public Library and asked her about Watts's borrowing activity. Since January, she reported, Watts had checked out seven books from the central branch in Copley Square: four hardback novels on the *New York Times* Best Seller List; two budget-travel guides to Thailand; and a how-to consumer volume, *The Complete Book of Insurance,* which Watts had returned in early March. Just before she'd added the ADB to her policy. It appeared that my subject was a very quick study.

Traffic was bad enough for me to polish off the *Bangkok Post* on the ride. Nothing but bad news: The Thai baht had dropped 20 percent against the dollar in just a week. The financial contagion was spreading, with speculators targeting Malaysia's currency. Cambodia's interior minister had been executed, as forces loyal to co-Prime Minister Hun Sen mounted a coup against his main political rival. And elephants were dying in Thailand's pineapple orchards, possibly from chemical poisoning. Financial crises and violent politics I could understand. But to kill an elephant? It took more than an hour for my taxi to reach the walled, near-windowless monolith that was the new American embassy. Already the wilting heat and humidity of Bangkok trumped any Carolina summer. A U.S. marine at the embassy guardhouse directed me across Wireless Road; Consular Affairs was in the old embassy complex. There, another marine collected my camera and admitted me to the shaded, landscaped grounds. I waded through a crowd petitioning for U.S. visas to reach the small room that housed American Citizen Services. A young Thai receptionist signed me in and told me that everyone in the ACS section was at lunch and would not return until one thirty.

I stood in the waiting area, perusing the posted travelers' advisories and drug-smuggling warnings and listening to another innocent abroad, a balding, fiftysomething man moaning about his stolen passport. It was nearly two o'clock before a preppy-looking man with thinning blond hair took me back to his office. Walker "Trip" Forbes III was standard-issue State Department: pressed khaki slacks, jaunty paisley-print bow tie, a light-blue button-down shirt with crescent-shaped sweat stains under the arms, and the faintly sour smell of a heavy drinker.

"Anyone had a look at your eye?" he asked solicitously. "I know a decent Bangkok hospital that takes Visa and MasterCard."

"I'm fine. But the other guy in the waiting room seems in a bad way."

"Him? Lucky to be alive. Got rolled down in Pattaya. Ghastly place: rip-off bars, underage whores, sewage all over the beach. The hookers smear a drug on their breasts; knocks the johns out cold when they have a tug. Then the girls clean 'em out: cash, credit cards, jewelry, cameras. This old sport is fortunate his whore didn't go for the jugular. More than forty *farang* were strangled and robbed like this in the past year."

"Any arrests?"

Forbes smiled.

"The police own the biggest bars in Pattaya. T-I-T. It means, 'This is Thailand.' Things are different here. Very different."

"Seems like even the elephants aren't immune from getting poisoned."

"Not when someone considers them a nuisance. This is a devoutly Buddhist country, except when it isn't. But what can I do for you?"

He settled in behind his well-ordered desk and gestured for me to take a seat as well. I gave him my business card.

"I'm conducting a life-insurance investigation of a woman named Linda Watts. She died in mid-June, over on Khao San Road."

"The female OD?"

"You remember."

"We get heaps of male ODs, Mr. Damon. Female ODs are still a novelty in Thailand. But before we go any further, do you have an authorization for this investigation?"

I pulled the paperwork from my case file and passed it across the polished expanse of tropical hardwood. Forbes gave it a cursory look. His affable behavior masked the officious soul of a foreign-service lifer.

"We haven't finished our report," he replied. "We have to wait for the toxicology work, and then we'll have to wait a little longer for the English translations." He shrugged. "We're a little short-staffed at the moment. This office only has three Americans, and there are other pressing consular matters."

"Insurance companies have a difficult time waiting for these reports, Mr. Forbes. A claim has been filed."

"I understand," the consul said coolly. "I deal with this sort of thing all the time. We'll have a file on this girl. Excuse me."

He soon returned with a manila envelope and slouched back into his well-padded chair.

"One of our new ACS people, Isabel O'Toole, identified the body," he said, reviewing the file. Forbes paused to regard a photocopy of Watts's passport.

"Pretty girl, once upon a time. This is who you're looking for, right?"

He handed me the Xerox: the same face, a little older, bearing a world-weary expression. But still attractive. Gorgeous, to be honest. Her silver hoop earrings were a nice ethnic touch; she hadn't forgotten where she came from. The picture was recent; the passport had been issued four months earlier in Boston.

"Yes. Did Miss O'Toole identify this person at the death scene?"

"Naturally. We make every effort in the case of American citizens. Other consulates just tell the Thai to deliver the decedent's passport to them. The Germans don't go out. The French don't go out. Even the Brits won't go out. But American Citizen Services goes out. Bangkok, Chiang Mai, Pattaya, we get around."

"Sorry we make it so difficult for you."

"More than seventy Americans die in Thailand every year. Car crashes. Drownings. Whorehouse robberies. But about half the deaths are ODs. Like I said, female ODs aren't common, but anything can happen on Khao San Road. Aside from her gender, the death was unremarkable."

"Anything else?" I pressed. "The condition of the corpse?"

"Bad shape, but that's not unusual. The heat, the rodents, and the medical examiners can do that. Miss O'Toole made the identification off the woman's passport. Standard procedure. Watts' body was then sent to the medical examiner's office for autopsy. Also standard. We contacted the next of kin listed in her passport. Again, standard procedure."

"Then what happens?"

"After the ME is through, the body's released. For Christian families, we normally recommend a funeral parlor in Chinatown, the Neck Fong Shop, if the relatives want the body shipped home for burial. They're really about the only undertaker in Bangkok up to the challenge. But there've been complaints lately of a few botched embalming jobs."

He regarded the report.

"Watts' next of kin chose to have her cremated here in Bangkok. Neck Fong handled arrangements. Wat Klong Toey Nai did the cremation. They're down in the docklands."

"Is Miss O'Toole available?"

"Out all day, I'm afraid. Gone to Bang Kwang Maximum Security Prison, clear past the airport. The other, pressing duties I mentioned."

"How pressing?"

"More than sixty Americans are imprisoned here in Thailand, mostly for heroin smuggling. It's very hard time—they do thirty years or more. It could be worse: some drug traffickers get the death penalty. The executioner at Bang Kwang uses a stand-mounted machine gun. Saves on hiring a firing squad, but it does make a hell of a mess."

Forbes shook his head.

"Poor bastards didn't listen. Thought they'd pull an easy score, that the embassy could pull a few strings if they got pinched. We try to visit at least once a month."

"Where did they score heroin in Bangkok?"

"Khao San Road, of course. Pattunam's also bad news. Place is crawling with Nigerians trolling for drug couriers. They used to do the muling themselves, until Royal Thai Customs caught on. Did you know that over seven hundred Nigerians are imprisoned here in Thailand? Do you think their consuls visit them? They don't give a toss."

He drummed his fingers on the desktop.

"Could Linda Watts have gotten involved with the Nigerians, Mr. Forbes?"

"She looked innocent enough to run customs. And drug smuggling is a big temptation: a free first-class ticket to the States and ten thousand dollars upon delivery. All to mule a few kilos. There are plenty of kids from good families doing life at Bang Kwang who thought it sounded like a great idea."

I'd have to check out the drug-courier angle. Months before, I'd read a *Boston Herald* story about a Nigerian smuggling ring that the DEA had taken down in Boston. The outfit recruited working stiffs—nurses, bus drivers, even two Boston cops—to mule heroin from Thailand. Sometimes the smugglers traveled in pairs. Sometimes they traveled with children. They looked like such ordinary tourists that no one suspected. It had gone on for years. It was probably still happening. Perhaps Linda Watts had somehow been recruited into a similar operation. The Nigerians were brilliant scam artists. Dolores Moyle had already indicated that the country was a hotbed of insurance fraud.

"First time in Bangkok?" He seemed to be staring at my bruised eye again.

"I wasn't injured here, if that's what you're asking."

"Thailand can be an overwhelming place. Perhaps I can suggest a plan. I have some experience, since so many of our citizens find the kingdom such a lovely place to die."

"Or to rot away."

"Quite right. The Bangkok police are organized by districts.

Chanasongkram station would have handled the Watts case. They're at the west end of Khao San Road. There's a Tourist Police post at the station, too. Tell the duty officer you need a copy of the paperwork and want to see the police log. If you want to speak with the investigating officer who handled this case, just ask. When it comes to information, the Thais can be very helpful.

"Your guidebook probably went over this, but politeness goes a long way over here. Act rude and people clam up. Take notes and people get nervous. Ask names and people leave. Here, indirection is an art form. And, off the record, it wouldn't hurt to slide the police a little tea money. Discreetly. Say, one hundred baht per favor. Only about three dollars now, the way the local currency is crashing."

"Another Asian art form?"

"Probably a bargain," he replied, "compared with the cops in Boston."

"Only some of the cops. Not my father."

"No insult intended, Mr. Damon. It's the same here. There are a few good apples. But they usually don't get too far on the force."

He leafed through the contents of the embassy's file on Watts.

"You'll find death certificates at the local *amphoe,* the Thai equivalent of a county courthouse. You'll want to make sure her death was also entered in the record book; that way you know someone didn't just make out a bogus certificate for a few hundred baht under the table. Look in the record book for an official's name with the entry; registrars must sign when they write in the death record."

"Anything else?"

He thought for a minute.

"TM cards, the arrival/departure forms from Thai immigration. You filled one out on the plane before arrival: a little white card about the size of a postcard. Every foreign visitor has to complete one."

I nodded. Immigration had collected half the card upon my arrival and stapled the departure portion to my passport.

"Watts would have completed one, too. Her TM card'll show her date of arrival and what hotel she planned to check in to. It could help track her movements, if that interests you."

"It interests me."

"You can find the cards out at the airport. Go to the international terminal. Thai immigration keeps the records in an office just beyond Passport Control."

He stood and handed me his business card.

"Office number's on the back. Try O'Toole tomorrow. One more bit of advice. It's nearly three o'clock. Impossible to get over to Khao San Road at this hour. Your best hope for any further information is the medical examiner's office. They'd have handled the autopsy. They're just west of here, on Henri Dunant Road. I'll have the receptionist write out the name and address in Thai for you. Give the card to any taxi driver. The fare shouldn't be more than fifty baht."

"I could've used you last night. I got ripped off big-time on the ride from the airport."

"Don't feel bad. Everyone gets hustled their first time in Bangkok."

"T-I-T," I said. "This is Thailand."

Forbes smiled.

"Please try and stay out of Bang Kwang. We're busy enough."

I had barely settled into the *tuk-tuk* when the low, roiling clouds released waves of warm rain that pounded the vehicle's roof like a thousand deranged sheet-metal workers. The flimsy vehicle's open-sided construction offered little shelter; I was soaked within a minute. There was nothing to do but sit there and take the downpour and the car exhaust. We plodded along in near gridlock for forty-five minutes before reaching the nerve center of Thai law enforcement—a secondary road lined with dreary, ferroconcrete office buildings standing like a row of cavity-riddled teeth. The Institute of Forensic Medicine was the last in line, beyond the Scientific Crime Detection Division and the Central Investigation Bureau.

Outside, an ancient, withered woman sold days-old garlands of jasmine. The pungent flowers and the astringent scent of disinfectant in the lobby could not chase the indelible stain of death. The place smelled like a slaughterhouse. A registrar who spoke a bit of English took my request. While she went to make me an official copy of the autopsy report, I killed time in a hallway lined with glass-covered display cases that held luridly colored Polaroids of the nameless dead, gruesome portraits of disfigured, bloated, and decayed corpses that had met their maker in lonely, violent ways. Drowned in a *klong*. Thrown from a bus. Crushed by collapsed scaffolding. Anxious families scanned the horrific pictures, at once hopeful and repulsed. I made it through two gory display cases before the receptionist returned with a copy of Watts's autopsy report. I took the file outside, to a small garden with a Buddhist shrine. A young woman in a bloody hospital coat sat on a concrete bench, smoking a cigarette. I approached her cautiously.

"Do you speak English?"

She stared at me, as if trying to determine the blunt object responsible for my colorful facial trauma, then tossed a half-smoked cigarette into a trash basket full of red, hairy rambutan skins resembling tiny, bludgeoned skulls.

"Some English, yes."

"Do you work here?"

She nodded at the Thai-language name tag on her lapel.

"Assistant medical examiner."

"I don't read Thai. Could you please tell me what this document says?"

As she scrutinized the report, I watched while two white Toyota pickup trucks swung off the road and onto a lane bordering the garden, then backed into the coroner's loading dock. A half-dozen porters appeared. They shouldered a corpse wrapped in blood-soaked sheets and cardboard and carried it inside.

"The report says her body had started to lose water. It's the weather. And the decay . . ."

"I saw your portrait gallery."

"Yes, the unknown dead. But when a *farang* dies, officials become very concerned. It is very bad for tourism."

"I'm trying to learn as much as I can about her death."

"Do you have an old picture? I am always interested in the lives of the dead."

I produced the graduation photograph of Linda. She regarded the picture as if trying to imagine a scenario that would leave such a beautiful young woman dead and bloated in a cheap Bangkok youth hostel.

"I'm sorry. She was very pretty. But she doesn't look like a *farang* lady."

"She grew up in Laos."

"You've traveled very far. You must care for her very much."

"I represent an American insurance company. That makes me interested in her death."

She consulted the report.

"This girl was physically normal. No tumors. No defects. The body was beginning to swell, but that is natural in Bangkok weather. Only now is our hot season ending."

"Any sign of heart problems?"

If Linda had known about a physical defect and had lied on her insurance application, then my client might have a contestable claim.

"No, her heart appeared normal."

She pointed at the bottom of the report.

"The alcohol level on her blood test was very high. The drug level on her urine test was also very high. The coroner listed 'addictive drug.' Her lungs had congestion and edema—very common with opiate intoxication. Her death resulted from respiratory and circulatory failure, caused by extreme opiate abuse."

In other words, a classic OD.

"I thought you didn't speak much English."

"I spent a year in Los Angeles, high-school exchange program. I'm okay."

"More than okay. One more thing: can you tell how long she'd been using drugs?"

"Impossible to say."

"The heroin habit surprises me, and my client."

"It always surprises people. But I see it so much: young girls dead from drugs or AIDS. I don't know why they make bad choices."

She stood and nodded toward the loading dock. Another Toyota pickup had pulled up to disgorge its bloody cargo.

"I must go now," the medical examiner said. "The work here never stops. Bangkok drivers see to that."

I watched her walk back through the waiting room, down the gallery of death, and through the swinging doors that led to the cutting rooms. Then I headed back to my hotel in the early-evening rush hour, the gritty, yellowish smog casting Bangkok in an alien, sepia-toned glow.

The autopsy report checked out. I'd have to examine the death certificate and police report tomorrow. It was too late today for any further Thai bureaucracy. There was time, however, for a little phone work. Before I'd left, a Bell Atlantic source had given me a breakdown of all the long-distance calls Linda Watts had made since the beginning of the year. There were three calls to Bangkok—all in late May, just before she had left Boston. The first and last of these calls had been brief: two minutes apiece. The second call had lasted ten minutes. Linda Watts had also received a twenty-minute collect call from Thailand in early March. My guidebook placed the area code of this call in Ubon Ratchathani, a province in the remote northeast of the kingdom. A second, eleven-minute collect call to the States had come from the same number in early May. Who had Linda called three times in Bangkok? And who in Ubon Ratchathani, more than four hundred miles from here, knew Linda well enough to call her collect on two separate occasions? A distant relative? An old friend from the refugee camp? Linda had been away from Thailand for more than fifteen years.

I dialed the long-distance number in Ubon: busy. I then dialed the Bangkok number Linda had called three times from Boston. The man who answered spoke enough English to tell me I had phoned the Front Row Hotel. Location? Thonglor district, he replied, and hung up. I rang down to the Grand Babylon's front desk; the receptionist said the Front Row was off Sukhumvit, on Soi 33. But was something wrong with my room here? Was I thinking of checking out? I assured the woman I was quite satisfied with the Grand Babylon and only wanted to meet a man on business at the Front Row. She hummed knowingly. I could take a cab, she told me. In this traffic, the ride would take twenty minutes. Or I could walk to the Front Row in ten minutes.

I thanked her and then redialed the Ubon number. Still busy. I tried three more times over the next ten minutes without success, then decided to call my father. He refused to subscribe to the Internet; he'd left his computer in the Somerville office when he moved to Florida. One less distraction. Before leaving Boston I had called, asking him to look into Linda Watts's credit-card activity. It was morning along the Gulf Coast, but he was an early riser—an old army habit he maintained in retirement. He answered the phone in the middle of a Camel-fueled coughing jag.

"Damn Red Sox got me smoking again. At least they can't lose for a few more days, what with the All-Star break."

"I'd love to chat about baseball, Dad, but my client is paying for this. Since you don't have e-mail."

"It'll never last. No security. Where the hell do all those words go once you hit Send?"

"Someplace cheaper than the two dollars a minute I'm paying to speak with you."

"That AOL's no bargain, either."

"I appreciate the IT advice, Dad. But can you tell me if your financial guy came through?"

"Of course Quinlan delivered. He got all the credit agencies: Equifax, TRW, Fidelity. Took some time, but he gave me a breakdown on all the credit charges Linda Watts made this year. I'll fax you the Thailand stuff after we hang up."

"Anything in those charges seem suspicious to you?"

"Not really. No big cash advances, no major purchases. Just meals and hotels."

"Any charges come through for a place called the Front Row?"

"I'm down by the dock, on the cordless. Damn thing's nearly as big as a walkie-talkie. I don't have the paperwork in front of me."

"What was the date of her last credit-card charge?"

"Hold the line," he sighed, "while I fetch the report."

"Let me call back."

"Only take me a minute, son. Your client can afford it. Stand by."

I could hear only the rumbling of inboard engines and the screeching of gulls and then, after a silence that would cost Mather Mutual ten dollars, he finally picked up again, wheezing slightly.

"Thought you said a minute."

"I meant a Florida minute. Looks like she stayed a bit at some place called the Mermaid's Rest Guest House. Had a pretty good meal at the Dusit Thani Hotel. Also had a hell of a time over at the Oriental Hotel. Here it is: the last charge was for some place called the Fun Frog Guest House in Kanchanaburi. That was June seventh. No activity after that."

A week before her death.

"How much she charge there?"

"Fifty dollars. Still worth checking out, son. Maybe something happened in Kanchanaburi that has a bearing on this case. It's not that far from Bangkok. You could knock it out in a day. Pretty town, too. Least it used to be."

"I plan on looking into it. The subject also accepted two long, collect calls from Ubon Ratchathani before she left the States. Ever been up there?"

"Ubon? Big air base there during the war. That's all I know."

"What about Laos? The subject grew up there, some burg in the mountains."

"Haven't thought about Laos for years. Nothing but a big, bad, black hole."

He went quiet.

"Anything else, Dad? Advice? Criticism? Second-guessing?"

"One name for you: Sam Honeyman. He was my old One-One—sorry about the army jargon—my assistant team leader. Covered my ass plenty of times over there. Still in Bangkok, last I heard."

"Doubt I'll need him."

"Don't get too cocky. Find yourself in a bind, look up Sam. Used to hang out at a German beer garden near Soi Cowboy. Any expat can tell you how to find the Cowboy. How to find Sam, that's another story. Thinks he's the reincarnation of Hank Williams, plays guitar in some of the local titty bars. He moves around, but what do you expect from an old Green Beret? He's good people. And he owes me a few favors."

I heard boat horns and irate voices and my father yelling at somebody to wait just a goddamn minute.

"Gotta go, son. I'll fax you the credit-card report this morning. Give me a number."

"It's already evening over here."

"Then you'll have some bedtime reading. Just a few pages. By the way, Quinlan told me you're nearly living on repo time, that you've already fucked up the line of credit I left."

"Thanks for running a credit check on me, too. It's not like I planned it. Business has been slow."

"If you're having problems, come to me. All right? I'm here to help."

My older brother, John, could use the old man's help more than me, but he wasn't even half-way through a three- to five-year sentence at MCI-Concord for an assault conviction. I kept quiet.

I tried the Ubon number twice more: busy. Then I lay down on the bed, intent on resting for a few minutes before walking in the infernal heat over to the Front Row Hotel, where Linda's trail apparently began. I never made it out of bed. Sleep mugged me. It was the thunder that awakened me, and the rain pouring like sustained applause outside the open balcony door. I groped for my watch: it was after midnight. Too late to visit the Front Row, even to order a room-service meal. I sat in the dark for a while, listening to the wild storm. Then I raided the minibar for a half-pint of Jack Daniels, hoping to summon sleep. I needed to have a better day tomorrow.

MEMORANDUM FOR THE FILE

Re: Watts, Linda (Case 97-013)
Subject: Interview with Bryan Ward
Date: Thursday, July 3, 1997

I met Bryan Ward, Linda Watts' former fiancé, at Mr. Dooley's, a Broad Street saloon favored by the Young Turks who work the Financial District. Ward is employed by BankBoston as a financial analyst; he had met Linda Watts there in early 1996. He is 31, approximately three years older than the subject. They became engaged in September 1996, six months after they met, and planned to marry in the fall of 1997. Watts insisted that her uncle, Bounliep Yanglong, described by Ward as a shaman, officiate part of the wedding ceremony. Ward said he and Watts planned to honeymoon in Thailand. He was eager to see Asia, hoping it might help him understand the difficult past of his bride-to-be.

But Watts called off their engagement in early April of this year. She told him she wasn't ready to commit to marriage; the cultural differences were too great. She refused to consider counseling and completely broke off the relationship, to the point of returning her engagement ring and never even speaking to Ward at work.

Ward said he never knew Watts to use heroin. Her

behavior had progressively worsened this year, however. She had started to drink heavily: always Chivas, always neat. She couldn't hold her liquor; there had been a few scenes at Mr. Dooley's before she called off the wedding. Ward believes Watts was haunted by her past, although he couldn't provide any specific details. He told me that she avoided talking with him about her childhood in Asia and glossed over the details of her American assimilation. He said he barely knew a woman he almost married.

Four

I stood uneasily on my balcony, drinking thin, lukewarm room-service coffee to chase the low-grade-whiskey funk. Below, two Thai women in Day-Glo thongs splashed in the hotel swimming pool while their patron, a balding, sunburned *farang* man with an in-denial ponytail, ate breakfast. I had already spoken with Isabel O'Toole. She was new to Thailand, in the country just four months, but adamant about the details of the Watts case. The Royal Thai Police had notified American Citizen Services about the discovery of the body; Chanasongkram police station was less than one hundred yards from the Marco Polo Guest House, where the body had been found. Watts had been dead less than a day, but in the summer heat the stench had soon become unavoidable. The body had begun to bloat, while rodents had already gnawed away some of the soft tissue: lips, eyes, ears, and a bit of the nose.

O'Toole had identified Watts from her passport, which the police had found with the girl's effects. They had also discovered the American girl with a hypodermic syringe still embedded in her left arm. What could the death be other than a hot shot? O'Toole said she had seen about one-half dozen similar ODs already in Bangkok, most of them around Khao San Road. This was the first female OD she had worked. If there had been a robbery, Watts's credit cards and passport would have been stolen, she reasoned. Besides, there was no sign of a struggle or an altercation.

Working from Linda's passport, O'Toole had contacted the next of kin, the uncle in Rhode Island. Because her relative didn't speak English, a Thai woman in the office had translated the conversation. Thai and Lao were similar enough, O'Toole said, like Spanish and Portuguese. And the woman at the embassy hailed from Isan, Thailand's northeastern region, where many locals spoke Lao. The consul had mentioned that the Chinatown funeral parlor had experience embalming bodies, but the uncle insisted upon cremation. His decision made sense for a lot of reasons, O'Toole explained. Owing to the heat, the rodents, and the medical examiner's autopsy, Linda's body was in terrible shape; the undertaker had lately developed a reputation for sloppy work. Besides, it cost more than two thousand dollars to embalm and ship a body back to the States for burial; a bill for cremation ran around three hundred dollars. After she had notified the uncle, O'Toole canceled Linda Watts's passport. When the medical examiner had finished the autopsy, the undertaker handled all the cremation details with the temple in Klong Toey. Then the ashes were placed in an urn, crated, and shipped home to her next of kin in Providence, Rhode Island.

Sometime during my whiskey-basted night, a hotel clerk had slid the expected fax from my father under my door. Now I studied Linda Watts's credit-card activity in Thailand, which only deepened the mystery of her disappearance. She had charged nothing at the Front Row, the hotel she had called repeatedly from the States. Her first charge was at the Mermaid's Rest Guest House—a place off Sukhumvit Road, according to my guidebook—in the same general neighborhood as the Front Row. Judging from the date and the amount of the bill, she had stayed at the Mermaid's Rest her entire first week in Bangkok. During that time she had also put down her plastic at the Oriental Hotel, the Dusit Thani Hotel's Hamilton Steak House, and the Central Department Store. Then, no more activity, except the Fun Frog Guest House in Kanchanaburi. I would check out as much as I could today.

I was in a *tuk-tuk* headed west for Khao San Road by half past ten. The hotel receptionist had written the address for the Phranakhon district office in Thai for my driver, who took it as a personal challenge to his manhood to deliver me across town in under an hour. We rode for miles through a dull gray canyon of office buildings, crossed over the festering waters of a *klong,* and disappeared into a warren of Chinatown streets. The breakfast aromas of kerosene, wet bamboo, and steamed rice steeped the old, crowded neighborhood. Buildings stained and pockmarked with age held a bustle of tire changers and lantern makers, noodle sellers and chemists, jewelers and tailors. Clusters of old men squatted in narrow doorways and smoked cigarettes; wrinkled women in high-collared jackets and silk trousers of another era swapped the first rumors of the day. We finally broke from the crush and skirted a broad canal lined with flame trees, then turned right onto a major road that carried us on a high-arching bridge over the waterway.

"Samsen Road," the driver announced.

I consulted my Bangkok map. The district office had to be just a few blocks away. He turned into a narrow lane and halted in front of a fenced compound several hundred yards later. Behind the elaborate ironwork stood a small Buddhist shrine and a gracious wooden building overshadowed by a gaudy five-story concrete addition.

"Amphoe Phranakhon," he said.

The district office. Alone, I wouldn't have found the place in a month of Sundays. Across the lane, a quartet of indigo-skinned men sat in the shade of a flame tree on the patio of a guest house. Nigerians, perhaps. Mustering all my nonchalance, I entered the *amphoe,* Watts's death certificate in hand. Three bureaucrats later, I found the vital-statistics office: a large ground-floor room with twenty clerks sitting behind twenty neat desks. If paperwork came here to die, it wasn't apparent. The first clerk I addressed didn't understand much English; she summoned a colleague who did. It was no problem, said the second clerk, to examine the record book or to make a certified copy of the death certificate. She pulled the volume and ran through the pages, looking for the pertinent entry. I watched her carefully as she searched, looking for a reaction that might indicate something amiss with the record. Nothing. If a local civil registrar had faked the death certificate, the odds were that he wouldn't have entered the death at the district office. The clerk would have to sign the record book, which would leave an incriminating paper trail should someone come asking.

And there it was, she gestured: Linda Watts's name, followed by the name of a registrar. The entry number matched the number on my copy of the light blue death certificate. And the entry signature matched the name on the death certificate of the assistant registrar, Phinthip Wetchasat, who had received the death notification. I asked the clerk if I could speak to this registrar. My questions didn't rattle Mrs. Phinthip, a serious-minded, middle-aged careerist. The paperwork for Linda Watts's death was normal, said Mrs. Phinthip, who added that she had personally entered the record. *Farang* died all the time on Khao San Road. She was sorry they came to Thailand and never left Bangkok. There were so many nicer places to tour, places like Chiang Mai, her hometown.

I made a documentation photo of the register. The death certificate looked solid enough to stand up in court.

"Go to Chiang Mai," Mrs. Phinthip advised as I turned to leave. "You see Chiang Mai before you die, you live a good life!"

From my map, Khao San Road looked to be about a half mile south of the *amphoe*. Short enough to tackle on foot. I walked out to Samsen Road and retraced the thoroughfare back over the old bridge, where a group of school-age boys were diving into the turgid canal, then gleefully surfacing and waving the crabs they had caught. Beyond the bridge the buildings grew taller, the motorists more militant, the vendors more brazen. Every square foot of the sidewalk teemed with lottery-ticket agents, beggars, freelance barbers, and while-you-wait tailors. Chanasongkram police station stood a few blocks south of the *klong,* a no-frills concrete box that told the dopers and scam artists that no nonsense would be tolerated, except at a hefty price. Inside the station, Bangkokians crowded a ground-floor waiting room to pass the day watching Thai soap operas and real-life *farang* drama. Against a long wall several clocks marked time in various cities: Sydney, London, New York. It was nearly midnight in Boston. At some point this evening, Bangkok time, I needed to check in with my client.

Off the lobby I found an empty desk with a Welcome sign. But an angular space beneath the broad staircase housed a booth staffed by an attractive young woman in the navy-blue uniform of the Tourist Police. She listened intently as a German trekker talked of an incident on the night train from Chiang Mai: he had been robbed after accepting a drugged drink from a Thai passenger. The tourist finally walked off, muttering to himself; he would beg to differ with Mrs. Phinthip about the wonders of her hometown. I sidled up to the booth and gave the policewoman my best pickup grin and the only bit of Thai I knew.

"Sawasdee."

"You speak good Thai."

"You speak better English."

She smiled serenely. How many *farang* men gave her the same tired compliment every day?

"I'm looking for the Royal Thai Police. No one else seems to be down here. I'd like to check a police report."

"You are a tourist?"

"No. I represent an American insurance company."

She was quiet for a moment, as if assessing my injured face. Then she smiled again.

"A businessman. Where are you from?"

"Boston, Massachusetts."

"My king was born in Massachusetts," she said. "His father studied at Harvard. Is Harvard in Boston?"

"Just across the river, in Cambridge. Like Bangkok and Thonburi."

She brightened.

"You know Thailand?"

"Only what I've read."

"Do not believe everything you read," she scolded.

"I hope to be pleasantly surprised."

"Someday I want to go to college in America."

She seemed like a sweet, guileless woman. And it behooved me to create some trust, especially if I needed further information or a small favor.

"There are many schools in Boston. If you give me your address, I can mail you some brochures."

"I would like that very much."

She wrote her particulars on a business card and exchanged it for one of mine, which she studied carefully.

"Where is Somerville, *Khun* Sebastian?"

"Next to Cambridge."

"Somerville is nice?"

"It is not the birthplace of kings."

She smiled her perfect smile and put my card in her breast pocket.

"Police records are on second floor. Tell Sergeant Wiwat what you like."

"You've been a big help, Miss Sirilaksana. Can I take you to lunch? We can talk more about Boston, and Bangkok."

"Today I am busy."

"Tomorrow, maybe?"

"The day after tomorrow, *Khun* Sebastian. At one o'clock we can go to lunch."

Whatever good vibe from my encounter with Miss Sirilaksana was quickly dissipated upstairs by the spit-and-polish appearance of Sergeant Wiwat, who wore a razor-creased umber uniform. He completed the intimidating kit with a holstered 9 mm pistol, black-leather jackboots, and expensive-looking aviator sunglasses. The sergeant didn't speak English; a lower-ranking officer translated my request for a copy of the police report and a glimpse of the police log. Sergeant Wiwat nodded: no problem. He permitted himself a Marlboro cigarette while his assistant retrieved the paperwork for my review. If only the police could apply the same efficiency to traffic control that they took to record keeping. Each police case had its own green, legal-size folder. Incident reports that comprised the police log were entered in date and time order and contained in another folder; each day had its own file. The police document number that appeared on the death certificate jibed with the number of the police-report document. There was also a police-log entry for June 14: an Asian female dead from a drug overdose at a Khao San Road guest house.

"But the woman was American," I noted.

The sergeant frowned and looked at the police report. The assistant translated his reply.

"American citizen, yes. But Asian."

"May I speak with the investigating officer?"

The assistant looked to the sergeant for a reply.

"The inspector is not here today," he finally said.

"What about tomorrow?"

Sergeant Wiwat permitted himself a small grin. Maybe tomorrow. Then again, maybe not. It was not possible to make photocopies, the sergeant said, since the machine was broken. I used my camera to make photographs of the log entry and the police report and left the office. Downstairs, another traveler burdened Miss Sirilaksana with a woeful tale. She met my gaze and smiled: the day after tomorrow.

Once outside, I turned east, heading to Khao San Road. It was time to get a good look at the neighborhood where Linda had allegedly died. The street ran about two hundred yards and was filled with double-parked cars and idling *tuk-tuks* that forced pedestrians to sidewalks crammed with stalls that sold knock-off designer clothing, pirated compact disks, and fake media-ID cards. The entire strip catered exclusively to the transient trekker mob doing Thailand on a few dollars a day. Used-book stores. Tattoo parlors. Budget-travel agencies. Nothing about the street seemed to reflect the Thai character. Khao San Road only mirrored the Western culture that backpackers said they wanted to leave, yet instinctively sought out.

Every few paces brought another cheerily named world-traveler dive: Hello Guest House, Buddy Guest House, Land of Smiles Guest House. Most had ground-floor lobbies that doubled as restaurants and attracted feral-looking couples in budget-tourist mufti: tank tops, drawstring pants, cheap sandals. A few eateries were patronized by small groups of aloof, nattily dressed African men who seemed to regard the trekkers as so many fresh, ready marks. Several storefronts held money-changing agencies that doubled as calling centers and Internet shops; if Linda had phoned the States from one of these operations, there was nothing I could do to trace her calls. My phone-company source had found no evidence of collect calls from Linda to her uncle from Bangkok, nor any long-distance charges from Thailand made to Linda's calling-card number.

I wasn't the only one searching Khao San Road for a missing person. Many of the support pillars in the guest-house lobbies and restaurants were papered over with flyers of young adults gone missing in Asia: smiling high-school and college pictures, biographical data, distinguishing physical characteristics, addresses of worried parents, anguished pleas for help. This down-market street seemed the last stop many other travelers made before dropping out of circulation forever. A small sign marked the alley to the Marco Polo Guest House. It was the third rooming house on the lane, with clean air-conditioned rooms priced at ten dollars a night. Nearly top of the line for this area. I rang the bell and waited until a young Thai man appeared from a room off the lobby.

"Sawasdee," I said.

The man didn't respond.

"I'm looking for information on a girl who died here last month."

The man frowned, shook his head.

"No girl die here," he replied. "Only German man. He die in March."

"American girl," I said. I pulled the paperwork from my knapsack and dropped it onto the registration desk. "This says she died at the Marco Polo."

The man studied the report.

"Yes, she die at Marco Polo. But she not die here. On Khao San Road, two Marco Polo guest houses. This number-one Marco Polo. She die in number-two Marco Polo. They steal name from us, try to steal customer. Other side of Khao San. Then down a dirty little *soi*. The small street. Hard to miss."

He gave a gesture that was part dismissal, part directional. I retraced my path with a tinge of embarrassment and crossed Khao San Road, where I found the trash-strewn *soi*—a small, paved alley perpendicular to the main street—and a tiny yellow sign announcing the hostel. It stood beyond a slight dogleg in the *soi*, past several other flophouses and beyond a young backpacker junkie on the nod, all but invisible from the bustling road. This place seemed an insult to the famed explorer: a two-story concrete shoe box with grit-caked glass-louvered windows and an exterior wainscoting of dark brown paint to mask the filth of the street. I entered the empty lobby, rang the desk bell, and waited. From a back room came the crackling sound of a Thai TV game show. The lobby held no clues, just cheap furniture: two rattan chairs and a plywood reception desk, a small wall-mounted television set, a few generic Thai travel posters, and a homemade sign for a tour agency. There was a rate card: small rooms went for seventy baht; large rooms, one hundred ten baht a night, a little more than three dollars.

The manager finally emerged, stifling a yawn and flicking long, greasy black tresses that fell in her face. Her lips were smeared a candy-apple red with hurriedly applied lipstick. I consulted the Thai death certificate.

"I'm looking for the manager, Mrs. Antiporn?"

She nodded.

"You reported the death of Linda Watts?"

No reaction.

"The American? The girl died here three weeks ago."

"Yes."

I gave her my card and explained my purpose.

"I tell police everything," she said with a hint of irritation. "They say nobody bother me."

"I'm not with the police. I only want to know about the American girl."

She considered my statement.

"What you want?"

"I want to see the room where the American girl died."

She seemed tense and dubious, like the effort would be a bother.

"All right," I persevered. "I want to rent the room where the girl died. For one hour. I'll pay you two hundred baht."

I slid two blood-orange bills across the reception desk. Her mood quickly improved. She fetched her master-key ring and led the way up a narrow staircase.

"She die in number six."

It didn't get much grimmer than this in Bangkok. A small room, a cubicle really, no more than seven feet by eight feet, located immediately at the top of the stairs. There was little floor space for much besides a bed, a chair, and a slight nightstand that held a small electric fan. The guest-house rooms were separated by plywood partitions that rose to within two feet of the ceiling. The resulting gap was screened, which allowed for ventilation at the expense of privacy. There were several holes at the base of the wooden walls and scattered animal droppings: the rodents Forbes had mentioned to me at the consulate. A reeking communal toilet stood at the other end of the dim, narrow hall.

"How long did she rent this room?"

"She stay one week, then she die," Mrs. Antiporn replied. "But she pay two weeks: one thousand baht. Cash. She not sleep in room. I know. I sleep downstairs. Every day, every night I am here. But she not come home at night. Maybe she go with *farang* men."

She clucked disapprovingly.

"She paid and never came to the room?"

"Sometime I see her. Morning time."

"Did you ever talk to her?"

"Just hello, goodbye, how are you, lady?"

"What's your security arrangement?"

She looked at me quizzically.

"Do you lock the front door at night?"

"No more. Many *farang* stay out late." Mrs. Antiporn sighed. "They get *mau,* very drunk. They bang on door, wake me. 'Hello, Mrs. Antiporn. Open door, please.' So I leave door open. Now I sleep. Young people, they come and go. But I only give room to good people. No thief here."

"When was the dead girl found?"

"Afternoon. Time like now."

"How did you know the girl died?"

"*Farang* man in number seven. He tell me about bad smell. I knock on door for number six, no answer. Door is closed. *Farang* man get chair, stand on chair. He look over wall. Lady on floor against door. She dead already."

She pointed to a narrow space between the bed and the plywood partition.

"I touch nothing. Right away I call police. They come."

She patted the door.

"The policeman, he look to see if lady dead. Bad smell. She very dead."

"What did the inspector find?"

"Not inspector. Policeman. He come quick, then call Chanasongkram. Then inspector come to Marco Polo."

"Do you know the inspector's name?"

"Colonel . . ." Mrs. Antiporn smiled sheepishly. "Sorry, I do not know. First time *farang* die at Marco Polo."

"And the inspector came quickly?"

"Maybe he come one hour later."

"A foreigner dies in Bangkok and it takes an hour for a detective to respond? The police station's just up the street."

"Maybe inspector go to eat first." She shrugged. "The lady very dead. Nothing change that."

"What did he look like, the detective?"

"Not too young, not too old. He always wear sunglasses. He want everyone go away from room. He stay long time in room. Then doctor come, they take away body."

"Did he say anything about the dead girl?"

"Inspector say lady die from bad drug. Heroin. He show me needle. This is Khao San Road—bad drug happen all the time. But first time somebody die here. I have good business."

"How many rooms do you have?"

"Twelve room."

"You said another guest discovered the body of the girl?"

"Yes. Number seven. *Farang* man."

"Does the man have a name?"

"Yes. In guest book."

"May I see the book?"

"Okay, downstairs. But no help to you. I write book in Thai."

"Does number seven still rent a room here?" I asked.

"Yes," she finally said.

At last, a break in the canvassing.

"But he not here today," said Mrs. Antiporn with more than a trace of satisfaction. "You come back later."

The tinkle of a bell floated up the stairwell, announcing a prospective guest. Mrs. Antiporn excused herself. I shot a half-dozen documentation photographs of Linda's room, then sat on the mean, hard bed and wondered. What had possessed Linda to stay here? Surely she could have afforded someplace better, even on a modest budget. What was she running from in Thailand, let alone the States? Had she used this room as a safe house, a crash pad, a shooting gallery? Had she meant to OD?

I passed Mrs. Antiporn on the stairs as she led a potential lodger up to review the cell-like chambers. I had a few minutes in the lobby before they would return, so I went behind the reception desk and pulled out the guest-house register. I leafed through the broad, weather-wrinkled pages of the book to the most recent entries, then worked my way back, photographing the pages until I had exhausted the roll of film. Then I went out to the road and hailed another *tuk-tuk*. I wanted to check out several of Linda's credit-card charges on my way back to the Grand Babylon.

It took five hundred baht to get the concierge at the Oriental Hotel to answer my questions; no amount of money, however, could restore his selective memory. He spoke with hundreds of customers a day. Many of them were attractive; some were Thai. This woman had probably come for drinks at the Bamboo Room, he said, examining the credit-card statement. Beyond that, he could not say. His hotel attracted only the best sort of people, the kind willing to pay for discretion. I slipped him an extra one hundred baht. Could he find out if she had been alone? He pushed the money back into my hands. A lady like this, he said, never drank alone.

I didn't fare any better at the Dusit Thani Hotel; their steakhouse maître d' couldn't place Linda's face. She must have come for dinner, he offered, and probably not by herself, unless she had ordered a good bottle of French wine. The bill was quite large for one person. I must have looked discouraged, for he gave me this information for free.

When I returned to the Grand Babylon, the receptionist handed me a message: call Miss Dolores. My client had left her home number; it was still very early morning in Boston. Upstairs, I tried the Ubon Ratchathani number again: still busy. I consulted my guidebook for details about Kanchanaburi and got lucky. It rated the Fun Frog Guest House: a no-star place with spartan rooms and a "soothing" river view. The woman who answered their phone spoke very limited English. It took nearly ten minutes to determine that I would have to talk to her boss, who was out rafting the Kwai Noi River and would not return until tomorrow.

Upon reaching Dolores Moyle, I found her late for work and in a curt, foul mood. She wanted to hear from me every twenty-four hours, she scolded. She had stuck her neck out by hiring me. The Claims Committee would have a field day questioning her decision to hire Damon & Son instead of Insight Security. She needed results, ASAP. So far, I had done what any competent PI would do. Now I needed to do more, she said, something outside the box.

Outside the box. People always talked about unpredictability in the most predictable fashion. That sealed my decision to go to Kanchanaburi. After Dolores Moyle had hung up, I dropped off my film for processing at a Sukhumvit Road camera shop a block from the Grand Babylon and continued walking west, toward the Front Row. In the waning light, scores of food hawkers had erected woks and braziers on the clogged sidewalks, charging the air with the scent of fried meat and fresh coconut, lemongrass and cooking oil. Mototaxi drivers, young families, and shopgirls sat on low stools on the cracked concrete walkways and spooned up their evening meal. It seemed as if half the city subsisted on street food. The hotel, a drab, six-story concrete box, was well marked and poorly decorated. No "soothing" views would ever be mentioned in the guidebooks for this dump, which had all the charm of a downtown bus terminal at three in the morning. Dodgy characters squatted on threadbare furniture, idly reading old newspapers, smoking, watching, waiting. For what? The receptionist couldn't remember a six-week-old phone call from America or Linda Watts's face, even after I showed him the photograph and offered a one-hundred-baht note to restore his memory. Maybe, he said, maybe not. He smiled and pocketed the money. That Linda Watts had repeatedly telephoned this low-rent dump mystified me. Why had the Front Row Hotel merited three international phone calls?

A short *tuk-tuk* ride later, I landed at the Mermaid's Rest. The man working the reception desk had a two-hundred-baht memory. He described Linda as a nice lady tourist. She stayed a week, did all the nice lady-tourist things: Temple of the Emerald Buddha, Jim Thompson House, Ratchaburi floating market.

"Was she with anybody?" I asked.

"No one. One night old Chinaman come to see her."

"Trouble?"

"They talk like friend. They leave together."

"Where?"

"Who knows? No one question Chinaman. Powerful man. He ask. You answer."

The mystery gnawed at me through dinner at a Cajun-theme restaurant off Sukhumvit's Soi 22. What man had Linda Watts befriended? Why would she have stayed at such a budget-conscious hostel but then racked up huge bills at the Oriental and the Dusit Thani? Had she gone there with the Chinaman? If so, why had she paid? The Cajun restaurant's owner, a retired Louisiana oil worker, didn't know much about the Front Row. Americans never stayed there; the place catered to low-level businessmen from across Southeast Asia. The Mermaid's Rest attracted *farang* because it had a swimming pool and a restaurant that served passable Texas barbecue. He did have a better handle on the local nightlife: Nana Plaza was the place to see tits and ass; Lumpini Boxing Stadium put on the best ass kicking. I hadn't seen Bangkok until I'd done both.

I elected to pass on the Nana nightlife and an hour later found myself outside Lumpini. I bought a grandstand ticket from the first scalper I saw and joined the mob surging down an alley and into a dilapidated, two-story concrete building. The stadium had all the hallmarks of a Third World fire trap: a handful of exits, overflowing bleachers, virtually no windows. I took an aisle seat as close to an egress point as possible. The crowd stirred as a pair of boxers entered the ring. The barefoot fighters were thin and slight, diminutive as children, weighed down by oversize boxing gloves and garlands of orchids. Bookmakers pushed through the cheap seats, signaling the fluctuating odds. The prefight buzz built as the boxers bowed and danced and postured to the jangling accompaniment of percussion and woodwinds. Then the bell rang and the ceremonial headbands, flowers, and rituals fell away. The two boys bobbed and wove rhythmically as the orchestra continued its recital. Soon the musical tempo rose and the boxers fell on each other in a street-fight flurry of punches, pushes, and kicks. The soundtrack grew discordant and agitated spectators surged forward, rattling the chain-link fence that separated the bleachers from the well-heeled fans sitting ringside.

The fights culminated in a big-purse bout between a lightweight Thai champion and a young, inexperienced *farang*—a Canadian, to judge by the red maple leaf embroidered on his white satin boxing trunks. The champion meted out a frightful beating that made the rounds seem to last an eternity, pummeling the challenger with jabs to the face, elbow punches to the temple, knee hooks to the groin, roundhouse kicks to the solar plexus. But the referee made no effort to stop the fight; he seemed to enjoy the mismatch as much as the crowd did. And the *farang* kept getting off the canvas; I could make out his mouthed comment after a crushing roundhouse kick had again sent him crashing to the canvas: Bring it on. The shrill din swelled. The Thai champion waded into the breach, only too happy to oblige.

MEMORANDUM FOR THE FILE

Re: Watts, Linda (Case 97-013)
Subject: Interview with Bounliep Yanglong
Date: Friday, July 4, 1997

Bounliep Yanglong met me at the doorway of his apartment, 1109 Westminster Street, Providence, clutching a freshly decapitated rooster. Linda Watts's uncle is short and spry, with skin the color of weathered saddle leather. His blood-spackled torso is covered in indigo tattoos—triangles, swastikas, circles—and the figure of a dancing girl permanently etched into his forehead. His teeth are stained black and filed to the gums.

Bounliep has been on welfare since arriving with Linda in the United States in 1980 as refugees. His one-bedroom apartment is sparsely furnished with a scrounged sofa and mismatched chairs; the only items of quality are several expensively framed photographs of his niece. Bounliep does not speak English. I had to conduct this interview with the assistance of a Lao teen-aged boy, Souvath Sissaphong, who lives across the hall, as a translator.

Bounliep told me the spirits called him at a young age to become a shaman. As a traditional healer, he apparently has little concern for money. A handful of other elderly Lao immigrants occasionally pay him to perform sacrificial or ceremonial functions. Providence police cited Bounliep last week after a bleeding pig escaped from his apartment and was run over by an SUV passing by on Westminster Street. Bounliep said that accident explains why he answered the door while in possession of a dead rooster—it was important that he appease the spirits.

According to Souvath, such voodoo is confined to the hill people, or Lao Theung, of his country. Lowlanders like Souvath are Lao Loum; they are also Buddhists. More than one dozen different tribes, all considered Lao Theung, occupy the mountains of southern Laos, where Linda spent her early childhood.

Bounliep is of the Katu hill tribe, and proud of it. Souvath said the nomadic Katu are the most warlike of the Lao Theung. Every other tribe in the mountains avoids the Katu, if at all possible. The uncle told me that the name "Katu" is only used by outsiders; the tribesmen refer to themselves as "Monui" (people).

He and his niece formerly lived in Ban Katu ("Katu village" in Lao), Xanxai district, Attapeu Province, far east of the Mekong River, near the Vietnamese border.

Bounliep is Linda's uncle on her maternal side. His father was the village headman of Ban Katu. Bounliep said Linda's father had died after the Communist victory in Laos in 1975; he wasn't sure of the date. He also said he didn't know anything about the family of the subject's father.

Among the photographs of Linda Watts in her uncle's possession is a recent corporate portrait. In this picture, the subject wears a small silver watch on her right wrist. The placement of this timepiece suggests that Watts might be left-handed. [Note: The evidence seems to indicate that the woman who OD'd in Bangkok was right-handed—the syringe was embedded in her left arm, according to the Bangkok police report.]

Watts didn't give Bounliep an itinerary for her trip to Thailand. Her uncle believes she met someone in Bangkok and decided to extend her stay there. He says he never saw his niece use narcotics.

He didn't consider Linda an observant Monui. He said she had lost her way, like many young immigrants in America, and had been unhappy for many years. Bounliep said his niece returned to Asia "to find her soul." Her "bad death" had upset the spirits and would cost him many pigs.

Five

I watched sunrise from the train station at Thonburi, the dawn a smear of rouge behind Bangkok's skyline. The gurgling Chao Phraya River was already alive with activity: freighters and ferries tilled the turbid water into furrows; long-tail boats kicked up rooster tails of fine, brown spray. From the open-air market squatting beside the headhouse, the chatter of vendors, the sweet perfume of overripe papaya, and the stench of durian drifted on the rising heat into my train car. I had decided to make the eighty-mile trip westward to Kanchanaburi by rail; the Thai newspapers held too many stories about horrific traffic accidents, accounts that ran with color photos in great, grisly registration. And so I sat and sweated on a pewlike seat in the third-class morning train.

Early-morning commuters poured from the coaches and hurried to the Bangkok-bound ferries, manic pedestrian wedges that scattered dull-witted food hawkers and skittish, mange-ridden dogs. Amid the rush-hour frenzy on the next platform, a beggar slept on a thin reed mat with his paltry belongings—a hardback book, a comb, a plastic bowl—arranged in a neat arc around his head. Another pauper down from the countryside, confident of finding work but confronted now with the rising financial panic. I had seen his dispossessed brethren all across Bangkok, sleeping on sidewalks, in parks, beneath highway overpasses. A salaryman passed, surveyed the sleeping man and his belongings. Then he stooped, grabbed the book, and vanished into the crowd.

A bit after eight o'clock, the train pulled from the station at a walking pace, easing through the rail yard and the gridlocked traffic, crossing dirty *klongs,* rattling the corrugated-metal shacks of laborers. The journey west soon settled into a pleasant rhythm as we skirted ponds covered with lotus in bloom and fields bursting with sugar cane and small orchards of tamarind, mango, and banana. Every few minutes, whistle-stops broke the gentle syncopation of the rails: ancient Nakhon Pathom, with its immense, bell-shaped stupa rising toward the heavens; Nong Pladuk Junction, where another track led all the way to Singapore; Thung Thong, where jagged mountains first rose from the green plains and unfurled toward the Burmese border.

The aging railcar was less than one-quarter full for this weekday run and, with the exception of an older, well-dressed man who sat a few rows ahead of me, held no other *farang.* In the faces of passengers I saw city folk bound for a holiday and countryfolk returning home from the markets of Bangkok. And then there were the faces of mountain people, darker and harder than their lowland brethren. Faces that reminded me of Linda's uncle. Of distant, desperate souls.

It took three hours to make Kanchanaburi. Only a handful of *tuk-tuks* had staked out the station; they were immediately commandeered by the locals. The old foreigner from the train caught my eye and shuffled across the crumbling, empty platform to where I stood. He was thin and gully-chested, with lank gray hair framing an angular face set off by a nose like the prow of a warship.

"The drivers look for *farang* at the bus station, not the train station," the man said. He spoke with an English accent. "Only backpackers ride the rails, and they never have any money. They always want to argue over the fare."

"But you hardly look like a backpacker, sir."

"Neither do you. On holiday?"

"Business."

"You've come to the wrong place." He permitted himself a smile. "No business for *farang* in Kanchanaburi, unless you're after teak. Or you work with Burmese refugees. You don't look the type for either."

"Guilty as charged. And you?"

"I live here."

"Then why not take the bus?"

"I'm the sentimental sort."

He broke off the conversation to hail a passing vehicle of the style that Thais called a *song-thaew,* a pickup with two wooden benches bolted to the truck bed. Although the vehicle already held a half-dozen schoolgirls, the driver veered to the curb, where he and the old man began talking in Thai. A few moments later, the Englishman waved me over.

"We'll give you a lift. I know how disconcerting it can be, alone in a strange place."

He grabbed a handhold and swung himself gracefully into the mass of prim, giggling girls in starched white shirts and pleated blue skirts.

"Come along then. The name's Thompson. Leslie Thompson."

He relayed the guest-house address to the *song-thaew* driver and we drove along a main road eviscerated by construction, lurching between earthmoving machinery and stacks of concrete culverts.

"This road used to be no more than a bullock cart," Thompson said. "Across the river, there was nothing but jungle. Now there's talk of building a superhighway from here all the way through Burma to the Andaman Sea."

And then Thompson told me about the Death Railway. He had been a young corporal with the British Eighteenth Infantry Division, posted to Singapore. When the colony fell in early 1942, he was shipped to Thailand to labor on the railroad the Japanese were building through the green hell to link Singapore, Bangkok, and Rangoon. The work went quickly to Kanchanaburi, but then turned deadly as the line entered the hills. Although Japanese engineers predicted the project would take five or six years to complete, the slave laborers—sixty thousand Allied POWs and four times as many impressed Asians—finished the job in less than eighteen months. Thompson somehow existed on a starvation diet, without clean water, medical attention, or decent shelter, until liberation in late 1945.

He brushed a lock of wet hair from his sweat-glistening forehead and nodded toward a large, well-tended cemetery. Neat rows of low headstones spread across an immaculate greensward: nearly seven thousand Allied soldiers who had not survived the trials of malaria, cholera, dysentery, and malnutrition.

"I worked all the way up, right to the border," Thompson said. "Before Singapore my battalion stood at one thousand men. Only two hundred sixty-seven of us saw it through the war."

"How on earth did you make it?"

"I'm stubborn as they come," he replied. "The Japanese said they would keep me forever: I would work until I died, then other prisoners would take my place and work until they died. But I never lost hope we'd somehow win the war. Oh, I had my low points. But I never wanted to give my captors the satisfaction of killing me. And now I've stayed on. The Thai are happy enough to turn the whole thing with the bridge into a bloody tourist attraction. But I won't let people forget what transpired in this place, the evil that men can inflict."

We followed the main road into the town center, where the schoolgirls alighted. The intersection was a jumble of buses, *tuk-tuks,* and trucks overloaded with huge logs and sections of pipeline. A knot of people had formed around three policemen who were shouting at a dark-skinned young man wearing a windbreaker and a checked sarong. Thompson said something to the driver in Thai and we passed through the intersection and a bustling marketplace beyond.

"The latest scandal," said Thompson. "They round up these Karen boys and send them back to Burma. The Thai used to support the Karen guerrillas, traded them guns for timber. Do you know the Karen refuse to fight on Sundays? They're American Baptists, of all things. But the Thai have cut all the forest the Karen controlled. Now only the Burmese have teak. So the Karen don't get any more guns in trade. They get deported. Another hill tribe buggered."

The traffic eased a bit and we cruised by a large Buddhist temple, its gilded finials glittering in the sunlight, and a string of downmarket guest houses lining the Kwai Yai River.

"You'll be up here, 'round the corner," he said. "We were quartered right across the river, once upon a time. The view could bring you to tears—just the thought of dying out here alone in these magnificent mountains."

We turned from the road down a short, unpaved alley that ended in a cluster of shops—laundry, snack bar, tour agency, dry-goods store—flanking the gated entrance to the Fun Frog Guest House. When I got out, Thompson refused my money.

"I've enjoyed our conversation."

"I'll try to visit that cemetery."

"Never forget: don't give anyone the satisfaction of your misery. Above all else—"

And then his voice was lost in the whining acceleration as the *song-thaew* raced away.

I entered the guest house's fenced-in grounds and found the registration desk in a corner of a shaded, open-air restaurant. It was approaching noontime and perhaps a dozen young backpacker types occupied the tables, watching a jumpy, pirated videocassette of *The Bridge on the River Kwai*. In this cheap hostel, it would be a while before management upgraded the electronics. I rang the desk bell and waited. Above me, a pair of small ceiling fans barely moved the wet air, laden with the scent of river mud, clove cigarettes, and a hint of marijuana. When the manager appeared I requested a one-hundred-baht room. Then I slid an extra banknote across the desk, along with Linda's picture. The manager nodded. Yes. She had registered here; she spoke Thai with an accent. Isan region, he thought. And she was very pretty. He remembered a woman like that.

Had she checked in to the guest house with anybody else?

She traveled alone. A *farang* man, a German, had tried to pick her up in this restaurant one night. He had watched the scene unfold from the desk. The *farang* thought she was a local girl—they sold themselves now, at the hotels and the floating restaurants near the center of town. Kanchanaburi was changing. Linda had thrown a glass of water in the German's face and gone to her room. He remembered a woman like that.

Had he spoken with her during her stay?

The next morning, during breakfast. She said she had come to Kanchanaburi to forget a love affair. It was a mistake to have come here. Kanchanaburi was for lovers.

Her mood?

Quiet. Sad. Like something bad had happened to her.

Had he seen her using drugs?

He rolled his eyes, amused. Here, all the tourists used drugs. Linda Watts had stayed at the Fun Frog for three days and then booked an overnight raft trip down the Kwai Noi River through the guest house. Such trips were popular. When the trip was over, she had left the guest house. Beyond that, the manager could not say. Maybe she went to Bangkok. Maybe to Chiang Mai. Maybe to Three Pagodas Pass. Maybe even to Burma. Who knew? Tourists came and went. He hadn't seen her since. He remembered that and gave a mock sigh.

He excused himself to wait on another new arrival. I took my room key and decided to have lunch and consider my options. The guest-house menu, written in English on a large chalkboard, seemed palatable. I took a seat at an empty table and gave the waitress my order for chicken fried rice. Another time, perhaps, and I would gladly have spent a few days here, lazing by the river, dining on a floating restaurant, breathing the cleaner air. The Bangkok salarymen and foreign backpackers had not yet destroyed Kanchanaburi, although the traffic and the sex workers were a troubling portent. What was my next move? I'd gone to the U.S. embassy and the Bangkok coroner's office, the *amphoe* and the police station, the Front Row Hotel and two guest houses. I'd turned up nothing to indicate that Linda Watts was still alive. I was quickly exhausting leads.

The waitress returned with a large bottle of Singha beer.

"I didn't order this."

"The lady order for you."

The waitress nodded toward the rear of the restaurant, where a young woman with skin the color of pressure-treated pine, streaked blond hair, and the lanky build of a lifelong beachcomber sat smiling. My beer benefactor looked like good company; I had a few hours to kill before the train returned to Bangkok. I asked the waitress to bring another glass and waved the woman over.

"From the looks of it, I thought you could use a beer," she said, sliding into a chair across the small table. She gave my face a closer inspection. "Hate to see the other guy, though."

"Just an irate husband."

"And you're a bit of a larrikin."

I couldn't place her accent. Not English. South African, maybe.

"Sebastian. From the States."

She smiled.

"That obvious?" I asked.

"Afraid so," she replied. "The name's Charlotte. From Adelaide, once upon a time."

Charlotte poured herself a small glass of beer. I toasted my improving fortunes.

"What brings you to Thailand, Sebastian?"

"A woman."

"Would this woman have something to do with the condition of your face?"

"Another woman, actually."

She cocked her head and ran a hand through her hair. The humidity gave her mane a wild, Pre-Raphaelite quality.

"A dangerous man."

I produced Linda's photo.

"Seen her around town?"

Charlotte regarded the photo, smiled conspiratorially.

"Is she here now?"

"That's what I'd like to know. She was here a few weeks ago."

"I can understand why you've followed her to Thailand. Your girl is beautiful."

"She's just someone I'm trying to find. Let's leave it at that."

The waitress brought the steaming plate of fried rice and another large bottle of Singha. Charlotte declined the offer to eat in favor of a cigarette. I squeezed lime over the meal and polished it off in a dozen quick bites.

"What did she do, this woman who lured you all the way from America to Kanchanaburi? Did she steal something from you?"

"She died. At least, that's what her family believes. Other people think she's alive."

"And what do you believe?"

"I'm paid to believe she's alive. But all the facts indicate she's dead and gone."

"Dead and gone happens over here with alarming frequency."

"I wish more people understood that." Namely my client. I took a long pull on my beer. "You here for the rafting?"

"For the manpower." She pushed her chair back from the table and arched her back, stretching. "Singha always gets me knackered."

We sat silently for a few minutes, watching the movie. It was the scene where William Holden is shot while attempting to escape from the Japanese prison camp, falls into a river, and is swept downstream, only to be rescued by Thai villagers.

"Fancy going somewhere, Sebastian?"

I finished off my beer, mulling the offer. Today had been a dead end. Kanchanaburi had gone nowhere and I was running out of time. I had to remind myself: not every lead would pan out, but they all had to be checked. The old man would have come here as well. There was nothing else to do here, just return to Bangkok and catch hell from my client. The next city-bound train left at three o'clock. Mrs. Moyle's castigation would come tonight, when it would be morning in Boston. My father had mentioned an old army buddy who lived in Bangkok; maybe it was time to look up Sam Honeyman when I got back to the city.

"What do you have in mind, Charlotte?"

"I've got a joint in my room that'd choke Bob Marley."

"I haven't smoked in years. But don't let me stop you. I'm happy to just hang out for a few hours."

I paid the tab and followed Charlotte to her quarters, a small, second-floor cubicle that was cheaper in every way than the guesthouse cells I had seen on Khao San Road, except for the vistas of the broad, green Kwai Yai River. A frayed rattan nightstand held a few dog-eared paperbacks and the remnants of a fat beeswax candle and a mosquito coil. Two batik-print sarongs and an expensive-looking blue backpack hung from nails in the wall. That seemed to be the sum total of Charlotte's possessions. She turned on a floor fan and sat on the bed beside me; there was no other furniture in the room.

"Nice place," I said.

Charlotte rummaged through her backpack and produced a cigarillo-size joint.

"Took the room for five hundred baht a week," she said, her voice a strained whisper as she lit the dope. About sixteen dollars, at the rate the Thai baht had already plummeted. I waved off the joint; I would need all my faculties when speaking with Dolores Moyle. My client was not the type who suffered half-baked fools.

"You live here, Charlotte?"

"I keep a place in Bangkok. You know Khao San Road?"

"A bit."

"Convenient, and good value. I just take the train down to Malaysia every month to renew my visa. And I take a little something else to pay the bills. I didn't come up here for the scenery."

"I heard on good authority that Kanchanaburi's for lovers."

"I'm looking for entrepreneurs."

She winked and exhaled sweet, blue smoke.

"Isn't that a bit dangerous?" I asked. "I've seen the warning posters. The Thai and the Malaysians won't fool around if they catch you smuggling dope."

"They have to catch you first. You're fine if you don't look the part. When I put my mind to it I can look quite demure. Or not." She drew a hand slowly across my injured face. "You could do it too, Sebastian."

"I don't plan on spending my golden years inside Bang Kwang Prison, counting down the days until my consul's monthly visit."

"You'd be surprised how lucrative the work can be."

"You couldn't afford my fee. Better find someone else."

"I've been here for nearly a week. Nobody looks the part. Just cheeky backpackers."

"The woman I'm looking for also spent a bit of time on Khao San Road. Ever see her there?"

Perhaps Linda had somehow gotten herself involved in a smuggling racket like this. Maybe she had agreed to mule a load, then OD'd when she decided to knick it for a taste.

"Khao San's a big, messy place, but I would have remembered her. She's the type I keep an eye out for. Like you. If you're interested, I could introduce you to some people in Bangkok."

"And who are these people?"

"They know other people."

"Will you introduce me to them, too?"

"They're very shy."

Charlotte was compartmentalized, just a link in the food chain. I'd never find Linda Watts this way.

"Nigerians?" I ventured.

"When it comes to money I'm color-blind."

"I don't think I want to meet your people, Charlotte, or the people behind your people."

"It's big money," she persisted, taking one last enormous hit on the joint. "Low risk. You'd be perfect."

"I've already got too much work in Bangkok."

"Maybe I can change your mind."

She smirked and coughed a cloud of pot smoke in my face. Then her arms were at my neck, pulling open my shirt, and her tongue danced on my chest. I didn't resist. The bed creaked like some nocturnal creature and I felt a rising, months-old longing as Charlotte worked to unbuckle my belt. If I didn't make the three o'clock train, there was always a bus. I could probably even expense a taxi. I rolled Charlotte onto her back, pulled her blouse over her head, and watched the folds of fabric ebb to reveal small, soft breasts. Only then did I see the junkie tracks that ran like sutures along the length of her bruised arms.

I was out of her room in less than a minute. Charlotte followed me outside, where she stood topless on the gallery, throwing down curses as I hustled across the grounds. Bloody Yank. Narc bastard. Poofter. The restaurant crowd began to notice the scene, so I did what I did best: I ran. Not through the restaurant, but back across the lawn, then along the rain-slick banks of the Kwai Yai River, sliding and slipping all the way to the next riverside guest house. I pushed through the surprised staff and made my way to the road, where I flagged down a passing *samlor* and collapsed in the seat of the pedicab. I didn't even argue when the driver gouged me for seventy-five baht to carry me to the train station.

We didn't pull into Thonburi until after six o'clock. It was Friday night, and crosstown traffic tortured me for another two hours, including a detour to pick up my photos from the camera shop. After a desultory meal in the hotel coffee shop and a lukewarm shower to chase the mud of Kanchanaburi and the grit of Bangkok's lethal atmosphere, I called my client and put my best spin on the case. I laid out the investigative steps I had taken in Boston, Providence, Bangkok, and Kanchanaburi, the people I had interviewed, the agencies I had visited, the documents I had obtained or confirmed. So far, I told Mrs. Moyle, nothing felt bogus. There was no indication of insurance fraud. Everything I had seen and heard stood up the drug overdose and the death claim submitted by Bounliep Yanglong.

"It looks like a good death," I concluded.

"Forget all that," she replied. "I have a feeling about this case. You work at this as long as I have, you learn to trust your instincts. You need to get that feeling, too. This case is far from over. Linda Watts is still out there."

"You still think she's alive?" I couldn't hide my exasperation.

"Isn't it obvious?"

How could I prove a negative, that Linda Watts wasn't dead? If she had faked her death, then why had she set the insurance scam up as a drug overdose, thereby forfeiting a quarter-million-dollar

ADB? How brilliant was that? Why had all the official reports of her death checked out? I found my voice rising.

"Shall I fax you the documentation, Mrs. Moyle? The autopsy report? The death certificate? The police report?"

"I'm sure the paperwork is valid. You need to think beyond the obvious. Linda Watts certainly does. How did she make her death seem so real? How could she afford this elaborate scam? Where can she go without money or an American passport? She has to surface someplace. The question is, where? Put yourself in her position. What's her motive? What are her means? Call me again in twenty-four hours. And please, have better news. I don't want the Claims Committee on my ass. Remember, I took a chance on you."

So there it was: one more unsuccessful day and I could book my return flight. I'd be back in Somerville, condemned to a career of spying on cheating husbands and malingering workers, if I was lucky. Maybe hunt down a few runaway teens or lost pets, just for variety's sake. Nobody was beating down my door. When I called my answering service, the only message it relayed was from a collection agency. Linda Watts would become nothing but a shameful memory, a big-league case I couldn't quite hack, even if I had done everything by the book. I had time to make one final out-of-the-box move: find Sam Honeyman in a city of more than six million strangers and one invisible woman. In light of my failed hunt for Linda Watts, the prospect seemed remote. I didn't have an address or telephone number for my father's old army buddy, just a lead about a German restaurant on a street with the unlikely name of Soi Cowboy. It was as good as any other tip I'd had in Thailand.

I caught a break: Soi Cowboy was only a mile from my hotel. At the east end of the garish, block-long strip of dance clubs and go-go bars I found an open-air restaurant that smelled of caged birds and canned sauerbraten. I made for a large gazebo just beyond the gated entrance, where I experienced a small miracle. For one hundred baht, the bartender immediately remembered Sam Honeyman. Why, Mr. Sam had been here earlier tonight. He'd be by again tomorrow night. He came every day for dinner. Five o'clock sharp. And tonight? Mr. Sam would be singing cowboy music over at Nana Plaza. And which club? The bartender smiled apologetically. They changed names constantly.

Another *tuk-tuk* carried me down Sukhumvit to just outside Nana Plaza, where a pickup truck had sideswiped a motorcycle, sending the bike's helmetless driver and his female passenger headfirst into a curb. They lay facedown in spreading slicks of dark blood. Pedestrians gathered to watch the police work the carnage: two new guests for the ME's office. I forced my way through the gawking crowd, following an alley that spilled into an enormous, neon-lit courtyard ringed by three levels of saloons, nightclubs, and restaurants. I would start at the bottom of Nana Plaza and work my way up. I had a Singha beer and no luck at both Santeria and Pretty Girls, two crowded clubs where sweating foreign men came to watch Asian women gyrate to techno-pop music, not listen to an old soldier sing country music. After three more forgettable bars, I moved up to level two. No luck. Three beers later and still no hint of Honeyman, I washed up at Hot Spot for a "shower show": a naked dancer lathering up inside a glass-sided booth. Still no Sam. Other strippers writhed atop a kidney-shaped stage to ZZ Top. The raw, grinding power chords of "La Grange" were revving up to full throttle when a topless woman stepped in front of my table. Bandoliers festooned with dozens of shot glasses draped her chest; over a pair of red hot pants she wore a large black leather belt with two holstered bottles of tequila. She tapped salt onto her left breast.

"Shooter?" she asked.

"You know Honeyman?" I slurred. "Mr. Sam?"

"No Sam here."

I was full of beer and flat out of ideas. I paid the cowgirl one hundred baht, then drank the rotgut liquor in a single gulp without the salted-breast chaser. Maybe that was how those tourists met their maker down in Pattaya, like the consular officer, Forbes, had mentioned. Death, with a twist of lime and tits. Now the stage dancers swayed to Steppenwolf's "Born To Be Wild." I paid the cowgirl again. Somewhere, Charlotte was hustling. Somewhere, Mr. Sam was singing cowboy music. And somewhere, if Dolores Moyle was to be believed, Linda Watts was hiding in plain sight.

Ignore the paperwork. The death was real. Forget the death. Look beyond the truth. That's where I'd find her. Somewhere behind the box. A thin, copper-skinned woman in a minidress slid beside me and smiled. Pretty, but no Linda. I bought another shot and ordered one for the woman as well. When she had finished with the salt and the tequila she turned to me, her face partially obscured by strands of black, shoulder-length hair, and began massaging my thighs.

"What your name?" she asked.

"PI."

"Why you look so sad, PI?"

"Bad day at the office."

"Tomorrow is new day."

"It'll probably be another bad day."

"But maybe tonight will be good for you. You like me?"

"In that dress, what's not to like?"

"Then you good PI," she said, smirking.

I bought her another shooter and rose unsteadily, bracing myself on the tables to make my way outside. Time to go to my hotel. The chatty bar girl followed me from Hot Spot across the courtyard and through the alley to the street. The churning music and the burning tequila had ruined my hearing and my equilibrium; walking through the swarming crowd felt like wading through crashing surf wearing swim fins. I swayed on the curb of a busy street, waiting for a break in the traffic. The bar girl sidled up to me.

"I help you make good night tonight?"

"I need to find Honeyman."

"Hanuman? Monkey god?"

And then I saw her, an apparition sitting with three Asian men in the back of a passing *tuk-tuk*. She wore a crimson dress and that fatalistic look.

"Linda!"

I thought I caught a flash of surprise cross her face, but she didn't startle, never even turned her head. The *tuk-tuk* sped off, swallowed by the night. I moved to give chase, stumbled. The bar girl caught me in her arms to keep me from spilling into the gutter. Tequila always sent me off the rails.

"She not your friend, PI. Good friend is me. Minh."

"Which way did she go, Minh?"

"She go on Sukhumvit Road. To where I don't know."

"I need to find her."

"Not tonight, PI. You very *mau*. Very drunk."

"Yes. *Mau*. Very stupid of me."

"You have hard time to find people in Bangkok."

"Like I said, it's been a bad day."

It got worse: I retched into the street. No one seemed to care. *Farang* puked all the time. It was inside-the-box behavior. Minh led me away from the road to an unlit lane. My good friend, *mau* friend. Drunk and aroused by the Hot Spot dancers, I fumbled with her shirt, trying to palm her breasts. Minh laughed as she warded off my clumsy advances, then pushed me against a cinder-block wall. It felt cool and hard against my back, like a hospital gurney. I stood as straight as I could to keep from falling while she flicked her tongue across my neck, my chest, my belly. The shrill whine of a thousand *tuk-tuks* dimmed to low, white noise, while neon signs cast harsh light against a dark opaque sky. My good friend. I could feel the warm, swelling expectation. The rains were coming soon.

MEMORANDUM FOR THE FILE

Re: Watts, Linda (Case 97-013)
Subject: Interview with Sister Tuyet Nguyen
Date: Saturday, July 5, 1997

In the fifteen years Sister Tuyet Nguyen has worked at the Emma Lazarus Center, she has seen more than six thousand refugees come through the doors. Linda Watts stood out like a beacon.

The nondenominational resettlement center is at 600 Potters Avenue, Providence, Rhode Island, a former parish school. Sister Tuyet is a Dominican nun; she teaches job skills and English as a second language. Having fled South Vietnam in 1975 on a boat, she seems to have a special rapport with the center's immigrant and refugee clients.

Sister Tuyet remembered Linda and her uncle Bounliep Yanglong as "the odd couple": a withdrawn little girl and an illiterate shaman who first came to the center in the early 1980s. Before Providence they had bounced around Lao-refugee communities in California and Minnesota for several years. Sister Tuyet said that the girl became one of the Lazarus Center's greatest success stories and told me all she could remember about her: a harrowing odyssey from Laos to a squalid refugee camp in Thailand, then a long climb from inner-city slums in America to a promising career at BankBoston. Her original name was Lin Wattana and she had left Laos with her uncle shortly after the country fell to the Communists in 1975. Bounliep Yanglong feared punishment under the new authoritarian regime. The shaman's concern was well founded, according to Sister Tuyet, who had witnessed the persecution of Catholic priests and Buddhist monks in Vietnam. So, Bounliep had escaped the mountains of the Lao-Vietnamese border. Lin—most likely six or seven years old at the time, no one knew exactly—went with him.

Sister Tuyet explained that Lin's mother (who was Bounliep's sister) could not leave Laos. Their father, the village headman, was ill with malaria; it was a daughter's duty to care for a sick parent. Lin and Bounliep walked through the jungle for more than a week to arrive at the Mekong, where they found a pirogue on the riverbank and paddled across the waterway to northeast Thailand. There they were taken into custody and sent to Ban Na Pho refugee center, in Nakhon Phanom Province.

Ban Na Pho was a crowded camp where the displaced fought one another and their Thai "protectors" preyed on everyone. Lin had a hard time of it, said Sister Tuyet, watching girls not much older than herself sell themselves to the guards for food. With no relatives overseas, it took almost five years before Bounliep and Lin were sponsored by a charity to come to America. By then, according to Bounliep, Lin's parents had died in Laos.

Lin arrived in Providence with a certain hardness of spirit, the nun said. Even in a dirt-poor place like Laos there is a social pecking order and Lin and her uncle were hill tribers, the bottom of the barrel. Lin had no Asian or American friends; she spoke virtually no English. She took Sister Tuyet's ESL classes for two years, then began to excel in several subjects, particularly mathematics.

Bounliep Yanglong was another matter. He had even fewer marketable skills than the elderly Hmong refugees, said Sister Tuyet. He couldn't complete the center's programs in food service or auto mechanics. And his idea of hospital-orderly duties involved sacrificing live poultry, the sister said.

After ESL classes, Lin went through "a phase," the nun related, going so far as to legally change her name to "Linda Watts." Lin acted out, became a punk, and dyed her hair red. Lin seemed confused about her own identity. When I asked about Lin's drug use during this rebellious phase, Sister Tuyet said that Lin had confessed to experimenting with marijuana, alcohol, and a few pills, not unlike numerous other Asian-immigrant teens she encountered, but nothing on the order of cocaine or heroin. Lin was never affiliated with any of the prominent Asian street gangs, like Tiny Rascals. Even they looked down on hill tribers. But by the end of her junior year in high school, the girl seemed to have found herself. Lin focused on her studies, scored nearly 800 on the math portion of her SATs. Sister Tuyet believed that Lin finally realized she would have to provide for herself and her uncle.

When Lin attended Boston College, she often returned on weekends to volunteer at the Lazarus

Center. After graduation she became one of the center's biggest private donors. She also worked as a volunteer, taking a special interest in Asian adolescents going through the same difficult cultural adjustments or having problems with their parents.

Six

The hotel maid shook me awake, giggling to find a *farang* fully dressed and stretched out on top of the bedcovers. The bar girl from Hot Spot was nowhere to be seen. Had she come home with me, melted into the night, or returned to Nana Plaza to hustle another tourist? I checked my pockets: somehow, I still had my passport and wallet containing two hundred dollars' worth of Thai baht. My head pounded; my bowels churned. After ushering the maid to the door, I barely made it to the toilet to suffer the indignity of concurrent vomiting and shitting. Then I administered a small pharmacopoeia—Lomitil, Advil, Cipro, and aspirin—and considered my worsening situation. It was after ten o'clock on a Saturday morning and I was hung over, probably sick with food poisoning, but finally beyond self-flagellation. I had seen Linda or her doppelgänger, I was almost sure of it. And I now had less than twelve hours to find her again and to document her existence before Dolores Moyle would pull the plug on Damon & Son.

Trip Forbes had mentioned the TM cards; it was an angle I hadn't pursued. I decided to go out to the airport, then return to Khao San Road and speak with the police detective who had investigated Linda's death and the Marco Polo guest who'd found the body. And I hoped that lunch with Miss Sirilaksana might yield some useful information about Khao San Road. The route to the airport highway passed Nana Plaza and I ordered the driver to stop; I wanted to retrace last night's movements. But for a pair of dogs lounging in the shade of an awning, the alley was deserted, the courtyard barren. Metal shutters covered the club entrances. Only after sundown did Nana spring to life. In the daylight, nothing looked familiar.

The cab headed north again, the antic urban sprawl fanning out on both sides of the superhighway. Empty office towers and skyscrapers seemed to erupt everywhere, on busy commercial streets and in neighborhoods where old, raised, wooden homes still stood and children swam and fished in green-gray *klongs,* the fetid canals that carried cargo and passenger-boat traffic and drained the summer storms into the Chao Phraya River. At the airport, the international terminal was relatively empty; the late-evening crush from Europe and the United States was still many hours away. I took an escalator up one flight from the cavernous baggage-claim area to the arrival level and explained my request to a Thai Passport Control officer. The small man sized me up, ignoring the one-hundred-baht note I had laid in my opened wallet, and pointed toward the nearby immigration office. Go there, he told me. Inside immigration, a clerk who spoke English took Linda's particulars—name, nationality, passport number, and arrival date—and entered them into a computer. In moments he had retrieved an electronic file with a referral number for her TM card. He smiled, then left the room. I leaned against the counter, sweating profusely, thinking how lousy I felt.

After a small, painful wait, the clerk returned with a small piece of paper. I regarded the white, postcard-size record, filled in with the careful block letters of someone who had studied English as a second language. The data at the top of the card checked out: name, date of birth, passport number. Farther down, the card had new information.

FIRST TRIP TO THAILAND?

NO, Linda had ticked.

TRAVELING ON GROUP TOUR?

NO.

LENGTH OF STAY?

FOURTEEN DAYS.

PURPOSE OF VISIT?

TOURIST, she had checked.

ADDRESS IN THAILAND?

FRONT ROW HOTEL, SUKHUMVIT, BANGKOK.

There was no paperwork for the return portion of Linda's trip. That information was recorded on a part of the TM card that would have been detatched and inserted into her passport. I had a similar pale stub stapled to my passport.

"This what you look for, yes?" the clerk said with a sly chuckle. "To find somebody in Thailand? Easy. No problem."

It was a problem, though, when you chased a ghost. He made me a copy and refused my tip. I felt the sour bile, the legacy of last night, burning in my stomach, hurriedly thanked him, and hustled from the office to puke in the nearest toilet. Then I took a solemn oath: no more street food. No more bar girls. And no more tequila.

By now it was half past noon; with Bangkok's traffic, I was going to miss lunch with Miss Sirilaksana. On the taxi ride into town I tried to figure Linda's moves and motives. It was possible that she had gone to the Front Row Hotel, been unimpressed with the amenities, and then checked into the nearby Mermaid's Rest. She had then gone to Kanchanaburi before returning to Bangkok, where she checked into the Marco Polo Guest House for the last week of her life. According to her TM card, she had arrived in Thailand nearly three weeks before she died. She had stayed longer than intended.

Had she met someone and decided to extend her visit? Had she gotten into serious trouble? Had she gone on a heroin jag? Or had she just gone underground? If so, why would she ride around Bangkok in a *tuk-tuk* with three Thai men?

Linda had repeatedly telephoned the Front Row Hotel before she left Boston. Had someone recommended the place, which failed to rate even a line in my guidebook? There had to be hundreds of sketchy establishments just like it strewn across Bangkok. Why was the Front Row so important? And why hadn't the clerk there seen Linda? Had she bought his silence? Had she changed her mind about staying on the ride from the airport, then gone to the Mermaid's Rest instead? Or had she simply lied about the Front Row on her TM card?

Another vexing question: if Linda Watts was still alive, why had she scuttled her promising career? Given her earnings potential, even $500,000 seemed like short money. I had read Linda's case file, talked to her friends and family, and seen her credit reports. I didn't want to believe this scam all boiled down to the usual, venal reasons. I wanted her to have a compelling excuse for fraud, some mitigating circumstances. And then I caught myself. The reasons for her actions didn't matter. The old man's advice was always to ignore a subject's motivation. You risked sympathy, he counseled, and sympathy was a weakness, an indulgence, a potentially fatal flaw. Only your clients mattered. They paid your bills.

I arrived at Khao San Road after two o'clock, too late for lunch with Miss Sirilaksana, and decided to stop by the Marco Polo to check on the lodger in room 7, the one who had found Linda's body. Mrs. Antiporn did not look pleased to see me again, but one hundred baht was enough to compel her to go upstairs to retrieve the witness. In a few minutes she returned with an owlish, redheaded man in his early thirties who looked to have been stirred from a sweat-drenched siesta.

"Are you with the embassy?" he asked, stifling a yawn. "Or a journalist?"

"Private investigator."

"Even worse."

"At least I've spared you the trench coat."

"I've already spoken to the police."

"I've come all the way from the States on this matter. I haven't really enjoyed my stay in Bangkok so far. So how about a few minutes, pal?"

He drew back. My bruised, agitated state made me look like I was not above resorting to my fists to get answers.

"All right, I suppose. Too hot to go back to sleep anyway."

I shot an exasperated look at Mrs. Antiporn, who eavesdropped from the registration desk. She scowled and disappeared into her back room to watch television.

"You're in room seven?"

"How'd you—"

"I don't consider you a suspect. Relax. Can you tell me where your room is in relation to room six, where Linda Watts died?"

"Next room down the hall, closer to the toilets. I never knew her name before. Linda." He paused, rolling the name over his tongue as if at a budget-wine tasting. "She didn't look like a Linda."

"Expecting something more exotic?"

"I suppose."

"How about Lin?"

"Not even close."

"This her?" I handed him Linda's college-graduation photo.

"Perhaps. Old picture?"

"Six, maybe seven years."

"People change. The girl I saw was thinner, less concerned with appearances."

"What do you mean?"

"Greasy hair, funky clothes, bad skin."

His description jibed with the drug-use story. Hard-core junkies didn't give a damn about anything except their next fix. Not food, not sleep, not hygiene, not style. Only heroin.

"What about this picture?"

I showed him a copy of Linda Watts's passport photo.

"Once upon a time, maybe. But like I said, the girl I saw was skanky."

"How did you discover the body?"

"The stench. Sweet and sour at the same time. You couldn't ignore it, really. I alerted the front desk, and then I climbed on top of a chair to look through the chicken wire. That's when I saw her dead on the floor, slumped against the door. A real mess. The rats had already done a job on her face."

"What time of day?"

"Late afternoon. I had just finished napping when I noticed the smell."

"Ever speak with her?"

"Not really. Just passed her by in the lobby, nodded hello."

"How'd her mood seem?

"Hard to say. No interaction to speak of."

"Did you ever see her in her room at night?"

"She was a pretty girl, even in her condition, but I'm no voyeur."

"I'm not accusing you of peeping on her. I just want to know: did you happen to hear anything suspicious coming from her room? Anything at all?"

He considered the question.

"Well, I did hear a bit of noise once. Sounded like she had a man in her room."

"When was this?"

"The night before she died, I think."

"Do you remember what time you heard the noise?"

"Nine or ten, maybe. I had gotten up to go to the toilet."

"What did you hear? Talking? Fighting? Fucking?"

"More like whispers."

"Whispers?"

"Yes, a man whispering."

"Did you ever see this man?"

"Her door was shut."

"Could you hear what this man said?"

"Barely."

"And what did the man say?"

"Hey, I've only been in Bangkok a short while. I can't understand every word of Thai I hear. The only thing I could make out was *ramat rawang*. It means 'careful.' "

"Thai?"

"Strange, huh? Maybe she picked up a Thai guy. I mean, when in Bangkok . . . And she could pass for a local."

"Did you tell any of this to the police?"

"The detective in charge didn't seem interested in interviewing the guests. He took my name, asked if I'd been in the room or disturbed the body before the police arrived. That was it. He stayed in her room until an ambulance came. To tell the truth, he seemed pretty bored about the whole thing, like it happened all the time to *farang* in Bangkok. The guest-house owner acted blasé, too. Maybe it does happen all the time. Or maybe it's just a Buddhist thing."

"Maybe so, Mister . . . ?"

"Brody. Doug Brody."

I gave Brody the number for the Grand Babylon, in case he remembered anything else substantial. Then I headed for the Chanasongkram police station, trying to figure the distance between Brody's story, my tequila-fueled vision, and Dolores Moyle's twenty-four-karat hunch. Something had to give. I kept to the sidewalk, where cloth awnings had been strung for shade, and walked through a dazzling tunnel of counterfeit goods all the way to the end of Khao San Road. Inside the precinct house, two feral-looking trekkers spoke with Miss Sirilaksana, who sat inside her glass booth, listening beautifully. I waved to her and took the stairs to the second floor. Sergeant Wiwat seemed perturbed to see me again, crushing his cigarette in an ashtray and snapping his fingers to summon his English-speaking assistant.

"The inspector is not available," the aide said, even before his superior had uttered a word.

"Is the inspector out of the station at the moment? Or is he busy here? I can wait."

The aide turned to Sergeant Wiwat, then translated his reply.

"The inspector is away. He cannot spend his entire day waiting for *farang* who want to speak with him at a moment's notice, *farang* who make no appointments. Bangkok is a very busy city."

"When I spoke with you two days ago you didn't mention the need for an appointment. I've come all the way across town to speak with the inspector. A long, bad drive."

"You would need appointment in your country to see important official, yes? You think Thailand is any different?"

The only difference was the shakedown. I slid the aide one hundred baht.

"Can I reserve a time tomorrow morning to speak with the inspector? Say, eleven o'clock?"

The aide pocketed the money. Then Sergeant Wiwat gave me the bad news.

"Tomorrow is Sunday. The inspector does not work on Sunday."

"Can you please give me a telephone number where I can reach him?"

"He will contact you."

I gave the sergeant my business card, inscribed with the telephone number of the Grand Babylon.

"I will give him your request," the aide translated.

"Can you at least tell me the inspector's name?"

"It is included in the police report. You have a copy of the report, yes?"

"If you recall, your Xerox machine was broken on Thursday. I had to take a photograph of the report."

"So now there is nothing for you here," the aide said officiously. "The inspector has said everything about the dead American girl in the report. Maybe you should take the information and go home. Your Bangkok investigation seems finished. Good day."

Sergeant Wiwat and his aide left the counter. Interview over. I stalked downstairs to chat up Miss Sirilaksana. When she saw me she tried a mild, momentary pout to tease me, then broke into a wide smile.

"You come late today, *Khun* Sebastian. I think you find some other Bangkok girl."

"I'm sorry. I had to go to the airport. And then with the traffic . . ."

"Ah, Bangkok traffic. But I am free tomorrow."

"That's not possible, I'm afraid. But you can still help me."

I gave her the photographs I'd taken of the guest-house register and the police report.

"Can you read the writing? It's quite small."

Her lips moved silently as she scanned the pictures.

"I think maybe."

"Can you tell me who rented room six in the middle of June?"

Her golden brow wrinkled in concentration as she examined the images. Then she tapped a photograph.

"What's the name?" I asked. "Does it say Linda Watts? Or Lin Wattana?"

"No. Different name. This lady is Chang Tai. From Singapore."

"Singapore? Not Boston?"

"Yes, Singapore. Chang Tai is a Chinese name. Many Chinese people from Singapore."

"Could there be a mistake? Please look again. Do you see the name Watts or Wattana anywhere on the page? Linda or Lin?"

"No."

"Are any Americans registered?"

"Only people from Canada, Italy, Germany, Singapore. You want the passport number and address of Chang Tai? I will write them down for you."

I stood there dumbly, trying to make sense of this development. Why had Linda taken the identity of a Chinese woman from Singapore? Whom was she hiding from? What kind of trouble had she tried to avoid? When Miss Sirilaksana gave me the information, I handed her the photo of the police report from the Chanasongkram station.

"Can you read the signature? Who wrote this police report?"

"Colonel Nagaphit."

"Do you know the colonel?"

"Very big man."

"Very busy man, too. He's never here. Will he return this afternoon? Can you get a message to him?"

"Colonel Nagaphit will not return here today, I think. He works from Thonglor."

"Thonglor? What's Thonglor?"

"Police station."

"But not this police station."

"No, not here."

"Another police station? Where?"

She sucked air through clenched teeth, as though thinking her answer might disappoint me.

"In Bangkok, but very far away. In Klong Toey district, near the Eastern Bus Terminal, off Sukhumvit Road."

"Why would Colonel Nagaphit from Thonglor station come and work a drug-overdose case for Chanasongkram?"

"I do not know."

"Does this colonel come often to Chanasongkram station?"

"The colonel and Sergeant Wiwat are very good friends. They attend police academy together. Maybe you talk to Sergeant Wiwat."

The sergeant hadn't wanted to dignify any of my questions.

"Maybe I will do that. But I have a question I think you can answer: how long would it take to drive to the Thonglor station from here, from Chanasongkram?"

"One hour maybe in police car, maybe longer in *tuk-tuk*."

"Here's my card, Miss Sirilaksana. Please write to me if you plan to come to Boston, or call me collect. I will take you to lunch in Cambridge, and show you the hospital where your king was born. I won't forget your help."

"Be careful of Bangkok traffic, *Khun* Sebastian."

Even on the back of a motorcycle taxi it took more than an hour to wend our way through the shoppers who clogged Bangkok's streets and sidewalks on Saturday afternoons. I clutched the bike's seat and tried to take my mind off our near-miss commute by considering the investigation so far. Perhaps I hadn't seen Linda Watts outside Nana Plaza after all. Had she adopted another identity, become Chang Tai from Singapore? Possibly, if she had gone into hiding. But could she then have come to grief so quickly in a cheap guest house? And from heroin? Why would Colonel Nagaphit, a high-ranking officer at the Thonglor police station, work an OD case on the other side of town in Chanasongkram's jurisdiction? How had he determined that the dead woman inside the Marco Polo was Linda Watts? From her passport? If she was masquerading as a Singaporean tourist, why had he not mentioned this detail in his police report? And why had he not interviewed other Marco Polo lodgers?

The Thonglor police station was less than a mile from my hotel, a two-story whitewashed building in a quiet neighborhood of old trees and foreign embassies. The kind of tony place a policeman assigned to a grungy backpacker district aspired to work, not vice versa. But maybe Colonel Nagaphit had a taste for budget travelers behaving badly. There was a fortune to be made by arresting and then extorting these knuckleheads, who didn't believe Thai law applied to their dim-witted actions. In his sunglasses and pressed uniform, the Thonglor desk sergeant looked the mirror image of his obdurate Khao San Road counterpart. He didn't skimp on attitude, either, allowing my request to speak with Colonel Nagaphit to hang an interminable time before he replied.

"Appointment, sir?"

"No, but it's very important that I see the inspector."

"Colonel Nagaphit very busy, sir."

"Then I will wait."

"Colonel Nagaphit very busy long time, sir."

"Then I will wait a long time."

"As you wish, sir."

He went back to studying a bus-crash story in his Thai newspaper. Colonel Nagaphit finally appeared at five o'clock. He had the short, powerful build of a lightweight boxer and the air of a skilled counterpuncher, a dangerous man to back into a corner. He accented the attitude with a neatly groomed mustache, a starched uniform, and a constitution unbowed by Bangkok's climate. The personification of a rising law-enforcement star, he barely broke stride to shake my hand, then motioned for me to follow him outside.

"I'm sorry but I've been called away, Mr. Damon," he said with a faintly British tone to his voice, the kind that effortlessly conveys both boredom and superiority. "I have only a few minutes. Please, walk with me to the car park."

"Colonel, I've come all the way to Bangkok to look into the death of Linda Watts, an American girl who—"

"I'm very familiar with the case of the American girl," he interjected, "and why you're here. Sergeant Wiwat rang me. He said you came by Chanasongkram station."

"Twice."

The inspector chuckled faintly.

"Does such persistence work in America?"

"Not always."

"The same holds true in Thailand, I'm afraid. You have seen my police report. Everything is there. I regret I can add nothing to it."

We exited the building and walked quickly to a small parking lot shaded by rain trees.

"I'm still confused about a few things, Colonel. I hope you can clear them up for me."

"Please continue."

"The girl you found at the Marco Polo Guest House was Linda Watts?"

"Certainly. It's in the report."

"How did you identify the woman?"

"From her passport, of course."

"But she registered under another name—Chang Tai—and she used a Singaporean passport as well."

The colonel smiled and kept walking.

"Your thoroughness is impressive, Mr. Damon. Perhaps you should come to work for the Bangkok police. If the American girl did engage in such subterfuge, the guest-house owner never told me. The false name is a moot point anyway. As I said, I determined her identity from her American passport, which I found in her possession."

"You don't think it strange that she may have registered under a false name?"

"People come to Bangkok to run away from many things. It is too late now to question Linda Watts about her reasons."

"One last question, Colonel, a minor point really. You are assigned to Thonglor station?"

"Yes. Going on five years."

"Yet you investigated a case out of Chanasongkram. All the way across town."

"I had gone to visit a colleague, Sergeant Wiwat. The station happened to be short of staff that day. When the death was reported, I agreed to help."

He walked to a late-model Mercedes sedan and produced a key.

"It was a favor," he continued. "You're in Thailand now. As professionals, we try not to worry too much about turf battles. We help each other in this way. We cut through the red tape, as you Americans love to say. And the death of Linda Watts was no mystery at all. Drug overdose. A very quick investigation. Cut and dried."

"Yet it took you an hour to arrive at the guest house from Chanasongkram. That seems like a very slow response time. Even allowing for Bangkok traffic."

Bristling, Colonel Nagaphit removed his sunglasses. His coal-black eyes blazed.

"The American girl died of a heroin overdose," he said, punctuating his comments by jabbing the sunglasses at me. "What is it about America that compels so many of its citizens to come to my country to die? And my methods of investigation are none of your concern. If new information becomes available, I will contact you at your hotel. The Grand Babylon, I believe?"

He repositioned his sunglasses and permitted himself a small, humorless smile: I know where you sleep. Then he attempted a different, avuncular tack.

"You have the official reports. There is really nothing else you can do. You should leave Bangkok before it becomes too late. Many *farang* wait too long. I see them everywhere: in bars, in streets, in tatty guest houses like the one where the American girl died. A shame. Such a pretty girl."

He slid into his expensive Mercedes and offered one last bit of advice before starting the car.

"Please don't become a burden to your embassy, Mr. Damon."

MEMORANDUM FOR THE FILE

Re: Watts, Linda (Case 97-013)
Subject: Some notes on the Katu
Date: Sunday, July 6, 1997

In the follow-up to my July 4 meeting with Bounliep Yanglong, I determined to read up on the Katu, a Southeast Asian hill tribe previously unknown to me. Perhaps there was something about their folkways or customs that would prove useful in ferreting out Linda's fate, or explaining her state of mind. Compared to other Southeast Asian ethnic-minority groups such as the Hmong, who are spread across the mountains of Thailand, Laos, China, and Vietnam and much studied by anthropologists, there isn't much documentation to be found about the Katu. What little information I discovered is buried in the stacks of the Boston Public Library and Harvard University's Widener and Tozzer libraries. The most useful books are Robert L. Mole's *The Montagnards of South Vietnam: A Study of Nine Tribes* (1970) and *Minority Groups in the Republic of South Vietnam* (1966), published as part of the U.S. Army's Ethnographic Study Series.

From Mole:

"Long considered to be one of the most warlike tribes of South Vietnam, the Katu have a history of violence among themselves, against other tribes and toward foreign peoples. They have resisted 'pacification' by the Khmer, Chams, French and ethnic Vietnamese. Not only are they geographically inaccessible, but also are known as a very unfriendly group. Their name Katu, 'savage,' acclaimed by their neighboring tribes is indicative of an attitude which the Katu have earned by tribal action through the centuries."

Mole went on to say that neighboring hill tribes had been unsuccessful in fostering friendly relations with the Katu, who were considered moody, hostile, and easily riled to murderous violence. And the kicker:

"Beware of involvements with women of the Katuic people."

From the U.S. Army:

"Annamese records of the mid-19th century mention the Katu as an aggressive tribe engaging in blood hunts—ritual murders to appease evil spirits—against the Annamese in the lowlands.

"Blood hunts were also perpetrated against neighboring tribes and even against Katu villages. When their enemies finally fought to stop the bloodshed they showed the Katu no mercy, so savage were the Katu during their blood hunts.

"In patriarchal Katu society the female members have lower status than the males. The male is undisputed head of the household and administers all punishments. Women walk behind men, often carrying heavy burdens such as a load of wood while the men carry only a crossbow.

"Katu have a subsistence economy and are dependent

upon agriculture for the bulk of their food. Upland rice, manioc, and corn are grown by slash-and-burn cultivation. After exhausting all possible sites in the vicinity of the village, the Katu then move their village to fresh, available land. Presumably such moves occur every few decades.

"One of the most warlike Montagnard tribes, the Katu were never completely pacified by the French—even now it is believed that they engage in blood hunts, attacking weaker or unsuspecting victims with much relish and bloodletting.

"The Christian and Missionary Alliance established a mission in the Katu area in 1941. Prior to this time, missionaries attempting to work among the Katu had been either driven away or killed.

"It may be noted that not until 1935 did the French open up the Katu area and establish six guard posts there. The difficulty of travel in the Katu area enabled the tribespeople to live in isolation and maintain only minimal contact with the Government.

"Little is known about the Vietnamese clans. Of those in Laos, almost nothing."

Seven

I returned to the hotel to change into fresh clothes; Bangkok wrung the life out of my shirts within minutes, reducing them to sweat-soaked rags. The night watchman, a Bangkok cop, was already on the clock in the lobby; he eyed me all the way to the elevator. When I came back downstairs, the receptionist gave me a message slip: Byron Peters of Insight Security had called around noon. Dolores Moyle didn't waste time. Mather Mutual's Claims Committee must have gotten wind of the Watts case. Well, good luck to Insight. I crumpled the note and threw it at a potted palm, then stormed outside and shook a driver dozing in his *tuk-tuk*.

I had one more chance to find Sam Honeyman. We headed downtown at a fair pace, driving against the stalled Saturday-evening traffic simmering on Sukhumvit Road. A few minutes into the ride, the chainsaw whine of a motorcycle announced the appearance of a motorcycle policeman, a malevolent insect in his bulbous helmet, dark visor, and grit-caked surgical mask. He pulled alongside my *tuk-tuk*; I sensed a shakedown coming for some imaginary traffic violation. The policeman sped ahead, then suddenly popped his motorbike into our lane. My driver shouted and swerved, coming to a sliding stop in a deep, curbside puddle. Had I not been holding on to the backseat I might have found myself splattered across Sukhumvit Road, more fresh meat for the coroner's office. The errant motorcyclist accelerated and disappeared between two buses.

"Bad policeman," my driver muttered, then kick-started his *tuk-tuk*. "Thonglor police no good. Bad driver. Bad man."

"No good," I concurred.

The encounter could have been just a coincidence. At the medical examiner's office I'd already seen the evidence that grisly road crashes happened in Thailand with frightening regularity. But I couldn't rule out the chance that Colonel Nagaphit had tried to frighten me off, or worse. This was Bangkok; I didn't know how things here worked. The accidental and the intentional were impossible to distinguish.

I paid off the irate driver, waded through the dirty water to the curb, and walked the rest of the way to Soi Cowboy, passing pubs filled with expats who were already half drunk and bar girls hoping to turn a short-time trick while the evening was still young. I arrived at the German restaurant to find other customers sucking down happy-hour Heinekens and plates of pale, overcooked sausages. A radio station at the bar played big-band music above the screeching of parrots; a muted television broadcast local-news coverage from Pattaya, where bodies were still being retrieved from a Thursday hotel fire that had killed more than ninety people. The bartender smiled at me, remembering a good tipper. I passed a fifty-baht note across the long, beer-slickened countertop; he pointed to an open-air structure across the courtyard. Beneath a thatched-roof pavilion a middle-aged man sat with an attractive Thai woman of indeterminate age. Their table held a half-dozen empty amber Singha beer bottles, half a bowl of sticky rice, and the remnants of a joint of roast pork.

"Sam Honeyman?"

The man pushed his white plastic chair back from the table and regarded me with a gambler's suspicion.

"I'm watching the news," he drawled. "Who wants to know?"

"Sebastian Damon. I'm Tom Damon's son. He said I should look you up if I ever made it to Bangkok."

That set him back for a few seconds and then he rose, an imposing physical figure even in his sixties, and grinned and shook my hand, his grip strong and slippery with pork grease. Framed by light, freckled skin and a military-style crew cut, his eyes looked rheumy and haunted.

"Hell, Stonewall's kid. Heard a lot about you."

"None of it's true."

"How'd you find me? Bangkok's a big place."

"My dad had a notion."

"I'm getting too set in my ways," he said with a chuckle.

He pushed the food aside and gestured for me to sit.

"A hell of a mess down in Pattaya," he said, nodding at the TV. "The hotel had padlocked the exits, to prevent guests from skipping out on the bill."

"T-I-T," I replied. "Or so I've heard."

"Shit happens," he answered, "and then it happens again. And again. This is Thailand."

"I stopped by last night. The bartender suggested I look for you at Nana Plaza. No luck."

"I play up on level three, the Beverly Hills Bar."

"I only made it to level two."

"Still impressive. Most new guys never get past level one. Too many temptations."

"Guess I don't know my limitations."

He handed me his business card, illustrated with an American eagle gripping an acoustic guitar in its talons.

"You wouldn't have found me anyway. Slow last night, and I met this girl. She convinced me to leave after my second set."

He nodded toward the woman, who gave me a gap-toothed smile.

"Bangkok can be a very friendly town." He signaled for another beer. "What brings you to Thailand? Did Stonewall recommend it to you for R-and-R?"

"No fun and games. Just business."

"The same business as your pops?"

"He got out a few months ago. I'm running the show now. And this is a different kind of investigation: life-insurance fraud. But I've hit the proverbial wall. I'm hoping you can help."

I produced the picture of Linda Watts from my shirt pocket and laid it on the table.

"I'm looking for her. According to every bit of official evidence I've seen, this woman OD'd on heroin in Bangkok three weeks ago."

Honeyman regarded the photo carefully, like a pawnbroker assessing estate jewelry.

"She don't look Thai."

"She's originally from Laos."

"She don't look too Lao either."

I was impressed with his appraisal.

"She's from the mountains."

"Thought she looked like a Montagnard."

I sketched the outlines of my subject's life from Lin Wattana, Katu hill-tribe refugee, to Linda Watts, model immigrant, from a shaman's apprentice to an executive banker, from the perfect fiancée to a pile of cold ashes.

"Who requested cremation?" Honeyman asked.

"Her uncle, the shaman. Her only kin."

"Katu, you said."

"Yes. He's got all the crazy tattoos to prove it. Scarier than an inked-up Yakuza body suit."

A waitress brought a cold beer and a glass, which Honeyman filled and slid my way.

"Anything about the case seem unusual to you so far?"

"Linda Watts registered under an assumed name at a Khao San Road guest house: Chang Tai, a Singaporean national. And the detective who handled her OD doesn't work at Chanasongkram, the police station with jurisdiction for that area. He's actually stationed near here, at Thonglor, all the way across town from Khao San Road. The investigating officer is a Colonel Nagaphit. I went by his office at Thonglor this evening. He had an excuse for catching the Watts case; he also gave me some serious attitude. Then I nearly got run off Sukhumvit by a motorcycle cop on my way here this evening. Somehow I don't think it was bad driving."

I pushed the foaming glass of beer aside.

"I think I saw Linda Watts last night in the back of a *tuk-tuk* near Nana Plaza. It was late; I was loaded. Maybe the tequila helped me see what I wanted to see. But so far the official documentation is solid."

Honeyman went silent for several minutes, then signaled for a check.

"Whoever the police found dead over on Khao San Road isn't your girl," he said flatly.

"What do you know that I don't know?"

"I know the Katu don't believe in cremation. They bury their dead, like most mountain people. The Katu would consider a drug overdose a very bad death. If they didn't bury the girl ASAP, her wandering spirit would make big trouble for them. A Katu, especially a shaman, would never sanction a cremation. It's a complete sacrilege."

I shook my head sheepishly. The source material I'd found at Harvard about the Katu had specifically described their funeral rites. And I had missed the inconsistency.

"No, I was never an anthropologist," Honeyman contined. "But I spent a couple of my army tours with the Montagnards, running recon teams in the Central Highlands during the war. That's where I met your pops. Kontum was our forward operating base. It's almost nothing but mountain people up there. We called 'em Yards—short for 'Montagnards.' They were good, tough-ass soldiers. And they hated the Vietnamese."

"Like the bad blood between the Lao Loum and Lao Theung."

"The Lao Theung and the Yards are one and the same. My old hooch girl was Jeh tribe. Her people lived just north of Kontum. And the Katu lived to the north of the Jeh. The Jeh gave them a wide berth. Nobody messed with the Katu—not even the North Vietnamese. Real shitkickers."

"So I've heard," I replied. "But my subject would have to be one hard customer to pull off this scam."

"If she's Katu, she's more than capable. What kind of money we talking about?"

"She's going for a half-million dollars."

"That'd buy a hell of a new life in Thailand, especially with the exchange rate now. How long does it take to collect on this kind of life-insurance claim?"

"Companies usually pay out in two or three months. If they don't move quickly, lawyers tend to get involved. That's why I'm up against it."

I described her itinerary: Front Row to Mermaid's Rest, Fun Frog to Marco Polo, then straight to a slab at the medical examiner's office.

A smile broke like sunlight across Honeyman's face.

"I believe she's reinvented herself, Sebastian. The Front Row is *the* place to go in Bangkok for false documents. Foreign passports, Thai ID cards, guest-worker visas, whatever you need. You can get a South African passport there for eighteen hundred American dollars, a Thai ID card for eleven hundred."

"The cops found her U.S. passport with the body."

"What was the condition of this body?"

"A mess, thanks to the heat and the rats."

"The embassy still made a positive ID, right?"

"They did. I have their report."

"Anything interesting in the autopsy report?"

"Slight variations in weight and height from her insurance application. But people shade the truth."

"They do indeed. What about money?"

"Some traveler's checks. About five hundred dollars' worth. The check register was among the effects found with her body. The checks were all gone and there was no log showing how they were spent. She also withdrew twenty-five-hundred dollars from her accounts before she left Boston. That wouldn't be a huge amount of money for a two-week vacation, especially if she intended to do some major Bangkok shopping. Or, I suppose, tweak heroin. There's no indication she was traveling with serious bucks. She hadn't cleaned out her bank accounts before she left the States. They still held a substantial balance."

"I assume a large withdrawal might tip you off?"

"Unusual bank activity is one of the first things I look for."

He went quiet, lost in thought for a minute.

"We know she's smart, this girl," Honeyman said. "She needed a new identity, one that would buy her time until the life-insurance company cut the check. Why not get a Thai ID card? She could pass for an Isan girl, down from the northeast. That'd give her an excellent reason to go to the Front Row."

"Are these Thai ID cards difficult to acquire?"

"Easier than getting a bogus driver's license. The old Chinaman who runs the Front Row operation has agents all over Thailand. For example, they buy IDs from poor rural farmers who have retarded kids that are never going to leave their villages. Or they go to border provinces like Kanchanaburi and bribe the district clerks, who then issue ID cards for residents who don't exist. This country is drowning in illegal workers: Lao, Burmese, Khmer. There's a huge market for Thai IDs."

"Linda did go to Kanchanaburi for several days."

"Sounds like she may have bought herself a new life."

"I spoke with the guest-house owner on Khao San Road where Linda's body was found. But she had registered under another name, Chang Tai, and claimed to be from Singapore. According to Colonel Nagaphit, the Thai police inspector, she later overdosed at this backpacker dump."

"Or not."

"What do you mean? They found her dead on Khao San Road."

"No, they found somebody dead at the scene. Some body. This colonel is up to no good. Why is a high-ranking police inspector way out of his jurisdiction and working a run-of-the-mill OD on Khao San Road, which is literally the other side of town? Backpackers die there all the time. The cop has a personal interest in the case, that's why. He also has the rank and the authority to control the crime scene. To what end?"

"I'm still working on that. It doesn't make sense."

Honeyman smiled.

"Well, try my theory on for size: body shopping. It makes a lot of sense." He paused to drain the last of his beer. "Don't look so surprised, kid. If your girl is alive and she's bought a new identity, she needs someone to take the fall for her, as it were. Someone to make her death look conclusive."

"I guess that could explain the body at the guest house—the girl from Singapore, Chang Tai, who registered for the room."

"A corpse makes a pretty damn convincing case for death, don't you think? Your subject needed a body to pass for her at the autopsy. This Chang Tai was close enough. Then the corpse is cremated. It's fucking brilliant: no burial, no evidence that can be exhumed later. Nothing but ashes."

"So the police just went out and found a body double?"

"Everything's for sale here. T-I-T. Remember? The Bangkok police are on the lookout for many things, bodies included. Not everyone's on the take, of course, but there are enough crooked cops to form a pretty effective network. They even carry along photos, statistics like height, weight, body type, ethnicity. They'll cordon off a death scene if they think they got a good match. Then they lift all distinguishing evidence and replace it with their client's ID and effects. The weather and the vermin do their part, too. It's easier than it seems."

Then the U.S. embassy would send out a new consul, Isabel O'Toole, to identify a body that had been rotting for nearly a day. By the time a clever, dishonest detective like Colonel Nagaphit got through salting the death scene, Honeyman added, all signs would have pointed to a straightforward OD: a bloated, gnawed corpse that had to be that of Linda Watts. And how could it not? There was more than a passing physical resemblance. A valid American passport, which no citizen left lying around overseas. And several eyewitness accounts. It would have been nearly impossible for an overworked consular officer like O'Toole not to believe the subversion.

"Your Linda Watts is alive and well in Bangkok."

"In that case, Sergeant, you think you can help me find her?"

"If we're going to work together you better start calling me Sam."

He rose and casually rained baht notes on the table to cover his meal.

"Only if you call me Bass."

"You've spoken with this inspector, Colonel Nagaphit, so I'm going to assume he's onto you. Seems like his people may have already tried to hurt you, too. He might stand pat now, or he might make a more-lethal move. We can't assume we have much time. We gotta find this girl. You ready to pull an all-nighter, Bass?"

"What about your gig tonight?"

"Stonewall's kid asks me for a favor? Hell, let's get busy. It's Saturday night in Bangkok. We've got a lot of ground to cover."

He peeled off three hundred-baht notes for his dinner companion for a taxi, kissed her lightly on the cheek, and led me out of the restaurant to a mob of *tuk-tuks*. Soon we were darting down a secondary soi, then entered a maze of narrow, darkening roads that ran between ash-colored high-rise apartment buildings. All the paperwork was real because the death had been real. My client had nearly said as much. But the Marco Polo Guest House victim wasn't Linda Watts, just some poor young junkie from Singapore used by the Bangkok police to run this insurance scam. Had the Singaporean woman died accidentally of a heroin overdose, as the coroner concluded? Or worse, had she been murdered, via a lethal injection, in the rush to obtain a body double? How far had Linda, or the Bangkok police, been willing to go to get the life-insurance money? How much desperation and depravity were required?

After nearly an hour of epic Saturday-night traffic we made the docklands of Klong Toey, Bangkok's crowded port, and the editorial offices of the *Bangkok Post*. Honeyman sweet-talked a lobby receptionist and gained us entrance to the newsroom. I felt a pang of nostalgia as we wove through the institutional chaos and first-edition energy of the city room to the disheveled desk of a balding, goateed *farang*.

"How's it hanging, Slink?"

"Hanging out to dry, Honeyman. I'm dying on deadline."

The harried reporter looked like Burl Ives after about a two-year bender. Honeyman made the introductions.

"Slink here writes the *Post*'s 'Night Crawler' column. A must-read for every reprobate in the kingdom. Ain't a bar girl in Bangkok comes down with the clap Slink don't know about. Give us some news we can use, fat man."

"New fuck show over on Patpong," Slink pronounced in a nasally voice, sounding like an old Walter Winchell newsreel. "Inspired by the Kama Sutra. Very artistic. A fresh batch of Isan ladies just down from Sisaket Province and now bumping and grinding on Soi Cowboy. And there's a crazy old *farang* still singing at Nana Plaza, cracker style. Very bad, unless you like Hank Williams that way."

Slink smirked and kept on typing.

"Yeah, the hell with you, too," Honeyman retorted. "Listen, I came over 'cause I need a quick favor. Something right up your dark little alley. Show him, Bass."

One look at Linda's photograph was enough to make Slink slow his typing to twenty words per minute.

"Ever seen her in the demimonde?" Honeyman asked.

"Think I'd remember a honey like this. New talent?"

"No more than a month in the game," said Honeyman.

"You won't find a girl like that within ten miles of Patpong," Slink said. "Or Nana Plaza. She looks too classy. If she's in the life, she's working the Cowboy. Fewer dip-shit tourists and cheap Charlies over there. Present company excepted, of course."

"Makes sense," Honeyman said to me. "The cop who's running the little caper you're investigating works out of Thonglor. This Colonel Nagaphit. Soi Cowboy happens to be in Thonglor district, so it would be in his jurisdiction. Beaucoup tea money to be made there."

"Tea money?" I ventured.

"The shakedown," said Slink. He continued to type as he talked. "Every go-go bar, pub, and street vendor in Bangkok has to cough up. Thonglor cops control the Cowboy rackets. They send over a bagman the first of every month. Pay up, or get raided. T-I-T."

It was an expat mantra: this is Thailand. Slink stopped typing and looked at us as if to say, *class dismissed.*

"*Now* can I go back to filing my column, Honeyman? Thousands of whoremasters hang on my every word. Bastards would be lost without me telling them where to get lost."

"Slink, I owe you."

"If you ever play the Shangri-la Hotel, I want to be the first to know."

"You'll have the best table in the house, Slink. And the driest martini."

"Your talk is cheap, Honeyman. As always."

Honeyman explained his hunch on our return ride to Soi Cowboy.

"Your girl needs money, no questions asked. You said she's Katu, spent years in the refugee camps. So she could pass for some Isan hick—it's all ethnic Lao and hill people up there in the northeast. If she's working with a heavy hitter like this Colonel Nagaphit, she's plugged into the scene. And a bar's a perfect setup. It's a cash business. Most of the bar girls here come from Isan. And with a Thai ID card, Linda could work. She could hide in plain sight, make some cash money, at least enough to tide her over until the smoke clears and your insurance company pays off."

"She wouldn't have much money left if she bought the Thai ID card," I argued. "She only withdrew twenty-five-hundred before leaving Boston. So how could she afford it?"

"Maybe she persuaded this colonel to do it on spec, or for a small deposit. Or maybe something else. Maybe he gets off on sleeping with an American girl, even a semi-American girl."

I couldn't help imagining the colonel, wearing only his aviator sunglasses, screwing Linda behind dark windows in the backseat of his Mercedes. I found my face reddening.

"To go this route—a fake ID, body shopping, consorting with

crooked cops—she'd have to be hard-core, Bass. One-hundred-percent Katu."

"Maybe she has her reasons."

There I was, worrying about her motivation.

"I'd say she's got a half-million good reasons."

It was after nine o'clock by the time we hit the Cowboy. Half-drunk *farang* milled about the street, buffeted by music pouring from forty different clubs and ogling off-duty dancers. Many of the strutting bar girls wore polyester kimonos emblazoned with their club's name with the swagger of high-school cheerleaders in their letter jackets. They tried to steer me inside to see the sleazy wonders of the kingdom. Best girls, they sang. Best show. No rip-off. Garish neon signs beckoned: Pink Pussy Cat. Midnite. Suzy Wong's. I followed Honeyman as he bore a steady course halfway down the block-long bazaar of bared flesh. Just beyond a pharmacy stocked with little more than cigarettes and condoms we entered Club M-16. Through the Marlboro haze I made out an immense bar girdling a raised runway that held a dozen half-nude women writhing to the beat of decade-old dance music. The tables nearest the entrance held clusters of Western men, while single guys slumped in banquettes along the shadowy periphery. The rear booths were crowded with Thai women waiting to take the stage. Several gazed our way in a desultory, half-bored attempt to make eye contact. None looked like Linda.

"This bar's the exception, kid, the only Cowboy club that doesn't pay tea money."

"Why's that?"

"The cops own it, that's why."

"T-I-T, right?"

"You're a quick study." He pointed to two unoccupied stools. "First expat rule: always sit at the bar. You get hassled less by the girls for lady-drinks that way. What'll you have?"

"Your call."

I couldn't think about cocktails. Directly above me, a nude woman swayed to the music, her eyes dull and drugged. Her body was a living canvas for a fluorescent-orange dragon whose claws encircled her ample breasts. The monster's tail ran down to disappear in the fine black thatch covering her sex, then rose between her buttocks and wrapped around her wide, brown hips.

"There's a helluva lot more money to be made here than your average Bangkok office job," Honeyman said, handing me a Coke and Mekhong whiskey. "A dancer gets paid about four dollars a night. She gets a man to buy her lady-drinks, she splits that bill with the bar. Fifty-fifty."

"And the sex? The women split that money with the bar, too?"

"You want to take a girl home before closing time, you have to pay a bar fine. On the Cowboy, that's about ten bucks, which the house keeps. Anything after that belongs to the girl. If I recall, snake lady here charges about thirty dollars for short-time love, forty for long-time, 'cause she'd have to screw you again in the morning."

"And after the party's over?"

He pointed to the low ceiling.

"The girls usually live upstairs. Most of 'em send all their money home to Mama and Papa back in Isan. Their families want TVs, refrigerators, motorcycles. They crave that material shit way more than they care about the virtue of their daughters."

Onstage, the dancers had given way to a nude, slightly overweight woman. She nonchalantly lay down on her back, inserted a clear plastic tube into her vagina, and then used her powerful diaphragm muscles to propel small, needle-tipped darts toward a cluster of balloons floating against the ceiling. With impressive aim and muscle control she burst several balloons, then left to scattered applause and was replaced by another squad of half-nude dancers. I scanned the shadows: no sign of Linda Watts.

"Let's give her one more drink to show up," Honeyman said.

We did; she didn't. Exiting M-16, we nearly collided with an Asian elephant standing in the middle of the crowded street with its mahout. The sun-browned handler, barefoot and dressed in a filthy blue tunic and tattered trousers, accepted three ten-baht coins from a pregnant bar girl, who then crouched beneath the animal while several of her colleagues giggled.

"No more forests, so no more work," Honeyman said. "Even the timber elephants and their masters have to come here and hustle. It's considered good luck to pass three times beneath an elephant's belly. Care to try?"

"Not yet."

We rounded the gaunt animal and crossed the street to Red and Black. Two barmaids shouted Honeyman's name in unison and led us to an enormous mirrored bar. Above us, a cluster of seminaked vamps pouted and swayed to a thumping dance track. Honeyman explained the entertainment concept: cheap beer and a cheaper bar fine. But no pussy tricks. The police-owned Club M-16 had a monopoly on the nude shows. Honeyman ignored my protests and handed me another Mekhong and Coke. A barmaid marched over with a bamboo cup, rattled its contents, and spilled five dice onto the countertop. Honeyman smiled at the challenge and slapped a one-hundred-baht note on the bar; the woman matched the bet.

"Six, five, four," said Honeyman. "You get three chances to roll a six-five-four straight. The remaining two dice are your score. Easy game."

He shook the cup theatrically, threw down only a four, three, and one. The barmaid applauded her good fortune. Honeyman slapped another one hundred baht on the bar, tossed back his drink as if trying to summon luck, rattled the dice cup, and unloaded another bad throw. Half-drunken concern scored his brow, but he brightened when he spotted a rotund, moon-faced woman in a printed-silk caftan at the end of the bar.

"That's Cham, the mamasan. She runs these girls. Give me Linda's picture."

I followed Honeyman to where Cham was scolding a young dancer. The criticism seemed to involve the girl's costume: a high-waisted, two-piece bathing suit in a garish floral print. What seemed the height of provincial fashion was apparently not acceptable Cowboy attire. The girl slunk away.

"What can I do, Honeyman?" The stout woman lit a cigarette, exasperated. "These farm girls, who bloody dresses them?"

"Give her a few months and a decent haircut and she'll be married off to some German," Honeyman answered.

"I'd like a German," Cham said. "Long time I don't see you, Honeyman. I think maybe you become a monk."

"There isn't a robe big enough to hide this beer gut, Cham. Besides, then I couldn't afford your bar fines. I've been singing for my supper."

"Central Plaza?"

"That was three jobs ago. I'm over at Nana now. Least I was till tonight. Gotta keep moving. Can't handle that nine-to-five."

"Always the butterfly."

"Whatever the flower, Cham, I always dream about feasting on you."

"*Bak waan*. Still the sweet mouth."

"Sugar always works better than vinegar." Honeyman nodded my way, then handed Linda's picture to the mamasan. "This is Bass, my new fishing buddy. We're looking for this girl. It's important. Anything you say goes no further than us."

She studied the photograph.

"Why are you looking, Bass? You fall in love with her?"

"She might be in trouble," Honeyman interjected.

"Bloody Isan girls all big trouble," Cham said.

"She's from Laos," I corrected.

"Lao girls even worse," Cham retorted.

"Have you seen her around?" I asked.

"Not at Red and Black. But you wait here. Let me ask."

Cham approached a quartet of dancers waiting to take the stage. She soon returned, smiling crisply.

"The girl in the black dress, number seventy, said to try Mia Noi Bar. You know the place, Honeyman?"

"Ain't been that long."

"One last question, Cham," I said. "Ever heard of a Colonel Nagaphit? Royal Thai Police?"

She smiled.

"Every Cowboy mamasan knows the colonel."

Then Cham went back to the dancers and resumed her fashion critique.

Outside, the good-luck elephant had attracted a large crowd. Two bar girls had filled a pitcher with beer and were holding it for the elephant, who drank as noisily and sloppily as a soccer hooligan. Honeyman handed the elephant's mahout a few coins for luck and we wove our way through the mob. My righteous quest had somehow unraveled into a pub crawl. Nearly one in the morning and the place hummed with desire. Groups of sunburned *farang* stumbled by, howling an English club-football song—Liverpool's "You'll Never Walk Alone," by the sound of it. Go-go dancers waved and wiggled for customers. All had a word for Honeyman, who seemed to know every bartender, to have patronized every food cart, and to have drunk, rolled dice, or slept with every bar girl in Bangkok.

The Mia Noi Bar stood awash in fluorescent lighting near the west end of the block, another harsh club with the requisite long bar and inner, raised stage. We grabbed two stools with a good view of the room and ordered a pair of Mekhong and Cokes. While Honeyman went looking for the mamasan, I scanned the club for Linda. No sign. Halfway through my drink I felt large, warm hands massaging my neck and shoulders. I turned to greet my mystery masseuse: a tall, dark-skinned girl wearing a white dress shirt and a thigh-high black-leather skirt. Unlike the other women crowding the Mia Noi, she didn't wear a number.

"Hello," she said a voice worn hoarse from years of loud bar talk. "You like?"

"Not so much."

She moved closer, rubbing her hips against my right knee.

"How much you like?"

"You're not my type." But by now I knew the drill. "Want a lady-drink?"

She frowned.

"No lady-drink. Whiskey. Jack Daniel."

She smiled, pleased at her worldliness. I signaled the bartender. The bar girl resumed her clumsy kneading.

"You like me much?" she insisted.

"No. I like the girl in this picture very much. Have you seen her on Soi Cowboy?"

"Why her?"

"I need to find her. She is in trouble."

"Not so pretty like me," she retorted. "Cannot smoke you like me. Cannot—"

"Fuck off, asshole."

It was Honeyman. He slapped the girl firmly on her fanny, sending her scuttling out the door of the Mia Noi Bar. Then he slumped beside me.

"Goddamn *katoey,*" he muttered.

"She might have told us about Linda."

"Her?" Honeyman said incredulously. He sighed and leaned close to my face. "She's a *he,* kid. A *katoey.* A ladyboy. A blow-job

queen. Did you see her wearing a number? Or rather, him? No—that means a freelancer. Lady-boys work all the bars. Welcome to Bangkok."

"*All* the bars?"

"You name it: Soi Cowboy, Patpong, Nana Plaza. Especially Nana."

I thought of last night, the girl from the Hot Spot. The one with the husky voice. Minh, my good friend from the alley. The bartender brought the shot of Jack Daniels. I downed it in a single gulp and called out for more. The prettiest women in Bangkok were all men. What a place.

"One of the dancers said she recognized Linda from the picture. But she called Linda by another name: Thien. She said this Thien was pretty stuck-up for a bumpkin from Mukdahan Province."

"Mukdahan?"

"About four hundred miles northeast of here. The end of the fucking earth, even by Isan standards. Thien spoke good English, too, for a Mukdahan girl. The dancer said Thien started here three weeks ago."

Right around the time Linda Watts had supposedly died.

"So where's this Thien? Somebody already bar-fine her tonight?"

"Thien lasted here less than a week. Gave a lot of the clientele a very hard time. Very picky about being bar-fined—not considered good manners for a girl in the game. Thien even stole money from a *farang* who short-timed her and then passed out in his hotel room. He came back to the Mia Noi and raised hell, made a huge scene. So the bar let her go. More trouble than she was worth."

"Where do we go from here, Sam? Did this dancer have any leads on where Linda's working now?"

"Not a clue. Linda could still be in Bangkok. Or she could be hustling down in Pattaya, even Phuket. Any one of a thousand bars. More bad news: a cop came by here Thursday—two nights ago—asking for Thien."

"Colonel Nagaphit?"

"More low-level, a Sergeant Tao. The Thonglor flunky who collects the tea money every month."

A bagman who took his marching orders from the colonel. The colonel probably thought I would go back to Khao San Road to spin my wheels again. We still held a slight advantage, until he learned through the bar-girl grapevine that two *farang* were nosing around Soi Cowboy. If only we knew where to find Linda Watts. The case required far more proof than the liquid words of a Bangkok bar girl about this elusive "Thien" to keep Mather Mutual from paying off the policy.

We straggled from the Mia Noi at the two o'clock closing with no sight of Linda or further leads on Thien. We were off to the West Virginia, an after-hours club on the Cowboy, Honeyman leading the way, warbling "Jambalaya" in a high-pitched, half-crazed, country twang. The West Virginia was the most popular witching-hour hangout on the Cowboy, a place where unattached *farang* men and dateless bar girls mingled in hopes of striking pay-for-play bargains. If Linda was freelancing out of desperation, she just might come here, Honeyman had reckoned. The West Virginia was a buyer's market, where women outnumbered men at least two to one. A long bar occupied the left wall; across the low dance floor, a small stage held a Thai rock band plodding through the Eagles' "Hotel California." Swaying couples crowded the small dance floor in front of the combo. Everyone cast hungry, appraising looks—everyone but the pair of plainclothes Bangkok policemen at the bar, regarding the scene. We drank in silence, enduring the band, which had decided to butcher a string of Creedence Clearwater Revival hits. "Proud Mary," "Born on the Bayou," and "Lodi" all got the phonetic-vocal treatment.

"This shit takes me back," Honeyman said.

"A bit before my time."

"Then you really missed something."

He went quiet again, lost in the music.

"How's your pops?" he finally asked.

"All right. Moved down to Florida last winter. Hates the cold weather."

"Your mom there, too?"

"She passed away three years ago. Liver cancer. Dad never discusses it. When we talk, it's about the firm. He has lots of advice. Can't let go of the business."

"His way of caring."

"You'd know better than me."

I had known only the broad, rough strokes of his life. Hurriedly scrawled, weeks-old letters from the field. Strained reunions in Honolulu budget hotels when he got an R&R break from Vietnam. And the irregular years when some of his postings came with dependent housing and we all chafed against his anal-retentive regimens, especially John, my older brother.

"You know he saved my life."

"He never mentioned it."

"He never would, but I will. Must've been sixty-eight or sixty-nine, sometime after Tet. We'd been in the woods for nearly a week. A North Vietnamese Army counterrecon hunter team was right on our asses, and we were fighting a running gun battle with these bastards. I got clipped in the leg by an AK round about a kilometer from our designated pickup zone. He humped me under fire all the way to the bird. If he hadn't, I'd have been a goner. The NVA weren't in the mood to take prisoners in Laos."

"But you two were based in Kontum. That's Vietnam, not Laos."

The beer and the whiskey had him talking now.

"Officially, sure. But the usual rules didn't apply to SOG. Your pops was a One-Zero, a team leader. I was his majordomo. We had a five-man RT, a recon team. All Yards. It was very unofficial, of course. Sterile uniforms, no dog tags. We always went over the fence."

"SOG?" It sounded like a villainous outfit from an Ian Fleming novel.

"Studies and Observations Group. You wouldn't guess from the name, but we were the baddest of the bad asses: scouting, sabotage, prisoner snatches. The greatest hits of covert special warfare. We wreaked all kinds of havoc."

He went quiet, not wanting to throw a brighter light on that clandestine corner of his life, nor that of my father, who'd never said anything to me about SOG, let alone his tours of duty in Vietnam. I had always assumed that the silence was because he had just been counting time in the rear, trying to earn another service ribbon to add to the fruit salad he wore on his dress uniform. The old man had even more stones than I'd imagined. And he could keep a secret. I wondered what other need-to-know exploits I hadn't heard about.

"What kept you here in Asia, Sam? Why not retire to the States? Live the quiet life."

"Your dad had a good family waiting for him. There wasn't anything for me but two pissed-off ex-wives. I'd been to Bangkok a few times on R-and-R. Different place back then—damn near livable. And Thailand was as close as I could get to Vietnam without being shot. There's something about that place I can't shake. I carry it with me. It's a chronic condition, like malaria or an intestinal parasite. So when I got out, I settled here. I didn't want to retire completely. Figured that'd leave me dead—or dead drunk—in a matter of months. I was half right. Found a job on the Cowboy managing a bar. But I kept my hand in."

"A hand in what, exactly?"

"Running a bar, you see and hear a lot of stuff. When something seemed interesting, I'd tip off the embassy. Drug smuggling. Illegal weapons shipments. POW leads."

"Yeah?" I had to smile at the mention of the last subject. "Inspiration for those Chuck Norris *Missing in Action* movies?"

Honeyman's demeanor grew icy.

"With SOG, we caught our share of search-and-rescue missions, mostly other recon teams and downed pilots. Sometimes we got them out; sometimes the NVA got there first. Then you'd sweep an area and there'd be nothing. No bodies, no blood trails, no gear. Our guys were just *gone*. We left people behind, Bass. That bugged the hell out of me. You never leave anyone. *Ever.* Your pops felt that way, too—I wouldn't be here if he hadn't come back for me. So I started helping private groups in Bangkok. All very illegal, but that didn't make it wrong. Too bad these so-called POW hunters mostly turned out to be bar-stool commandos. They scammed money from families of MIAs and blew most of it on booze and Patpong pussy. I got out for good after the Starr photo."

I nodded. The photograph had been all over the news in the States that summer of 1991: a picture of a jug-eared, Caucasian man who was a dead ringer for a U.S. Air Force pilot, Ronald Starr, shot down over southern Laos and MIA since the late 1960s. Even the Pentagon had gotten excited when the Starr photo surfaced. But a few months later the image had proved to be bogus. The man in the picture hadn't been an American POW after all, only an East German national who'd previously been arrested in Bangkok for smuggling exotic wildlife.

"The Starr photo was yours, Sam?"

"Guilty, with extenuating circumstances. I was given the picture by a former Lao guerrilla, Savan Voumi—a bad, fat boy who still had a serious network across the river."

"The Chao Phraya River?"

"No, the Mekong River. Back in the sixties, Voumi's father

actually ran Laos for a bit, courtesy of the CIA rigging an election. I met Voumi while running the bar on Soi Cowboy. Voumi traded on his intelligence connections, which made him a go-to guy for any private POW hunter or family member who came through Bangkok and wanted a briefing on Laos. Where do you think Voumi got a picture good enough to fool the Pentagon? Think he cooked it up all by himself over a few beers? Someone fed it to him, and he fed it to me. He was used, too. The Starr photo pretty much destroyed me. I lost the bar, got frozen out by lots of vets. I bailed out of the hero business. I leave that to Chuck Norris. These days, I stick to music."

He drained the last of his drink.

"So who set you and Voumi up?" I asked.

"Who the hell knows? Probably some intelligence agency. Maybe ours. Maybe theirs. It's a wilderness of mirrors out there. Everything's deniable. I know I sound like a conspiracy nut. These spooks know how to build up a case, get everyone all excited. Then they knock it down, and everyone gets disillusioned. If the best MIA leads turn out to be lies, doesn't it stand to reason that everything else is bullshit?"

A sardonic smiled creased his lips.

"Or maybe it's just my paranoia, kid."

What did I know? Linda's death seemed legitimate. The documentation indicated a good death, for which Mather Mutual would have to pay out. But Dolores Moyle, Sam Honeyman, even the Mia Noi bar girls told me otherwise. They offered nothing concrete to believe in, just hunches and hearsay. Everything they said could be bullshit. Or it could be the truth, elusive as morning fog. Honeyman considered his empty beer, then the band, which was playing an appalling version of "Purple Haze." Linda would not show here tonight. We left the bar and walked around the corner to Soi Asoke, a major Sukhumvit cross street. The *farang* staying at high-end hotels where it was difficult to walk garishly dressed working girls through glittering lobbies filled with fountains, concierges, and business executives had lined up with their short-time lovers along the cracked sidewalk, waiting for rooms-by-the-hour at the VIP Love Hotel.

"There's a few more places to check out," Honeyman announced. "A bit further downtown. Sooner or later every prowler, every freelancer will pass through. They're the final stops before sleep, or sex."

Honeyman bartered with a *tuk-tuk* driver and we clambered into the back, barely in time to grasp the side rails before he swung into traffic, ran a stoplight, and bore west on Sukhumvit. The broken pavement jolted the lightweight vehicle, sending Honeyman thudding into my shoulder.

"What'll it mean if we find her, Bass?"

"It means better work."

"Bet it'll mean a lot to your pops, too."

"Maybe he'll finally get off my ass."

"Hell of a girl to be looking for, if she's anything like her picture."

I looked away, at the blurring streetscape of dark shadows and liquid neon.

"I don't need any extra motivation, Sam. Just help me find her."

"She's easy on the eyes," he said, leering. "Just sayin'."

"Believe me, Sam, I've noticed."

Not five minutes later, the driver delivered us to the Grace Hotel. Honeyman ordered him to wait while we headed downstairs for a quick once-over. The darkened room was choked with cigarette smoke and half filled with African and Middle Eastern men and freelance hookers gyrating to 1970s Euro-disco music. There was no sign of Linda Watts. We would make our last stand at the Pompeii, a nearby after-after-hours club. The driver raced back to Sukhumvit and headed east for a few short blocks, finally skidding to a halt in front of a darkened lane. Honeyman led the way up the alley, which ended in a large courtyard. We passed a couple copulating in the backseat of a taxi while the driver stood outside his vehicle, smoking a cigarette, amused. His fare couldn't wait even for a love hotel. Honeyman snapped his fingers to get my attention and pointed to a shaft of thin light beaming from a throbbing, subterranean hole in the back of a bleak office building. I strode past the love taxi and crossed over the threshold into the Pompeii, the inner ring of Bangkok's demimonde.

What struck me first was the stench; the club's entrance ran through the men's toilet. A narrow, connecting staircase led past a cramped, dirty kitchen and into a pulsing cave rank with sweat and ammonia, vomit and beer, piss and perfume. Hell would smell something like this, I thought. Honeyman pushed his way to a small, crowded bar and grabbed us two bottles of Singha beer; he didn't trust the dishwasher or the icemaker to be clean enough for him to order a cocktail. According to Honeyman, this was a constellation, an after-hours meeting place like the Grace Hotel. All the night crawlers eventually washed up here: bar girls, freelance whores, even office workers who came to turn a few tricks when they couldn't make the rent.

I scanned the dim, smoky room for Linda. No hint of her among the banquettes running along the left wall or the few circular tables in the center of the room. Against the back wall stood a small stage overflowing with amplifiers and instruments. The band was nowhere to be seen. On break between sets, no doubt. No sign of Linda in a brick-lined alcove to the right of the stage, where a vintage Rock-Ola jukebox pumped out techno-funk dance music. A quartet of women swayed in a trance around the shining machine, as if worshipping an industrial god.

"Deaf mutes," Honeyman said. "If that's your scene."

The Pompeii filled me with unease: its subterranean gloom, its hissing kitchen, and especially its silent, desperate women. One day I'd pick up the *Herald* or the *Globe* and read a short item about this firetrap on page two, the space where editors gave horrific foreign disasters a few column inches of ten-point type. I surveyed the room for an emergency exit. Only the staircase through the men's room offered a means of escape. But I wasn't going anywhere at the moment, with a head full of rice whiskey in a crowded bar on a Saturday night and the perfect Bangkok woman ascending the Pompeii's bandstand. She wore black hose and heels and a black, knee-high sheath dress that seemed poured over her slender body, all of it set off by a mandarin-collared, scarlet jacket that burned like an incandescent lamp through the fumy room. She brandished a microphone like a rock star, and turned to banter with the crowd, her English quiet and halting, her Thai like a sigh. This was no fever dream. Linda Watts had just sauntered into my life.

Eight

Standing onstage, the staid banker now looked every inch a torch singer. She had shorn her hair back to shoulder length and dyed it black and wore lipstick the color of dried blood. But the Balinese-style hoop earrings, the ones she'd worn to such good effect in her passport photo, betrayed the remarkable metamorphosis. The devil always lurked in the jewelry. I collared a waiter and had him deliver a glass of Chivas—neat—to the stage, where the band, a quartet of long-haired Thai hipsters, was fiddling with amplifier dials and tuning their instruments. She accepted the drink with a bemused smile and gave a subtle *wai* bow in my direction when the waiter pointed me out. She probably thought me just another horny, calculating *farang.*

When the band launched into "Hurt So Bad," I knew I had badly underestimated my quarry. The combo at the West Virginia couldn't compare to this group, and for good reason: Linda Watts sang with conviction and phrasing, a plaintive soprano who did justice to Little Anthony, the Eagles, the Eurythmics. I had sold her short when considering her possible evasive action. She was a whip-smart survivor who had quickly found a way to survive in a cash-only world that didn't involve working as a bar girl. She had faked her death to give herself another life. Now her talent and guile had staked her to another chance. She closed the set with an old Hoagy Carmichael melody, "Skylark," a song that had been one of my mother's favorites. Whenever it came on the radio at home my parents had stopped to dance, Mother resting her head against the old man's broad shoulders. And when it floated from the radio and he wasn't there, I knew she'd soon find the gin.

I worked my way to the front of the bandstand and took two available-light photographs. Then I stood there on the crowded, clouded floor, surprised that I didn't feel a greater sense of accomplishment. Against the odds, I had found her. The feat would save Mather Mutual hundreds of thousands of dollars. I'd pocket a nice fee for Damon & Son, maybe even prompt the old man to quit meddling. Perhaps my success would convince Dolores Moyle to send more life-insurance-fraud cases my way. I knew now I could handle the overseas work. Yet, a part of me felt lousy about making the case, even as I was about to demolish Linda Watts and her elegant scam. It meant that my brief time in Bangkok had almost run its course, before I'd had a chance to get beneath the salacious surface. What lay beyond the sleaze of Soi Cowboy, Nana, even Khao San Road? I knew nothing beyond the lobbies of a few hotels, the law and disorder found in the waiting rooms of police stations and coroners' offices. I'd soon be back in Somerville, meeting with potential clients about matrimonial investigations, forcing myself to look concerned about their spouses, bastards one and all. And for short money. It was the worst kind of work: predictable, prosaic, depressing.

Then the music stopped, the lights came up, and the jukebox resumed thumping like a metronome. A diminutive young woman in bar-girl evening wear—leather miniskirt, red tube top, and black crochet vest—towed a drunken *farang* toward Linda. By way of introduction, the ruddy man sputtered nonsense and waved a five-hundred-baht bill in Linda's face. She gave him a stony look, then spoke animatedly with the young woman, who replied in kind. The girl grabbed the *farang* by the hand and pulled him back into the crowd, heading for the stairs. Probably off for a session. Linda watched them leave with a look that seemed equal parts contempt and resignation.

Another drunken fan pushed his way through the mob, holding two beers above his head, presumably to make Linda an offer. That's when I saw the policeman coming down the stairs. It wouldn't take him long to find Linda in her heat-seeking red jacket. Honeyman had spotted the law, too. He also had a diversionary plan—he grabbed the beer-toting drunk by the shoulders, spun him around, and jabbed him in the gut. Not painful enough to floor him but hard enough to invite retaliation from someone just made to spill two costly Heinekens on the floor. Angered, the man leaped at Honeyman, who effortlessly parried his blows. The crowd jeered and hooted as they pushed and shoved like a pair of rutting stags, ignoring the policeman blowing his whistle to call the fracas to order. The lawman hopped into the throng, jabbing his black baton like a cattle prod.

I looked to check Linda's reaction but she had vanished from the bandstand. There was only one way out of the Pompeii. I caught a flash of scarlet on the crowded staircase and began pushing my way toward the exit. Above the din I thought I heard Honeyman shout, "Don't lose her." By the time I resurfaced in the courtyard, Linda had already found a *tuk-tuk*. I ran to the nearest cab and waved five hundred baht at the driver. He hurried to open a back door and I dragged out a half-naked couple canoodling on the seat and then jumped in, ordering him to follow Linda onto Sukhumvit Road. My luck held. At nearly four in the morning, the road lay empty but for the taillights of Linda's *tuk-tuk*. The wind freshened; the sky rumbled. A hard, brief rain had fallen while I was inside the Pompeii and the neon reflections writhed like coral snakes on the wet streets.

We zipped beneath the expressway and then turned north into

the Pattunam district, the part of central Bangkok that Trip Forbes had called Little Lagos. A few minutes later Linda's *tuk-tuk* stopped behind a large, multistory market. I watched from outside the Overlook Hotel as she walked through the lobby, nodded at the night manager, then disappeared into an elevator. The Overlook seemed like the kind of *farang*-friendly place where no one asked too many questions. I waited a few beats, then entered the hotel and used one hundred baht to break the ice with the manager. He couldn't tell me where Linda had gone, only that she was not a registered guest. A lady like that, he never questioned. She knew her destination. I could wait in the lobby if I wanted. The coffee shop opened at six o'clock. Only unregistered women were allowed above the ground floor.

I slid the man another hundred baht and used the desk phone to call my client. I reached Dolores Moyle's voice mail; I'd forgotten it was Saturday morning in Boston. I left her a terse message: "It's a bad death. Details to follow. You can call off Insight." Then I sat down to wait for Linda. I didn't really have a plan. In my line of work, surreptitious surveillance was the norm, not face-to-face confrontation. I had chased her halfway around the world, not knowing what I'd do if I found her. How would she respond once I informed her that her scam had run its course? That Mather Mutual would never pay the half-million-dollar claim? Would not even pay the original policy? That she had thrown away her career for nothing? Would she offer one last, poker-faced denial—or attempt a sucker punch, even seduction? Fight, flight, or fuck? I wanted to tell her this wasn't personal, only business. But why did I even care how she might react? It had never mattered before. Now it hit me: I had carried a vague, nervous hunger for more than a week, ever since I'd first seen her photograph. Her beauty and mystery had animated my investigation. I was heartened that she was still alive, and not just because it proved my worth to my client.

I had violated the old man's cardinal rule: I had gotten too close.

Less than fifteen minutes after she had disappeared into the hotel, Linda Watts stepped out of the elevator, now accompanied by the young bar girl she had spoken with at the Pompeii, and hustled through the lobby. When they passed, my PI instincts overruled my personal interest.

"Hello, Linda."

She turned, instinctively, and regarded me. She knew that I knew. And so she bolted for the door, overturning lobby chairs in her wake. The young girl shouted and grabbed my leg like a terrier. I pried her loose and headed outside. Linda had shed her heels and was a hundred yards ahead, running barefoot, heading for the market. At a quarter-miler's pace, I made up more than half the distance by the time she entered the building, and then tracked her through the labyrinth of darkened stalls bulging with clothing and home goods. *Don't lose her now,* I told myself. A flash of red beyond the denim jeans and plastic colanders and then she exited onto a main street for half a block before turning into an alley where a few people were already setting up their open-air stalls of fruit and vegetables. Just a few yards ahead of me. *Kick it in.* Linda looked back, pulled down a pile of papayas, overturned a crate of durian—anything to slow my pursuit. I leaped over the mess and tackled her and we tumbled into a stand of rambutan, burying us in a pile of red, hairy fruit. I sat on her back, pinning her to the street, as the shopkeepers congregated like a flock of angry gulls. It took one hundred baht apiece to placate them.

"You're a very difficult woman to find, Linda."

"Me *Thien*!" she said in her most forceful bar-girl English. *"Thien!"*

"The same Thien from Mia Noi Bar? The same Thien who steals from *farang*?"

"Leave me. Boyfriend get angry." Still thinking she could somehow brass her way out of this predicament. She tried to shift my weight. "Leave me, mister."

"You'll just have to explain yourself. Better yet, I'll explain it to your boyfriend. Right after you tell me all about this little caper."

I had my left hand between her shoulder blades now. With my free hand I fished in my shirt pocket for her old college-graduation picture.

"Sorry about the mix-up. You're the same Thien from Providence. The same Thien from Boston College. The same Thien from Bank-Boston." I dropped the photograph on the mashed fruit in front of her face. "By the way, Uncle Bounliep says hello."

"I go now," she said softly, an edge of despair in her voice. "Please, mister."

People walked by and said nothing, as if it was perfectly natural for a *farang* man to be sitting atop a beautiful Asian woman and a pile of crushed fruit in the middle of a wet, filthy street. They probably regarded this scene as some kind of short-time/long-time disagreement between a bar girl and her customer.

"Why'd you run?"

"You scare me, think I someone else."

I dangled the photocopy of her passport.

"I know you're someone else. Now cut the bar-girl bullshit—very unbecoming for someone with a Jesuit education."

I felt her body relax, as if she had exhaled completely.

"I'm not going to hurt you. And I'm not going to dime you out to the cops here, either, if that's worrying you. That is, not if you play ball with me."

"Play ball? Who are you?"

The Suzie Wong accent had vanished. I eased off and she rolled over to regard me with those telltale blue-gray eyes, trying to figure another hopeless move.

"I'm the guy who was hired to find you, Linda."

"No one's looking for me."

"No one except your life-insurance company, Mather Mutual."

"Why should I believe you?"

"It doesn't matter whether you believe me or not. It only matters that Mather believes me."

I handed her a business card, which she regarded as if I'd handed her a fresh dog turd.

"You the Damon or the Son?"

Below me, she shifted her hips, trying to goad me.

"The son. And you, Lin or Linda?"

"Who says I'm either?"

"Maybe we should take a *tuk-tuk* down to Wireless Road and straighten this all out at the U.S. embassy. I asked you not to be difficult."

She considered the threat.

"It's Linda," she said finally. "And you?"

"Sebastian. And who's the other girl at the hotel?"

"Nok has no part in this."

"Looks like she's part of something."

"Not what you're thinking."

"You've got a lot of explaining to do."

"Can we get out of this fruit pile first?"

"Where'd you like to go, exactly? The Oriental?"

I didn't want to return to the Grand Babylon. If Colonel Nagaphit's henchmen were searching for Linda, it would be only a matter of time before they paid a call on my hotel. The colonel might be arrogant, but he was smart enough to cover the angles.

"The Overlook, Sebastian—the kind of place a man who hangs out at Pompeii would enjoy."

I ignored the insult.

"You have a room?"

"The current occupant won't mind."

"And the night manager?"

"Show him one hundred baht and he'll forget anything you want."

"But no more funny business."

"Is that how private eyes talk these days, or did you read it in a cheap paperback?"

It took two hundred baht to get the night manager smiling again. Then we took a creaky elevator to the eighth floor and walked to the end of a long corridor that stank of mildewed carpets and soiled sheets. Linda pushed open an unlocked door and led me into a room strewn with clothes, as if the place had been tossed. The fat *farang* who'd squired the young girl at the Pompeii and waved money in Linda's face lay faceup on the lumpy, unmade bed. He wore only black socks and blue bikini briefs, which were nearly obscured by his overhanging expanse of fish-belly-white flesh.

"What about the body?"

"Him? He'll be out for hours."

She drew the bedsheet over his comatose form.

"He looks dead."

"Rohypnol will do that."

"That's assault, if the Thai police find out."

"Nok is only sixteen. That's rape."

"Then what's she doing on the hustle?"

"Desperation. Family debt. Misguided dreams. All of the above. Take your pick."

"Where'd she go?"

"Took the money and ran, probably back to Soi Cowboy."

"And you? What's your motivation?"

She rummaged through the minibar, settled on a nip of Famous Grouse, and poured the contents into a plastic cup.

"Drink?"

"That what happened to this guy?"

"I'll behave," she said.

"I'll pass."

She studied my bruised face, my disheveled, half-drunken state. "Bet that's a first."

Then she sat in a chair by the open balcony door, her hair rustling in a slow, thick breeze. It had begun to rain again. I moved beside her with my camera.

"Look up, please. Mather Mutual's glad you're alive. I know I am."

"They *knew*?"

"My client had a gut feeling. Some sort of internal alarm that goes off when a case like this lands on her desk. And now her company knows for certain. Smile if you want."

I took two close-up photographs, three-quarter profile. She wore the same fatalistic expression she'd held in her college-graduation photo.

"You ought to think about letting your hair grow back, Linda."

"Shit." The realization that her brilliant plan had collapsed completely.

"You weren't going to get a half-million dollars anyway. The OD ruined that."

"So now what?"

"I can't speak for what the Thai authorities might do."

In a few hours, I could process and express-mail the photos to Dolores Moyle, then start arranging the logistics of my return flights to the States. Even with the damning evidence, I doubted that Mather Mutual would pursue charges against Linda. Her case, her looks, her story would drive Boston news editors wild; they would play any trial on page one in the *Globe* and the *Herald,* maybe even above the fold, for days. Especially the *Herald*. Insurance companies liked to keep the details of this sort of fraud in-house. That way, nobody else got any criminal ideas.

"You'll be on the Thonglor cops' shit list. You can't go back to

Soi Cowboy or Pompeii tonight. Colonel Nagaphit knows I'm looking for you."

"I have no place to go."

"No apartment or rooming house?"

"First place he'll look."

"My hotel is out of the question."

"Did I ask?" she retorted.

"Did I offer?"

Linda shrugged. I pulled my wallet from my hip pocket.

"Here's twenty dollars . . . make it forty. Take it. The way the baht's blowing up, it ought to go pretty far."

"So now you want to help."

"Let's put it this way: I don't want to hurt you."

"What's all this about then?"

"This is just business."

She stuffed the cash into her jacket pocket. Making a case had never felt so hollow. And then I asked her the question I had wanted to ask since Dolores Moyle first showed me that photograph: why? What in her life was so bad that she had to run away from success and affluence and love and reinvent herself as a provincial Thai girl singing with a cover band in an after-hours Bangkok club?

"I can't tell you."

"I'd really like to know, Linda."

"Too dangerous," she replied. "It'd jeopardize everything."

"This is off the record. Just you and me."

"I didn't run away from anything," she finally said. "I ran toward it. I did this for love. Can you understand that?"

"Your fiancé sure doesn't understand."

"No, I didn't do this for Bryan."

"Then who?"

"For my father. I want to bring him to America."

"Uncle Bounliep told me he's all the family you have."

"Uncle lied to protect me."

I shook my head at the memory of those sharpened teeth and angry tattoos. But even supporting Bounliep, and the additional cost of sponsoring her father, wouldn't explain this deception.

"Immigration shouldn't be a problem, Linda. Sponsor your father for a visa, he comes to America. Simple. Everyone lives happily ever after. You, Dad, Uncle Bounliep."

"I wish it were so simple."

"Tell me why it isn't."

"My father's an American."

"Then he has a passport."

"No."

"Then he's naturalized."

"He's as white as you. A veteran."

"He retired overseas?"

Maybe he had never come back, drifting instead through some Southeast Asian fleshpot. Just like Honeyman and scores of other expats I'd seen on Soi Cowboy and Nana Plaza.

"He never retired."

"A lifer then."

"I guess."

"Where's he now?"

She helped herself to another nip of scotch. I just watched her lithe, graceful form as she poured the drink. It really didn't matter what she did with her hair.

"He was a pilot during the war. Officially, he's dead. Unofficially, he's still alive. He has been for nearly thirty years."

"What're you saying, Linda?"

"I'm saying that he's still alive. In Laos."

"Why doesn't he come home then?"

"He can't. He's sort of a prisoner."

"'Sort of a prisoner'? What kind of POW bullshit *is* this?" Even as I said it I thought about Leslie Thompson in Kanchanaburi and Honeyman hissing at me, "We left people behind."

"What about your mother?"

"She was Katu tribe, like me. But dead a long time."

"So it's just your father you say you're after."

"Yes. And it's going to cost me plenty of money to get him."

"The life-insurance policy, then."

"Yes. In Thailand and Laos, many people want money."

"Now those hungry hands will be empty."

"A man called me this past spring."

"From Ubon Ratchathani. He called you twice."

"Yes. But how'd you know?"

"Phone records don't disappear just because you do. This man lives in Ubon?"

"I've never met Vannavong. He's a border trader who lives in Pakxe, a Lao town along the Mekong. He speaks decent English. He travels down to Cambodia and over to Thailand for work; Ubon's only about sixty miles west of Pakxe. It's the easiest place for him to contact me. Laos is so backward that the entire country has just a handful of international phone lines. Most are in the capital, Vientiane, more than a day's bus ride from Pakxe. Those phones are probably all tapped anyway. Vannavong went to Ubon instead to make the calls at an Internet shop. He contacted some of his relatives in the States, and they tracked me down. There aren't that many of us Monui—what everyone calls 'Katu'—in America. Word gets around the expat Lao community."

Especially, I thought, when someone looked as alien as Uncle Bounliep.

"What did this guy—Vannavong—tell you, Linda?"

"That my father is still alive, and living in my old village. He heard this from a Chinese trader who travels from Pakxe to Attapeu, the closest town to the mountains. A very difficult place to get to,

Attapeu. It's down in the panhandle, very near to the triborder with Vietnam and Cambodia. One of the most primitive provinces in one of the world's most remote countries. The road from Pakxe is really more like a trail. Sometimes it can take days, especially when it rains. Vannavong said the local people are either Communist cadre or survivors of the seminar camps, the hard-labor prisons where they sent folks for re-education. Everyone's suspicious of outsiders."

"Why are you telling me all this?"

"You asked me why I did this, right? The trader told Vannavong he could help take me to my father, but that it would cost a lot of money to buy his freedom. There were many people to pay—Lao and Katu—along the way. Vannavong ordered me not to go to the authorities, or the deal would be dead—along with my father. The trader also gave Vannavong something he said would prove my father was still alive. Vannavong mailed this to me from Thailand."

She opened her wallet and produced a large, tarnished coin about the size of a half-dollar and handed it to me. It had the weight of silver. The obverse side held the worn profile of a stern Caucasian man with an Old Testament–length beard and the legend "1888." The reverse side held a coat of arms—the symbol a lion on a shield—beneath an opulent, multiarched crown and the legend "JAMAIS CEDER." "Never yield," from what I remembered of high-school French. "I tried every coin shop in Boston. Nobody could place it."

"You contact the Pentagon?"

"What proof do I have? I can't remember that clearly, not even my father's real name. I was too young when we left Laos. Uncle told me people used to call my father 'Cut.' It could be a nickname or a phonetic approximation of his first or last name."

"Not Wattana?"

"That was just a family name my uncle invented for me when

we fled; he thought it sounded Thai and might help us in the refugee camps. I changed it to 'Watts' in high school."

"What happened when Vannavong contacted you?"

"What do you think? I felt shock. Joy. And anger at my uncle. Bounliep was upset and ashamed. He had lied to me about my parents, telling me they had died of malaria after the war. In that way, he hoped I would stop thinking about Laos and my family. Because we could never return."

"But now you intend to go back. That's what this whole scam was about."

"Wouldn't you do the same?"

"Nothing quite so devious. But you only mention your father, not your mother. What happened to her?"

"Vannavong said the trader was told she died a long time ago. So my uncle wasn't completely wrong. Mountain life is filled with hardships."

"If your father is a pilot, the Pentagon must have some missing-persons record."

"I wouldn't know where to begin. I only know the Pentagon would have classified my father as KIA-BNR–killed in action, body not recovered. After all these years, that's how they handle missing pilots. They're not going to do anything now. It's officially long over. The book is closed."

"They might ask the Lao government to investigate."

"You really don't know anything, do you? The Lao like to make their problems disappear. Forever. After the Pathet Lao victory in 1975, they took away Savang, the last king of Laos; no one ever saw him alive again. My story invites too many questions, makes too many people uncomfortable. It'd be more than an inconvenience—it'd be a big problem. No, I have to do this myself."

"You should've thought this through."

"I've thought of nothing else since Vannavong called me."

I had imagined that she'd created this subterfuge simply for the money, for a fresh start at a rich, soft life. I couldn't have been more wrong. Greed was the last thing on her mind.

"What were you going to do if your plans fell through?"

"I didn't count on anyone going to the effort of finding me. The insurance policy wasn't that big."

"There's not going to be any money, Linda."

"Not even the original benefit, the two-fifty?"

"Nothing."

"Maybe there's still a way."

She walked to where I stood and placed the mysterious silver coin, moist from her touch, in my hand.

"Make a wish, Sebastian."

"That would be a very long list, Linda. I wouldn't know where to start."

"Try."

"No one wants to listen."

"Then let me."

"It's too late, Linda. Mather knows you're still alive."

"Not that. Something else."

She stood so close that I felt her rich, warm breath, scented with good scotch and boundless possibilities. I faintly remembered the warning in that musty old anthropology text I'd stumbled across in a Harvard library: beware of getting involved with a Katu woman.

"I can read people pretty well, Sebastian," she said, her voice nearly a whisper. "It's part of being a banker. You're a good man; I feel this. I believe you have a big heart, and far more talent than you think. You found me, even in Bangkok. Now, please, help me find my father."

Nine

Without any pending work, I told myself, I could take some time off. It wasn't pro bono idealism: maybe it was the idea of inscrutable Asia, or of exotic escape with a beautiful, complicated woman. It felt too soon to head back to Boston, to the same steady diet of matrimonial stakeouts and workmen's comp cases. Here was Asia, beckoning like a billboard. None of the amenities and attractions I'd enjoyed on the European track circuit, but the potential for adventure was undeniable. Laos? It sounded like Albania, but with tigers and palm trees. Maybe I could even fill in a few of the huge blanks regarding the old man's classified career. And this time around, I wouldn't be just a rabbit. The chase was on, and I didn't intend to drop out. Linda Watts had just dangled the ultimate missing-person case in front of me. Maybe it was all another con, maybe not. Or perhaps she was just playing me, too. I intended to find out. The academic advice about the Katu was almost thirty years old; the world it described had to be obsolete.

We left the Overlook before the fat man came out of his Rohypnol stupor and the night manager lost his two-hundred-baht cheer. A *tuk-tuk* screeched to a halt at the sight of that spectacular little black dress. Linda gave him an address on Khao San Road and the driver didn't even try to overcharge her on the price.

We needed to hole up for a day or two and figure our next move. It would have to be the right move, too, since Colonel Nagaphit very well might have had a network of dirty cops spread across the city. The night rains had flushed the streets and sky, uncovering a brilliant spangle of distant, rarely seen stars. At this hour, when the roads were nearly empty and the air actually contained more oxygen than grit, Bangkok seemed almost inhabitable. Soon we hit the east end of Khao San Road, away from the police station and the sirens' wail. A few restaurants already held slack-jawed backpackers. Linda found a just-opened clothing shop and, when the owner complimented her outfit, began bargaining for a discounted "morning price"; the first sale of the day was considered auspicious for business. In a few minutes she emerged from a back room wearing a batik-print sarong, a sleeveless blue blouse, knock-off sandals, and a baseball cap drenched in sequins. She had shed the chanteuse image as easily as a snake molting its skin, all except those Balinese earrings.

"What do you think?"

"You look ready for a Phuket holiday."

"That's the idea, Sebastian. Now let's talk about your wardrobe."

"I already look like a tourist."

"Yes—a sex tourist. Who dresses you?"

"What else would a *farang* wear to Pompeii?"

"Your wife doesn't dress you like this, right?"

"There's no wife anymore, okay?"

"You've got more than just fashion issues."

"Right now, I've got hotel issues. How about picking us a decent guest house? And this time, make sure it isn't a heroin-shooting gallery. We want to avoid the police."

I ushered her out into the Sunday-morning light. Halfway up

the road, near the alleyway to the Marco Polo Guest House, a crowd had gathered around a wailing ambulance. We kept to the other side of the street until we were directly across from the scene. Policemen shouted, pushing the spectators apart. Two white-clad men moved through, carrying a slightly built corpse swathed in a bloodstained sheet.

"Another *farang* OD. Just like me."

"Too messy," I corrected. "Probably a suicide."

The sheet fell back as the men struggled to load their vehicle and I could see that the corpse's face had been crushed in, as if from the force of a baseball bat or a fall of several stories. But the sight of that mop of marmalade-colored hair brought the gastric acid churning halfway up my throat. Doug Brody had looked a lot better when I'd spoken with him the day before.

A crisply uniformed police officer wearing aviator-style sunglasses accompanied the stretcher bearers. Even as he oversaw the evacuation, Sergeant Wiwat scanned the crowd, a bland smile fixed beneath twin, lifeless patches of darkness. I shouldered Linda into the nearest *soi,* which ended at a guest house. We didn't stop in the lobby but continued through the owner's back room, the kitchen, and another alley that fed onto a small street, where we snared a *tuk-tuk* with a one-hundred-baht note and ordered the driver to take us around the park near the Dusit Zoo.

"Suicides freak you out?" she asked.

"Just corrupt cops. Especially those who murder to order."

"The dead guy back there?"

"I interviewed him yesterday at the Marco Polo Guest House. He was one of the last people to see you alive."

"You mean the other girl."

"The other girl had a name. Chang Tai. She was from Singapore. The dead guy we just saw? He found her body. He had a name, too. Doug Brody."

"You knew who she was?"

"It's my job."

"You think this man died because of me."

"You seem to have that effect on a lot of people in Bangkok."

"We don't know how he died."

"I've got a pretty good idea it wasn't natural causes."

"This Chang Tai, I didn't know her either."

"I suppose that makes it easier for you."

"Not really. I've wondered if she accidentally OD'd or—"

"Or if she was suckered into it, or even forced to inject herself?"

"Yes."

"I think Doug Brody died because he talked to me, or because Colonel Nagaphit needed another body double. Maybe both. The colonel is a very efficient, multitasking bastard."

She took my hand in hers and sighed.

"I didn't plan for it to get this heavy," she said, searching my eyes for any sign of doubt or distrust. "You've got to believe that."

"You keep asking me that: to believe you."

"Can you?"

"You talked me into helping to find your father. What does that tell you?"

We couldn't drift long like this in an open *tuk-tuk* through downtown Bangkok. And I realized that any hotel or hostel would mean registration, passports, questions. Calls might be made, prompting an unpleasant visit from some nameless henchman, or perhaps Sergeant Wiwat, even Colonel Nagaphit. I pulled Honeyman's business card out of my wallet. Inside of fifteen minutes we were climbing a sagging, ill-lit staircase to his third-floor apartment in an ancient Chinatown building redolent of cooking oil and garlic. Honeyman opened the door like he'd been expecting us.

"Looks like you've been running since we split up in Pompeii, Bass.

You gotta slow down. Stop and smell the *klongs*. Good morning, Miss Watts."

"He knows about me, too?"

"Sam Honeyman knows all, sees all, sleeps with most of it. Linda, this is Sam. Sam, Linda."

"Loved your band, lady, all except the keyboard player. Too much reverb."

"It's his group."

"A stage hog. That's always the way, isn't it? But you're the star, hands-down."

"*Was* the star."

"You sing too sweet to ever go silent."

"It would seem my Bangkok career is over before it started."

I ushered Linda into the tomb-quiet living room, under Honeyman's bemused look. A pair of beeswax candles glowed in front of a small altar, throwing faint shadows on the walls, infusing the fading photographs of army buddies and a dark-skinned Asian woman in wistful tones. Everyone appeared young and thin and full of bravado, standing against a silhouette of sandbags and dark, distant mountains. The old man was featured in a few of the photographs—floppy boonie hat worn at a rakish angle, a Soviet-made AK-47 slung casually over his shoulder, an unfiltered cigarette dangling from his lips. The barefoot young woman looked nearly as striking as Linda: a dark, stovepipe sarong and camouflage-print short-sleeved shirt, thick, shoulder-length hair, and pouty lips blooming into an insouciant smile. I took her to be the hooch girl Honeyman had mentioned, the one from the Jeh hill tribe.

"Old friends, old ghosts," said Honeyman. He lit a joss stick, then a cigarette, and motioned for us to sit on the silk cushions scattered on the wide-planked floor.

"Just got in a little while ago myself," Honeyman continued.

"Took five hundred baht for the cops to develop amnesia after the dust-up at Pompeii. That cleaned me out. Not even enough scratch for a *tuk-tuk*. Good thing it's less than a two-hour walk from Sukhumvit back to here."

"You should start fewer fights," Linda said.

"A VA doctor once told me it's a personality disorder. I've got anger-management issues."

"We all have our problems," she replied. "Yours sound self-inflicted."

"And yours, I believe, are cash-flow related," Honeyman parried.

"You hardly look like a financial expert," Linda said sarcastically.

"I could say the same thing about your talent for fraud," Honeyman retorted.

"I can't really say anything more about you, Honeyman. You're talent-free."

"C'mon you two," I interjected. "The enemy isn't in here."

Linda stood.

"If you two will excuse me, I smell like spoiling fruit. No wise-cracks, Honeyman."

"Shower's through the bedroom. There's a box of kitchen matches for the pilot light if you want hot water."

"At least the bathroom's in your apartment and not down the hall. Classy."

When the water started running, Honeyman cackled.

"You hound! Looks like you'll follow a pretty girl anywhere. Even *this* piece of work."

"It's complicated, Sam."

"What woman ain't?"

"This one more than most. She told me why she tried the scam."

"And you believed her."

"Enough of it, anyway."

"Enough to jeopardize your case?"

"My case is good, Sam. This doesn't affect the case. Which reminds me: I need to call my client. It's Saturday evening in Boston."

I borrowed Honeyman's phone and reached Dolores Moyle at home, where she was treating her gut instinct to a generous dose of single-malt scotch.

"So glad to hear from you, Sebastian," she said with a throaty chuckle. "And I'm sorry I brow-beat you earlier. It's a last resort when the Claims Committee is chewing on my ass. But they'll be very pleased with your work. Very pleased."

"I'm sorry my camera isn't digital, Mrs. Moyle. I'll FedEx the photographs today. You'll have them by the middle of the week."

"When will you be back in town?"

"Not for a bit. I thought I'd take a few days off, have a look around as long as I'm here. After all, it's my first time."

"You've earned it. I'm adding a twenty-percent bonus to your fee. Enjoy yourself."

"Thank you, Mrs. Moyle."

"Just be careful. Don't blow it all on one night in Bangkok. And if we're going to continue to work together, you must call me Dolores."

"Yes, Mrs. Moyle."

"And my best to your father. He should be very proud."

"I'll let him know."

When she hung up, Honeyman met my gaze.

"Planning a little holiday in Thailand?" he asked. "I can recommend a few places: Chiang Mai, Koh Samui, Phuket. All very popular with couples."

"None of the above, Sam. We're headed up to Isan. And then Laos."

Honeyman considered the news.

"That doesn't sound like R-and-R," he finally said. "Not Isan. And certainly not Laos."

"I wouldn't consider this trip to be a vacation."

"I consider Laos a complete waste of time and effort. What about your firm?"

"What I learned last night could put Damon and Son on the map. Mrs. Moyle likes to speak of 'big-game hunting.' This would be the most incredible trophy ever."

Then I recounted everything Linda Watts had revealed to me about Laos, about her childhood, and about her missing father. When I had finished, Honeyman sat silently in the shadows. The water had stopped running in the shower.

"That's a hell of a story, kid."

"You probably heard a few like it when you had that bar."

"Nothing like this."

"Not since the Starr photo, I bet."

"And how did that turn out?" he said, his voice rising. "I don't want to see you played for a sucker, too."

"I've got my eyes wide open."

"What's she paying you?"

"We never discussed money."

"A makeup call, huh? How do you know she's not just some quick-thinking little schemer who's gonna take you for a ride?"

"She's might be that, too. But her story sounds too detailed, too dense, too damn real to dream up on the fly. And it explains her behavior over the last several months."

"I got my doubts about her motivation."

Linda emerged in her new blouse and sarong, with a towel wrapped around her damp hair.

"Are you fellows through talking about me?"

"Not even close, lady," Honeyman retorted.

"What did you tell Honeyman?"

"Everything I know about Attapeu."

"And you, Honeyman? You don't seem too convinced."

"I think you're full of it. This sounds like just one more POW scam. Difference is, at least the other shit-bums were creative enough to cook up phony dogtags and doctored photographs. Some hard 'evidence,' at the very least."

"I don't care much for you either, Honeyman," Linda countered. "Bangkok's full of men like you, living in shithole apartments, riding two-baht buses, pinching their pensions so they can get laid on the Patpong once a month."

"I prefer the Cowboy, sweetheart. And I manage my money well enough to afford long-time at least once a week."

"Neutral corners," I said. "Linda, show him that silver piece."

She scowled, but rummaged in her purse, then flipped the large coin his way.

"Tails, you lose."

Honeyman snatched it with feline grace as it sang through the void, then he sat back on the floor pillows to regard the design.

"Tails it is," he said. But the doubt and cynicism soon vanished like smoke from his manner.

"What is it?" I asked.

His grip tightened around the coin, until the veins in his right arm bulged like cables.

"A ghost of Mayrena," he muttered finally. "I can help you."

"What can *you* do," Linda taunted, "besides drink and get into fights?"

"I win those fights, remember? When I hit people, they stay hit. That's a talent."

"That's all you got?"

"I can provide security, weapons, even intelligence. I've forgotten more about where you want to go in Thailand and Laos than you'll ever know, lady."

"I seriously doubt that."

"You don't ever want to bet against me."

"We want him along, Linda," I said.

What little Honeyman had told me of his Special Forces experience was still a powerful argument: his gallery of absent friends and the old man's endorsement left me no doubt. She finally nodded, shook hands with Honeyman, and retrieved the coin.

"What do you suggest, Honeyman?" Linda asked. "Impress me with a plan."

"We beat feet out of Bangkok. We're now all PNG: persona non grata. I say we head up into Isan, then cross into Laos and meet your source in Pakxe. We don't bother messing around here at the Lao embassy for visas. It'll take at least a day to process and it might tip off the Thai police. We'll just pay the tea money to Lao immigration when we get to the border. For one thousand baht, they'll issue us tourist visas on the spot. We just say we're headed for Champasak, going to take a boat trip down the Mekong, see the old Khmer Empire ruins of Wat Phu. But we push on for Attapeu instead, then head into the mountains and smoke out this deal."

"Not bad," Linda answered. "Except that I don't have a passport, only a fake Thai ID card."

"These are just details," Honeyman replied. "Here's the thing: we need to leave Bangkok. Pronto. There's a third-class local train for Isan at a quarter to noon. That's the last place the Thai cops will look for *farang*. Go and grab your gear and meet me at half past eleven outside Hualomphong Station. Second column from the right as you face the entrance."

"Too much like a *Casablanca* farewell," Linda said. "Hualomphong may be busy, but it's also crawling with the law. Better we take a taxi and meet you at Bang Sue Junction, near Chatuchak market. All the Northeastern-Line trains service the station. Two stops out of town."

"Not bad," Honeyman said, with a hint of a smile.

We hired a *tuk-tuk* for the remainder of the morning and drove back to Thonglor, where we parked around the corner from the

Grand Babylon. Linda then charmed the driver into fetching the hotel's bellhop for us. Within thirty minutes, the boy had sneaked the room key from the reception desk, packed my suitcase, and gotten the luggage past a Bangkok policeman staking out the lobby. It was the best one hundred baht I ever spent on room service. While we were waiting for my bag retrieval, I left the *tuk-tuk* and walked a block to a camera shop, where I paid a premium to rush the developing and printing of last night's film, the roll including the Pompeii and Overlook images. The pictures would be decent enough for Mather's purposes. Next time I shot available light at night, I'd try using ISO 800 film. Or maybe it was time to finally consider going digital.

Linda kept insisting we swing by Soi Cowboy; she needed to speak with Nok, her young Isan girlfriend. I finally relented, but only after demanding we park off-site near the German restaurant and send the driver to collect the bar girl. While we waited for Nok, I composed a short, handwritten cover letter to Mather Mutual detailing the enclosed images; I'd FedEx it and the film documentation from the business center of the nearest four-star hotel on the way to Bang Sue Junction. A typewritten account would look more professional, but I didn't have the time or office equipment. Besides, Dolores Moyle seemed the type of executive who appreciated bottom-line results more than business etiquette.

The underage bar girl finally returned with the driver, walking with small, defiant steps. Nok looked even younger in daylight, somewhere in the middle-school throes of sexual development. A brief, animated discussion followed; I didn't have to comprehend Thai to understand the gist of the argument. Linda wanted Nok to come with us, to return to her village. But the dancer refused, waving the baht she had taken off the drugged German the night before. There was more easy money where that came from, and she was smart and pretty and brave enough to take it. She dropped a five-hundred-baht note—commonly known as a Purple King—on the *tuk-tuk* seat and stomped off toward Soi Cowboy, not looking back or even bothering to avoid the rain puddles. We stopped in Siam Square to express-mail my package, then rode to Bang Sue Junction in silence.

At the station, Honeyman looked at my roll-on suitcase, shook his head in mock disgust, and then tossed a spare olive-drab rucksack and a floppy canvas hat my way.

"Try not to stick out like a damn tourist."

"You too, Sam?"

I dumped the contents into the canvas pack and left my good luggage on a concrete bench.

"Don't feel so bad, Sebastian," Linda said.

"I know: you gave up a dress and jacket this morning."

"DKNY. It nearly killed me to do it."

"I'll buy you a knockoff the next time we hit Khao San Road."

I purchased a tourist map of Indochina, a prestamped postcard of a Hmong hill-tribe woman, and a copy of the *Bangkok Post* at the station newsstand. Grim news filled the paper: the Thai stock market was on the verge of collapse; O. J. Simpson's California mansion was up for auction; the Red Sox had fallen seventeen games behind Baltimore. It was going to be a bad, long season. When the half-mile-long train to Ubon rolled into the station, we found two facing benches in an old coach full of glum peasants heading back to Isan without much to show for their backbreaking labors in the capital. The overhead racks were stuffed with inexpensive suitcases, recycled cardboard boxes, and baled plastic sacks of clothing, cheap gifts, and overripe fruit. A few small fans hummed and rattled but barely moved the air inside the steaming, metal-roofed car. Right on schedule, we pulled away from the train platform; soon, food hawkers moved down the aisles, touting the quality of their glazed ducks and flavored ices. Honeyman handed us each a ticket.

"These are good as far as Surin," he said, "but we'll be getting off a few hours earlier in Khorat. Just in case the conductor remembers us."

"You're not too bad at the tradecraft," I remarked. "You ought to think about PI work."

"Here's more cover: the *Collins Field Guide: Birds of South-East Asia*. Might help explain our whereabouts if we're stopped somewhere we shouldn't be. Just wave the book and tell the authorities we're crazy-ass bird-watchers. Twitchers will go damn near anywhere for a new sighting."

He tossed me the heavy, inch-thick volume.

"Why Khorat?" Linda asked.

"Got an old army buddy there, Frank Myers. He married a local girl; met her on the Cowboy, of course. The next thing I knew, he'd moved up to Khorat so she could be with her family. He does a little import-export work to keep his sanity. Timber and gems, animals and antiques. If anyone can get us some firepower on short notice, it'll be Frank."

"Is that really necessary?" Linda asked.

"Where we're going, lady, I intend to be packing. So I need to see Frank. Won't take long. He's usually at the VFW. Khorat's still got a real-live post. Big air base there during the war."

We cleared the city and ran alongside the superhighway for a few miles. After the airport station we slowly picked up speed, running between long, thin plots of paddy. The wet air smelled of mud and manure. Here we were, a pair of cynics caught up in a beautiful woman's knight-errant quest. Then again, cynics always made the deepest romantics.

"Back at your apartment, you mentioned a name, Honeyman. Something to do with Linda's coin."

"That name's Mayrena. But known to his loyal, thoroughly confused subjects as King Marie the First of Sedang."

"Never heard of him, or the kingdom of Sedang."

"Very few people ever have," Honeyman replied. "This all happened more than a hundred years ago. I only heard about Mayrena from an old French priest in Kontum, during my tour up there with your pops. Open up your map and I'll show you where I'm talking about."

Then Honeyman spun a story worthy of Conrad or Kipling. In the late 1800s, Marie-Charles David de Mayrena fled the law in Paris, as he was wanted for embezzlement, and headed for the Far East, where the usual legalities didn't always apply. He somehow persuaded the French authorities in Indochina to send him into the Central Highlands to win over the Montagnards before any English explorer got to them first. The governor-general loved that sort of Great Game pluck and audacity. So Mayrena rode off into the Annamite Mountains, ran up the Tricolor, and signed treaties with the highlanders in the Kontum area. He always kept the gold concessions for himself. But the Frenchman made the mistake of getting stranded upcountry when the rainy season struck. The mind plays strange tricks during the monsoon, especially in the mountains. Mayrena soon crossed the line. Before the French knew it, Mayrena had proclaimed himself king of Sedang, drafted his own constitution to rule over tens of thousands of subjects, declared war on surrounding hill tribes, even designed a flag and issued postage stamps. This was the first coin Honeyman had ever seen, but he was certain that it was legitimate. The date on the silverpiece—1888—jibed with Mayrena's reign; the coat of arms on the reverse matched that of some Sedang kingdom stamps that the priest in Kontum, a philatelist, had shown Honeyman from his collection.

The French became alarmed—Mayrena had begun courting the British and the Belgians—and put him out of business in less than a year, Honeyman elaborated. The adventurer died soon afterward in British Malaya; some people said he was killed in a duel, others said he died from snakebite. Mayrena was just a footnote now in the roll call of Imperial Age scoundrels and pikers. But he was more than The Man Who Would Be King. Mayrena had been the goddamn king.

"How do you think this is connected to my father?" Linda asked.

"Your father was an outsider who lived in those mountains, too, so he could be familiar with the king of Sedang legend. Maybe he's made a name for himself up there, like Mayrena, and this coin's some sort of signal that would get by the authorities if the messenger was ever stopped and searched. There are plenty of old French piasters still floating around. The Montagnards use 'em as jewelery."

"I knew it was important."

"It's priceless on every level," Honeyman said.

"Is it enough for us to go on, this coin and those phone calls from some guy in Pakxe?" I asked.

"I had a very interesting morning before I caught the train," Honeyman said. "I still know a few people it pays to know, like this old boy who used to work out of Stony Beach—the Defense Intelligence Agency outfit in Bangkok that looks into POW/MIA live-sighting reports. Retired now, but he's still in the loop. Guess what he heard? Seems that a few years ago Stony Beach had its eyes and ears on an old American pilot they thought might be living up in the mountains of Attapeu Province, way east of Pakxe."

"Did they have a name for the pilot?" Linda asked.

"Not a name that shows up on any POW/MIA lists. The locals apparently call him 'John Man.' The live-sighting report came from a Lao hunter who said he saw John Man. The witness said John Man was married to a headman's daughter. Somewhere back in the mountains of Xanxai district."

"Would Xanxai be on my map?" I asked.

"Not a chance. It's basically just a blank spot in the mountains."

"What else?"

"Nothing else. The DIA boys dropped the ball on the follow-up. They filed a request with the Lao authorities to visit the area—three weeks before they planned to come down from the embassy in Vientiane. How's that for a snap investigation? Plenty of time for the Lao to get on a shortwave radio to the provincial capital—there's no other communication out in the bush—and give the heads-up to the local Public Security Service: make sure the Americans don't find anyone in Attapeu to question about this John Man sighting. My buddy said a Thai listening post picked up the communication to Attapeu on electronic intercepts and forwarded it to U.S. intelligence. But DIA didn't consider the information valid, because the Thai are a third party. No matter that our National Security Agency had trained the Thai. It's mind-boggling. After a few weeks the DIA finally sends out a rookie from Vientiane and, surprise, no one in Attapeu has ever heard of or seen John Man. Plus, the Pentagon's MIA list doesn't carry anyone named John as missing in this area. So, case closed."

"What do you think, Honeyman?" Linda asked.

"You think I'm tall, Linda?" Honeyman replied.

"A little taller than average, sure."

"What about in Laos?"

"You're much taller than the average Lao, of course."

"I'd be goddamn Gulliver in Laos. Here's another question: how would a Lao describe someone who's tall?"

"Chon mein," she said. "That's one way. 'The tall one.' "

"Chon mein," echoed Honeyman. He smiled thinly. "The tall one. *Chon mein.* John Man."

"Chon mein," I repeated. "John Man. They sound almost the same."

"Don't you see?" Honeyman asked. "That's where the name comes from. They're not calling him by his first name. 'Chon Mein' is a nickname, because of his height."

"My God, this John Man might have been my father," Linda said.

"We're gonna find out," said Honeyman. He patted her shoulder with surprising tenderness. "And we're sure as shit not gonna file our travel plans with the Lao authorities. Or even our people."

Linda squeezed his forearm.

"I had you wrong, Honeyman."

"You had me pegged right, lady. But outside Bangkok I'm a much better person."

Along the railway, a buffalo resting up to his nostrils in a brown canal gazed dully at our passing. The heat shimmered off the tiled roofs of new homes. We were coming into Ayutthaya. Once one of the largest, most prosperous cities in the world, it had been destroyed by the Burmese in the late eighteenth century and never recovered.

"One more story, and then I'm taking a nap," said Honeyman. "It's about a place called Nhommarath, and anyone who knows about it is sick to their stomachs. This was back in late 1980, just after Reagan got elected. A source with some pretty serious contacts said that maybe thirty American POWs were working on a road gang near Nhommarath in Khammouane Province. That's in the Laotian panhandle, in a river valley about halfway between the Mekong and the Vietnamese border. Our intelligence confirmed there was a recently built prison camp of an odd design: an outer camp and another, inner camp, as if to hold high-value detainees. It got more interesting: satellite photos of the complex showed someone had arranged logs on the ground to form the figure 52 and the letter *K*. This symbol happened to be a standard distress signal a U.S. pilot might make after a shoot-down or a crash in enemy territory. How's that for coincidence?

"Recon photos were taken repeatedly for almost a month over Nhommarath, and the ground signal was always visible," he continued. "Shadow-length analysis of humans and tools in the pictures indicated the workers were taller than your average happy Lao rice farmers. How many? Thirty non-Asians by measurable shadow: that was the official intelligence verdict."

"Thirty guys like John Man."

"Sure as shit, kid. Reagan authorized a Delta Force raid. Choppers, satchel charges, chainsaws, the whole nine yards. They were going to train on a full-scale mock-up in the Philippines. They even had a cover story: they were filming an action movie. But some of the brass got nervous. Remember, this wasn't too long after the Desert One fuck-up in Iran that killed a bunch of our people. What if there was another helicopter crash? What if the long shadows were cast by Russian advisers, not American POWs? A raid would blow up into more than a major international embarrassment. To cover their ass, they wanted their own recon."

A hawker came through with bags of pomegranates and roasted chickens folded into newspapers with small bags of sticky rice.

"This doesn't end happily, does it?" Linda ventured.

"The CIA insisted on using its local operatives to take a look. One American was supposed to go along with the team, but it never happened. The recon was a clusterfuck from start to finish. They ran into Communist Lao patrols as soon as they crossed the Mekong. It took them more than a month to reach Nhommarath, which was only forty miles away. The team leader didn't have any commando experience. But he knew the area and the Agency liked him. How do I know? Because it was Voumi—the same fat bastard who fed me the Starr photo.

"Voumi is a coward and a shit-bum. He got hammered at the bar one night on the Cowboy and told me all about it, thinking I'd be impressed. He never got closer than five hundred yards to the camp. He stayed just a few hours, shot a few blurry pictures that didn't show a damn thing, and then got spooked by guard dogs. The Pentagon briefed Congress about their findings and then the whole thing leaked like a damn sieve. More than a few people, government and military, wanted it all to just go away. When the *Washington Post* broke the story, Operation Pocket Change got shit-canned. We had satellite photographs. We had electronic intercepts. Nhommarath was our best chance—ever. And we blew it. We left them."

"You think my father was there?" Linda asked.

"Probably not," Honeyman continued. "More likely it's the John Man scenario I mentioned, developed through live-sighting reports and electronic intercepts: a U.S. pilot living in a remote hill-tribe village in the mountains, inaccessible even to the Lao."

"What's our government say about this?" I asked.

"Well, the official line is that no American serviceman is being held against his will in Southeast Asia," Honeyman said. "Note the lawyerly distinction: 'held against his will.' If some MIA was to be found living in a mountain village in Laos, it'd allow the military investigators some cover for their screw-up. They could argue that the guy *wanted* to be there, that the detention wasn't against his will. Of course, no one ever went in and asked *him* if he'd like to come home."

Outside, the landscape had changed. We were climbing through low, denuded hills beneath fat gray clouds. This was scrubland, a marginal place that would never move poets. A place of quarries and sawmills, a place where things were extracted and never replaced. I fell asleep as we sat on a siding, waiting for a Bangkok-bound express train to pass. If there were dreams of deaf-mutes, drunken elephants, or giant men who cast long shadows, I don't remember. When I awoke, the hills had spilled onto a low plateau divided into fields of rice and maize and we were nearly in Khorat. It was almost six o'clock. The west-side station was less than a half mile from the VFW post, but Honeyman insisted we take a taxi. Fewer people would see us.

The VFW club occupied the ground floor of the Siri Hotel.

Beyond the grit-caked glass door stood a small vestibule, with a wall that held about twenty wooden lockers, each labeled in English with a Western surname and holding a combination lock. None listed Myers. We passed another doorway into a garish main room done up like a kitschy European acid trip: floor-to-ceiling color photographs of Dutch tulip beds, support columns papered with scenes of Bavarian pine forests and rustic Swiss chalets. There was a bulletin board for VFW business but most of the place was given over to a greasy-spoon restaurant, where Thai customers ate charred hamburgers and watched Bangkok soap operas. However, there was one older American, a short, sturdy man in pressed, faded jeans, a weathered, checked shirt, and two-tone iguana-skin cowboy boots. He was bald, with a unkempt hedge of curly silvery hair that fell over his collar. Linda and I took another table and let Honeyman do the schmoozing. Inside of ten minutes, Honeyman gave us the bad, improbable news.

"Frank used to live about an hour out of Khorat until six months ago. His wife had been sick for quite a while. Ovarian cancer. When she died, he fell apart. Frank blamed himself for not getting her an earlier diagnosis. He closed his business, gave away his motorbike, cleared out his VFW locker."

"So where'd he go?" Linda asked.

"He's entered a forest monastery outside of Ubon Ratchathani. Place called Wat Pah Nanachat. They get a lot of *farang* looking to atone for their sins, real or imagined. The abbot was a combat vet, too."

Ubon: the town where Linda's Lao contact had twice gone to call her collect in the States. I asked about our next move.

"We get a room upstairs," Honeyman said. "Stay off the streets. Clean up, shower, rest for a few hours. There's another local train that comes through just before midnight. We keep on going to Ubon."

"What about your buddy?"

"I'm hoping Frank didn't give away his stash of AK-47s when he renounced the material world."

We had to go outside the building to access the hotel lobby. But when we left the VFW post, a Royal Thai Police officer was waiting for us on the sidewalk. He must have attended the same academy as Colonel Nagaphit, but he had skipped the class on elegant menace. He needed to find a better tailor to let out the waist of his trousers, buried somewhere beneath a belly that had welcomed too many snifters of cognac.

"Looks like your friend Nok gave us up, Linda," I said. "Who else knew we were headed to Isan?"

"Linda Watts?" the cop asked. "Sebastian Damon? You come."

"And me?" Honeyman asked.

"You I don't know. You go away."

"What's the charge?" I asked.

"A *farang* die on Khao San Road."

"So what?" I replied. "*Farang* die all the time in Bangkok."

"Different. This time, someone murder *farang*. Maybe someone like you."

"Well, not me. I'm innocent."

"No problem then, Sebastian Damon. We all go to Bangkok. You answer questions from the colonel."

"Colonel Nagaphit?"

"He has friends in many places. Like me."

"Seems like everyone knows your Colonel Tea Money," Honeyman said.

"This is a setup," I complained. "A frame job."

"We go," the policeman insisted. "No problem."

Linda fumed and looked up and down the otherwise empty sidewalk. Then she blurted something in Thai, and when the policeman turned, she kicked him in the groin. Hard. He buckled, and then Honeyman dragged him into a side alley and knocked him cold with a flurry of punches. I stood dumbfounded over the unconscious cop with Linda while Honeyman casually walked into the Siri Hotel and paid cash to rent a room for two nights. To the desk clerk, he'd be just another old *farang* vet, come back to visit Khorat.

"What'd you tell this cop, Linda?"

"To go fuck himself with the colonel's gun," she replied.

"Now we're screwed," I said. "This is just further confirmation."

"If we have to go back to Bangkok to face the colonel, we're fucked—and with a rusty pipe. This is the best option."

When Honeyman returned, we carried the policeman up a back staircase to the second-floor hotel room, rigged a gag, bound his feet and hands, and then used the cop's handcuffs to secure him to a bedpost. I turned on the TV and hung a Do Not Disturb placard on the door. With any luck, the maid wouldn't open the room and find him until at least late tomorrow. I regarded Linda and Honeyman, bantering easily as they double-tied the knots around the policeman's wrists. The sudden attack had been instinctual, their commitment unwavering. Damn the consequences. We were in this all the way to the end.

Ten

The roar of a Bangkok-bound express train startled me awake. I bolted upright and looked out the open window. A pinkish-red tincture spilled over the eastern horizon, dusting a low haze of wood smoke. We had stopped on a rail siding overlooking a still pond where a flock of geese floated among mauve lotus blossoms. A faint smell of sweet steamed rice and bananas hung inside the coach. Linda slept beside me, her head resting against my shoulder. I looked around for Honeyman, then quickly caught myself. We'd split up in Khorat. In an attempt to divert the Thai police, Honeyman had taken another, more northerly train line toward Nong Khai, a few miles downstream from Vientiane, the Lao capital. Once he reached the border town along the Mekong, he would hire a local boatman to sneak him across the river to Laos after nightfall and then look up an old crony in the Lao resistance. The man now worked as a tour guide in Vientiane, but rumor had it that he kept a cache of automatic weapons buried in his backyard. Some things had changed for the better in Laos, Honeyman had told me as we bade him farewell on the train platform in Khorat, and some things would never change.

Once we got to Ubon Ratchathani, we would get what we could

from Frank Myers at the monastery, then somehow enter southern Laos at the Chong Mek border crossing. How we got across the frontier was our challenge; we needed to avoid any scrutiny by both Thai and Lao immigration officials, so visas and passports were out of the question. We would meet Honeyman in Pakxe, a Lao provincial capital along the Mekong, in five days. While we waited at the Champasak Palace Hotel, we would pose as tourists while scouting the feasibility of possible exfiltration routes from the Lao interior to the Thai border. If we couldn't all meet at the set date in Pakxe, the Laithong Hotel in Ubon Ratchathani would be our fallback position.

Around midnight, we had retightened the policeman's bindings, retied his gag, and then sneaked out of the Siri Hotel. At the train station, Honeyman bought three tickets for Nong Khai.

"That's only for the stationmaster's benefit," Honeyman had said as we walked to the far end of the platform. "If the police ask, he'll remember we were all heading north. But you all will be on the next train for Ubon, heading east. Just pay the fare onboard. Only about sixty baht apiece. Not even two dollars."

"Another hard seat in third-class," Linda said.

"Beats the local buses," I replied.

"Take a good look at that bird guidebook," Honeyman suggested. "It might come in handy at the border."

"Du nok," said Linda.

"You got that right." Honeyman grinned. "Look at birds."

A longing cry and the slow, blazing star of the train's headlight as it approached from the west.

"Right on time," said Honeyman. "I'll see you all in Pakxe. Behave now."

"No promises," Linda replied.

We had boarded a muggy car near the back of the train, stepping over men sleeping in the aisle on plastic mats, and finally found an open bench at the very rear, next to the toilet. All the overhead fans were out of order; only the soft purr of Thai love songs from a passenger's cassette tape deck stirred the still air. We were headed for the hinterlands, where obsolete electronics still held on, where *tuk-tuks* probably came equipped with eight-track-tape players and guest-house sitting rooms featured Betamax VCRs.

Leaving Khorat, we had passed unlit shanties of rusted metal and scavenged wood, then plunged into the mosaic of paddy and plains. I had wondered aloud if we'd seen the last of Colonel Nagaphit's henchmen.

"I don't know," Linda had replied. "When he casts his net, he covers the entire pond."

It was a good thing we were heading for a new pond. Something about train travel elicits intimacy. Sitting together on a dark, rocking bench, it wasn't long before Linda had volunteered more details of her attempted insurance scam. We were now on the same team, no longer the quarry and the hunter. Her failed fraud scheme seemed a moot point. She'd gotten the idea from a newspaper story in the *Boston Herald,* she explained. Some immigrant, maybe a Haitian, had faked his death back home to collect a life-insurance policy. In the wake of a ferry sinking, the man had bought a death certificate and then put in a claim. It wasn't that complicated in a place where lots of people died and no one asked too many questions. While volunteering at the Lazarus Center in Providence, Linda had met a Burmese refugee who told her about the Front Row Hotel and the bogus-document ring in Bangkok. When she arrived in Thailand, she went immediately to the Front Row to acquire a fake ID card. Then she looked for a job that paid in cash; no one cared about employer references on Soi Cowboy.

"I couldn't just go missing and expect my uncle to collect on the policy," Linda said now. "I could doctor up official forms and certificates, but that wouldn't be foolproof if the company decided on a closer look. When I got to Bangkok, I realized I needed a body double. Working Soi Cowboy, it didn't take long to learn that Colonel Nagaphit ran the local rackets. He agreed to help, for a price: he wanted one thousand dollars up front, plus ten thousand dollars when the policy paid off. Between his advance and the money for the ID card, it wiped me out. Then the colonel took my US passport, so he could plant it on my double. Incredibly stupid of me to let him have it."

"Then he had control."

"He added a new demand: I had to pay one hundred dollars a week in 'interest' on the ten thousand I owed. What could I do? There was no one I could turn to in the States for a loan; I was supposed to be dead. Working in a bar seemed more anonymous, more low-profile than anything else. Hustling lady-drinks, playing six-five-four with drunks. I tried to be careful. I didn't live above the bar. I rented a cheap room in Thonglor, in a building full of girls down from Isan. I only allowed the drunkest, most affluent older tourists to bar-fine me. I delayed the sex as long as possible: take a long, hot shower first, raid the minibar, give them a back massage. They passed out before I had to sleep with them. Then I took their money, but I always left a few dollars. That way they wouldn't think I had robbed them—they just got hammered and couldn't remember how much they spent on drinks and bar fines. It was a nightmare. And then my luck ran out. One of the johns I ripped off did come back to the club. There was a big confrontation and I got fired on the spot. But by that time I'd made a few musical contacts at the after-hours clubs on Soi Cowboy. That's where I heard about a cover band looking for a female singer. It paid better. No more bar fines, or mamasans, or drunken customers. I'd be more visibile, though, so I changed my appearance.

"The colonel was having a hard time finding a good match. I don't know what he told his people to do. I only hope the Singapore girl on Khao San Road died accidentally. I made a horrible mistake,

Sebastian. And the heroin OD wiped out the double-indemnity clause, which I'd counted on. Of course, the colonel didn't see how he'd cost me a quarter-million dollars. He found me a body: that was his end of the bargain. He still wanted payment, and his interest. Then you showed up, asking too many pointed questions. And you had to go to Pompeii."

"Blame that on Honeyman."

Across the aisle of the train, a barefoot old woman stood and thrust her head out the open window, singing crazily into the black rush of wind. When I looked again at Linda, she had fallen asleep. I leafed through the bird guide for a while, marveling at the sheer beauty and bounty: barbets and bee-eaters, serpent-eagles and cranes, woodpeckers and even a storklike creature called a greater adjutant. Somewhere on the hot plateau, sleep overtook me. An hour after sunrise, we pulled into the Ubon terminal, located in a suburb south of the provincial capital. While a happy mob of relatives, porters, and drivers pounced on the train, we used the confusion to get a taxi to take us to the Laithong Hotel, the place Honeyman had recommended for a fallback rendezvous. It seemed decent enough: a nine-story pile a bit north of the city center that catered more to Asian businessmen than the few *farang* who made it this far into Isan.

"We checking in?" Linda asked.

"Only for breakfast. Just a bit of misdirection, in case the cops canvass the station."

"You and Honeyman, with your bobbing and weaving."

"I've seen what happens to people who forget to duck their heads in Thailand."

After a hurried hotel meal of runny fried eggs and scorched toast washed down by bad instant coffee, we hired a *song-thaew* for the ride to Wat Pah Nanachat. On the return drive through downtown, I had the driver wait outside an Internet shop while I tried to make an international call to the old man. Just a busy signal: my father had never figured out the call-waiting or voice-mail features on his telephone. The one computer in the establishment with Internet access was broken. The old man had a low opinion of e-mail anyway. I would have to send this dinosaur the postcard, the one of the Hmong woman, to let him know my whereabouts.

The monastery turned out to be back across the river and beyond the train station, a few miles west along the main highway toward neighboring Sisaket Province. Fresh new homes with stucco as white as an egret's feathers rose along the shoulder, but mostly the road ran through paddy land that stretched out on either side all the way to the far horizon. Half-drowned fields in an endless spectrum of green hues, from jade and cephalon to tourmaline and emerald, steamed against the sun. The forest temple stood about a half mile off the roadway, beyond a hamlet and further rice fields. We followed a paved road through the shade of old trees to a clearing with a cluster of low, wooden buildings. After paying the driver, I gave a young Australian monk a letter of introduction that Honeyman had written and asked him to deliver it to Frank Myers. Then I took out the postcard from my pack and a ballpoint pen and dashed off a few quick lines to the old man:

"Case closed. Client happy. Money in the bank. Honeyman semisober. Now in Ubon, but heading over the fence and across the river and through the woods. That big, black hole you mentioned. Maybe even following your footsteps. Will call if I can. Of course I'll be careful."

Ten minutes later, a tall, middle-aged man walked up a freshly swept dirt path through the jungle to greet us.

"You've missed the prayer and meal for visitors," Myers said apologetically. Gray stubble flocked his shaven head and I saw the outline of his rib cage where his saffron robes fell below his shoulders. Diet, prayer, and grief had rendered the recent widower a gaunt ascetic.

"We just got in on the Bangkok train. We ate in town."

"Seeing the sights of Ubon?"

"Passing through, actually."

"Most tourists come next month, for the big candle festival. But there's a good provincial museum, a few silversmiths, and some fabric shops. That's about it for Ubon."

"We're shopping for something else," I said. "Something with stopping power. Honeyman suggested we see you."

His brow began to knit itself into a frown.

"Walk with me."

We followed Myers through the forest to another clearing with a large bodhi tree surrounded by beds of heliconia. Myers gestured toward a nearby, empty pavilion and we sat down.

"Honeyman is a very good friend," he said softly, "but I can't help you. That was another life. A bad life."

"And if we promise you that what we want will be used for a just cause?" Linda asked.

"We cannot presume to know what is just," Myers countered. "And automatic weapons cannot be put to good use."

"Not even to help an old friend?" she pursued.

"Especially for an old friend. But I can't blame Honeyman for trying. He knew what I was."

"Do you know why he asked?" I said.

"I haven't spoken with him for several years. Your visit comes as a surprise."

I told Myers we were headed for Laos, where the guns might come in handy, especially in the mountains.

"I used to run Lurp operations—pardon the acronym, a long-range recon patrol—across the border, too," Myers said. "I understand your concern. I felt like a hunted animal every time we did an insertion. But all the firepower in the world doesn't matter. Your time is either up, or it's not. Weapons won't protect you from your destiny."

"They might delay the inevitable for a little while," I said.

Myers only smiled.

"Honeyman won't have a problem. He's a resourceful man, one who's made more merit than he'll ever admit to anyone. I can't give you guns, but I can help get you into Laos."

"I hope so, because I don't have a passport anymore," Linda said. "And Sebastian doesn't have a Lao visa. Besides, the authorities may be looking for us at the border. We had a run-in with a cop in Khorat. It didn't end well."

"How bad was it?" Myers asked.

"He'll be sore for a few days," Linda replied, "and very pissed for a lot longer."

"I've been reading up on Thai bird life," I said. "Amazing diversity. I've never seen a lineated barbet. I think the countryside along the frontier might be a good place to spot one. Or at least a good excuse for a cross-border foray."

Myers smiled again, and I thought I glimpsed the old life he'd tried to shed.

"An old monk's blessing and a few baht can loosen the rustiest gate. Tomorrow we'll go to Chong Mek and see if we can't take a walk and find you that bird. Stay with us as long as you like today. We don't have accommodation for women, but I'll arrange something with one of the villagers if you don't want to go back into town."

There was no sense in returning to Ubon, where the local authorities might be searching for us, and then driving back out here tomorrow. So we stayed and helped Myers sweep the buildings and haul water, then dozed off in the shade of the pavilion to the sonorous, purposeful murmur of chanting monks. In the late afternoon, Myers walked us across the heavy muck of a waterlogged paddy dike to a small hamlet, where our presence scattered thin chickens and swaybacked dogs. An elderly widow who had gone blind from cataracts agreed to put us up, but refused payment. To make merit was reward enough, she told the monk, then let fly with an enormous gob of betel juice.

The widow led us to her house, a raised, old-teak affair with split-bamboo walls and a thatched roof. Below, pigs snuffled in the shade, raising halfhearted squeals every time the crone spit between the cracks of the flimsy floor. Our host began cooking the evening meal over a small charcoal brazier: rice with fried squash, onion, chili peppers, and fish paste. She spoke softly with Linda, who translated.

"She apologizes for the food. If she had known we would be here tonight she would have gone to the market to buy something special."

"Tell her I'm sorry we didn't bring anything for the meal."

"She says our presence is honor enough."

A pair of Royal Thai Air Force fighter planes from Ubon tore through the sky ahead of thunderheads glowering to the west. The old woman spoke again and Linda laughed.

"She asked if you are married. I told her not anymore."

"My wife left six months ago, right before Christmas."

"She wants to know: how can a wife just leave a man like that?"

"In America, no problem. They just start driving. My ex took everything but the bills."

As Linda translated, the widow cackled in amazement.

"There are no more prospective wives to be found here," she told me. "All the young women have gone to Bangkok."

The third-class train delivered them to bleak lives as housemaids or laborers or bar girls. This village sheltered the old, the infirm, and the indolent young men who preferred to live on the money their sisters sent home from the capital rather than work the thankless land. The soil here was poor, full of sand and salt, and good for just one rice crop a year. The fish had nearly vanished from the river since the new dam had been built. Everything was disappearing, or dying. The hard life had killed her husband two years earlier. Our host spooned the stir-fried meal into three plastic bowls and nodded for us to eat.

"Just like old times, Linda?"

"The fish paste tastes better here, Sebastian."

"My friends call me 'Seb' or 'Bass.'"

There was a thump of thunder and the rains began with such intensity that the forest of Wat Pah Nanachat vanished behind a thick, pewter-gray deluge.

"You look almost comfortable yourself, Seb."

"Eight schools in twelve years will make you adaptable."

"You know what it's like to always be on the outside, too."

"I was just an army brat, never a refugee. Was it anything like here?"

"Here? This is fabulous. Ban Na Pho, now that was the pits. Corrupt guards, a leaky tent, barely any edible food or clean water. People sold whatever jewelry they had, even gold fillings, just for moldy rice and half-rotten fish paste. What I remember most was the rows of airplane seats. Some NGO had brought them in and set them up in the schoolhouse, so we would be prepared and know how to act when we would finally be allowed to leave and fly to America. I must have practiced sitting in those plane seats for years."

She paused and absently pushed a dollop of rice around her plate with a spoon.

"There were some older kids, Hmong girls, who had come to the camp by themselves," she continued. "After they sold all their silver bracelets to the Thai guards, they had nothing left to offer for rice. Just themselves, their young, frightened bodies. You'd see them walking toward the barracks as if toward an execution. They never looked up. . . ."

Her voice quavered.

"I was angry at my parents for allowing me to leave the mountains. I hated my uncle for taking us there, for the years we were trapped in Na Pho camp. For a while I even hated him for bringing me to America."

"It had to be difficult."

"It's hard to describe that loneliness."

"Why did you wait so long to come back here?"

"Bounliep told me my parents had died after the war. He said it was best if I tried to forget them."

"What do you remember about your father?"

"I remember that he was tall and had dark hair and eyes as blue as a dry-season sky. Uncle told me everyone called him 'Cut,' and that he was very clever. He taught himself the Monui names of every animal in the mountains, every bird and every tree. One of my most vivid memories is of him carrying me on his back through the forest. We followed a fresh trail made by wild elephants, until we found the herd bathing in a river. He didn't try to kill them; we must have watched those elephants for hours. The only time I recall him getting upset was when airplanes or helicopters flew overhead. He would fire his crossbow, throw stones, yell out letters and numbers. It seemed like crazy talk; the aircraft were always so far away. Eventually he stopped looking up altogether.

"Uncle said the village elders respected him, even my grandfather. Cut knew a lot about medicine and farming and the stars, things no one else in the village knew. It must have seemed like magic to my people. And my father could make my mother laugh. That's what I remember most about my parents. How happy they seemed together."

The old woman spoke above the downpour. Linda replied in a rising voice, and the two of them giggled. She may have spent the majority of her life in the States and become a bank executive, but

Linda Watts seemed completely at ease here in the sticks of Thailand, without a hint of pretension or prima donna behavior. Perhaps my Somerville three-decker would suit her just fine.

"She says she doesn't understand what we say when we talk together," Linda related, "but our voices fit together like lovers holding hands."

"Tell her she is very wise," I replied.

"Bak waan," the old woman said, laughing, taking care to cover her mouth with a wrinkled hand. *Sweet mouth*.

Linda regarded me, without any of the acrimony that had informed our first encounter.

"Tonight you sleep on the veranda, Detective."

Twilight had collapsed from the rain and the only illumination came from the twinkle of a few smoldering coals. While the widow prepared a sleeping area, Linda helped me roll out a mat beneath a well-thatched section of the roof.

"You know what I missed most while I was living in America, Seb? The rain. It never pours like this in the States. You can sit here and not do anything for hours but listen to the power and the anger, wondering if the monsoon's going to break down the roof and drown you."

"We lived in the Panama Canal Zone for a couple of years when I was a boy. My father was a jungle-warfare instructor, stationed at Fort Sherman. It used to rain like this almost every afternoon in the wet season. It sounded like the end of the world, especially when the howler monkeys went off."

"There's nothing scarier when you're a kid. Remember?"

She squeezed my hand and shifted quietly off to a space in the shadows. The coals faded to ash and then there was only silver-black darkness and the monsoon's metallic, hissing song. This was one evening. What would it be like to endure an entire rainy season, or five seasons, or thirty seasons? Mayrena hadn't lasted a summer in the Central Highlands before going rogue. What about Linda's father? Had he wanted to be there, year after year? If not, could he have held up without going mad? But Leslie Thompson had somehow survived the horrors of the Death Railway and still lived in Kanchanaburi. Never yield. *Jamais ceder.* Maybe anything was possible.

Sometime during the long, hot night, the old woman shook me awake and pulled me to where Linda lay, asleep and weeping, her tough exterior eroded by unconsciousness. She was beautiful, no doubt, but we hadn't exactly met under ideal circumstances. Women could fall for firemen, their piano movers, even policemen who wrote them speeding tickets. But someone who'd been hired to stalk every corner of her life? It would take time, and a special woman. I cradled her in my arms, feeling the sobs rack her body, until the rain finally carried away the nightmares of Ban Na Pho.

Myers came by at dawn, his saffron-robed figure glowing like an ember across the paddies. The widow dropped a scoop of cold sticky rice into his alms bowl and then we followed the monk across the mist-capped fields toward Wat Pah Nanachat. The abbot met us in the front of the *bot*, the ordination hall of the forest temple. Beside him idled a late-model Range Rover, a gift to the order from Myers.

"Please stay longer next time," the holy man said. "You're always welcome here."

The abbot looked to be in his late fifties, thin and muscular, with a jagged scar along his throat and the growl of a former heavy smoker.

"Maybe after we've taken care of business. Your temple is a very peaceful place."

"Brother Frank told me where you're going."

"Please, keep it a secret. Our safety may depend on it."

"You have my word. But Laos is not a safe place," he said, wiping sweat from his pink scar. "Never has been. We will pray for you."

The abbot recited a blessing in Pali, then gave us a lucky number.

We loaded into the truck and Myers drove through the forest, chuckling as he shifted gears.

"He always gives the same number."

"Superstitious?"

"It's the ID number on his old Cobra gunship. Shot down twice, and he walked away both times. One very fortunate bastard."

The route to Chong Mek took us back past the train station, where I slipped the postcard into a mailbox, then onto a good four-lane highway lined by cinder-block houses and sections of concrete culvert strewn along the road like the vertebrae of some giant, broken animal. Shops and small businesses gradually gave way to rice fields and small pavilions where dark-skinned laborers waited for city-bound buses. When the road narrowed to two lanes, Myers ordered us to lie down in the backseat beneath a thin cotton blanket. A few minutes later, he slowed the vehicle.

"Checkpoint," he said.

"We're ready," Linda whispered.

In the heat beneath the blanket, her breath felt like a warm, sweet bath. We heard the mechanical hum of a power window, then brief chatter in Thai, followed by laughter. Then the hum again and the air conditioning blasting as we gained speed.

"Free and clear," said Myers. "Come on out."

"They looking for us?" I asked.

"Didn't say. Checkpoint's been here forever. They ought to name it after me. I've paid enough tea money over the years to buy 'em all new scooters."

Soon we skirted an enormous reservoir where bamboo platforms held huge, saillike fishing nets. Beyond the shimmering water lay green, rolling hills, the last spasms of the Dângkrêk Range, the jungle-clad mountains separating Thailand from Laos and Cambodia. Chong Mek lay east of the man-made lake, busy with the naughty energy of an open-air bazaar. The north side of the road held a cluster of small shops selling cigarettes, liquor, candy, clothing, bronze Buddhas, small appliances, and plastic housewares, everything a Lao border trader might want to purchase. Myers pulled into the scrum of commerce and exited the vehicle. Above the merchant babble was the shrill din of cicadas from the surrounding scrub forest.

"Say your prayers," the monk advised. "And wait in the Rover."

We waited and watched two Thai mechanics try to resurrect an ancient Chevy Impala while Myers disappeared into the market. A few minutes later, he returned, smiling, and motioned for us.

"The monkhood has its privileges," he said when we joined him. "Didn't even have to grease any palms."

"What sort of divine intervention did you arrange?" I asked.

"Wander into the market like you're here to shop," Myers advised. "Out back behind the spice seller's stall, a young man will be waiting for you. His name is Lek. He's agreed to guide you into Laos. I said you would pay him five hundred baht. He'll take you around the checkpoint to a place on the road where you can flag down a bus to Pakxe. From there it's about a one-hour ride to the Mekong ferry. There's no bridge across the river down here. This is Laos, after all."

"You've brought us good luck," said Linda.

"Glad to help. Sorry about the guns, or the lack thereof."

"Honeyman'll turn something up," I said. We shook hands.

"Say hello from me when you see him. Tell him I am doing well. As the Buddha preached, *Vaya con Dios*. Now go find your bird."

"Please chant for our safe arrival," Linda said. "It can't hurt."

"I will, but I fear Laos is beyond even the Buddha's powers," the monk said.

It was almost noon and Thai immigration officials were knocking off for lunch, strolling to a collection of noodle shops on the south side of the road. Their Lao counterparts would probably being doing the same on the other side of the border. Security would never be slacker. We shouldered our packs and walked nonchalantly into the bazaar, eyed a few pairs of sandals, and followed the scents of cardamom and curry powder to the spice stall. We found Lek out back, as promised. Linda greeted him in Lao, and the wiry, barefoot young Isan man in jeans, a Metallica T-shirt, and a disco-era Members Only windbreaker replied in kind.

"He said no problem," Linda relayed. "He makes this trip almost every day."

"But not guiding *farang*," I noted.

"I told him you wanted to see a special bird. He said he knows its song and will try to find it for you."

We set out to the north. Lek set a brisk pace despite the heat, pausing every fifty yards or so to wait for us. Last night's downpour had left the the route muddy; there were hundreds of shoe- and footprints set in the reddish muck, evidence that this was a well-used end run. We steadily worked our way up the western edge of a large hill, eventually turning eastward until we confronted a barbed-wire fence. The official border. A section had been tramped down to allow passage for pedestrians.

"He says there's never a guard here, Thai or Lao."

We stepped over the fence and into Laos. The pathway continued its gradual ascent through a stand of dry forest. A web of secondary trails met and crossed our trail, and we negotiated several switchbacks. Every few minutes we encountered a smuggler, either Lao or Thai, on the trail. No one said a word, although one or two young men acknowledged Lek with a nod as they passed us on their way to Thailand. After we'd walked about twenty minutes, the hike gradually leveled off. I was grateful for even a speck of shade in the dense heat. An occasional peep, warble, or cackle of an unseen bird broke the hot silence. Then, a manic, trilling call, like that of a loon, floated up the hill. Lek halted and smiled: it was my lineated barbet.

I produced the *Collins Field Guide* from my pack and showed Lek and Linda the bird: a foot-long, big-headed brute with a stout bill, a stubby tail, and a light-green body with distinctive buff-brown streaks covering its head, throat, and breast. A bird that looked like it could take care of itself.

"More handsome than I imagined," remarked Linda.

"I'll take it as a good sign."

Lek lit a cigarette and resumed hiking. At a break in the trees, he pointed down to a large, sandy area to the south, just north of the two-lane roadway that ran from the border eastward to be swallowed by the horizon. Even from a distance of at least half a mile, I heard the overstrained engine of a Lao bus as it labored westward toward Chong Mek. As we came down off the hill, thorny brush supplanted the open forest, and we soon encountered flatter, sandier terrain, but no further people. Even the birds had gone silent in the midday heat. We crossed the buckled road and found a bit of shade beneath a lone cassia tree. I mopped my brow: the two-mile walk had left me drenched with perspiration. Linda and Lek, however, were barely glistening. Within fifteen minutes, we heard the whining approach of an eastbound bus. I paid off Lek with a Purple King and he waved down the vehicle. He bounded aboard the bus and spoke briefly with the driver, then motioned us aboard. At Linda's instruction, I peeled off two one-hundred baht notes for the man—far more than the regular fare, but still a bargain for a no-questions-asked passage.

Lek hopped down to the shoulder of the road. We left him in a plume of blackish exhaust. The bus, nothing more than a cab crammed with wooden benches bolted to a Chinese flatbed truck that had been built sometime during Chairman Mao's regime, struggled along a narrow, half-collapsed causeway through grids of flooded rice paddy. We moved to the back to share a plank with two women who carried woven baskets filled with unhappy ducks. Every rut and pothole brought an eruption of dust and down and indignant quacking and shitting, much to the amusement of the other passengers. Along the roadside, stilted houses clung to the embankment like a host of feeding mosquitoes. Every few miles we were nearly swept off the road by a convoy of overloaded timber trucks speeding to Thailand. The hour-long ordeal ended at a river landing, where the road disappeared halfway down the side of a concrete revetment into brown, swirling water. Two miles across the Mekong, Pakxe slept at the foot of a saddleback mountain. With the next scheduled ferry departure still hours away, Linda bartered for a private longtail boat for one hundred baht. We clung to the gunwales as the boat bucked across the racing river, finally nosing into the mud beneath a sandy bluff dominated by a derelict colonial building.

"A much better Mekong crossing than last time," Linda said. "Then it was dark and raining. We were somewhere upstream, I think. Uncle was afraid the current would push our boat down here, and someone would discover us."

"But you made it."

"Sometimes God smiles on foolish shamans and small children." She nudged me playfully in the side of my stomach with her elbow. "And even on wayward private detectives."

There was no checkpoint when we disembarked at the Pakxe landing. Just a riverside restaurant and a few rusting, three-wheeled motorcycle taxis. This was where *tuk-tuks* went to die. We hired a fume-spewing vehicle for a short, slow drive through streets of sagging, colonial-era shophouses to the freshly whitewashed Champasak Palace Hotel, an ornate pile that had been the home of the last prince. But then the war came and his subjects picked up AK-47s; the prince had fled to Paris and died in exile, far removed from his pleasure dome. The government had recently leased the palace to a Thai company, which had cleaned the patina of neglect that twenty years of socialism had brought to the structure. The six-story Champasak now shone like a Mississippi River steamboat. On the front lawn, a worker slapped more fresh paint on an old bunker, now half hidden by flower beds, that commanded the sweeping hotel driveway. The purple bougainvillea lent a cheery touch to the narrow, menacing gun slits. Some things had changed in Laos, Honeyman had said, and some things never would.

Eleven

Perhaps the prince of Champasak had once used our corner room on the fourth floor for a favored mistress or palace functionary, but it now looked more suited to a well-attended interrogation. A pair of twin beds sat across a ten-yard gulf of blue tiles. Aside from a writing desk with peeling laminate and a plastic Beer Lao ashtray, the room was unfurnished, not even a telephone. Somewhere, an air conditioner moaned, but the temperature remained prison-oppressive. I parted the thick curtains and discovered the reason: the windows had metal screens and wooden jalousies, but no glass panes. The heat seeped in at will.

"What did you expect?" Linda asked. "Some customs official back in Chong Mek has a hell of a set of picture windows in his hut."

"It's hotter inside than out."

"So let's stay outside."

"Let me shower first. Travel makes me feel like a dirtbag."

"You'll be sweating through clean clothes in ten minutes. Shower later. Who do you have to impress?"

"Not you, I guess."

Linda didn't want to wait any longer to check out Pakxe's central market. Any substantial settlement in Southeast Asia has such a spot: the timeworn place where everyone goes to get his daily fix of fresh fish and meat, fruits and vegetables, rumor and gossip. In a city with just a handful of telephones, it would also be the easiest locale for Linda to track down her Lao contact, Vannavong, the man who had twice traveled across the border to Ubon Ratchathani, Thailand, to call her in the States.

By early afternoon, the stench of dead carp and overripe durian permeated the gray-grim concrete market building a few short blocks from the Mekong. We made two circuits of the dimly lit dry-goods stalls; Vannavong was nowhere to be found. From an ethnic-Chinese gold merchant, Linda learned that Vannavong had left Pakxe and gone south to the Cambodian border on business a few days earlier. There wasn't any telephone service along the frontier but the jeweler said he could send a reliable messenger boy down to fetch Vannavong. Linda sighed. Laos was a low-tech, labor-intensive place. She unfurled two one-hundred-baht notes, a lordly amount by Laotian standards, for travel expenses. The Chinese merchant clucked and rolled his eyes. It took six hours to get to the border, he argued. The road was terrible. He'd be without his best worker for at least two days. Linda peeled off another hundred baht for the effort.

"No stopping to visit relatives on the way down," she instructed. "The boy must find Vannavong at once. I want to see him tomorrow night at my hotel. The Champasak Palace."

The Chinaman nodded. Of course we stayed at the Palace. Where else would foreigners stay in Pakxe? He was decent enough to give us a good exchange rate, so we turned in a thousand baht for a six-inch-thick brick of musty kip, the nearly worthless Laotian currency. Then Linda led me through a clutter of fabric stalls to the street, flagged down a Toyota 4WD truck, and began negotiating a price to hire the young driver and his vehicle. She haggled hard, knowing the truck driver had high-balled the initial price when he saw me, a foreigner who could presumably afford to pay more. The man shook his head and counteroffered. Linda offered a pained look and turned, taking my hand. We began to leave.

"Okay okay okay," the driver sputtered.

"You drive a hard bargain," I said admiringly.

"A fair bargain," she said. "The secret is to always be prepared to walk away."

After a wad of kip changed hands, we drove east, climbing slowly onto the Bolaven Plateau. As we'd discussed with Honeyman before splitting up in Khorat, we would scout road conditions and possible routes leading from the mountains to the Mekong River. The most obvious natural feature to explore was the Bolaven Plateau, an enormous mesa rising up like a wave just beyond Pakxe.

The air gradually cooled as we passed small plantations with roadside displays of papaya, rambutan, and longan. The driver rolled down his window and blew his nose. These people were Lao Theung, he said, as Linda translated. Mountain people. The government had moved them from the borderlands and given them a bit of land, but couldn't be bothered to name the new settlements. This was Kilometer Eleven Village. Everyone living here was Alak. Farther up the road, where coffee trees grew, lived the Suay, in Kilometer Fifteen Village. The Lao Theung were lazy, the driver complained. The men preferred hunting to farming. A Lao Loum farmer could grow many more crops on the same land than these backward hill people. And they wouldn't send their children to school, didn't boil their drinking water, even refused to use a proper toilet. They were all stupid, never had any money, and seemed always to be sick.

"What about the Katu?" Linda asked. "Do they live here, too?"

The driver smiled. The Katu were different. Most of them still lived in the mountains, untamed. Government officials never traveled there except in pairs. The Lao military rarely left Pakxe or Attapeu, and then only in helicopters. It was too difficult, too dangerous in the mountains. There was bad weather and sickness. Tigers and old American *bombis*. And the Katu themselves.

Up on the Bolaven Plateau, the air felt at least ten degrees cooler and sweet with the scent of flowers. The fractured pavement frittered out a few miles east of Paksong, the run-down district seat, and we bounced along a muddy, rutted track through forest with ghostly, half-scale spirit villages. After a half hour of steady jolting, we took a break in a small village with the look of long-time poverty. The settlement held one roadside refreshment stand, run by a crone with an inventory far beyond expiration dates. She served us warm cans of Coke, then went back to berating a barefoot man. We watched the scolding while sipping syrup-thick soda. Linda finally explained.

"The man is Ngeh. A Lao Theung tribe. This village is Suay, another hill tribe. The Suay don't trust the Ngeh. The Lao government took Ngeh land for a dam and dumped them here, in Suay territory. The Ngeh man wanted some store credit. He has no money. The government promised him rice rations and a plot of land to grow coffee, but they gave him nothing when he moved. The Ngeh are very untalented farmers. He is desperate. Now his daughter sells herself at the camp of the Korean dam builders."

We paid the old woman and continued east along the track, finally skidding down an escarpment on a poor road through a narrow, stream-cut valley to a junction just west of the Xe Kong River. I consulted my tourist map and found the stream, the Namnoy, which fed into the Xe Kong as it flowed south toward the broad plain that held Attapeu, where it was joined with the mountain-fed waters of the Xe Kaman to form a powerful river that ran down into Cambodia and eventually emptied into the Mekong. Six peasants waited on the roadside for a southbound bus to Attapeu. From the looks of the hammocks and cooking fires it appeared that they'd already been waiting several days. Had we seen any buses from Pakxe? a young man asked Linda. She shook her head, then inquired if the young man had seen any vehicles come north. So far only two vehicles today, he related, both logging trucks. Yesterday, there had been five logging trucks. The road was still passable. But the rains had already cut off the unsealed roads beyond Attapeu. In the mountains across the Xe Kong River, the travel situation was even worse. Flooding had made the rivers too deep for trucks to ford.

"How is the drive to Attapeu?" I asked.

"Maybe three or four hours, maybe a two or three days," Linda related. "It depends on the mud and the bridges."

"Then let's avoid Attapeu for now. Going that far off the grid, a *farang* like me is bound to get noticed. I could get away with posing as an adventure tourist the first time we went. But any return trip, especially so soon afterwards, people could get suspicious. If we have to travel this way with Honeyman, it'd be best to wait and not tip our hand."

Instead, we drove a few minutes north through scrub forest until a broad, swift river severed the unsealed road. There was no bridge across this lower section of the Namnoy, only a cable ferry tied up on the far shore, at least a quarter mile away. We yelled and honked the truck horn, without effect. The ferry pilot was nowhere to be found.

"Probably out hunting," Linda said. She nudged me, pointing out a tiny girl with platinum-blond hair and ghostly white skin playing with a mangy dog in the river's swirling shallows.

"Albino," she said, smiling. "A good omen. Uncle Bounliep would be pleased."

The day had been a good start. The road to Attapeu still seemed passable, but we could attempt it only once. On any return trip, we probably couldn't depend on taking the cable ferry across the Namnoy River and working our way around the northern flank of the plateau. I pointed to a double line on the map south of the Bolaven and had Linda ask the driver about road conditions in that area. He just laughed.

"Wishful cartography," she informed me. "There's no road. More like an oxcart path. Many swamps. I believe Uncle and I may have walked that way when we left the mountains."

"Tomorrow we'll check out the north side of the Bolaven," I said. "Then we'll have a clearer understanding of our options."

At the moment, there didn't seem to be many choices. There was only one barely drivable link to Attapeu. One way in; one way out. If we were lucky and the rains held off. Linda went quiet on the return drive over the Bolaven to Pakxe, traveling through a landscape of long-buried memories. The driver let us out at a restaurant overlooking the Mekong ferry landing, and Linda spent dinner gazing at the dark water, barely touching her meal of stir-fried vegetables. A pair of heavily madeup hostesses turned a tentative foxtrot on the small dance floor, moving to a karaoke tune while a Korean businessman botched the lyrics of "Am I Blue?" Less than a decade earlier, the dancing would have earned the women a lengthy sentence to seminar camp. Now they could work as bar girls and sell themselves to construction workers.

When we returned to the Champasak Palace, a desk clerk solicitously approached me.

"Sir, I still need your passport for registration."

"I'm so sorry," I replied, patting my back pockets and feigning exasperation. "I forgot yesterday when we checked in. I must have left the documents up in our room today. We're very tired now. I'll bring them down later."

Knowing that later would never come. I gave the man one hundred baht for his trouble. Another shift change or two at the front desk, I hoped, and the paperwork would be forgotten.

Linda slept deeply that night, without incident. I stayed awake until early morning, listening to her shallow, rhythmic breathing hang like moonlight. We'd been on the road for three days, moving so quickly that I hadn't had time to call my father. And there was no way to check voice mail from Laos, let alone change my message to let callers know I was still overseas. Any phone calls would have to wait. There was no point worrying about Dolores Moyle or Mather Mutual or whether I had any prospective clients. My client was satisfied. The fee, plus the bonus, had bought me some breathing room. There was room only for Linda, for Honeyman—and for Laos. And now we were planning to plunge into its outer limits. What had my father wondered about during those long, starless nights back in Kontum? Upcoming cross-border missions? Army buddies who'd been killed or gone missing? His distant family? Or just the readiness of his weapons, the diligence of his recon team? That would be all he could have controlled. Everything else was just fate—or luck. Then the rains struck and the clamor washed me down a long culvert of sleep.

The following morning, the driver returned with his truck. He first wanted to take us to a silk-weaving village along the Mekong upriver from Pakxe, but Linda refused. We needed to finish surveying the Bolaven area. She insisted on seeing Salavan, a small provincial capital north of the plateau and closer to the Annamite Mountains. Our wheelman sulked as we again drove east from Pakxe: there'd be no brick-o'-kip commission from any textile sales. We retraced the previous day's route for several miles, then turned north on a secondary road skirting the base of the Bolaven's western slope. This was fat, fertile land, with head-high fields of sugar cane, dense groves of bananas, clear, tumbling streams, and villages awash in racks of sun-dried coffee beans.

Salavan came as a shock—dusty, broken, still on its knees from the wartime pounding inflicted by American bombers against the Ho Chi Minh Trail, which once ran through the town. Whatever colonial buildings the French erected had all been obliterated, replaced with soulless cinder-block boxes. We got out to stretch our legs but my appearance prompted scowls at the market: the old people would never forget the terrifying B-52 raids. Linda bought a handful of lottery tickets for the driver, whose mood immediately improved, and we entered the dimly lit bazaar. For fifty baht, I bought a barrette fashioned from a boar's tusk.

"For when your hair grows back, Linda."

She kissed me lightly on the cheek.

"You're just piling up the Brownie points."

The smells grew more acrid as we made our way through the cheap merchandise to the rear of the shedlike building, where wildlife was sold. While a trio of hunters slurped bowls of noodles, Linda regarded a pair of cramped mesh cages: a silent, sad-eyed creature resembling a toucan and a purplish bird with a cry like screeching tires. I consulted the *Collins Field Guide*: a brown hornbill and a blue whistling thrush. We purchased the thrush and its cage for a half-inch-thick block of kip. The songbird thanked us with a loud, musical étude as we abandoned Salavan and retraced our route along the west side of the Bolaven Plateau.

"We'll make big merit, Seb, when we free the bird."

"Merit is a Buddhist concept," I said. "You're Katu."

"We're going to need all the luck we can muster."

"I thought you had a better plan."

"I do—I've got you and Honeyman."

"I stopped making plans back in Bangkok."

"Now you sound like a Buddhist monk from that Thai monastery. So enjoy the moment."

A few miles later, the driver turned off the highway and onto a smooth dirt road and drove through a tunnel of bamboo toward the plateau and the sound of falling water. The track ended at a small, open-air restaurant, rimmed with poinsettias and hibiscus, attached to a rustic resort overlooking Tad Lo waterfall. Linda took the birdcage and led me to a table overlooking the pretty, twenty-foot cascade.

"The bird can sing here," she said, setting the cage on the table and opening its door. "And we can have lunch."

When the thrush wouldn't budge, Linda tapped the wire mesh. The bird quietly crept from its cage to the table's edge, spread its broad wings, leaped—and then promptly fell to the ground in a tumble. Someone had clipped its spangled wings. While I gathered the stunned bird, a waiter appeared. Linda asked if the restaurant had a larger enclosure. She would donate the bird to the resort for safekeeping; it would sing and amuse the customers. But if someone killed and ate the bird, bad fortune would curse them. I cuddled the shaken, silent thrush and regarded the deer skulls displayed on the walls. It was a good bet that as soon as we left, someone would grill the crow-size bird, Buddha be damned. The waiter nodded at Linda's orders and spoke to a dark-skinned boy wiping down a nearby table. Not in Lao, however, for Linda gasped, then grabbed the waiter's arm. She blurted questions at him in the same rising, staccato tongue.

"These two are also Monui," she said excitedly.

"You know them?"

"Different clan, different province. They came down from the mountains three years ago. Now they live about an hour's walk from here. Their life was too hard in Xe Kong Province."

"Do they know your people?"

There was another flurry of foreign conversation.

"They heard a story during the last rainy season. There was talk of a headman farther south who had gone crazy. He ordered his warriors to attack any trespassers—Lao Loum, Lao Theung, even other Monui."

"Where?"

"Xanxai district."

The waiter struggled to pronounce the chief's name.

"J-J-John. John Man."

Chon mein. The tall one. Tears welled in Linda's eyes, and she stroked the thrush, silent and nestled in my arms. The nervous waiter bowed and left to hunt for a larger cage. We didn't eat lunch until we had gone back to Salavan and saved the hornbill, too, for display at the Tad Lo restaurant. After doubling our merit, we tackled the Bolaven Plateau from the north, poor roads the entire way. The few villages were all wretched, raised huts filled with relocated mountain people, though none were inhabited by Katu. A note from the Pakxe-market gold merchant awaited us at the hotel, but even the news that Vannavong was in Cambodia and couldn't return for at least another day didn't destroy her mood. The desk clerk didn't mention our passports. We had bought ourselves good fortune in Salavan. I only hoped the birds were still alive and singing at Tad Lo.

The next day, there was still no word from Honeyman. Linda had an alternate plan: instead of knocking around the Bolaven Plateu again, we would go south along the Mekong to Wat Phu, the site of an ancient Khmer Empire temple. On my map, the ruin looked to be directly across the river from the route on the south side of the Bolaven that connected to Attapeu, the trail the driver had dismissed as impassable. The boat was every bit as crowded with passengers and baggage and animals as the bus from the border crossing had been, with the added menace of unseaworthiness. We sat on the roof above the sweltering hold, where a weak breeze tried to offset the blazing midmorning sun. The pilot kept near the western shore, where the rising river already lapped at the dry-season huts of the farmers who had planted the banks with corn, squash, and long beans. Another ferry struggled upstream against the current; a trio of old monks sat cross-legged on the vessel's roof like figureheads.

"Another omen? Good or bad?"

"It's only a bad omen if the boat sinks," she replied.

The scattering of factories on the outskirts of town soon gave way to rice fields. Beyond the far bank reared a long, jungle-swathed escarpment. The little evidence of the twentieth century vanished as we rounded a bend in the river and Pakxe fell away from sight.

"What do you think, detective?"

"I hope we don't hit a rock and capsize. The river's running awfully fast."

"Not that. About Laos."

"It's different, rawer. I feel like a stranger, more so than even in Thailand. Maybe a little like you must have felt when you came to the States."

"I felt like a total stranger then, completely alone. I could hardly speak English. It took me a year to make any acquaintances. I couldn't bring anyone home. What would they say about Uncle Bounliep at school?"

The pilot eased off the throttle and allowed the main current to carry the boat through shoals and a maze of sandy, wooded islands toward the west bank, where a pair of dugouts darted out, tied on to the hull, and began hawking drinks and snacks. The chaos continued when we disembarked at a village screened by tall trees. Just upstream from the landing, a group of locals crouched on the riverbank, wailing. A funeral was about to begin, Linda related. A fisherman from a nearby, nameless hamlet had suffered a seizure, tumbled from his canoe, and drowned. The body would be cremated where it had been found; in this way, bad spirits would not find their way back to the fisherman's village. This was a world of ever-present ghosts and lethal beauty, where death took many forms: road accidents, land mines, drownings.

Linda haggled for a *tuk-tuk* and we rolled down the muddy streets of Champasak, passing the colonial wreckage of crumbling villas, sagging shophouses, and a traffic-free rotary holding a fountain that hadn't spouted since the de Gaulle era. Lush rice paddy spread behind the town all the way to a green horizon and a mountain capped with an enormous, natural column of stone.

"Wat Phu," the driver announced.

He turned away from the river and drove west, perhaps three miles, to the archaeological park. At the base of the holy mountain sprawled a derelict complex of Angkor-era temple structures. A trio of local men sat beneath a mango tree, playing cards and waiting for visitors to guide. I hired the best-dressed one to show us around.

"Song loy," I said, holding up two fingers. Two hundred baht. I didn't see any other tourists. The man grunted, lit a Lao cigarette.

"Good price," Linda said approvingly. "Fair for everyone."

"Vamos," the guide said, ushering us toward a ruined palace, where a wandering cow peered from a broken door. Years before, he explained, he had studied agriculture in Minsk and hung out with the Cuban students every free moment.

"Buenas dias, chica," he said to Linda, tipping his battered knock-off Yankees baseball cap. He grinned. "The Russian teachers, always they were angry with the Cubans for stealing their women."

"How far from here to the Thai border?" I interjected.

"Maybe thirty kilometers," he replied. "Less than a day's walk, if you know where to go."

"Over Wat Phu mountain?"

"Too difficult. Best to go south, around the mountain, and then west. But the *sendero*—the trail—is very bad."

"Anything to see?"

"No big temple. Just countryside. Rice fields and forest."

"And to the east. From here to Attapeu?"

"Maybe one hundred kilometers, maybe more. At least four or five days' walk. No mountains, but this road is the worst. Many streams and swamps. No one travels this way. You will die of fever before you make Attapeu. Or you will be arrested."

"Why is that?"

"It is off-limits to *farang*. It is not safe. Too many war bombs. Anyway there is nothing to see in Attapeu."

"Maybe the countryside is different."

"Same-same, but different."

Wat Phu was the exception. Its strange, phallic peak had made the mountain a holy place for thousands of years. Centuries earlier, the king himself would come to the temple and make a human offering to appease the gods and ensure a bountiful harvest. The villagers still held a buffalo sacrifice every June. This had been a great place—one of the three kingdoms of Laos before the French arrived—its rule unquestioned from Ubon Ratchathani across the Bolaven Plateau all the way to the Long Mountains, the guide related.

We followed a buckling causeway between a pair of abandoned Angkor-era reservoirs. After centuries of neglect, one of the formal ponds had silted in, become a pasture of lush grass. In the dark water of the other tank, small boys bathed their water buffalo. Tramped-down paths snaked through the unkempt grass choking the ruins. Eroded sandstone lintels of Hindu deities still rested above dark portals, while stone balustrades cordoned empty windows. A steep staircase shaded by a tunnel of frangipani trees led us onto the upper temple platform. The view from here was immense: pavilions and promenades and ponds, all laid out on a precise east–west axis that pointed across the river plain toward the Mekong. To the north of Champasak, wisps of grayish smoke from the fisherman's cremation curled upward, then dissipated. Despite the bird's-eye perspective,

I could not find any hint of a road on the far shore of the river—only the mountains, the jungle, and the rising, sweltering sun.

Following the guide's lead, we paused inside the temple's sanctuary to light joss sticks beside a life-size Buddha image. I was learning: never miss a chance to make merit. A short walk behind the altar, a trickle of water ran off the sandstone cliff and into a collecting basin. Linda held her head under the stream to wet her hair, then took a drink. The guide followed suit.

"Don't tell me, Linda. It's good luck."

"It's good for your love life. Drink up."

The guide showed us a boulder into which the devout had carved the forms of Hindu gods, a recently abandoned monastery where all the monks had died of malaria, and another rock, where an earlier, nameless civilization had chiseled out the form of a crocodile. They made the sacrifices here, the guide said. Hidden monkeys shrieked from the surrounding forest. When it came time to leave, Linda took my hand as I led the way down the staircase. Frangipani blossoms covered the worn sandstone treads; the crushed petals made the air smell sweet and dense. She kept scolding me to watch my step, not to worry so much about her safety. She took my hand again on the causeway, giving it a squeeze.

"Thought you'd like Wat Phu," she said.

"One thousand years ago, these people ruled the roost. And now they live in mud huts."

"Welcome to the Lao People's Democratic Republic."

"Any other insights, Linda?"

"We can rule out any other road to Attapeu. It'll have to be over the Bolaven Plateau. And you?"

"That if we have to leave Laos in a hurry, we'd better find a boat with an outboard to cross the Mekong. This time of the year, the current's too strong for an unmotorized dugout. And we'd probably want to avoid hiking around this mountain to the Thai border. The road from Pakxe to Chong Mek still seems the most direct way out of here."

"The most direct, and the most obvious."

"Maybe Honeyman's seen something better on the way down."

"I hope he shows up by tomorrow. I'm not going back to Ubon."

We roused the napping *tuk-tuk* driver and loaded into his ride as dark clouds loomed behind Wat Phu mountain. On the return to Champasak, the driver pointed out an old, ocher villa with green, half-rotting jalousies shut against the impending weather. A grand old man lived there, he said, the brother of the dead prince. He lived by himself, an exile in his former kingdom. There were worse fates, Linda observed. The Communists might simply have made him vanish, like the king.

Down at the landing, the next Pakxe-bound boat wasn't for hours. We found a pair of cramped seats in the bow of a north-bound barge overloaded with cattle and cargo. As Champasak fell behind the first bend in the river, it began to rain. A few fat drops at first, then a steady pelting. Thunder rumbled and the uneasy live-stock began to stir. The pilot brought the shuddering boat closer to the shore to avoid a maze of sandbars and small islands. The first crack of lightning exploded like a howitzer in the mountains some-where off the port side. The cattle bellowed crazily, without room to stampede. The boat shook nervously as the pilot throttled up, bucking against the strong Mekong current.

"Let's take our chances up top," Linda urged.

I took her arm and we carefully extricated ourselves from the press of nervous passengers and terror-stricken cows, then clam-bered over sacks of rice and coconuts and up through a small hatch in the roof, where the belowdecks scent of sweat, wet grass, and ma-nure was carried away by storm gusts. Another flash: a near-instant detonation. Way too close for comfort. Linda folded as easily as a Hindu goddess into a complicated meditation pose, ignoring the threat. A third flash and a tree exploded on a small island to starboard. As I moved to pull her off the wooden roof and back below, the boat pitched. Linda fell hard against me, her arms brushing past my face. She looked up at me through the torrent, conjured that same sad smile from her Boston College portrait. And then I ignored the storm and the malevolent Mekong intent on pushing us all the way to Cambodia. There was only the warmth of her kiss, pulling me into a whirlpool that held me down until my last breath, then flung me to the surface far downstream. I took a deep breath and let the current carry me away again, no longer caring about the rain or the boat and its crazed cattle and crazier skipper and panicked passengers or what lay around the next bend in the river, except that there was Linda beside me on the boat and then beneath me in bed and wind outside clattering the tamarind pods, the rain spurting through the hotel jalousies, and lightning flashing off the slickened floor tiles.

Twelve

The knock on the door couldn't have been the maid; I had hung out the Do Not Disturb sign last night. I pulled on a pair of shorts while the rapping continued.

"Honeyman?" Linda asked.

"A little early, but you never know."

"He shouldn't see us like this."

"He knew how I felt about you before I knew."

"And how do you feel?"

"I feel like going back to Wat Phu. I could use another gallon of that holy water."

She rifled a plastic ashtray from the nightstand past me as I headed for the door. It hit the wall and clattered to the tiles.

"You missed."

"I simply avoided hitting you."

"A shot across the brow."

The knocking had stopped.

"Honeyman?" I asked.

No reply. I parted the solid teak slab and squinted into the daylight. A bellhop wearing a white jacket and a confused smile backed off toward the balustrade. I beckoned him forward.

"We were still sleeping. I'll be down with my passport in a little while."

"Message for lady," he said in soft, night-school English.

"The lady is sleeping."

"A man downstair for lady."

"*Farang* man?"

"No, sir."

"Policeman?"

"No, sir," he replied, sounding almost hurt by my caution. "Lao man. Businessman."

Ten minutes later, Vannavong Sisaphong entered the room. He was tall for a Lao, nearly my height, and the only overweight local I'd seen since we left Thailand. He also seemed to disapprove of the sleeping arrangements.

"Border problems," he said in English. "If I know you here, Miss Linda, I come back early from Stung Treng."

"This was all last-minute," I interjected.

"You know why I want to see you, Vannavong?"

"Because of what I say when I call you from Ubon?"

"You can speak in front of my friend," Linda said, nodding toward me. "He has agreed to help me."

He snorted dismissively.

"You said the trader in Attapeu had very important news," she prompted.

"Did you bring the money?"

"It would be dangerous to carry so much money," Linda replied.

"The money is in a safe place," I bluffed. "We can get it in less than a day, no problem."

He shot me a perturbed look.

"No problem," he repeated.

"I'm disappointed you didn't bring the trader with you today, Vannavong," Linda remarked.

"Yes."

"Can you go get him now? Is he in town?"

"No," he said, shifting in his cheap plastic sandals.

"No, because he's traveling? Or no, you won't get him?"

"No, miss."

"Are you trying to get more money from me, Vannavong? I'll warn you: I get very mad when people try to shake me down."

He sat sadly on the edge of the other bed, fished in the pocket of a new pair of cargo pants for a pack of cigarettes, then lit up without asking. Marlboro. Whatever Vannavong's business was, business was good if he could afford American smokes.

"No more money," he said, sighing.

"No more money? You're not making any sense. There's more money. Bring the trader here from Attapeu. We have a deal. You'll get your money."

He shook his head.

"I wish I can bring you trader. But no way. Trader die."

"Now you're telling us that the trader's dead?" I said loudly, taking Vannavong by the lapels of his cheap button-down dress shirt and lifting him out of his sandals.

"Sebastian—"

"What the hell happened, Vannavong?"

"Let him down."

I pushed him away, then slumped on the clean bed beside Vannavong and tried to rub the mounting headache from my temples.

"Cigarette?" he offered.

"Shut up and talk," I ordered.

"Give him a chance."

"Two week ago, trader has bad crash in Paksong. Truck with teak log is much bigger than trader's Toyota. So trader die. But he have very big funeral. Two monk come from Vientiane. Trader a big VIP."

Linda paced the room. I don't know how long it stayed like this, her furious breathing and the rising morning heat.

"Sorry," Vannavong finally said. "I think maybe I go to Ubon to call you, but I do not know where you stay in Thailand. So bad news must wait."

"You can still help us."

"How can I help, Miss Linda? You are very angry with me."

"You can tell us everything the trader told you."

"He tell me only small thing."

"You are a clever businessman, Vannavong," Linda continued. "Successful, well fed. I want you to tell me everything you know and I won't ask my crazy *farang* friend to pick you up again and carry you outside and drop you over the railing. He will do it. He has thrown men out of helicopters who did not answer his questions."

"It works best if there are two men," I said, improvising. "Very messy for the first man. No parachute. But it has a way of concentrating the mind. The second man always talks."

I put an arm around Vannavong while Linda held the silver coin so close to his face that he had to look at it cross-eyed.

"Slowly," she said. "And from the beginning."

He sang as gratefully as that caged thrush from the Salavan market, a torrent of names, some that I'd never heard before. The trader had made contact with several Katu in the central market of Attapeu town. The tribesmen had journeyed from the mountains of Xanxai district—the same location Uncle Bounliep had mentioned when I'd interviewed him in Providence. The Katu men told the trader they wanted to communicate with the former shaman from their village, who was rumored to live in America with his niece. They had a *farang* who wanted to go home to America; they would sell him to the shaman for the right price. They offered the silver coin as proof of life. The trader hadn't described much more to Vannavong about the strange tribesmen; that way, any deal would have to go through him. The trader worked alone, without any sons in the business. Only Vannavong knew of the deal, and he hardly knew anything. He was just the middleman who tracked down Bounliep and Linda in the States.

Linda sent the glum man away, but not before giving him a thick block of kip.

"Forget everything that just happened, Vannavong," she ordered. "My *farang* friend likes to throw things when he is angry. He is sorry now. Stay in Pakxe for the next day or two. I may need to find you."

I frowned as he backed out of the room.

"No trader," I said. "No Honeyman. No—"

"No shit, Sebastian. But you know what? No Ubon Ratchathani, either. You can go back today if you want to. But I'm not leaving Laos. Not without my father."

"And Honeyman? The whole Thai plan?"

"If he's the hotshot soldier you say he is, he'll figure out where we're at."

"And where exactly will that be?"

"I don't know," she retorted, her voice cracking. "Maybe here. Maybe Attapeu. Nothing's going as planned."

She slid on a pair of sunglasses to mask her tears.

"We're not through, Linda. First, we canvass the Pakxe market again. We'll find another trader. Maybe even find a hill triber up from Attapeu. This place is like a small town. Someone's gotta know Xanxai district. We'll get to your father if we have to drag Vannavong all the way down to Attapeu. One American living in the mountains? It can't be any harder than finding a Katu runaway in Bangkok."

But we spent the next hour inside the sweltering market without turning up a decent lead. The scattering of hill people all hailed from the Bolaven Plateau. They came to town to sell cardamom, coffee, and vanilla and then used the money to buy medicine to treat their sick, potbellied children. From the Chinese merchant, we learned that no other Pakxe-based traders worked the mountains. It was too much work for too little profit, he said, unless you wanted to live in Attapeu. And who in his right mind wanted to settle in such a place? Attapeu smelled of malaria and seminar camps. The government zealots still broadcast propaganda every morning and suspected every outsider, especially a Chinese trader from Pakxe, as a counterrevolutionary spy. No way would he ever live in Attapeu, he huffed.

I absently scanned the dry-goods market while the merchant complained about Attapeu. The bazaar seemed typical: a retinue of gold dealers, money exchangers, shoe repairmen, purveyors of cheap, used electronics. But I nearly did a double take as I regarded a stall across the central hall, where an unwelcome acquaintance perused a display case packed with boom boxes.

Colonel Nagaphit had shed his police uniform, but there was no mistaking the aviator sunglasses, the bulge of a handgun beneath his olive windbreaker, or the official swagger. The colonel fingered a knock-off gym bag as he scanned the market.

"Walk, Linda. Don't run. To the right. The nearest exit. Go."

"Why?"

"We've just been made."

Something in our flustered movement must have caught the colonel's eye. A *farang* man, walking just a bit too hastily through a crowd of Lao shoppers. Moving away from where he stood. When I turned to check, the laser bore of the lawman's stare burned across the hall.

I grabbed Linda by the wrist and led the way at a trot through a steaming maze of food stalls and then outside between gridlocked *tuk-tuks. Think, Sebastian, think.* The colonel wasn't in uniform. He might be alone, though he could have a flunky checking out the hotels that catered to foreign tourists. We headed toward the old quarter, hoping to lose him in the narrow, crowded streets near the river. Then we could double back and try to clear out of the Champasak Palace, much the same way I'd left the Grand Babylon. I turned to check our nemesis: the colonel trailed a half block behind us, running easily, a leering flash of teeth and those blackout shades. Like it was only a matter of time before he caught up to us. As a rabbit in Europe, I had paced a lot of milers with the same cocky attitude. This time, I wouldn't be run down. I pulled Linda around the next corner, into a dim lane lined with old, French-era warehouses. I scanned the massive, louvered doors, found one without a padlock. It would have to do. We jumped inside and shut the door.

"All the way in the back," I whispered.

Faint light filtered through the rotted wooden jalousies; the dusky air reeked of urine, excrement, and spoiled meat. I bumped heavily into something large and metallic, prompting a soft, near-human bleating, followed by a chorus of growls and soft hooting. Linda led the way down a narrow passage to the far corner of the building. As my eyes grew accustomed to the darkened space, I made out several rows of small cages. A small tiger and a leopard, some gibbons, and an oryxlike creature I had never seen before. The rest of the cages were packed with black bears. The animal nearest to me moaned like an old man; embedded in its abdomen was a crude bamboo tap. In addition to trafficking in endangered wildlife, this dingy place doubled as an illegal bear-bile factory. There was the creak of an unseen door, a brief glow of light, and the animals stirred again. When I turned back, Linda had somehow vanished into the darkness. I didn't dare call out for her. I retraced my steps for a few paces; the nearest bears snuffled as I passed. Still no sign of Linda. Then a tiger erupted a few yards away, and the gibbons began screeching.

Something, someone was near. I squeezed between two cages to the next parallel passageway, so close I could feel another bear's sick, fetid breath, and turned to make my way back to the entrance door. It was a mistake. Colonel Nagaphit crouched beside the next bear cage, his pistol pointing at my torso.

"So many glaring errors, Mr. Damon. Very disappointing from a professional standpoint."

"I'm sure you'll want to use it as a case study at your next police-academy lecture."

"Too predictable, really," he said as he stood up, all the while keeping his weapon trained on me. "Isan was obvious. A few questions to railway personnel, to hotel staff in Khorat and Ubon, to merchants at the border, and I had a bead on you. These people remember a *farang*, especially a foreigner traveling with such a beautiful Asian lady. Deep down, local people don't like it, you see. They immediately suspect you are a sex tourist. Their resentment makes my job so much easier."

"If it was so easy, you would have delegated this job to one of your stooges."

"I prefer to lead from the front sometimes. Good for morale."

"Or for trying to save your own scheming ass, Colonel?"

His bluster belied the colonel's mounting concern. The Royal Thai Police have had a tarnished reputation, but even they would consider body shopping and tampering in a homicide investigation conduct unbecoming a senior officer. Given his gold-plated tastes and the ongoing economic meltdown of his kingdom, it stood to reason that the colonel was also experiencing a sudden cash-flow crisis. His corrupt, carefully constructed career had begun to unravel, to the point where he could no longer rely on less-competent subordinates to handle the dirty work. Now he had to personally rectify these problems, or risk losing everything.

"How badly did you treat Nok to get her to talk?"

"She is just another cheap girl from Isan. You seem to be on a first-name basis with all the wrong women, Mr. Damon."

"Not so many as you, Colonel."

"And you know all the wrong men as well. Sam Honeyman is a drunk and a scoundrel. He should have had his visa canceled years ago."

"I'm surprised you never tried to body shop him."

"There's no market for his type."

"You don't have any authority here in Pakxe."

"A few hundred baht and the Lao become very helpful to their Thai cousins."

"The baht doesn't go as far as it used to, Colonel."

"I'm in the process of diversifying."

"Linda's finished paying you. It's over."

"I'm afraid she has quite a lot to pay for now. Assault and battery of a Khorat police officer is a serious offense."

"So is murdering a Singapore tourist."

"I believe you have some questions to answer in the unfortunate death of Mr. Brody."

"We're not in Thailand anymore."

"Why quibble about jurisdiction?" the colonel asked. "Reveal yourself, Miss Watts, before I shoot your white knight."

No reply. The gibbons began chattering, which got the bears moaning. I realized in that moment that the colonel had no intention of taking us back to Thailand to answer any questions about Khao San Road, or even Khorat. It was easier to permanently eliminate the potential threat to his career, weather the money problems as best he could, then rebuild his tea-money accounts.

"Now, please. That's an order."

"She's left the building. Only looking out for herself."

Nothing, just a rising clamor from the caged animals.

"I'm quickly losing patience, Miss Watts," he said, his voice rising. "Your American friend is about to lose a great deal more."

He pointed the pistol at my chest and smiled. If this was how it was going to end, I would not beg.

"I hope the contact information on your passport is current, Mr. Damon."

"You can break the news to my ex."

"I look forward to it."

"She will, too. This must be very disappointing for you, Colonel. A dead *farang*, and no buyer waiting in the wings? What a waste."

"Don't worry. I'll arrange something special for—"

A shot exploded off the cage's iron bars a few inches behind the colonel's head. The bear inside roared. When the colonel turned, I leaped and drove a knee into his groin and a fist into his right temple. He hit the side of a cage and slumped to the floor, stunned. I grabbed a metal pipe that secured the door of the enclosure and swung it down to his skull with two hands, as if I were splitting firewood. There wasn't the crack you get when your ax strikes seasoned wood—only a soft, wet thud, like sinking a shovel into garden soil after a soaking rain. As the animals shrieked in alarm, the colonel flopped facedown on the floor. He was dead. Linda stepped from the shadows between two nearby cages.

"Just looking out for myself?" she asked accusingly.

"It was a ruse. I was playing for time."

She brushed bits of brain matter from my arms, then kissed me lightly on the cheek.

"You squirmed brilliantly."

"All this time, you had a gun?" I asked, incredulous.

"Honeyman took it off that policeman in Khorat."

"And he gave it to you."

"He didn't know if you'd use it."

"But he knew you would."

"I'm Katu, remember?"

"I just killed a Thai cop, Linda. And not just any cop. A senior Bangkok detective. This trip has officially turned into a world of shit."

Linda knelt and checked the colonel's pulse.

"I'd put a bullet in him, but it'd be overkill. Nice job. No one's going to know who he is by the time we're through."

She collected the colonel's service pistol and holster, then rifled through his pockets until she found his wallet and handed it to me. I knew where she was going with this: I removed all forms of identification, including his Thai ID card. And I took all his money, several thousand baht in Purple Kings. Now the dead officer looked like a scumbag businessman, taken down in a sketchy exotic-animal-smuggling deal gone sour. As Linda brushed past, I heard the crunch of sunglasses grinding into concrete. Then a low, rusted-metal groan, a heavy thud, and a large, heaving mass of fur and muscle and raw fury rolled past me and lumbered up the aisle. I stepped over the colonel's body to help her. We released the rest of bears, the deer, even the big cats and the odd, oryxlike creature. Then we found a side exit to the warehouse, and joined the bedlam coursing through the old quarter of Pakxe. I only hoped we had just made enough merit for what we had done, and what we were about to do.

We found Honeyman inside our hotel room, lying atop the spare bed and reading a days-old *Bangkok Post* he'd taken from the lobby. The news hadn't improved in the interim.

"Enjoying your Lao holiday?" he asked.

"Up until this morning," I replied.

"Sounds like there's quite a stir downtown," Honeyman continued.

"The circus just arrived."

"You don't say?"

"Police harassment." Linda shrugged.

"Well, this *is* a police state," Honeyman said drolly.

"This was Thai police," I said. "Our old friend, Colonel Nagaphit."

"He tracked you all to Pakxe?"

"It's okay now. The pacifist here took care of the problem," Linda said. "Permanently."

"Permanently?"

"Blew his mind out with a steel bar. Very impressive."

Honeyman whistled.

"A few days with a Katu woman could turn even a Quaker into a killer."

"I just had to clean up the colonel after Linda missed shooting him."

"I don't miss," she said. "Remember?"

Honeyman snorted.

"Anyone with the colonel?"

"It looks like he was flying solo on this."

"Good. Just to be safe, we hit the road now. Get your gear packed and in my truck. We leave in five minutes."

When we reached the lobby, Honeyman handed me a stack of newly printed business cards.

"Congratulations, Sebastian. You're now a hydrology expert for the Asian Development Fund, if anybody asks."

"And me?" Linda asked.

"Our faithful translator and guide."

"What about you, Honeyman?"

He produced another business card from his wallet.

"ADF's aid director. We're researching the feasibility of hydro-electric projects in southern Laos. God's work."

"I like it, Sam."

"I'd like a promotion," Linda said.

"Do a good job," he retorted, "and we'll get you your own tour company."

We rolled east in a late-model Land Rover that Honeyman had "liberated" from the motor pool of a Vientiane-based British mine-removal group. With its tinted windows and four-wheel drive, it was damn near ideal for a tough, clandestine job in the bush. As a bonus, the truck had a cache of detailed 1:100000 topographic maps in the backseat, including some covering the panhandle region. The maps of the Annamite Range looked like a million fingerprints, a cluster of tight whorls representing contour lines that promised violent, unforgiving terrain. As we passed a long line of overloaded logging trucks idling outside a stretch of timber-company compounds, Linda briefed Honeyman about Vannavong's news. Even as we climbed onto the Bolaven Plateau we knew there was only one destination: Attapeu. And we would have to travel with limited firepower, nothing aside from two Thai police-issue 9mm pistols that had belonged to the late Colonel Nagaphit and his Khorat flunky.

"My Vientiane connection was a washout," Honeyman said. "He unloaded all his guns last year to some Hmong guerrillas up on the Plain of Jars. There's a lot of bad blood between the lowland Lao and the hill tribers, and probably not just up there. We can't underestimate these mountain people. The French did, and they got their asses handed to them."

The Special Forces veteran had studied the complicated cultures and fractious history of these mountains, looking for any detail, any advantage that might help his mission, prolong his life. His knowledge of Indochina's obscure colonial-era figures didn't end with the exploits of Mayrena, either. While we drove onto the Bolaven, Honeyman described a bloody, all-but-forgotten revolt on this tableland that had resonated across southern Laos for decades. In 1901, a Lao Theung chief named Bac My experienced a vision that he had become an invincible holy man. Worse, as far as French authorities were concerned, was that Bac My convinced other tribesmen of his supernatural powers. Revolt quickly swept across the plateau, fueled by hill tribe grievances against the colonial government for unpaid labor and against the lowland Lao Loum for their centuries-old practice of raiding the mountains for slaves. Bac My's followers attacked the French garrison in Savannakhet, another Mekong River town farther north in the panhandle. The fighters believed Bac My's magic would turn French bullets into frangipani flowers, but three hundred highlanders were killed or wounded in the lethal assault. It took the French years to finally arrest the chief; Bac My was later bayoneted to death while still in custody. But his faithful followers kept up the fight on the Bolaven Plateau until 1936, when the French finally killed or imprisoned the last rebels. The Montagnards had waged a thirty-five-year guerrilla war, armed with little more than crossbows and cutlasses.

"Moral of the story: you don't screw with the Lao Theung," Honeyman concluded.

"From what we've seen, everyone seems to be screwing them now," I said. "The Bolaven is filled with displaced people. They're even messing with the Katu."

"Really."

"We met a few Katu working at a resort outside Salavan."

"Not my people," Linda said. "Different province. But they told a story about a *farang* in Xanxai district. And they called him John Man."

"Now we're getting somewhere." Honeyman cackled.

We made good time over the plateau, though yesterday's downpour had made the descent of the escarpment seem like a flume ride. A gaggle of peasants at the road junction near the Xe Kong River tried to wave us down for a ride to Attapeu, but Honeyman had no intention of stopping for anyone after the ruckus we had unleashed in Pakxe. Within a few miles, the road devolved into a rutted, muddy struggle through dense jungle. We fishtailed up and down slick slopes, eased across the trunks of felled trees that served as makeshift bridges over the dozens of streams spilling off the Bolaven. In a few weeks, everything would be at flood stage, sealing off Attapeu for the rest of the monsoon season. We encountered no villages, saw few people: a gang of tribesmen dragging a half-hewn dugout canoe along the road; a solitary man carrying the foreleg of some hoofed mammal. In a few spots the forest opened and we saw the emerald wall of the Bolaven to the west and, to the east, a blue-green battlement that the Vietnamese called "Truong Son"—the "Long Mountains."

"I spoke with your pops," Honeyman said. He tried to sound casual.

"When?"

"Called him from Nong Khai. Just before I crossed into Laos. Told him you had made the case, done an outstanding job. That your client was thrilled. Didn't really tell him where we were headed now, but I said you were doing the right thing."

"How'd he take it?"

"A little worried."

"About the firm?"

"The firm is just letterhead on stationery. He's worried about you. But I told him I got your back."

"And?"

"And now he's really worried," he said, laughing.

"He's not really the type. Complaining type, absolutely. But a worrywart?"

"Laos will do that."

"SOG, right?"

"Right out there was what we trained for," he said, nodding at the imposing landscape. "Complete and total Indian country: anti-aircraft batteries, surface-to-air missile sites, trackers up the wazoo. This shitty road we're on now? Back in the day, it was part of the Ho Chi Minh Trail. It ran south to Attapeu, and then split. One part continued down into Cambodia. The other route ran east, towards the Central Highlands."

"Which was where you guys were waiting. That Special Forces stuff you told me about."

"You've been here, Sam?" Linda interjected.

"A long time ago. We couldn't let 'em just waltz into South Vietnam. We had to make it a little difficult. We also wanted to keep our guys out of their hands, if we could."

"Like what happened to my father," Linda said.

"If he was a pilot downed over southern Laos in the late sixties, like you say, there's a chance I went over the fence looking for him. A lot of airmen got winged here. We did the best we could. Sometimes it wasn't enough. I've had to live with that."

The jungle finally relented, leaving a floodplain haphazardly cut into rice fields and distant clumps of palms announcing the town. Beside a weathered stone obelisk marking a large, untended North Vietnamese Army cemetery, Honeyman hopped from the truck to urinate in the weeds.

"Just paying your respects?" I asked when he resumed driving.

"Promise I once made, thirty monsoons and a thousand years ago," he replied. "I'm still here, and they ain't."

Attapeu lay gasping in the afternoon heat. A quick circuit of its few streets pointed to just one place we could stay, a government-owned guest house that hadn't seen a customer in months. Cattle and goats grazed the grounds; a flock of ducks roosted in an abandoned jeep. The caretaker scurried from a small cinder-block building behind a restaurant on the property; she filled the air with apologies as she kicked a huge sow from the doorway and led us into the damp building. A large ground-floor room was empty save for a flimsy cabinet that held a large portrait of Ho Chi Minh enshrouded in spiderwebs. I brushed the tangle aside and saw that his wispy beard had not been painted but rather created from actual human hair. Upstairs held a squat toilet and two sweltering bedrooms. Honeyman pushed open the wooden shutters. None of the windows had screens. What could you expect in a two-dollar-a-night guest house, except bed lice and malaria?

We unloaded our gear, then drove to the market to buy netting and mosquito coils. The broad, unpaved roads were flanked by lush fruit trees and ridiculous billboards of stout socialist youths clearing forests, lifting logs, harvesting rice. After making our purchases, the shopkeeper told Linda of an ethnic-Vietnamese trader across the street who did business with the Lao Theung. We found an old man dozing in a hammock in a small room crammed with artifacts on the ground floor of his house. He reacted as if we were his first customers in weeks. He called for his wife to make tea while he showed us thick bronze bangles, piles of tiger claws and boars' tusks and French-era silver piasters, a brace of rattan shoulder baskets, and an armory of wooden shields and crossbows. And a bolt of red-and-black banded cloth that Linda immediately wrapped around her waist.

"Katu," the trader said.

For twenty dollars, Mr. Le provided the sarong and its history. Every few months, the trader said, several young Katu men paddled down the Xe Kaman River in a red canoe to trade handicrafts and hunting trophies for salt, machetes, and Thai whiskey. The Katu slept on the riverbank near the provincial hospital and got drunk every night; all of Attapeu was too terrified to confront the tattooed men, even the police. After a week or so, the Katu simply left. They always disappeared during the night. It was rumored that they lived several days' journey up the Xe Kaman, beyond a waterfall guarded by a man-eating tiger.

"What about the trader from Pakxe, the guy Vannavong said was dead?"

"He's dead all right," Linda said. "Mr. Le confirms this. He says the Pakxe trader bought many things from him. Now that he is dead, no one comes to Attapeu to buy Lao Theung souvenirs. Business is very bad."

"And the silver piece?" Honeyman asked.

Mr. Le fingered the mysterious Mayrena coin Linda had pulled from her pocket.

"He says it is very old silver. He has heard the story of the crazy Frenchman but he has never seen a coin like this before."

"So it's news to him."

"Maybe the Katu went around this man and directly to the Pakxe trader, for a better price."

"It's possible."

"The coin's also possibly bullshit," I said. "The trader could have cooked this whole scam up."

"The coin is legit," Honeyman said flatly.

"We'll find out soon enough," said Linda, "because I'm going up that river tomorrow morning."

"No one said that was a bad idea, either."

We drove down to the waterfront, where the Xe Kong met with a large tributary, the Xe Kaman, that flowed out of the Annamite Mountains to the east. A one-car ferry chugged across the confluence to the far shore. At the Attapeu landing, a young boy plucked the feathers from a live, bloody, hysterical duck. Nearby, a dozen fishermen sat aboard their boats and mended nets. Tomorrow, one lucky waterman would make enough money to avoid fishing for several weeks. A pair of Lao People's Army officers rode by on bicycles. They looked straight ahead, even as they regarded us out of the corners of their dead eyes.

"No one smiles here," said Honeyman. "Not even the children. Like an old VC-controlled 'ville."

When the twilight failed, the town generator stirred, powering a few harsh streetlamps and battered public-address speakers lashed to the light poles. Metallic voices barked through the darkness.

"No news from Vientiane, or even Pakxe," Linda said. "Just local propaganda. Work for the people. Obey authority. Remain vigilant."

"These folks don't give a damn about Pakxe," said Honeyman. "Pakxe might as well be a million miles away. And Vientiane is a whole 'nother galaxy as far as they're concerned."

The one decent restaurant in town was nearly empty, but the young hostess seated us beside a table where another *farang* had built a small pile of empty Beer Lao cans. The man nodded with elaborate formality.

"You are the first *farang* of the year," he said in accented English. "My compliments."

"Don't get many visitors?" I asked.

He took a swig of beer and offered a small, bitter laugh.

"Eight months ago, a party of Germans. Before that, two *Francais*. And before that, no one."

"And you?"

"Yves Mouhot. Director, Water Unlimited, Attapeu Province."

"NGO?"

"Of course."

"Will you join us for dinner?"

"There is nowhere else for dinner," Mouhot said.

"Not even the market?"

"You ask many questions, monsieur."

"An occupational hazard," I replied.

"I hope you understand I must talk to maintain my sanity," Mouhot blurted. "A dialogue with anyone: the maid, my dog, a bottle. There is no television, of course, and no telephone. My shortwave radio is broken; I suspect the police. The post takes two weeks from Vientiane, if it comes at all after the authorities steam open my letters and attempt to read them. No one here speaks English; some of the old people remember a few words of French. I speak Lao like a disaster. The people here mostly experienced the seminar camps. After years of this reeducation torture, many believe it is best to remain silent in any language."

"Let me buy you a beer, friend," offered Honeyman.

"Rice whiskey, if you please."

He spoke at length in Lao to the hostess. She returned with an amber bottle and four clouded glasses. Honeyman made the first toast.

"To Attapeu."

"I drink to Attapeu every night."

"You drink because of Attapeu."

"Of course," Mouhot said, laughing. "I have been here two years already. One more year and I will drink to someplace else. Someplace more civilized. Someplace with Campari and soda and ice."

"You mentioned your work," I said.

"Mostly water wells, for drinking. Here, there is no concept of sanitation. Cattle wander through the hospital, defecating. It is even worse in the mountains."

The hostess soon set down a huge silver platter heaped with bowls of sticky rice, steaming vegetables, and grilled meat.

"The restaurant is usually safe," Mouhot said. "And the duck is fresh."

Linda and I stuck with the rice and vegetables. Honeyman piled his plate with hunks of greasy, gray-black meat.

"What about dams?" Honeyman asked. "Does your charity build them, too?"

"Dams will not help these people. They flood good farmland and kill the fish. What is the benefit? Electricity? Each day, Attapeu receives electricity for three hours only. The benefit is all to Thailand. You came over the Bolaven? The dam there is just the beginning. All over the Annamites, the mountain people are being evicted.

"The engineers will not stop until they have destroyed this place. After they remove the people, then they will cut the trees. It will be another tragedy. You have new animals here, not even known to science. Sometimes I see them for sale in the market. Also animals that are extinct almost everywhere else in Southeast Asia: elephants, big cats, maybe even a few rhino. When I plan to go to the mountains, my Lao staff becomes very worried. They think we will all be eaten by tigers."

"To tigers," said Honeyman.

"Oui."

We all toasted, then drained our glasses.

"And bears," said Linda.

"Oui."

"And ducks," I added.

"You have a business card? Maybe I will write you. The authorities in Attapeu will be fascinated to read our correspondence."

Honeyman gave him a card.

"Of what interest is Attapeu to the Asian Development Fund?" Mouhot asked.

"Feasibility," I said. "Of the hydroelectric projects you mentioned."

"On what rivers?"

"The Xe Kong," Honeyman ventured, "and the Xe Kaman."

"You are too late, my friends. The Lao government has already decided where to locate the dams."

"We have not guaranteed any funding."

"The ADF must have financial problems I do not know about," Mouhot continued. "The ADF always travels in Land Cruisers, not in the Land Rovers of the Halo Trust, a de-mining charity."

He smiled and poured himself another shot. "What is your recommendation for the height of the inundation zones?"

"The inundation zones," Honeyman repeated, stalling for time.

"How tall do you desire the dam faces? The higher the face, the deeper the reservoir, and the more surface of the river valley will be flooded. It is just an excuse, of course, to facilitate logging. The Australians proposed a dam with a two-hundred-meter face. Two hundred meters!"

"That's a shitload of trees," I said.

"I think I know why you come to Attapeu," Mouhot said slyly. "The same reason the Americans came last year from their embassy in Vientiane. They came with their tents and gas stoves and freeze-dried food and radios and shovels and mine detectors. And, of course, their Lao minders. Across the Xe Kong, they dug for one week, looking for the bones of a pilot. They found only small parts of the plane, I think."

"So they found nothing?" Honeyman asked.

"They looked in the wrong place," Mouhot said. "All the secrets are in the mountains. The Lao Theung chiefs know this. When I go to their villages, the subject often comes up."

"What subject?" Linda asked.

"First we drink a few jars of *lao-lao*. It is the custom in the mountains. Then the headmen ask me: 'What if an American lived here? Would the United States be angry? Would they bomb us again?' They think I must be interested."

"Then what?"

"We laugh. Then we drink more *lao-lao*. And we say no more about the Americans."

"What do you believe, Mouhot?" questioned Honeyman.

He poured himself another shot of whiskey.

"I will tell you a story," Mouhot said. "Last year after the rains, I had to go into the mountains, about two days upriver. I am walking along a trail in the forest, the middle of nowhere. I meet a young boy walking from the other direction."

"What tribe?" Linda asked.

"Difficult to say. He wore only rags, nothing ceremonial. I nod to the boy. No reaction. He passes by me. He is silent. Okay, no big deal. I continue walking, maybe ten paces. Then I hear the boy call to me, 'Hey, man, how's it going?' "

Mouhot paused, helped himself to another shot.

"I turn around and look at the boy. Now he is smiling. Then he waves at me and walks away. How do you like that? 'Hey, man, how's it going?' he asks me. Perfect, idiomatic American English he speaks to me. In Xanxai district, how is this possible? Who taught this boy?"

"We intend to find his teacher," I said.

"Look in the mountains. Your missing American is out there."

He laughed, drained his glass, muttered the boy's greeting like a mantra. *How's it going? How's it going?* There was no shutting Mouhot up. When the power cut off, the hostess brought us a candle. I kept pouring out the rice whiskey until Mouhot finally, mercifully passed out. The waitress didn't seem surprised, only cleared a table where we laid him out on the planks, as if for a wake, to sleep it off. With Monsieur Mouhot, she said, every night ended like this.

Thirteen

The roosters rousted me just after dawn. Through the dew-slick mosquito netting, I saw the empty beds of Linda and Honeyman. I felt for our gear, stowed beneath my rack. Still there. From the window, I made out the blurry, saffron-colored forms of monks padding down the empty street on their morning round to collect alms. A thick, cool mist clung to the town, obscuring tinny speakers that coughed up the Lao national anthem and the morning ration of hectoring propaganda. Then Linda and Honeyman materialized from the fog.

"Saddle up," Honeyman called. "We're leaving Attapeu in five minutes."

"Where to?"

"Know anything about boats?" Linda asked.

"That's the old man's department. I only know that I can't afford to own one."

"We're only renting this hulk," Honeyman said. "One hundred dollars. The owner thinks he got a helluva deal."

"Did he?"

"Told him we're just going upriver about one hour, to Ban Watloung. That we'll return his tub tonight."

"How'd he take it?" I asked.

"He said we shouldn't go any farther upriver. Too dangerous. A pair of Lao surveyors disappeared two weeks ago in a long-tail boat."

"Are we listening to him?"

"We are going up the Xe Kaman River, kid, but we ain't stopping at Ban Watloung. And we sure as shit won't bring back the boat tonight."

"Did he ask for a deposit?"

"A deposit? In the Lao People's Democratic Republic? I gave him a bottle of Johnnie Walker."

"Red or black?" I asked.

"Red label."

"Then I think we got a helluva deal."

The extra jerry can of gasoline we found stored in the stern of the dugout only sweetened the arrangement. The boat ran about twenty feet long, carved from a single tree with three roughhewn thwarts, and was propelled by a fifty-horsepower outboard engine. It would run slower and quieter than the long-tail boats of Bangkok; what it sacrificed in speed it would make up for in stealth. We would get where we were headed soon enough. And the less attention we attracted along the way, the better.

We quickly loaded our baggage and shoved off from the muddy embankment. While Honeyman pulled on the engine cord, Linda waved to fishermen mending nets along the ramshackle waterfront. She pretended to take a photograph of the scene with a disposable camera while I scouted the far shoreline with a pair of binoculars. To the official eyes of Attapeu, we seemed to be three tourists out to see the rural sights. The motor coughed to life, and Honeyman swung the dugout into the main channel of the Xe Kong and headed downstream. After a few minutes, he pointed the bow into a wide tributary along the left bank and we headed east on the Xe Kaman, toward the sunglow swelling through the fog. Attapeu quickly dropped from sight.

From the bow, Linda called out for sandbars or snags as we worked our way up the meandering course. Scrubby bushes lined the crest of the slick riverbanks, which were backed by rice fields and simple shelters. Within an hour we made Ban Watloung, a Lao Loum settlement substantial enough to support its own small Buddhist temple. A small ferry chugged across the river to the south shore. From there, a bad road ran all the way to the triborder area where Laos, Cambodia, and Vietnam collided.

"Take a good look at your last vehicle," said Honeyman. "We are now officially beyond the end of the line."

For the benefit of any government flunky condemned to Ban Watloung, I handed Linda the field glasses and pointed out a pair of stork-billed kingfishers shearing through the dark water. To any observer, we were just an intrepid group of obsessive bird watchers. We buzzed upriver all day, the rural scenery unrelenting. A few mango and papaya trees, an occasional oxcart or bicycle struggling along the muddy track, and paddy fields that stretched to the dark, green mountains.

"What did you think about Mouhot?" Linda finally asked me.

"If I lived here, I'd drink more than he does."

"What of his story, about the boy he met?"

"He's a drunk, not a liar," Honeyman interjected. "He was onto something, and it's eating him alive."

We ate a noontime meal while tied up to the branch of a massive teak tree that had been uprooted by the monsoon flood and collapsed into the river.

"Take a look at your last baguette," Linda said.

Honeyman popped open some tinned meat and handed the container to me, along with a Swiss Army knife.

"But not your last can of Spam," he said, grinning.

Then he jerked on the engine and we pushed onward. As the afternoon wore on, the Long Mountains gradually grew in size until they were a jagged jade-green wall running on a northwest-to-southeast axis as far as the eye could see. A few miles ahead, the Xe Kaman seemed to spill from a steep-sided gap cleaved through the range. Behind us, low, rain-swollen clouds mustered for an assault. Honeyman regarded the impending storm with distaste.

"We don't want to get trapped out in that."

A few minutes later, Linda glimpsed a high-pitched thatched roof through the skein of vegetation atop a bend in the river. Around the point, a small set of rapids churned up the water. Several topless, unsmiling women stood in the riffles, their ablutions interrupted by our arrival. A pair of young children clawed their way up the left-side bank and ran crying into a village.

"Not on my map," Honeyman said.

"Wouldn't be," Linda said. "It's too new."

"*New* is a relative term," I said. "This place looks totally used up."

"They're Lao Theung," said Linda. She hopped from the bow into the shallows and tied the bowline to another downed tree. There were no other boats in this village of mountain people.

"Katu, maybe?"

Linda regarded the raised houses that teetered on poorly plumbed posts, the threadbare thatch of the swaybacked roofs, the gauntness of the pigs and chickens.

"We would never live like this."

A barefoot old man appeared, clad in clean but frayed fourth-hand trousers and a shirt. Linda greeted him in Lao; the man responded haltingly. This was the chief, she explained. The headman beckoned us to enter his settlement—a dozen longhouses rising about five feet above the mud and arranged like a horseshoe around a common area with an enormous central sacrificial post. The sky erupted and we scurried with our bags to the largest platform.

"The mud, the rain," said Honeyman. "One whiff and it all comes back."

There was another sticky-sweet smell as well, like the stench of decay, or roadkill, hanging over the hamlet.

"They'll let us stay the night," Linda related. "They are Jeh tribe."

Honeyman looked startled.

"It'd be good if we had a gift for the chief," he said.

"Lao kip won't do him much good out here," I replied.

"I'm sure they'd appreciate any medicine you could offer," Linda suggested.

Honeyman rummaged through his pack until he found a bottle of aspirin.

"Tell the chief to take one if his head hurts," he instructed Linda.

"Do you have anything for malaria?" she asked.

"Then he can take two."

"What's our story if they want to know why we're here?" I said.

"They won't ask," Linda answered. "It wouldn't be polite."

"Thank them for their hospitality," Honeyman ordered. "But let's keep up our NGO cover. We're here to help develop Laos. Ask them about security, about unexploded ordnance. Do they ever find cluster bombs?"

She waited while the old man replied.

"They don't know much about farming," she related. "They only plowed the land one time. They stopped after a young man died when he struck an old *bombi* with a hoe."

"Must have been from one of the thousands of cannisters we dropped on Uncle Ho's trail." Honeyman sighed. "Thirty years later, they still kill innocent folks."

Rain dripped through the thatch overhanging the veranda. A

few buffalo skulls and a set of small deer antlers hung overhead from a crudely carved crossbeam. More smoke than illumination came from the cooking fire in the back of the space. An old woman, presumably the chief's wife, emerged from the shadows with a bamboo tray that held four steaming glasses.

"Take one, or she'll be insulted," Linda ordered.

She bowed, took a sip of the beige-colored brew, then spoke at length with the headman.

These people had lived here along the Xe Kaman for the last two dry seasons, Linda related. For generations before they had lived a day's walk upriver, in the mountains. But the Lao government had ordered them to leave, to make way for a hydroelectric project. Even though I didn't speak Lao, I sensed the chief's anguish.

"A district official told them their land would be flooded by the dam. They would have to move to get any compensation or electricity. They would have plenty of good land for farming. When they moved here, each household was given ten dollars and a bag of iron nails. The official came back once last dry season to give them some cans of fish. That was the last they saw of him. They try to grow wet rice, but they have no experience. It is the same with fishing. Their catch is very low and sometimes they get sick after eating the fish. The water here is bad. Many Jeh have stomach problems. Only half the families grow enough food for themselves. He wants to know why they were treated this way. I told him we didn't know."

The old man's voice caught, sounding almost apologetic.

"He wonders if you have any medicine to ease the shame in his heart, Honeyman. He misses the mountains."

A small crowd clustered in front of the veranda, standing in the rain to hear the chief's complaints and hoping Honeyman might also treat their ailments.

"These poor bastards can't catch a break," Honeyman said.

"Everywhere they've turned, somebody has screwed 'em. The Vietnamese. The Lao. The Thai. Us."

He slowly shook his head, then rummaged again in his rucksack for his first-aid kit.

"Haven't done a sick call for ages. Not since Kontum. Let's try and win a few hearts and minds."

Honeyman shook a bright pink bottle of Pepto-Bismol and the children laughed.

"The chief said he hopes the pink medicine will make them better," Linda related. "If it doesn't, then they will go under the houses."

"There's nothing under the houses but animal pens," I said.

"It's traditionally where they store their coffins. Lots of them."

Out here, people died unexpectedly all the time. Disease. Accidents. *Bombis*. A village could never have too many coffins, which were fashioned from the hollowed-out trunks of rosewood trees. But all the big trees around the new village had been cut down before the Jeh arrived, a bad portent that the tribe had to address immediately by floating down several huge rosewood logs from the mountains. Normally a coffin-tree containing a dead tribesman would be set out in the jungle. But the forest here had vanished. Their dead now rested in hard-carved coffins beneath their dilapidated huts, in a state of limbo. That explained the miasma hanging over the village.

"The chief says that one day they will carry the coffins back to their old village to be buried," Linda said.

Once again, the headman's wife appeared. This time her tray held a banana leaf heaped with steamed rice and an earthen jar with a fragrant soup of lemongrass and canned sardines. We bowed and ate gratefully. When the meal had been cleared, the chief barked an order and two adult men with gourd pipes sat down on the veranda. His wife brought out another earthen jar with several reed straws.

"It's *lao-lao* time," Honeyman announced.

We sipped the fiery moonshine while the musicians played a mournful reel. The chief got up and performed a slow, trancelike dance of a hunter. We all drank to his talent. We did the same for the chief's teenage daughter. Then Honeyman stood. The bamboo slats creaked beneath his weight, causing the children to laugh. He took the chief's wife and guided her in a slow waltz across the veranda. She was at once delighted and embarrassed, trying to hide her laughter behind the palm of her hand while the villagers hooted. Then Honeyman pulled a harmonica from a pocket of his trousers, sounded a few notes of a haunting, vaguely familiar melody, and pulled Linda to her feet.

"F major?" she asked.

Honeyman nodded and launched again into the old Hank Williams song.

" '*Hear that lonesome whip-poor-will/He sounds too blue to fly . . .*' "

Her voice was low and weary, drawing out every bittersweet syllable. She sang like someone tilling a fallow field, slow and stark. The rain had stopped but heat lightning still winked in the distance to the west.

Linda and Honeyman finished "I'm So Lonesome I Could Cry" on a long, yearning note. The villagers clapped their approval.

"Nice," Honeyman said. "You ought to add it to your set list."

"No more gigs," Linda replied. "Ever."

The chief's wife flourished another jar of *lao-lao*. We drank to Hank. Then Linda spoke with the headman, who grew serious under her quiet questioning.

"I asked him about the Katu," Linda said. "He said they live farther up this river. Where the river boils there is a trail to the north."

"Rapids?"

She questioned the chief again.

"Not rapids. A waterfall. The Katu live in those mountains, maybe a half day's walk from the Xe Kaman."

"Where in the mountains?"

"Hard to say exactly. They're slash-and-burn farmers: every few years they shift the village. But always the same mountains."

The chief continued, growing animated as he spoke.

"A half-moon ago he saw a pair of Lao Loum men go up this river by boat. They have not come down the river. He says we should be careful. The Jeh, the other Lao Theung tribes, are all afraid of these Katu. They are very angry people."

"We know that," I said.

"They are much angrier than me," Linda said.

"Seems like they have a lot to be upset about," Honeyman said.

To lighten the mood, the chief again called for music and *lao-lao.* Staggering to his feet, he tried to dance but soon knelt, laughing. His daughter took his place, skipping around the space and miming the harvesting of rice.

"Has the chief ever seen any *farang* before us?" I asked.

The headman just chuckled and sipped more *lao-lao.* Honeyman showed the silver coin to the old man, who responded by clutching the necklace around his neck. Three tiger claws; a good trade. Then he pointed to his ear. Yes, the coin could be worked into stylish jewelry. Honeyman smiled, then leaned forward until his face was just inches from that of the old man.

"How's it going, Chief?" he asked.

The headman seemed briefly startled, then offered a broad smile and the earthen jar of moonshine.

"Merci, Chon mein," he said, shaking his head. Then even the

animals and the dead below us seemed to join in the laughter that spilled from the village and across the failed fields.

Honeyman shook me awake before dawn. I had slept on the veranda, curled around Linda. The chief and his wife snored nearby. I counted at least four *lao-lao* jars scattered across the slats. We let everyone doze while we hauled our gear down to the boat.

"Some party."

"Pretty tame by Bangkok standards," Honeyman said. "I'm used to the Cowboy."

"My resistance is lower than yours."

"Only when it comes to booze, kid."

"And women?"

"I'm here, ain't I?"

"Because of Linda?"

"Because of unfinished business. Because of your pops."

"And maybe because of your old hooch girl. I saw that picture at your place. She was a looker."

"De oppresso liber," he replied with a smile. "To liberate the oppressed."

Honeyman didn't say so, but those long-ago search-and-rescue missions when his recon team had returned empty-handed to Kontum still gnawed at his conscience. "They were just gone," he'd told me. The old soldier also undoubtedly wanted redemption. Finding an American POW after all these years would make his critics finally shut up about the bogus Starr photo. It would vindicate years of effort by friends and family members of the missing in action. And it would make more than a few politicians and military and government officials look like incompetents or, worse, craven cynics for writing off these men. We tossed our bags into the boat. In the moonlight, the racing river gleamed like a freshly forged machete blade. Behind us, the first cock crowed in the village. A dog offered heated rebuttal.

"What day you think it is, Honeyman?"

"We left Bangkok about a week ago, Bass."

"I can't keep track."

"Imagine being here thirty years."

"I'd lose track of the seasons: drought, monsoon, drought, monsoon."

"If someone was tough enough and lucky enough, he might pull through."

"But could he make it out?"

"That's the million-dollar question, ain't it?" Honeyman answered. "We're not exactly going in with good intel and close-air support."

"All the satellite imagery and DIA investigations in the world have produced squat so far," I answered. "Maybe we've taken a page from the bad guys' playbook. Go in fast, light, low-tech. Hit 'em hard and get out before they know what happened."

Honeyman stooped to grab a small, flat stone, then skipped the rock upstream.

"Sometimes you sound just like your pops."

"I don't know about that. He can't be happy about what I've done to get here. Basically walking out on the firm."

"Relax a little. You just cleared the biggest case of your career. And when we're through here, your firm will never want for work again," Honeyman replied.

"And if this doesn't work?"

"Then we'll both be hiding out in Bangkok, won't we?"

The entire village came down to the water's edge to see us off. The chief insisted on sending two armed men along. They would escort us as far as their former village, then leave to hunt. After the Jeh hospitality last night we could hardly refuse, though we did beg off when the headman tried to give us another jar of *lao-lao* as a parting gift. Our new passengers laid their carbines and homemade slingshots in the boat and, along with Linda and me, pulled on the bowline to drag the boat up the rapids until we had cleared the largest rocks. Then Honeyman gunned the engine, we all loaded into the dugout, and, to enormous cheers from the children, we headed east toward the brightening sky and the misted mountains. The Jeh men rode in the bow, ancient guns in hand, scanning the horizon. An empty, rutted road soon appeared on the port side and followed the river's course. We avoided a sandbar, then tackled a small set of rapids without having to get out of the boat. Then we entered a deep, shadowy defile between twin, jungled peaks that vaulted up more than a thousand feet from the plain. The Annamite Range threw more whitewater and deadfall in our way, but Honeyman remained unfazed.

"This boat drafts less than a foot of water," he told me. "Plenty of freeboard. I'm surprised the chief didn't try to load us up with more hunters."

"Or send any occupied coffins back to the family plot."

The mountains gave way to a long, narrow, denuded valley of mud, exposed rock, and tree stumps that looked like black, rotting teeth. The Jeh pointed to the clear-cut hillsides and hummed angrily. There was nothing here. No people, no animals. Even the buzzards had vanished. We ducked beneath the rusted cable of an abandoned ferry crossing. Behind it stood a massive pile of logs and the weather-beaten huts of a timber camp shut down for the rainy season.

"These men say the dam will go here," Linda related. "This is the last road in Laos. From here, there are only the rivers and walking trails."

"Just what you always wanted, Honeyman. More Indian country."

He spit overboard, then tilted his head upward. Far overhead,

I saw a gleam of silver bearing northeast, leaving a long, thin contrail that seemed to stretch all the way back to Thailand.

"Looks like you missed your flight, kid. They're heading back to Narita without you."

We left the dead valley and threaded another river gorge, which opened onto a larger, lush plain. The river's course swung north, with occasional small rapids and pale sandbars. Even using the binoculars, the nearest mountaintop hamlets were miles away.

"Anything look familiar?" I asked.

"It was a very long time ago," Linda said. "I can barely remember my parents, let alone the scenery."

Seeing this resilient land, it was hard to believe that Laos had once been the most heavily bombed nation in the history of warfare, and that simple, innocent men and women had died out here on nameless peaks and in anonymous valleys. It would all be drowned and forgotten, just so that Bangkok could blaze with even more neon lights. The Xe Kaman swung east again, growing narrower and swifter as we approached another dramatic gorge. Just after noon, our escorts beckoned us to stop. We beached just downstream from a small brook tumbling into the Xe Kaman and a clearing half choked with vines. Fresh deer tracks crimped the rough sand at the water's edge.

"They say the waterfall is around the next big mountain."

"These mountains all look big," I replied.

The men laughed, shouldered their weapons, and soon vanished up a faint trail running beside the tributary. The chatter of hidden monkeys floated from the jungle while Honeyman poured the extra fuel into the tank. Through a break in the trees, I saw a hawk soaring on the rising heat.

"I understand why the Jeh miss this place," I said.

"Hell, I even miss it," Honeyman said. "When nobody's trying to shoot your ass off, and you can stop and smell the strangler figs, it's real nice. Although it's not quite Kontum."

He yanked the engine and the noise in the trees leaped to a fever pitch. We traveled another hour, bearing south and then east again around an enormous massif. Honeyman smoked a cigarette and said nothing, no doubt remembering some classified mission gone sideways in these mountains. An ambush, a particularly hairy extraction, maybe even a team member killed in action. I didn't push him. To pass the time, Linda taught me a few Katuic words. *Hello. Name. Father. Mother.*

Racing around a tight bend, we nearly swamped a small, outboard-motor-equipped boat paddled by a young boy. Honeyman throttled down and we swung our boat around.

"How's it going?" I called.

Linda hailed him in Lao, then Katuic. The boy looked at us implacably and remained silent. Then he dug his paddle into the water and disappeared downstream.

"What we used to call a big 'no comment' in the news business," I said.

"Did you notice the engine?" Linda asked. "You think that's the Lao Loum boat?"

"Maybe. It's definitely not the red boat the Katu take down to Attapeu."

"Two *farang* on the upper reaches of the Xe Kaman River," Honeyman posed, "and the kid's not surprised or interested at all? Why is that?"

"Maybe because he's afraid?" I answered. "Or he doesn't speak the language?"

"Or maybe because he's seen a white man before," Linda said.

We resumed our voyage. Perhaps a half hour later, I felt a dip in temperature and a tremble in the air over the loping outboard engine. Around the next reach, a waterfall churned out mist and foam that roiled on enormous boulders ten yards below its uneven lip. At the base of the falls, a track on the north bank seemed to lead through the thick vegetation and up the mountain. This had to be the landmark the Jeh chief spoke of. We unloaded our gear, then motored downstream a few hundred feet. Honeyman ran the boat ashore and we dragged it into the undergrowth and concealed it beneath tree fronds and elephant-ear leaves.

"Don't want to make it too tempting to steal," Honeyman said. He popped the outboard's sparkplug and slid it inside a side pocket of his pants. "Let's go hold that Watts family reunion."

Five minutes up the trail and my shirt was soaked with sweat. The thick forest canopy blocked the sunlight and any vestige of a breeze. The stench of mud and rotting vegetation infused the still, humid air. I kept my eyes warily on the slick path. I could handle falling down, but not the bite of a viper, like the one Honeyman called a "two-stepper."

Whoever had blazed this route believed that the shortest distance between two points was a straight line. To hell with switchbacks. As we grunted and slid and grabbed and crawled our way up the mountain, Honeyman regaled us with tales of the Ho Chi Minh Trail. Try this while pushing a bike loaded with five hundred pounds of rice. Try this during a B-52 strike. Try this while suffering with blackwater fever. The Americans had dropped bombs, mines, listening sensors, and chemical defoliants on the trail. Nothing had stopped the North Vietnamese Army from keeping the supply lines open or the Youth Volunteers from delivering the goods.

"Aside from your Montagnard mercenaries, how did the hill people treat you?" I asked Honeyman.

"The ones I knew in Kontum weren't political," Honeyman answered. "They didn't like the South Vietnamese, the VC, or the NVA. How was it here, Linda?"

"Everyone would have obeyed my grandfather, the chief. We have always just wanted to be left alone."

After a two-hour slog, the ski-jump-steep slope gradually grew sane. The forest opened up, revealing other rugged ridgelines in the distance. A low growl borne on an eastward wind meant that the rains would soon deliver their evening deluge. We quickened our pace for the next half hour but found no sign of habitation. Honeyman called a stop when he found a stand of young teak trees, where we strung a tarp and hung a pair of hammocks in the fading light. When Linda and I returned with two armloads of dead wood, he already had a fire going. Skewers he'd whittled from dead branches hung at an angle over the flames; some held sizzling slabs of Spam, others his steaming, stinking socks.

"Do the same if you don't want fungus all over your feet," Honeyman advised.

"The secret is to just go barefoot," Linda said.

"That works, right up until you step on a pit viper," Honeyman replied. "You won't feel so comfortable then."

She kicked off her shoes and knelt before the fire. The rain had begun to fall, but the tarp and the huge teak leaves kept our campsite relatively dry. Honeyman fluttered his rank socks at Linda like a fly fisherman making a deft cast.

"Keep waving them," she goaded. "See how the stench keeps the mosquitoes away."

"What's your secret then for avoiding hookworm?" he taunted.

"Spam," she replied. "Twice a day. Kills any parasite."

We all had a laugh, then a swig of water from the canteen while the food cooled.

"Hear anything?" Honeyman asked.

"Just thunder," I said. "Obviously."

"That and the rain," added Linda. "Nothing else."

"Nothing else," said Honeyman. "Exactly. It's too quiet. That may be a problem. Get out your pistol, Linda."

But by then it was too late for him to do anything but throw a few handfuls of wet leaves to douse the fire. Lightning burst as a dartlike arrow struck Honeyman in the back. I grabbed Linda and we dived behind a fallen trunk for cover. Honeyman staggered behind a nearby tree, yanked out the barbed point buried in his left shoulder, and collapsed. Small, silent men crept from the shadows.

More lightning exploded nearby, illuminating attackers who gathered around Honeyman. The bare-chested men were short and stocky, wore loincloths and carried crossbows. Among them was the boy we'd seen in the boat below the waterfall. The foliage rustled; a branch cracked on the forest floor. Other warriors pressed in on us with spears brandished.

"Now would be a real good time to use that pistol, Linda."

"No. Wait."

I rolled to a sitting position, my back resting against the log. At least I could give them the evil eye before they stabbed me to death.

"I'd feel a lot better, Linda, if we were back in Providence and these were just Tiny Rascals gangbangers."

A sharp order rang above the rain and a more muscular warrior strode forward and roughly shoved my shoulders. He was nearly a head taller than the rest of our attackers and wore a shirt resembling chainmail, with dark iron rings interlaced throughout the cloth. Then he kicked my legs and yanked my hair with mounting agitation until I stood up. When another bolt struck I saw his dark face: long, matted hair; wild, half-crazed eyes; filed and blackened teeth; and swirling, magical tattoos. I'd seen a similar visage before: Uncle Bounliep. In a single, powerful move he grabbed Linda by her shoulders and lifted her to her feet. Then he unsheathed a short knife, held it to my throat, and howled a question drowned out by the thunder.

"Ama?" Linda replied in Katuic. Father?

Fourteen

We did not die there in the rain and mud. Wild Eye withdrew the knife blade and gaped. Around us, dark voices murmured. *Ama . . . ama . . . ama*. What sort of dark magic was this, that a stranger could speak their language? Linda continued, slowly, evenly. From her tone I understood that she was trying to identify herself. But the war party's leader brusquely sliced the air with his knife, waving off further explanations. No female trickster would talk to him in this fashion. A terse order and a pair of his fellow tribesmen set about hacking nearby bamboo and liana into a crude litter. Two more men tore down the tarp, then rolled it tightly and gave it to the alpha warrior. Others searched our packs and patted us down for weapons, whooping when they discovered Honeyman's bottle of Johnnie Walker Black Label scotch, the two Thai sidearms, and the cans of Spam. A warrior found the outboard's sparkplug while searching Honeyman and regarded it quizzically like some exotic animal tooth.

"Give it back," I said, extending my hand. "It's worthless to you."

Wild Eye shouted at me. No translation needed: shut up, or die. He regarded the booze, the guns, the tinned meat, and the engine part, then stuffed them all into a woven-bamboo quiver slung over his left shoulder. We waited silently in the downpour while his men worked. If they had wanted to kill us, we'd have been dead already, unless they didn't want to carry bodies and booty too far. Or maybe something about Linda had kept them from violence, at least for the moment. Tribesmen tied Honeyman's arms and legs with thick lianas. They then used more vines to truss him to the bamboo poles of the litter like a big-game kill. Wild Eye pointed to Honeyman while several of his tribesmen effortlessly hoisted our packs.

"Grab the back, Seb. I'll take the front."

Honeyman groaned as Linda and I struggled to shoulder the load. Wild Eye bellowed and pointed his machete into the wet night: march, or die. I quickly lost all sense of direction as we followed the mountain's contours. About an hour into our trek, the rains suddenly subsided to a light drizzle, then fizzled altogether. The moon broke through the low clouds, casting the trail in dark, serpentine shadows. Occasionally Linda or I slipped and Honeyman landed on his back in the mud and wet grass. He stopped moaning after the third spill. Once the rain ceased, the men began singing. Their voices lacked the lilting, nasal quality of Thai or Lao and came instead in short, guttural bursts, like gunfire. The moment was all that mattered now. The path, the litter, the weight of the load searing my shoulders. Linda's village didn't figure. Neither did finding her father, or furthering the fortunes of Damon & Son Investigations. Staying alive was all that mattered. If we could avoid shedding our blood on the warriors' blades, there was hope.

When dawn finally came, the forest had faded to a scattering of ancient trees standing above an expanse of elephant grass rustling in a cool wind. To the east, ragged peaks jabbed at a papaya-pink sunrise. No villages stood in sight as we headed northeast, farther into the mountains. Weapons at the ready, our fierce captors trudged along silently, the only sound the dull clacking of their tiger-claw necklaces. None of the tribesmen stood above five foot two, except Wild Eye, or had an ounce of body fat. Muscles rippled beneath the black tattoos that began at their knees and flowed across their thighs, torsos, and faces. Some had swastika patterns or dancing girls on their faces, just like Uncle Bounliep. Many had also extended their eyebrows with a series of tattooed spots down to their jawlines. Everyone had the same bad dental plan.

Our route crested a ridge, then gradually descended through groves of banana trees and a patchwork of recently planted mountain-rice fields clinging to the slopes. We were nearing some sort of settlement. We overtook a pregnant woman struggling silently beneath an enormous bundle of firewood. None of the warriors stopped to assist her: wood collecting was women's work. Two young boys herding buffalo stepped off the trail and gave us silent passage through fields of corn, tobacco, and vegetables I had never seen before. Around the next fold in the mountain, three dozen longhouses huddled behind a stockade of sharpened bamboo stakes that looked tall and dangerous enough to repel any attackers or marauding animals. At the base of the fence, several women scooped mud from a shoulder-deep pit; nearby, a half-tattooed adolescent boy deftly chopped sections of bamboo into needle-sharp *punji* sticks with a gleaming machete. The spikes would kill or grievously maim anyone or anything that fell into the trap. Thick smoke seeped from the high-pitched roofs of the village, and there was a cacophony of voices and animal sounds.

"Krnoon Blo Mat," the leader proudly pronounced.

"Sunrise Village," Linda said.

"What about Ban Katu?" I asked. "Where's that in relation to this?"

"The same place," she explained, "but 'Ban Katu' is the Lao Loum name. This is our name."

Wild Eye drew his knife and tersely ordered us to stop speaking. Pigs and chickens scattered as our procession passed through the village gate, while a few mangy dogs barked their displeasure. Young women held indigo sarongs to their chests while topless old crones with pendulous breasts smiled, baring lacquer-blackened teeth as they wove baskets. They seemed nearly as tattooed as their men. Young children dashed up to welcome the warriors, then ran away shouting after sighting Honeyman and me. Not unlike the Jeh village, the longhouses inside the fortifications were arranged in an oval. But here the sacrificial pole in the center common area was elaborately carved with geometric designs and stained with recent blood. Nearby stood a short, stone pillar. On Wild Eye's command, we handed over the litter to a half-dozen young warriors, who carried Honeyman to the veranda of the largest structure in the village and then disappeared inside this high-pitched longhouse. Others followed with our packs. Wild Eye ordered us to sit in the enormous pole's shadow and stalked away. A half-buried bamboo cage was situated nearby. Inside, two filthy, emaciated men called to us in low, desperate voices.

"They are Lao Loum," Linda whispered. "The missing surveyors."

"It'll be a tight fit with all of us in there."

"I'm working to keep us out."

Word of our arrival spread quickly, for it seemed that nearly every villager not out farming or hunting soon clustered around us. The toddlers went naked in this dirt-poor hard place, while older children wore ragged scraps. The women dressed nearly in uniform, with indigo sarongs and necklaces of animal teeth and birds' beaks. Brass bracelets coiled like snakes along their forearms. An old, pipe-smoking man coughed up phlegm and a question, asking our names. "My father is Cut," Linda replied in Katuic. One young mother nearly dropped her baby in surprise. From Linda's gestures, I knew she was explaining her appearance and us, her companions. Murmurs drifted through the crowd.

"We've made it," Linda said. "This is my family's village."

"Where's your family, then?" I asked. "Why don't they came forward?"

"They left before sunup to work their fields."

"Your father, too?" I asked.

"They tell me I have to speak with *ta-ka*—the headman. The chief will tell us everything."

"What about Honeyman?"

"He should be all right now." She nodded toward the soaring structure the warriors had delivered him to. "They've taken him to the *gual*—the communal longhouse. The men there will care for him."

Wild Eye returned to shoo away the crowd, then ordered us to follow him beyond the *gual,* which was reserved for the village males. The support poles and the gables jutting from the thatched roof that towered more than thirty feet above us contained more fantastic carvings of animals and geometrical designs. On the veranda of the longhouse, several old men tended Honeyman's wound with a poultice of jungle leaves. As we passed, his eyes met my gaze and he nodded. Stay calm. We were doing better than the Lao Loum prisoners. Still, I worried. From what little I'd been able to learn about the tribe, the Katu had never welcomed strangers.

Aside from the *gual,* the chief's longhouse seemed the largest, most solidly built shelter in the village. Further figures of animals and human silhouettes embellished the wooden framework that rested on short pilings and stretched as far as end-to-end mobile homes. The overhanging eaves and the short, tightly plaited bamboo walls kept the interior quarters in perpetual shadow. There seemed to be no partitions, no furniture. At one arc-shaped end of the structure, a cooking fire smoldered in an earthen hearth beside clay jars of rice whiskey, bamboo tubes of water, and copper cooking pots. Without a chimney, wood smoke had glazed the beams, roofing material, and possessions hanging from the rafters—a bronze gong, animal traps, crossbows, and a recently killed deer—with a sooty veneer. The woman of the house sat beside the fire, crushing mint-scented leaves in a wooden bowl. Wild Eye spoke to her with surprising tenderness and she began preparing tea. He then reverted to form, gruffly ordering us to sit on the split-bamboo flooring. Below us, pigs snuffled for any morsel of food. A slightly taller and more muscular version of Wild Eye stepped from the shadows at the far end of the longhouse. He carried the two pistols.

"*Ta-ka* Kanam," Wild Eye announced.

Wild Eye knelt by the entrance's sliding door and laid his sparkling, well-honed machete at the ready. Chief Kanam silently stepped across the room, then sat cross-legged before us and placed the confiscated handguns beside him. He wore a loincloth trimmed with metal rings, several necklaces of tiger fangs and claws, and a body suit of tattoos, including the dancing-woman facial work. His oiled skin glistened in the half-light like a panther's coat.

"Ve mai," Linda said.

The chief flashed freshly lacquered teeth.

"Hello," he replied, in English. "How's it going?"

Wild Eye laughed as I gasped in surprise. Linda remained composed.

"Karo."

"I am also well," Kanam replied. "Your friend?"

"Achak ku Sebastian," I said, giving him my name.

"Achak ku Kanam," the chief said, pleased at my attempt to speak Katuic. "Let us speak English, Sebastian. It has been too long. I must practice."

"As you wish, *ta-ka,*" Linda answered.

A teenager without tattoos cautiously carried a bamboo tray with four cups of hot tea from the cooking area. The servant laid the steaming cups out silently, then bowed repeatedly as he backed away.

"Silly boy," Kanam said. He shook his head. "Jeh people."

He spit an order and the boy and the woman left the longhouse.

"My wife, Rudu," the headman said.

"Very pretty," I said.

"Pretty, yes," Kanam said, "but for Monui, cousin always make best wife."

Linda raised her cup.

"May your rule be long and wise, *ta-ka,*" she said.

"Thank you, cousin."

"Cousin," I repeated dumbly.

"Our parents also cousin," Kanam explained. "When we are baby, we very good friend. Then Bounliep take away Lin."

"You remember more than me, *ta-ka*. That was a long time ago."

"Village people always tell your story. They try to scare their children. Do not run away in the forest: you be lost forever, like Lin."

"Now I've come back," she answered.

"Good surprise. We think you dead forever."

"I never forgot my way home."

"You have strong feeling in your heart."

"I came home for a reason."

"Every journey has purpose. What about two white friend?"

"I come because of her," I said, nodding toward Linda.

"Pretty girl, my cousin," Kanam said with a smile. "And old man? Your father?"

"No. He is a friend of my father."

"Very good friend to come so far with you. His purpose? He love my cousin same-same as you?"

"Linda asked for my help," I answered. "My friend Honeyman comes because of someone else."

"He is soldier?"

"A long time ago," Linda answered.

"He fights in these mountains?"

"To the east," I said. "Beyond the sunrise. Vietnam. A place near Kontum. And the girl was Jeh people."

Kanam nodded.

"Jeh girl also very pretty. Old soldier cannot forget."

"We love what we cannot have," Linda said.

"Sebastian, you are soldier?" Kanam asked.

"No. I am too young. The war had ended."

"Monui must fight all the time. Vietnam people. Lao people. Bahnar. Jeh."

"My friends are not here to fight you," Linda said.

"Maybe you help Monui."

"I don't think our being here will help your people," I said.

"Talk your purpose, cousin," Kanam said.

"I come for *ama*."

"*Ta-ka* Curtis."

"He is also chief?"

"Only *ta-ka* ask question," Kanam said firmly. "What of Curtis?"

"A Lao Loum man from Pakxe contacted me in America. He said my father is alive in Xanxai district. He was told this by a Chinese trader who traveled to Attapeu."

"How does Chinese man know about Curtis?"

"The trader met some men from Krnoon Blo Mat," Linda related. "They came down the Xe Kaman to Attapeu in a red canoe. They said they could sell my father to him for a large ransom."

"Many boats on Xe Kaman," Kanam said quickly. "And many men."

"But not so many Monui," Linda retorted. "And only the men of the red boat had this."

She fished in a fold of her skirt, which the warriors had somehow overlooked in their search for our weapons, and extended the antique coin toward the chief.

"They offered this as proof, *ta-ka*."

The chief went silent. As he turned the coin over in his palm, the dancing-woman tattoo on his forehead seemed to flinch.

"Where you find this? Long time I have this silver. Then I lose."

Behind us, the flooring creaked as Wild Eye shifted position.

"Someone must have taken it from you to the Chinese trader in Attapeu."

"I don't believe my village has thief."

"Who among your people travels to Attapeu?"

Kanam paused, as if considering whether he should identify the warriors by name, especially with Wild Eye within earshot.

"Only my best men."

"Maybe some of these men had a plan you didn't know about, *ta-ka*. The trader gave the coin to an associate in Pakxe, who mailed it from Thailand to me in America. I was told it's a sign that *ama* is alive."

Kanam went silent, as if trying to process this information.

"No way," he finally said.

"I can get the ransom money for you," Linda said urgently. "Just not as much as the Chinese asked. And it will take a little time."

"Keep this money, cousin," said Kanam, handing her back the coin. "It is yours."

"Then what do you want?"

"Nothing."

"Nothing?" she asked, incredulous. "Everyone wants money."

"Nothing help you now. *Ta-ka* Curtis, he dead."

The chief stared past us at Wild Eye, and it suddenly felt hot and oppressive inside the longhouse, as if the air had been sucked from the space. Linda tried to stifle a sob.

"Yesterday hornbill fly to sun," Kanam said softly. "So bad thing come today. Spirit never lie."

"How?" Linda asked. "When?"

"Malaria," Kanam said apologetically. "Almost two years. Spirits very angry. Malaria also kill two more Monui at same time."

"But I was told my father was alive. That I could bring him to America."

"Chinese always lie."

"Somebody else lied to the trader. Somebody from Krnoon Blo Mat."

"Many bad people in Attapeu, not my village," Kanam said defensively. "They lie for money. They cheat Monui. I do not lie. *Ta-ka* Curtis dead. So sorry, cousin."

It was too late. There would be no reunion, no rescue, no redemption. No more John Man. No one asking how an American MIA could have had survived thirty years in a remote corner of Laos. No one asking why he was forgotten.

The tears pooling in Linda's eyes slid down her cheeks in rivulets, but she did not break down. Perhaps it was the shock of disbelief, or some steely inner strength. Perhaps she had already mourned enough. Perhaps the emotion would come later, prompted by some unspoken nightmare while she slept, as it had that night in the hut outside Wat Pa Nanachat forest monastery. I resisted the urge to console her as I had then, not knowing how Kanam would react. He didn't need to know we had become lovers. Not when he had been so blunt about considering his cousin an ideal Katu bride.

"Did he suffer, my father?"

"He die quick. One day. *Chet loq*. Good death."

A good death. There were those words again. But out here there'd be no paperwork to chase, no consular officials or police inspectors or medical examiners to interview. In these unforgiving mountains, people lived and then they died. No questions asked. Linda had walked away from a promising career and faked her death to find her father. And someone had faked her father's mysterious life to try to get away with a fortune in ransom money from her insurance policy. It was about as sleazy a scam as could be imagined, preying on a family tragedy. And despite Kanam's protestations, it seemed as if the key culprit, or culprits, in this swindle hailed from this very village. And now we had materialized without warning, upsetting whatever rip-off was planned and, worse, casting suspicion on the warriors' fealty to their chief. Linda may have returned to her ancestral village, but we would make few friends.

Kanam uncoiled himself into a stance. We rose as well. Behind Kanam, shadows flitted off the longhouse's center pole. Amid the carvings of jungle beasts was a shield that held an upturned, V-shaped lightning bolt. It didn't look like Katu handiwork, but rather a sort of military insignia, perhaps Curtis's old outfit. Then it hit me: this must have been the American's former dwelling.

"I keep your gun," Kanam said coolly. "Also the medicine you bring. Now Drak and I go to *gual*. We talk to elder. So many strangers come to Krnoon Blo Mat. Now you must stay in village. Later today I take you to see grave of Curtis. I miss him, my teacher. No one to speak English after he die."

Kanam and Wild Eye—his henchman, Drak—left us outside the longhouse. I watched as the strapping warriors strode away, Drak walking slightly behind Kanam as if in deference. It wasn't difficult to imagine Kanam's fierce-looking enforcer intimidating the townfolk of Attapeu. And now it seemed that Drak was more than just the *ta-ka*'s willing bulldog: he had the means and enough ambition and malice to cook up his own MIA con. His motives? An underling's usual desires, probably: greed, envy, lust for power, the desire to impress a woman.

Linda wiped away her tears and exhaled, as if surfacing after a deep dive. Across the clearing, some children had caught a small, emerald-green snake and were using it to tease a young man cowering beneath a nearby hut. One of the village's middle-aged, half-naked crones stalked up and snatched away the writhing serpent.

"Karboch!" she shouted at the children. A pit viper brought bad luck.

As they ran off, the man crawled from his muddy refuge, whimpering like a Bangkok pariah dog. He didn't have any tattoos, either, but that wasn't the first thing I noticed about his disheveled appearance. Tears poured from his crazed blue eyes, washing away the filth streaking his ghostly cheeks. The gibbering man was albino. The withered woman snapped the snake against a house post, exploding its skull, then placed the carcass by the hut's doorway. Then she hugged the terrified man, cooed in his ear, and brought him to see us. I thought I heard Linda catch her breath as the woman spoke to us.

"My auntie Bruang," she announced, then wrapped her arms around the smiling, wrinkled woman and the strange, albino man-child, who burst out laughing. "And she says this is my younger brother, Kase. He was born after I left."

Linda returned the old woman's smile.

"Finally some good news," she added. "I still have family."

Aunt Bruang led us into the hut, which backed up against the village stockade. Cracks of light pierced the poorly gathered thatch roof. Her pots and jars were dark and worn with age, and no weapons or fresh game hung from the rafters. She set about cleaning the snake on the bamboo floor, cutting it lengthwise and then dumping the guts through the floor slats. Kase peered through the cracks, babbling to the pigs and chickens squabbling over the offal. As Bruang worked, her words fell like the steady patter of rain.

Few people in the village were still alive who remembered when Curtis had come from the sky, she recounted while Linda translated. It was a very long time ago, when there was fighting throughout the mountains. The village hid Curtis from the Vietnamese and the Lao soldiers, but the chief could not bear to grant the flying man his freedom. The American had too much *ae,* or magic power: Curtis knew how to farm, how to hunt, how to read the weather. He was like a gemstone; the *ta-ka* would never part with such a treasure. At first, Curtis repeatedly tried to escape. But after several rainy seasons he understood he could never leave the village. The mountains were like a prison. His country had given up looking for him by then. He would have to put away his old life, forget his own people. His destiny lay with the Katu. He married Bruang's older sister, Yayong; both girls were daughters of the *ta-ka*. Four buffalo died at the sacrificial *chanur* pole during the great celebration. Curtis gave wise counsel to his father-in-law and worked the family's fields.

But the *ta-ka*'s son, the shaman Bounliep, constantly worried that the Communist Lao Loum of the lowlands would seek revenge on the neutral Katu after the war, especially the headman's family. Because of Curtis, Bounliep feared, they would be seen as collaborators and sent to seminar camp—or worse. He could talk of little else to Bruang and Yayong. Bounliep urged them to escape as well, but the chief was very sick. The dutiful daughters would not abandon their father. A foreigner like Curtis could never escape to Thailand, at least a week's journey on foot, without being discovered. Anyone captured with him would probably be executed as well. Besides, he was bound to Yayong; if she stayed, he would, too. Promising to send word to the family once he was settled, Bounliep had fled west with his young niece, Lin. The Thai would be less likely to refuse a Lao Theung refugee with a young child, he reasoned. They never heard from Bounliep again.

Aunt Bruang put a small clay teapot of water on the hearth to boil for tea. Then she began plaiting strips of bamboo to make a bird trap—there was always a chore to do—while she resumed her story.

After the war, the Lao Loum did not come to arrest the *ta-ka* or his family. But the mountains stopped providing the village with the animals and fish they had supplied for the ancestors. Life became even harder. Many buffalo fell beneath the blade to placate the *dyaang* spirits. For years, the family believed that Bounliep and Lin had died making their escape. There were scattered rumors, however, that the two had survived and made it down the mountains and across the Mekong to Thailand. There were even claims they had somehow settled in America. Curtis and Yayong mourned their missing daughter. Yayong became pregnant again, but had died giving birth to the magic, white child whom Curtis had dubbed Kase, a name that meant "Moon."

Chet biik. Yayong had died a bad death. The Katu elders believed the spirits did not want the boy to have a mother; her sudden passing meant the village became taboo. Yayong had been hurriedly buried in an unmarked grave far from the settlement. The family abandoned their longhouse for a month-long *dieng* period and lived in the jungle. When they moved back to the village, Curtis even accompanied the warriors in a successful blood hunt against a Jeh settlement. The *dyaang* were pleased; that year the harvest fed everyone. Curtis placed Kase in the care of Bruang, who never married. He loved the boy as deeply as he had loved his late wife and his lost daughter. When the headman finally passed away, the elders chose the stranger from the sky to succeed him as *ta-ka,* considered the cleverest person in the village. Curtis never took another wife.

The teapot was steaming now, but Bruang was caught up in her tale.

Kase had barely started walking when the *dyaang* seemed to steal his soul. When the boy spoke, it was in grunts and screams or a strange tongue that no one, not even his father, understood. Kase would sit for hours on his haunches, lost in a trance, and then suddenly begin dancing with a pig, or just as quickly attack a warrior with his bare hands. In most cases, the Katu dug a small hole and buried alive anyone who had serious mental problems; it was their custom to prevent a deranged person from destroying the village by fire or to avoid further angering the *dyaang*. But Curtis had rejected such action. The boy's striking pigmentation was evidence of special gifts, he had argued. Kase saw and spoke to a world of spirits.

The people had listened to Curtis, Bruang told her niece. The animals and fish slowly returned to the forests and rivers where the Katu hunted. *Ta-ka* Curtis had good *ae,* although some men in the village, such as Kanam's father, were jealous of his wisdom and physical strength. They worried that he might take one of their women for his new wife. But Krnoon Blo Mat prospered under Curtis. The tigers killed no one in the forest. No children were abducted by other villages. It was all here, Bruang said, contained in the pale leaves that Curtis had covered with strange symbols. She rummaged in the sleeping area, where Kase pulled back a bamboo mat and proudly produced a moleskin-covered notebook. Curtis had kept a journal.

But since Curtis's sudden death two years ago, Bruang continued, the village had struggled. There was withering drought, followed by heavy rains. Kanam became the new *ta-ka,* but under his leadership the village fought with other tribes, even other Monui clans. Now the Lao Loum and their army threatened to remove their people from the Long Mountains forever. Kanam was brave, Bruang admitted. He had killed his first leopard when just twelve years old. But he was too hotheaded to be a good leader.

"Kah ae," the old woman concluded. Kanam had no magic.

Bruang finally rose to prepare the tea. As she crouched by the fire, a shadow filled the threshold of the hut.

"How's it going?" Kanam asked. "Now we see Curtis."

He spoke brusquely to Bruang, who bowed and placed the cooking pot on a stone to cool. Our tea, as well as Curtis's diary, would have to wait. Kanam led us north from Krnoon Blo Mat along a well-worn path, walking briskly in the wet afternoon heat through more stands of banana and papaya. There was a cry, then Kase skipped up the path to join us. He shyly took Linda's hand and led the way. Soon elephant grass enveloped the trail, then forest, and we walked in the shade of ancient trees.

"Our world has three layers," Kanam told me. "The earth, for Monui. The sky, for *dyaang*. And *arde,* for dead souls."

"And what for *ta-ka* Curtis?"

"Good death, good spirit."

"Uncle would talk of this," Linda said. "First, you need a coffin tree."

"Yes, the *lieng sarieng*. We cut tree in two pieces, top and bottom, dig it out like boat. Then the *taram* is finished. We keep it in big cave. When someone die, we use this tree coffin."

"For bad death, too?"

"For *chet biik*? No coffin tree. Only bamboo blanket. When someone die from murder, from tiger, from having baby, bad spirit are very close. You see sign of bad spirit: cobra, peacock egg on path, rooster sing at night. You must take body far away and bury quick. No *taram* for bad death. No funeral. In this way, bad spirit cannot find village."

Kanam stepped from the main trail to a path that descended through old-growth forest. In the hidden valley below I heard the rush of falling water and the chattering of monkeys. By a grove of towering teak trees the lower canopy thinned, revealing a collection of small, raised huts that were well built and as lovingly decorated as the longhouses of Krnoon Blo Mat. The tombs, or *pin,* had thatched roofs but no siding; inside each shelter lay dozens of dark, hand-carved coffins. This was the village of the Katu dead.

"For good death we have good funeral," Kanam said. "For *ta-ka* Curtis we have big party. Many buffalo die. We drink much *tavaak*. Then we come to forest."

"Please show me my family's tomb."

"Curtis not here. Come."

We followed Kanam a few dozen yards beyond the necropolis to a deep, open grave flanked by stands of torch ginger. At the bottom of the pit lay a thick rosewood log, darkened even further by exposure to the weather. A rusting machete, a clay jug, and an old crossbow lay atop the massive lid of the tree coffin.

"*Ta-ka* Curtis."

Linda squatted beside the edge of the grave. Kase whimpered and did the same.

"Why haven't you buried his *taram*?" I asked. "Or built a shelter for it?"

"First his soul must go home—protect Kase, protect Bruang. This the Monui way. Coffin stay like this way in ground two, three years. Then we make new funeral. We make better *taram*. Then coffin go to *pin*."

"I want that for my father."

"You come home, cousin. Very good. So now spirit of Curtis can stay with *dyaang* in mountains. I give your family two buffalo for his funeral."

"We are so poor and you are so kind, *ta-ka*. Thank you."

"No problem, cousin."

Linda removed her trademark earrings, then knelt and dropped them onto the casket. Kase pulled at his ears as well, then laughed softly. Linda began chanting, while I walked back to the open-sided houses of the dead. Kanam was smarter than I had presumed. He had ideas. Maybe he just wanted to put on a big, generous show for the village. Or maybe he also wanted to impress Linda. He could afford to give up two buffalo. What could I, her broke-dick American friend, provide?

While Linda continued to pray, Kanam joined me by the cluster of tombs.

"You like?"

"It is a good place to die."

"Spirit like this land."

"I can understand why."

"Lao Loum also like to have Monui land. But not to farm or to hunt or to fish. They only want to push away Monui and cut the big tree."

"But the *dyaang* would be very angry."

"You know Monui good."

"I don't think I will ever completely understand."

"It is good we make Lao Loum our prisoner?"

"No. I think if you hurt them it will only anger the Lao government. They will still come here and force you to move."

"Drak tells me same thing. You both wrong. When we kill them, it scare many more Lao Loum. They stay away."

"Their deaths will hurt your people even more."

"Me *ta-ka,*" he said sharply. "*Dyaang* tell me do this."

"If you kill those prisoners, not even the *dyaang* can keep your village safe."

"We very safe, Sebastian," he said, throwing an arm around my shoulders and smiling slyly. "Now we have two *farang*. Maybe we keep you for ransom. Or maybe we keep you forever."

Then he laughed. I don't remember much about the hike back to Krnoon Blo Mat. Kase sidled up to me on the trail, humming tunelessly. While Linda and Kanam spoke in Katuic about funeral arrangements, I took in the deep forest, the meager fields, and the mountains that unfurled as far as I could see. Kase whistled and almost immediately a curious oriole swooped overhead to investigate the flute-like call. The boy smiled; at least the birds understood him.

"Don't try to escape," Kanam had told me. "You have nowhere to go. We treat you like guest. No cage like Lao Loum. You stay in *gual* with Monui men. Now you friend. Someday maybe you become *taka*. Just like Curtis."

It sounded like a living death. Dark clouds rumbled with the promise of rain as we returned to the village. Smoke from cooking fires seeped through the thatched roofs, casting the village in a pall. Kanam bade Linda good day, with a pledge that tomorrow he would select a pair of buffalo for slaughter. When the headman had disappeared into his longhouse, I walked Linda to Aunt Bruang's hut. Several Katu men were in the central plaza, adding wooden wings to the *chanur* killing post. Kase ran over and began dancing happily around the wooden column. Linda, however, looked apprehensive.

"They're preparing for a sacrifice," she said. "Maybe human. You and Honeyman have to leave."

"How? Where? Kanam calls us his guests, but we're just prisoners under house arrest."

"I'll talk to him."

"He doesn't seem to listen to anyone. Those two Lao Loum in the cage are as good as dead."

"And if you and Honeyman stay, you'll be dead, too. The next time there's a blood hunt, the village may take you instead. The blood of another hill tribe, or even a Lao Loum, will do. But my people consider the blood of a foreigner to be best of all."

Kanam and his warriors would feed us and shelter us. And then one day the *dyaang* would whisper their wishes to the shaman and the headman would have us butchered at the stake, just like a buffalo.

"If we leave, Linda, what will happen to you?"

She brushed the hair from her eyes and gave me that look I'd seen in Bangkok.

"What do I have to go back to, Sebastian? No job. No reputation."

"We could go back together."

She regarded Kase, still swaying by the *chanur,* chattering to no one.

"And what about my aunt? And my brother?"

"They could come with us."

"It would never work. You saw my Uncle Bounliep in Providence. You know how horrible it is for him away from these mountains. It would be the same for Bruang and Kase."

"So you plan to stay."

"Kanam will do me a favor."

"What are you prepared to do?"

"Whatever I decide will be my choice," she said, slightly agitated. "And it will be what is best for my family, not just for me."

"This is a dangerous game, Linda. Can't I get you to change your mind?"

"Why can't I convince you to take Honeyman and leave? It is your only chance."

"We're not going yet, Linda."

"I can't thank you or Honeyman enough for coming here with me. But this isn't your place anymore."

"It looks like it's my place for now. So we'll be seeing a lot of each other."

Hidden thunder cracked and I turned and left Linda, walking through the first, sharp raindrops to the communal house.

"Look what the Katu dragged in."

It was Honeyman, conscious and back to his caustic old self. He sat propped against the longhouse's thick, carved center pole. Above us, all manner of weapons, hunting tools, ceremonial masks, and animal skulls hung from the smoke-darkened beams and rafters of the *gual*'s vaulted roof. Quivers of arrows and mountain axes, steel-pointed spears and hand-woven fishnets, carved wooden likenesses of human and monkey faces, the dried heads of buffalo and strange, fang-toothed deer. It was as if a Stone Age tribe had built an Elks Club or an American Legion post.

"Feeling better, Honeyman?"

"I've felt worse, kid. But not for decades."

"Getting shot will do that to you."

"And by a damn crossbow. That's a first. They tip their arrows with some sort of drug like curare."

In the shadows of the room, several tribesmen passed around a jar of rice wine. The boy we'd encountered on the Xe Kaman lay on the bamboo slats while an old man tattooed his back with a soot-blackened spike and a wooden mallet. Someone brought us a large banana leaf that held clumps of nutty mountain rice and clawlike bananas.

"Mighty hospitable folks," said Honeyman, "once you get past the initial ass-kicking."

"They're treating us like veal calves, Honeyman. We're no better off than those Lao surveyors rotting out there in the cage."

"But we are, kid. We're not *in* the damn cage."

"We met the chief, Kanam. He won't let us leave the village."

"How can you tell?"

"He speaks some English. A bit headstrong and erratic, but Kanam's no dummy. And he told me the Katu can keep us here forever—just like they did with Linda's father."

I thought Honeyman was going to choke on the food.

"So he *is* here. When can we meet him?"

"*Was* here. His name was Curtis. He died two years ago. Malaria."

"Shit. The poor bastard almost held out long enough."

"Almost. Linda and I saw his old house, and his grave."

"You sure about that?"

"I think I found his old outfit's insignia, carved into a support post inside the house. Kanam lives there now."

"What did it look like?" Honeyman asked eagerly.

"Like a shield. And inside the shield was a V-shaped lightning bolt."

"A Thunderbolt," he replied. "The Fifty-sixth Special Operations Wing."

"So he was a pilot."

"The Thunderbolts were based out of Nahkon Phanom. That's in Isan, right along the Mekong, a few hours north of Ubon. They called in airstrikes all up and down the Trail. Very ballsy stuff. But they were sitting ducks in those little prop planes. I bet this Curtis was a forward air controller. I looked for a few downed FACs in my time. Maybe even him."

I told Honeyman what Bruang and Kanam had described about the long, strange life of *ta-ka* Curtis. The repeated escape attempts. The eventual marriage to the chief's daughter, Yayong. Her unexpected death in childbirth with Linda's albino younger brother, Kase. Curtis's own reign as village headman. And finally, his sudden death and repose in the village of tree coffins. When I finished, Honeyman remained silent for a several minutes while the rain mashed against the thatched roof and the old men drank and laughed. In the far shadows, Drak instructed the young bachelors in the art of woodworking, all the while watching us.

"I feel for Curtis," Honeyman mused. "Alone. Forgotten. No chance of rescue. How'd he keep himself going for all those years? He made the best of it. And we will, too. When it's time, we'll make our move."

"And what's that move going to be?"

"I haven't gotten that far yet. But we sure as shit won't wait thirty years—or even thirty days. What about Linda? How's she handling all the news?"

"It's going to be a problem. She wants to stay with her aunt and her brother."

"When the time comes, she goes with us."

"She won't leave. There's some unfinished village business I haven't quite figured out. And she wants to give her father a proper burial, so his soul is at ease."

"You told me you saw his grave."

"I saw the first grave. They need to transfer his remains to another tree coffin, then store Curtis in the family tomb."

"Think it'll be a big funeral?"

"Curtis used to be chief, believe it or not. Kanam, the new headman, is coughing up two buffalo for the sacrifice."

"Chief?" Honeyman asked. "I guess Curtis did make the best of it."

"His funeral will probably happen soon. Curtis hadn't attacked any other villages in years, either. It was just a 'John Man' rumor floating around the Bolaven Plateau. The loose cannon is Kanam, the new chief, who's ordering all the raids. I think he's going to whack those Lao prisoners soon, probably close to the funeral. I'm also picking up on some tension between Kanam and his right-hand man, Drak—the big lout who captured us. I think Drak was behind the scheme to ransom Curtis. The Mayrena coin belonged to Kanam. But it seems likely that Drak stole it, perhaps with the help of someone with access to Kanam's house, and brought it to the Chinese trader in Attapeu. Drak would have acted as the go-between on any deal for Linda's father. With Curtis dead, the whole plan was a lie, of course."

Honeyman considered all this.

"Take a look around this longhouse, Sebastian. These mountain people don't do anything before drinking a shitload of rice wine. It's just like those *lao-lao* sessions with the Jeh, only the moonshine here will probably taste even nastier. So we watch, and we wait. We'll make our move soon—maybe during this funeral for Curtis."

Those rites couldn't come fast enough. I felt a slight fever; I hoped it wasn't malaria. At Drak's insistence, the old men proffered us the jug of *tavaak*. There was nothing to do but smile and sip the foul brew and hope that it somehow also inoculated us against the bad spirits that brought on typhus, cholera, dysentery, tuberculosis, and parasitic infections. As the rains raked the village, two warriors stood and performed a drunken dance relating the capture of the Lao surveyors. Then Drak and the newly tattooed boy did a jig to celebrate our abduction. An old man staggered to his feet, pulled a darkened tiger skull from the wall, and mimed his epic, ancient hunt.

Honeyman pointed to his pack and looked at Drak expectantly. The dour warrior nodded and Honeyman searched an outside pocket of the rucksack, produced his harmonica, and began blowing another old Hank Williams tune, "Your Cheatin' Heart." Everyone hooted and shouted in delight, even Drak. I stumbled to the *gual*'s doorway and gazed outside. Kase was still there in the clearing, dancing near the prisoners' cage, oblivious to the downpour. More *tavaak,* until the moonshine ran out. Drak then pulled the bottle of scotch from his quiver; we passed the Black Label around until it, too, was gone. By then the fire had faded but the eyes of the dead animals gazing down on us burned with malice and the wooden masks twisted with deathly scowls. Sometime after midnight, when the rain had stopped and the frogs had emerged to sing, I found myself shivering. Not a good sign, the chills. A rooster crowed from beyond Bruang's hut. Kanam had told me, but I couldn't remember what bad news it foretold.

Fifteen

Wake up, ass head!"

I could see only black teeth and bloodshot eyes. Kanam had me pinned to the floor of the longhouse, his knees sinking into my ribs, as he leaned in to hiss his wake-up call. Then he backed off, awakened Honeyman with a kick to the side, and marched us both outside into the cool, fog-bound dawn. A cluster of wailing villagers surrounded the cage near the sacrificial stake. I broke into a run when I saw Linda and Aunt Bruang, now crying hysterically. The Lao prisoners were no longer trapped in their fetid enclosure. Instead, Kase sat propped against the back of the cell, unmoving, his head lolling sideways at an unnatural angle. I stuck a hand through the bars: the boy's body felt cold and stiff, and his arresting blue eyes held the horrible realization of his own death. I walked to Linda, who was shivering with shock, and wrapped an arm around her shoulders.

"I should have gone looking for him last night," she said softly. "Poor Kase."

"You can't blame yourself."

"He shouldn't have been out there in the storm."

"Even your aunt couldn't control him."

"But this . . . He was harmless. He had the mind of a child. Why?"

Honeyman ducked inside the muddy cage to examine Kase's body.

"He's probably been dead for five or six hours. This was quick. He didn't suffer long."

"Where did the Lao go?" I asked.

"Drak leave now," Kanam interjected. "He take five fast warriors to Xe Kaman River. But maybe too late."

"What if the Lao Loum head north?" Honeyman asked.

"Then we catch them and they wish they never leave Attapeu." Kanam glowered. "Same for you."

"Sebastian and Honeyman had nothing to do with this," Linda said.

"Maybe your American friends tell Lao Loum go for help," Kanam answered.

"And not try to escape ourselves?" Honeyman asked. "You can see for yourself what happened here, Kanam. The Lao tricked this poor boy into opening the cage, and then they strangled him and escaped."

"We were sleeping, Kanam," I said. "Ask Drak. Ask anyone in the *gual*."

"Bad death," Kanam muttered. "Very bad death. *Chet biik*."

Chet biik. I'd heard those words before. A bad death. A half-dozen hungover tribesmen emerged from the longhouse, brandishing a small armory of crossbows, spears, and machetes. Kanam's wife, Rudu, and several boys rubbed liniment on the bared arms and legs of Drak and the warriors to ward off evil spirits while the shaman chanted a hurried blessing. To the encouragement of the enraged villagers, Drak and his surly posse then trotted out of the stockade gate in hot pursuit. With their departure, Kanam spoke forcefully in Katuic to Linda and her aunt and then disappeared into the *gual* with the village elders.

"No villagers will touch Kase now," Linda said flatly. "Not when someone has been murdered. It is a bad death."

"No funeral?" Honeyman asked.

"We believe every person has two souls—one good and one bad," she said. "How you die determines how your soul survives. A good death from natural causes brings a good spirit who watches over your family, protecting them from the dangers of the forest. A bad death from violence or illness or childbirth brings a bad spirit. This must be avoided, at all cost."

Aunt Bruang began to wail again. Linda scolded the onlookers, and they slowly drifted away.

"There won't be a proper funeral," Linda said, her voice barely above a whisper. "We have to bury Kase in the forest as soon as possible. Otherwise the people here believe his bad spirit will wander and make more trouble for the village."

"Will these folks harass you and your aunt?" Honeyman asked.

"Probably," I said. "Their lives are governed by anxiety and fear. Fear of bad spirits, bad omens, a bad death."

Linda spoke briefly with Bruang. Still weeping, the old woman trudged to her hut. We watched her departure in silence. The woman had raised Kase from infancy; he might as well have been her own son. I wondered if the Lao Loum had headed south and made it to the river. If they managed to escape the mountains, would they report our presence to the Attapeu authorities? And what really worried me: would Kanam try to scapegoat Honeyman and me for their escape and Kase's death?

"The village expects the same thing will happen as when my mother died," Linda finally said. "The family must go into *dieng* for one month. During this time it is forbidden for us to stay in Bruang's house. We must go and live in the jungle."

"During this monsoon season?" I protested. "That's suicide."

"It is our way," Linda replied. "It would be suicide to try and stay in the village. The elders would never allow it. The *dyaang* are too powerful."

"Your aunt won't survive," Honeyman said. "Not through the rainy season."

"She did this once before, after the death of my mother. And this time, I will be here to help her."

"How can you help?" I asked. "You're a banker."

"I was once a banker, Sebastian. But I will always be Monui."

Bruang returned and unfurled a thin floor mat she had brought from her hut. Honeyman and I extricated Kase from the cage and laid out his slight, ghostly body on the plaited bamboo surface. Bruang fell upon the dead boy, covering his pale face and shock of chalk-white hair with kisses. A few villagers stood on the periphery and hurled epithets, presumably at the mourning women or gathering evil spirits. Several scowling elders came out of the *gual* to regard the scene.

"We must hurry," Linda said. "Bad spirits will not be far away."

She hugged her aunt while we rolled the matting around Kase. Then we tied his bundled corpse to the sturdy length of bamboo Linda and I had used to carry Honeyman.

"Your wound, Honeyman. Can you handle this?"

"Don't worry about me, Linda. Take care of your aunt."

I hoisted the front end of the litter, with Honeyman balancing the pole on his good, right shoulder, and we followed the women out of the village. We'd be all right walking along the mountain path; Kase couldn't have weighed more than one hundred pounds.

"You look like crap, kid," Honeyman said, panting.

"Fever, then chills last night," I answered. "But it seems to have broken today."

"Let's hope there's no reoccurrence."

"And if there is?"

"Then you pray like hell it ain't falciparum malaria. Out here, that's a serious problem."

As we walked, I helped Honeyman get his bearings: we were heading north on the same route I'd taken yesterday with Linda and Kanam. If the Lao Loum chose this path for their escape, they would only travel deeper into the mountains—a guaranteed death sentence. To the east, the sun had begun to burn through the mist. And far below, from the hidden valley, came the sound of rushing water. Honeyman studied the terrain.

"That river below us flows south," he said. "It's gotta feed into the Xe Kaman at some point."

"It doesn't sound too navigable."

"In a boat, no."

"Like there's any other way."

"You can swim, can't you?"

"Not all the way back to Attapeu."

"We'd find a canoe, or a log," Honeyman said. "With any luck our boat's still hidden below the falls."

"Whatever floats had better hold four people."

"Linda and her aunt?"

"She won't leave without the old woman."

"The aunt ain't gonna make it. I hate to say it."

"Bruang's all the family's she got now, Sam."

"Linda may have a very tough choice to make."

"I don't think it'll be a hard decision. She's already made up her mind. She's staying."

We followed the women off the trail and down a slope through a grove of ancient trees; we had returned to the graveyard of good deaths. Soon Linda and Bruang would have to fend for themselves in this forest—and we would be at Kanam's mercy during their banishment. Bruang led the way to the open grave that held Curtis's coffin. She gestured for us to lay down Kase atop his father's casket.

"He was a good son," Linda said. "The only evil belongs to the people who killed Kase. And who murdered my father."

"Kanam said Curtis died of malaria."

"It's a lie. From the symptoms my aunt describes, my father didn't die of malaria. He was poisoned."

"How?" I asked.

"There are many poisons, and many ways. But Bruang has seen many people die of malaria. My father did not die like those people."

"So who do you suspect?" Honeyman asked.

"You know all about motives, Sebastian," Linda said. "You're a detective. *Qui bono*? Who stood to benefit if the *ta-ka* died? If his family went into *dieng*? If his survivors had to sacrifice all their animals, abandon their longhouse, let their fields go untended?"

"The same person who took his house and his position as *ta-ka*—Kanam."

"My father feared the same. It's here, in his diary. I read most of it last night. He worried about many things."

She opened the weathered notebook and flipped to a page she had dog-eared.

"He made the first entries with a ballpoint pen. When that was used up, it looks like he wrote with indigo ink and a quill pen. He was a resourceful man, my father. But after the first year, 1968, he stopped giving the exact dates for his entries.

"Here's an entry, sometime after 1975. 'Spotted a large commercial airliner today, unknown model—four engines, but profile is wider than B-52—bearing ENE, altitude at least thirty thousand feet. If they bothered to look out the windows, what would those passengers make of Laos? Would they even see this village? Or wonder about its people, what sort of lives they lead? The war must be over. The larger world forgets, and moves on. No one remembers the dead or the missing but their families. Eileen would have broken off our engagement and married someone else by now. At least I hope so. Every now and then, maybe she still wonders about me. Maybe not. But my parents: their eldest son, MIA in Laos for more than a decade. Will they ever have closure? Have they already passed away, never knowing the truth? I can comprehend that pain and emptiness. I feel the same agony over Lin. Did she and Bounliep get away from here? How far? Attapeu? Pakxe? Maybe even Thailand? Did they make it at all? Wherever they are, I only hope my daughter is safe—and happy. I never wanted to let her go.' "

Linda halted for a moment to gather her emotions. She flipped through the pages and then continued.

" 'It has taken years, but I am finally at peace in this lonely place. Kase is a great comfort. His total innocence, his perpetual delight—it is difficult to complain when he is so happy about everything. Bruang is a fine woman who honors her sister in her every action. I would marry her, but she fears Yayong's spirit would not approve. In loving Kase, however, she believes she makes her sister's spirit happy. This is enough. I must accept the will of the *dyaang*. Bruang and Kase depend on me. I cannot abandon them. The village still looks to me for guidance. I will never be a despot like the king of Sedang. That is why I carry Mayrena's coin with me—a wedding gift from my father-in-law and a reminder of an ego run amok. There are some promising young men here. The brightest is Kanam, a cousin to Bruang. My Lin would be about his age. The spirits called upon his father to become shaman after Bounliep left with Lin. I am teaching English to Kanam. He is a quick study and an excellent hunter, of course. Kanam asks many questions of the world beyond the mountains, questions I can no longer answer with certainty. Much of the world I came from must no longer exist.' "

She turned several more pages.

"Here are my father's final entries, written just before his death. 'Another shouting match this evening after supper with Kanam. I have tried to tell him our crop failures are caused by drought—not from angering the *dyaang*. There are forces beyond these mountains—weather patterns, international politics, hydropower schemes—that we cannot control. He takes his father's side in these arguments. The shaman's solution is always another sacrifice. Chickens, pigs, buffalo—or worse. I will never sanction another blood hunt. The innocents always suffer the most. Kanam has told me all outsiders deserve their fate. He believes the *dyaang* have chosen the Katu as judge, jury, and executioner. He has convinced many other villagers here as well. It is a dark, angry force, built on fear. I have misjudged his character. As *ta-ka,* I now stand in his way. If something terrible happens to me, what then becomes of Kase and Bruang?'

"'Very bad stomach this A.M.—fatigue and neuropathy. Maybe from fever, maybe from Kanam's food. Cassava? Cyanide? High pulse rate. Dizzy. Very tired. Must rally. Kase—' "

Linda closed the journal. Honeyman looked shaken.

"What happens now?" he asked.

"When someone is killed by an outsider, like Kase, my people believe that the *dyaang* demand a blood hunt," Linda explained. "Failure to avenge such a murder would bring dishonor. First we hold a feast with a sacrifice, and then the village is taboo for a day. No one can enter. No one can leave. Then the warriors set out to spill blood."

Krnoon Blo Mat was unraveling. We wouldn't have to watch, or wait, very long to make our escape. Through her tears, Bruang launched into a bitter tirade.

"She says that Kanam is a bad seed, that jealousy gave him a black heart," Linda related. "She says Kanam poisoned Curtis to get power. Kanam might even have released the Lao Loum surveyors last night and then killed Kase—it would force us into *dieng* and give him a convenient excuse for a blood hunt. Kanam wants to make war on everyone. He has big problems with Rudu, his wife. Some of the warriors have doubts about his leadership. Many of the elders are frightened for the village. The Lao are eating the forest. The animals have disappeared. Now we kill our own people. We have lost our way. Our world is ending."

"Chet biik," Aunt Bruang concluded.

There would be only more bad death.

Late that afternoon, a grim-faced Drak returned to Krnoon Blo Mat with the war party. The Lao Loum had fled southward toward the waterfall, not into the mountains, and escaped down the Xe Kaman, presumably in their outboard-equipped boat, the one we'd seen the Katu boy paddling on the river as we approached the landing below the cascade. The Katu had tracked the surveyors to the water's edge, but couldn't keep up their pursuit: the Lao had also taken the tribe's red canoe as they retreated. Honeyman caught my gaze and nodded: the warriors had not found our concealed boat. We still had a means of escape, if we could ever sneak away from the village.

Drak and his men had returned to participate in the rituals that colored the impending blood hunt. Preparations were already apparent. On our return from the grove of the tree coffins, we encountered wooden statues of grotesque, gargoylelike figures set down in the path to deter evil spirits. Felled saplings also lay across the trail and barred the village gates—a warning to outsiders to avoid the taboo settlement.

Kanam met us on the village plaza, reeking of rice wine. Behind him, several old men stood unsteadily. They, too, had been drinking.

"You take long time," Kanam said. "Maybe you bring bad spirit from forest."

"The bad spirits don't belong with Kase," Linda replied. "He had the mark of purity."

"You leave mountains long time, cousin. You forget our way."

"I have not strayed, *ta-ka*. Uncle Bounliep taught me well."

"Many things have changed since Bounliep go away," Kanam retorted. "Big funeral for Curtis must wait. Kase die, so now we have blood hunt to make spirit happy."

"How long must I wait to bury my father?"

"*Dyaang* tell us," said Kanam.

"Before or after Bruang and I go to the forest and make *dieng* for Kase?"

"For you, cousin, maybe no *dieng* in forest."

"But that has always been our way."

"Shaman speaks of new way."

"What do the *dyaang* tell your father?"

Kanam smiled.

"They tell him evil spirit cannot enter house of *ta-ka*. They tell him you can make *dieng* in this house, not in forest."

"In your longhouse."

"Yes, now I am *ta-ka*. And Bruang can stay, of course."

"And what does your wife say of this plan?"

"Rudu has no say. *Dyaang* do not speak to her."

Linda glanced at her aunt.

"Many things have changed, *ta-ka*. This is all very new. You must give me a little time to decide."

"I ask you today," Kanam said firmly. "I do not ask you tomorrow."

One of the elders from the *gual* handed Honeyman the clay pot and nodded. Drink. We sipped, then passed back the *tavaak*. The boy we'd encountered on the river in the canoe appeared, carrying a furious black rooster by its feet, and delivered the bird to Kanam's father. Another elder produced a pair of python-skin drums, while several of the boy's friends brought over pots. In the shrill tumult that followed, the shaman pressed the squawking bird into the ground and, amid a flurry of feathers, cut off its right foot with a single stroke of a machete. While the one-legged bird shrieked and spun in the mud, the old man held up the amputated limb for inspection. The main spur lay between its remaining two claws. The villagers shouted approval of the augury: the ancestors had blessed the blood hunt. The shaman caressed the claw, then consulted Kanam. His son nodded.

"The *dyanng* have spoken," Kanam said. "We honor them tonight. Tomorrow, village is taboo. Then we march two days toward setting sun, toward Attapeu. On morning of third day, we shed blood."

"Whose blood, *ta-ka*?"

"Whoever we find, cousin."

The chief anticipated my question.

"You stay here in *gual,* you and Honeyman, your old soldier friend. No trick—or maybe you two also go make *dieng* in the forest. Or maybe you stay in cage—like Lao Loum."

Kanam grinned, then took the rooster's claw from his father and drew its talons down his bare, greased chest. Blood beaded in the raised welts.

"Remember, cousin: today. Not tomorrow."

"Then I have until dawn," Linda replied. "And there's one less cock to crow."

Kanam regarded her, livid about something unspoken. Then he dropped the rooster claw in the mud and walked with his father to the *chanur,* where several men were tying a buffalo to the blood-spattered post. Thunder began rattling beyond the mountains in the west. Beneath an ash-colored sky, the remaining villagers made their way from the fields to the killing ground. Many carried firewood, which they piled a short distance from the sacrificial pole.

"Correct me if I'm wrong," Honeyman asked Linda, "but was that Kanam's idea of a marriage proposal?"

"It was some sort of proposal," she answered. "He needs to save face."

"What's going on?"

"Drak's been having an affair with Rudu. Auntie says most of the village knows. It's been going on since the last dry season, but Kanam only caught them in the forest two days before we arrived. As *ta-ka* it is a big embarrassment for him. Now that Kanam has asked me to make *dieng* in his longhouse, he will want to marry me. We Monui consider a cousin the best spouse."

It didn't matter if the warring couples were six-figure Boston professionals or penniless hill tribers from the backwoods of Laos. Marital problems almost always came down to jealousy and sex.

"Got any choice in the matter?" Honeyman asked.

"Linda can string Kanam along," I said. "Believe me."

I earned a harsh look.

Kanam directed the warriors to attach a pair of large wooden arms to the pole at an upward angle. Betel-red carvings of hornbills and serpents covered the rising, winglike additions, giving the *chanur* the profile of a crucifix. I hoped the modifications weren't meant for us. The wind freshened but the rains held off. As darkness gathered, village elders lit the bonfires. The python-skin drums thumped, joined by jangling tambourines and soft wooden flutes. Then the musicians fell silent. Drak stepped into the center of the plaza, accompanied by Rudu. The warrior stared glumly at the ground, while his lover glared defiantly at the gathering crowd. Kanam joined the pair and began lecturing them in a loud, indignant tone.

"They have brought him great shame," Linda related. "Since they were little boys, Drak has been one of Kanam's closest friends. They hunted together, came of age together in the *gual.* Now he hopes Drak will be happy with Rudu—a wife who never bore him any children. Two buffalo is a high price to pay for such a woman. One buffalo to Kanam, for his suffering. And this second buffalo at the *chanur,* to be offered to the village."

Kanam suddenly struck Drak on the right temple, a jolting hook that buckled the warrior to his knees. Drak did not retaliate, but knelt there, torso sagging, head lolling. As divorces go, it was a hell of a lot quicker and cleaner than the nasty, prolonged legal wranglings back home, and infinitely more satisfying for the wronged party than a no-fault split. The cuckold had his very public revenge—and a pick of Drak's buffalo. Rudu sniffled, trying to stifle her humiliation, pulled her woozy lover to his feet, and led him into the shadows. There was nowhere else for the pair to go. The *gual* was out of the question. Her family hailed from another village. They would not accept her back anyway. But Kanam wasn't through. He then announced that the couple had committed an even graver crime.

"Drak stole something very valuable from me, with the help of Rudu," Kanam proclaimed in Katuic. "Something that once belonged to Curtis. He took it to Attapeu. He made a big lie. That town made him dream of big money. For what? Maybe Drak also wants power, to make himself *ta-ka.* But he is not so clever. I know of his cheating, his thieving. We Monui know what the punishment should be. His fate will be decided after the blood hunt. My friends, we have had many new problems. For now, let us try and make the *dyaang* happy."

"Will Drak have to pay another buffalo?" I asked.

"He only wishes that were the case," Linda replied. "For my people, theft is the worst possible crime. Rudu will be banished. And Drak will be buried alive for stealing the silver coin of Mayrena."

The music resumed; rice wine flowed from dozens of clay jars.

This time, it wasn't just the grown men who drank. The boys raised the jugs to their lips, then handed the *tavaak* to mothers, old women, young girls. Someone pushed a full jar into Linda's arms. Warriors lurched around the *chanur,* wildly waving spears as they recounted past blood hunts. The buffalo shuffled nervously, straining at the rattan line. Then Kanam hoisted a strange covered basket of woven rattan onto his shoulders and stalked around the clearing; the children screamed and scattered whenever he approached and pulled off the lid.

"For little ones," said Linda.

"A papoose?" I asked.

"It's not for carrying your own children," she explained. "It's in case the warriors can kidnap a small child."

"So the children can become slaves, like that Jeh boy in Kanam's house?"

Linda shook her head.

"I remember it happened once before I left with Uncle. A raiding party returned with a small boy, not much younger than me. Maybe he was Lao, maybe Jeh. The boy cried and cried. He missed his parents and his village. They made the boy squeeze the blade of a knife until his hand bled. The shaman offered his blood to the *dyaang*. Then he slaughtered the boy."

"The shaman did this?"

I immediately regretted asking the question.

"It is something Uncle lives with every day," she said quietly. "Maybe it is really why he ran from this place."

Kanam produced a clay jug from the shoulder basket and forced more *tavaak* on us, then stumbled around the muddy grounds in a drunken trance. After the shaman sprinkled lustral water around the base of the *chanur,* a dozen men stabbed their spears at the pole. The panicked buffalo pulled the tether taut, bleating like a toddler as the warriors then pricked its hide with their weapons as they circled the *chanur*. The music and singing swelled like a storm surge, hoping to propitiate the *dyaang*. On Kanam's order, the shaman brandished his machete and slashed the buffalo's leg tendons. As the animal collapsed, two of the men held its muzzle to keep the buffalo from bellowing or touching its mouth to the ground. That would not please the *dyaang*. The shaman finished the animal off with a single spear thrust to the heart, then the men clustered around the body, drawing blood from the mortal wound into bamboo tubes. While life drained from the buffalo, the crowd's wailing reached a crescendo. The spirits would be pleased.

As heat lightning rippled in the distance, the men set upon the buffalo with knives and machetes. The shaman daubed the pole with fresh blood and reeled around the killing ground, chanting. We rose to join the women and children who pulled pieces of smoldering wood from the fire; they cast embers as they circled the *chanur*, bathed in flames and butchery. Then the onlookers pushed closer to be anointed with gore and to grab the bamboo tubes. Unknown hands smeared my face with warm, soft tissue: a buffalo's ear. Someone pulled my right arm and I turned to confront a wild, blood-streaked face: Linda. She led me from the mob and into the shadows behind the *gual*. Villagers stumbled by, carrying dripping hunks of raw meat. Others splashed the tubes of blood onto the poles of their longhouses. The entire place smelled of death.

"Where's Sam?" I asked.

She gestured to the chaos around the fire.

"I saw him dressing the buffalo," Linda said, her words slightly slurred. "Don't worry. Now come with me."

She pulled me into a raised hut. It smelled of old, musty hides and seemed too small to be a living quarters. Despite the darkness, I sensed Linda's presence next to me.

"I dreamed last night about the big trees near Father's grave," she said. "We believe the trees don't speak, but that they still see and hear everything. After we left this place in my dream, the trees fell and broke apart, even though there was no big wind. Then I awoke. *Pharlang pano*—it was a bad-luck dream. I should have known today would bring tragedy."

"There's not a lot of time left, Linda."

"I know. You and Honeyman must leave as soon as possible. If Kanam returns from this hunt without a victim, he'll tie you both to the *chanur*. And I won't be able to help. I must go to the forest with my aunt. I will not live with Kanam under the roof of my father's house."

"Please come with us. The village is imploding. Kase. Kanam. Drak. Rudu. These punishments. This blood hunt. If those escaped surveyors make it to Attapeu, the Lao government will return here in force, with chainsaws and guns and soldiers. They will drive away the Katu forever."

"No one cares about my people," she said, the rice whiskey making her morose. "They only care about the timber. But the *dyaang* live in these mountains. We can't honor them if we leave. Who then will tend the tombs of our ancestors?"

"Only the Katu will remember."

"You saw the Jeh village," she said. "They are lost and dying."

"And now the Katu have only Kanam to lead them. He's about to eliminate Drak."

"I'm afraid for our future," she said with a weary sigh. "All Kanam knows is fighting. This will end very badly. Auntie was right: *chet biik*. A bad death. Then everyone will forget our people. The mountains will become empty, filled only with our ghosts."

"Your spirit will always be here, Linda. And those of your family: your mother, your father, your brother."

"That's the *tavaak* talking."

"No, that's me talking."

I felt her warm arms searching out my hands, and then the cool silver coin in my palm. Mayrena. A long time ago, it had ended badly for the explorer in these very mountains as well.

"I gave this to you before, Sebastian, to convince you to come here with me. Now I give it to you again to take with you, to always remember me. You must always be prepared to walk away."

I took the coin and ran its smooth edge gently up the contours of her body until I found the hard cords of her neck, and then my mouth was on her and we were falling into a place too deep and dark for any tree coffin. The heat lightning burst again, illuminating the walls of the hut and its contents: the butcher's bill of past Katu war parties, including the severed, dried heads of buffalo and enemy chieftains and innocent children. I kissed her hungrily, even as I felt her tragic spirit moving to join the rootless *dyaang* somewhere in the lost folds of the Long Mountains.

Sixteen

I lay awkwardly in the bottom of a dugout, gazing up at the brilliant night sky, the canoe too narrow for my shoulders. The vessel was still, unmoving, as if stuck on dry land. Then came the dull grind of wood sliding against wood, and the star-filled sky began to vanish as if someone were drawing down a shade. I could just make out the glint of Kanam's bared, filed teeth as he strained to push the heavy hardwood lid atop the tree coffin that held me. I couldn't move, couldn't shout. It was as if I'd been drugged and could only watch mutely as I was buried alive. I awoke with a start, my clothing soaked in sweat. Linda was no longer in the hut. Outside, it was still dark and drizzling lightly, though moonlight threatened to break through the thin clouds. I skulked through the deserted common to the *gual,* where I found Honeyman sleeping just inside the doorway. In their drunken state, the tribesmen had neglected to reshackle him before they passed out. There would never be a better chance for escape. Honeyman grunted when I jostled his bad shoulder.

"We gotta make our move," I whispered. "Now."

"What time is it?" he mumbled.

"Maybe a few hours before sunrise. And from the looks of it, everyone's sleeping in today."

Honeyman rose as quietly as possible. No one stirred inside the longhouse; the tribesmen snored deeply, as if they all suffered from sleep apnea. We crept across the village clearing, where the remains of the bonfire smoldered beneath the *chanur.* Nothing remained of the buffalo but a bloodied rope. Entering Bruang's hut, I shivered in the damp highland air, then softly called Linda's name. Nothing. Just the dripping of water through breaks in the thatched roof onto the floor planks, where the seepage pooled and mixed with something dark and slick. Blood, still warm to the touch. In the faint moonlight, I spotted a crumpled form by the hearth. Too big to be Bruang or Linda. We moved in quietly to examine the body. It was Kanam. His throat had been expertly cut.

"Looks like Linda won't be playing house with the chief," said Honeyman. "She's left us and bolted with Bruang. Think they're headed for the river?"

"No. They would've gone north, toward the burial ground."

"There's no way out in that direction."

"Linda's not interested in getting out, Sam."

We left Kanam's corpse in the hut. A dog snuffled but didn't bark as we stepped quietly over the saplings laid at the village gate to announce its taboo status. I grabbed a long branch to use as a walking stick and followed Honeyman down the trail, heading toward the Katu cemetery.

"This is gonna screw up everything," he said. "There's not going to be enough time to double back to the river before the village wakes up."

"We can't just leave them."

"I never said we would," he replied grimly.

Somewhere in the murk ahead of me, I heard Honeyman gradually increase his pace. Stars were finally peeking through the rain clouds. A quarter hour down the trail, I heard a thump and cursing as Honeyman skidded in the mud.

"Tripped over something, kid. Be careful."

Heat lightning flickered, and I made out a broken, facedown body at my feet. It was Bruang. I knelt and shook the old woman's shoulders. No response. I felt her neck. No pulse. Checked her breathing. Nothing. Her small corpse was still warm. Defensive wounds scored her forearms; there was a nasty cut across her throat. And then there was a rustling from beside the trail and someone pounced on my back before I could react, kneeing my kidneys and grabbing my hair from behind.

"How it's going?" the attacker hissed.

I struggled to turn and land a blow with the walking stick. My assailant fended off the strikes and held tight as we twisted, pulling my head back by my hair to bare my throat. At any moment the killing blow would fall from his machete. So this was how it would end: a bad death on a muddy path in the back of beyond. But suddenly I felt the man lurch, followed by the sound of a sickening crack. The warrior went limp and slid off my back and into the mire, dead from a broken neck.

"It's going great, Drak," Honeyman replied. "Just fucking great."

I fell to my knees and retched, my throat burning from bad *tavaak* and stomach acid. That's when we heard the dull, dreadful explosion farther down the trail. Then I was up and running blindly through the darkness, Honeyman hot on my trail. *Let it be wandering livestock, a prowling leopard, or even some stranger. Not Linda.* We found her perhaps a half mile farther on, lying on her back in a patch of tall grass just off the path. Shrapnel had peppered the left side of her body and shredded her arm. Dark runnels of blood drained from a deep gash on her neck onto the wet earth.

"Booby trap," said Honeyman. "Drak must have rigged a *bombi* last night on the trail while everyone else in the village was getting hammered."

He tore off a strip of his shirt and tried to stanch her horrific bleeding.

"Auntie," she moaned. "Is she—?"

"Gone," I said. "I'm sorry."

"Drak?"

"He's dead now."

"Where's Kanam?"

"We found him inside Bruang's hut," Honeyman said. "We thought you killed him."

"No."

"It was Drak then," I said. "He must have followed Kanam."

"So many bad deaths . . ." Linda gasped.

"There's no explaining all of this to the village," Honeyman said. "We have to move out. Now. Can you walk, Linda?"

"I—I don't think so."

"I'll carry her, Honeyman."

"With that malaria, you can barely take care of yourself. I got her."

"Leave me, you two. Please."

"No way," I replied.

She trembled and coughed up blood.

"Almost dawn," she croaked. "Save yourselves. Walk away."

"We all go together," Honeyman said.

The night was lifting. By now, the roosters and the dogs had probably awakened the villagers. Kanam's body would soon be discovered. The headman's murder and a *bombi* explosion couldn't be blamed on the spirits. Despite the taboo, the first Katu warriors would soon be on our trail, spoiling for revenge. It was fruitless to go back and try to hide the bodies of Bruang and Drak in the bush. We had perhaps twenty minutes, thirty at most, before these expert hunters tracked us here. Honeyman scooped Linda into his arms and led the way along the trail.

"The river's the other way," she insisted.

"This is our only chance," Honeyman replied. "The village will be on the warpath."

"I'm sorry," she added. "I didn't know Drak would follow us."

"He had to make it look like you and your aunt killed Kanam," I said. "Then, if he killed both of you to avenge Kanam, maybe the village would forgive his adultery and theft. Maybe he wouldn't be so ostracized. And with Kanam gone, he would save himself a buffalo. There'd also be fewer complications if he married Rudu. In his mind, maybe he even had a chance to become *ta-ka*."

"Drak would've killed us next, in our sleep," said Honeyman.

"What people do for love," Linda said faintly.

"Just about anything," I said. "I know."

Linda groaned, then fell silent. She had lost a frightening amount of blood. We kept marching. The small plots of vegetables flanking the trail soon gave way to elephant grass and then we entered dense, old-growth forest alive with birdsong in the final hour before dawn. Linda said something to Honeyman, and he soon stepped off the main trail and onto a side path. Even in the dim light I recognized the route: it led to the Katu graveyard. I followed them down the hill, toward the sound of the hidden river below, until we reached the sacred grove of the coffin trees and the pit that held the bodies of Linda's father and brother.

"Now lay me down, Honeyman."

He knelt and gently delivered her to the damp, leaf-covered forest floor. Her breathing had become shallow and labored.

"We can still make it out of here, Linda," I said, nearly pleading.

"You make it for me," she answered. "And take this with you."

She pulled a small, bloodied notebook from her clothing. It was her father's diary.

"The river just below us leads to the Xe Kaman," I said, bending to brush her hair from her eyes. "From there, we can get our dugout."

"That'd be nice—another boat ride with you."

She squeezed my hand, then rolled over and retched more blood. A hornbill dived from the cavity of a nearby tree, swooping so close to us that I heard the breeze rush through its feathers, then cawed and flew off toward the swelling sunrise.

"Ravai dai apleng," Linda said calmly, a faint smile pursing her lips. "My soul will be in the sky."

And then she was gone. I shook her shoulders. Nothing. Then I straightened her matted hair and brushed her eyelids closed and then we carried her to the open grave. There we laid her out with Kase atop Curtis's coffin as the first shards of sunlight cut through the forest canopy, bathing the scene in an otherworldly, Arthurian glow. I fumbled in my pockets for the silver coin but couldn't bring myself to place it in the open grave. It was my only tangible memento. Instead, I plucked three long stalks of torch ginger and placed them atop the bodies. For the earth, the sky, and all the wandering Katu souls.

"It was a good death," Honeyman said, breaking the silence.

"There's no such thing."

I shivered from the building fever as tears welled in my eyes. I'd hardly known her, yet my loss felt immense. Everything had gone to hell: the case that would cement my PI career; a woman I had finally cared about. It had all peaked and just as suddenly vanished in a few short weeks. From the south came a faint, but swelling, howl: the search party from the village must have found Bruang and Drak. I didn't have any more time to feel sorry for myself or for Linda. We had to leave.

"We got two moves," Honeyman stated. "You're going straight downhill and into the river. No arguing. From there, you've got a decent chance to get to the boat and back down to Attapeu."

"And you?"

"I'm going back up to the trail and lead these Katu boys on a wild goose chase all the way to Kontum."

"That's suicide. They know these mountains."

"So do I, Bass. It's like a flashback, but in a good way."

"Thanks for everything, Sam. For saving my ass back there."

"Buy me a beer next time we meet on the Cowboy," he said, slapping me on the shoulder. "Now get the hell outta here."

He turned and walked briskly uphill, bound for the Long Mountains, for the land of the Jeh, whistling that crazy old Hank Williams tune, "Jambalaya," and scattering iridescent sunbirds from the trees. I watched as he was swallowed by the forest understory and then I scrambled downhill, mindful of not leaving tracks or broken branches in my wake. Over the rush of water I made out a low, mounting, mechanical throb from the west, followed by the crump of explosives and the unmistakable blurt of machine-gun fire. It sounded as if Krnoon Blo Mat was under heavy assault by the Lao army's Soviet-era helicopters, retaliation for nearly killing those surveyors. Curtis had come from the sky, bringing magic and hope to the Katu. Now the sky brought only bad death, a bitter end. The hill people would never win. The irate shouts of the war party soon faded from the ridgeline; the searchers had retreated to defend their doomed village from attack. Maybe Honeyman would make it to Kontum after all.

At water's edge, I wrapped my arms around a stout section of a fallen tree branch, then slid out into a cool current that felt like balm to my feverish body. The rains had increased this anonymous tributary's depth and speed, carrying me at a walking pace between the tops of giant boulders, smoothing over now-drowned dry-season rapids. Distant, thunderous eruptions occasionally rolled down the mountains. Krnoon Blo Mat was in its final death throes. I closed my eyes, felt myself borne along. When I came to, I spotted the contrails of a jumbo jet cutting through a cloudless sky far overhead. Its passengers would spend the afternoon in Tokyo or Taipei, Hong Kong or Manila. I floated downstream, not knowing what lay one hundred yards ahead. Woodpeckers darted in and out of the dense forest along the steep banks and, far overhead, a vulture effortlessly rode the thermals. And then the boulders and the riffles subsided, the sky and the forest and the water opened up, and I was delivered to a broader, still-surging river. I thought this must be the Xe Kaman. I kicked my way clear of the main current in the middle of the channel, swimming for the shallows near the right bank. Somewhere ahead lurked that waterfall and I wanted to avoid getting swept over its edge. I don't know how long I drifted—maybe an hour, perhaps two—before I heard a ceaseless, hidden roar from around a sharp bend. The falls. I released the bough and swam for the right bank, pulling myself out of the river with the help of a dead limb dangling overhead. Chills racked my body almost as soon as I made my way into the shade of the forest. I thrashed about until I found a faint, steep path and slid down the mud-slick slope flanking the falls. Curtis's notebook, which I'd placed in a rear pocket of my trousers, was now a pulpy mess.

Luckily, my clumsy descent attracted no attention. The riverbank stood empty. I staggered along at the water's edge, peering into the undergrowth until I found the boat Linda had rented in Attapeu, still hidden beneath a tangle of leaves and branches. It took all my strength to wrestle it into the water and shove off. But the engine wouldn't start when I yanked the outboard motor's cord. I tried several more times, half in a panic, and then remembered that the Katu had confiscated the sparkplug. I grabbed a paddle and pulled weakly for a few strokes, just enough to catch the main current. And then the malaria was on me again and I slumped down in the hull and drifted along in a fever dream. I saw Linda and Kase and Curtis standing along a sandy bank of the Xe Kaman, laughing and waving as if at a picnic. But around a rocky point, bruised and angry corpses stood thigh-deep in the water, awaiting my passage. Kanam. Drak. Colonel Nagaphit. Chang Tai. Doug Brody. They waded out into the channel toward the boat, until an undertow pulled them beneath the surface of the racing river.

It was the Jeh hunters who found me and shook me awake, my boat aground in an eddy close to where Honeyman had dropped them. How long ago was that? Five days? A week? I'd lost track. The tribesmen held open their hands and pointed upstream as if to ask, *Where are your friends? What happened to Honeyman and Linda?* I could only shake my head and offer an exhausted wave of my arm: Gone. Dead. MIA. And then I passed out as they loaded their stiff, bloody catch into the boat: a brace of quaillike birds, a wild boar, a pangolin, and a small deer. The mountains still treated the Jeh well.

The dead animals in the Katu hut accusing me. The dead animals in the boat mocking me. And then the chief of the Jeh village praying over me, sprinkling *lao-lao* on my boiling brow. Another boat ride to Attapeu. The shocked, sober face of Yves Mouhot. How's it going? I had discovered that old, terrible secret buried deep in the mountains. Now I, too, understood. Some medicine and a long, lurching trip through the mud in Mouhot's overheating truck to Pakxe, then a crossing of the brown, monsoon-broad Mekong aboard a car ferry. A deep, exhausted sadness when I glimpsed Wat Phu's peak in the distance, then a rough, suffocating ride hidden beneath a rubberized tarp in the back of Mouhot's truck through the Chong Mek checkpoint to Ubon Ratchathani. Finally a clean, hard bed beneath a ceiling fan at Wat Pah Nanachat, the mantric chanting of Frank Myers and his fellow fallen angels. How's it going? *Jamais ceder . . .*

Epilogue

It feels like rain today. Even in the small hours of a moonless night, I can sense its presence, heavy and ominous, the intruder in a darkened room. There is nothing to be done. The rain will come. First the warm, sluggish wind, then a few fat, teasing globules, and suddenly the liquid-silver sheets beating like timpani against the monastery's steaming tin roof, a torrent that splays the paddle-shaped leaves of the banana trees, swells the cisterns to overflowing. The wet, white noise sloughs away distractions, centers me in the chant. With the rain I lose myself in the core of the mantra, a whirlpool draining into the void. But her image in the forest remains.

Every misted morning I join the saffron-robed line: the few, the proud, the devout. The abbot leads us from the cool sanctuary of the forest temple to make the daily predawn circuit of the hamlets in this vast, skillet-flat land where stooped men and wrinkled women wear the stoicism of peasants in tragic novels. I am mindful enough to feel each bead of sweat gathering upon my shaved head. The pious drop rice and fruit and the occasional morsel of chicken into my alms bowl.

This is the hard-won bounty of Isan. Here the rains will wash away the sandy soil to stain the rivers the color of tea and cream. Here the dry-season sun will bake the earth without mercy and then call up the winds to blow it all away. *Anicca,* the abbot teaches us: the transience of all things. Another novitiate, an Austrian, tells me that Isan means large and prosperous. A cruel joke, says Myers. The land yields only hardship and heartache. No wonder peasants call it the Weeping Prairie. This year it seems the rains will never end.

The forest here vanished long ago except for our small patch of green, the dying echo of a jungle that once held tiger and elephant and rhino. The city creeps inexorably closer. Across the rice fields I see new homes rising along the highway to Sisaket. It takes only an hour to walk the wooded perimeter of our monastery, but the air still holds animal chatter and the songs of unseen birds. Last week I witnessed a miracle—a small barking deer—in our little forest. It must have wandered all the way from Cambodia, fifty miles to the south, where the Khmer Rouge has scared away all but the greediest loggers and desperate poachers.

My malaria has subsided. I have not yet learned to hate this land.

Every day I find myself drawn to the bodhi tree that vaults from a clearing a quarter-mile walk through the forest from our simple quarters. Beds of heliconia surround the holy tree; their brilliant red flowers glow like gas flares. To build my strength I come here most days after the abbot's dharma talk and meditate in the shade of the new pavilion we *sangha* have built. I have nearly learned to ignore the banshee howl of the Thai fighter planes on patrol over the borderlands. I remove myself from desire, from the source of all human suffering. I concentrate on the rain. Memory is a stagnant pond where a lotus rarely blooms. The strongest image is of her crestfallen face—from that night at the Overlook Hotel in Bangkok—staring past me toward something unspeakable, unavoidable. Fate, perhaps.

I have been here nearly a month. Myers says I am almost well enough to go home. I can't forget, but I have begun to earn forgiveness. The silver coin still weighs heavily in the charm bag dangling from my neck. *Annica,* I remind myself. All things must pass. Life. Love. Illness. Anger. Remorse.

The rain, he says, will wash it all away.

Acknowledgments

Not unlike a permanent watermark left by a cold beer bottle on an expensive wood table, this book is the residue of more than twenty years of travel in Southeast Asia. In the course of wandering this region, I've encountered numerous colorful residents, indigenous and expatriate, and witnessed extraordinary landscapes—all of which I hope imbue this novel with a certain degree of verisimilitude and sense of place. But this book is, foremost, a work of fiction. Any resemblance of the characters that inhabit these pages with actual private investigators, insurance experts, hill-tribe shamans, Thai policeman, former prisoners of war, Special Forces veterans, and Bangkok bar girls, among others, is purely coincidental.

What is not a fluke is the constant support I have received from my family, especially my wife, Maria, my son Timothy, my parents, Nancy and Gerald, and my two sisters, Deborah and Pamela, during the years it took to produce this work.

Although my newspaper career and magazine freelance assignments delayed this project much longer than I ever anticipated, my literary agent, Thomas C. Wallace, never ceased to offer encouragement as I slogged through numerous drafts and revisions. He also suggested several invaluable improvements to the narrative.

I'm fortunate that Anne Bensson, an associate editor for Thomas Dunne Books at St. Martin's Press, saw the potential in the convoluted story of a first-time fiction writer, and then worked with me to tighten the narrative and fine-tune the characters.

Linda Tischler, Sonia Turek, and Linda Kincaid, my former feature editors at the *Boston Herald*, were kind enough to green-light my various story pitches, including numerous profiles of Southeast Asian refugees and Boston-area private investigators, which provided the inspiration for this novel.

A huge round of thanks to my friend, Jay F. Sullivan, with whom I've traveled to Southeast Asia since 1991, including trips to Thailand, Burma's off-limits Shan State, and several excursions into Laos. Jay's good humor and enormous duffel bag of freeze-dried food, vodka, duct tape, and Lomotil sustained us on a 1994 4WD adventure down the Ho Chi Minh Trail to Attapeu, where we became the first Americans to explore the province since the end of the Vietnam War. Jay also provided encouraging feedback on several drafts of the book.

Thomas P. McCarthy, Steve Biondolillo, and Heidi Barron, three longtime friends, also read the manuscript and offered invaluable advice. Nam Van Phan, CEO of Dorchester's Vietnamese American Initiative for Development, vetted the details of a young Asian immigrant's banking career.

Michael Szpuk, a Boston-area private investigator, allowed me to tag along on several matrimonial stakeouts and also explained state-of-the-art surveillance technology in the late 1990s. Private investigator Diane Kellner explained the ins and outs of health and life insurance fraud and introduced me to PI extraordinaire (and proud Marine) Byron Bales. Byron was kind enough to supplement my book "research" with an epic, weeklong pub crawl of Bangkok, where he introduced me to Mekhong whiskey, dice games and the bar girls, mamasans, and expats of Soi Cowboy and Nana Plaza. Byron also advised me on the procedures and protocols for investigating overseas life-insurance fraud, especially in Thailand.

Harvard University granted me reading-room privileges at the Widener and Tozzer libraries. Their collections were invaluable in providing ethnographic and folkways information—even a comparative dictionary—about the Katu that informed my descriptions of this little-known people and other embattled hill tribes inhabiting the Annamite Mountains. Even in the Age of Google, there is no substitute for this old-fashioned scholarly material—monographs, handbooks, obscure journals—almost all of which is unavailable on the Internet. I am also grateful to the Boston Public Library, Bangkok's Siam Society, Hanoi's Museum of Ethnography, and Kanchanaburi's JEATH War Museum and Thailand-Burma Railway Centre for providing information on a variety of historical and cultural topics.

Steven Emerson's 1998 book, *Secret Warriors: Inside the Covert Military Operations of the Reagan Era*, contains a chapter on the tragicomic efforts to search for POW/MIAs in Laos, including the aborted raid on the Nhommarath prison. Major John L. Plaster's *SOG: The Secret Wars of America's Commandos in Vietnam* is a riveting account of the incredible valor demonstrated by the clandestine warriors of the Studies and Observation Group in Southeast Asia. The definitive account of the life of French adventurer Charles David Mayrena is Gerald Cannon Hickey's meticulously researched *Kingdom in the Morning Mist* (1988).

During a newspaper career that extended almost twenty years, I had the opportunity to interview scores of Asian refugees who had resettled in the United States. Among the most unforgettable encounters were with Arn Chorn-Pond, Loung Ung, and Tai Tang, who were all kind enough to share their experiences, however traumatic, in Thai border camps and their often painful adjustment and assimilation into American society.

Air Force veteran Vern Pall of Tucson, Arizona, provided information on the still-active Veterans of Foreign Wars post in Khorat, Thailand. I am also indebted to several intelligence officials, who shall remain anonymous, for speaking candidly with me about the U.S. government's efforts in the search for American POW/MIAs in Laos.

Wat Pah Nanachat is, in fact, a lovely forest monastery on the outskirts of Ubon Ratchathani that attracts numerous foreigners with an interest in practicing Buddhism in a monastic setting. But none of the monks I describe in my novel bear any intentional resemblance to the *sangha* of this special, sylvan space.

And, finally, my deepest gratitude to Dr. Dimitrios Tzachanis and the rest of the physicians, nurses, staff, and volunteers of the Bone Marrow Transplant Unit at Beth Israel Deaconess Medical Center in Boston, as well as Dr. Paul G. Richardson and the nurses and staff of the Jerome Lipper Multiple Myeloma Center. I wouldn't be here, typing these words, without their help and expertise.